BECOMING
Mrs. Lockwood

K.I. LYNN

BECOMING Mrs. Lockwood

Chapter One

OUR CHANCE ENCOUNTER

For my fall break I wanted to go see the Grand Canyon. I wanted to take a helicopter ride to see it from above or a mule ride inside. Instead, my mom convinced me to go to Las Vegas.

She went on and on about all the sights we'd see and the shows we'd go to.

Tourist stuff.

Maybe even drive out to see the Hoover Dam.

We were going to make our way down the strip one casino at a time, starting at Mandalay Bay, and I was excited to see all the lights. After two days, we had yet to make it out of the Mirage's front door.

Secret Garden? Done by myself. The pool was boring after a few hours of reading and tanning alone.

It'd been "five more minutes" for the last two hours, and I was beyond aggravated.

Bored out of my freaking mind.

It wasn't the great girls' getaway I thought it would be. It would've been better if my stepdad, Mike, was in my place, and I had just stayed home. Instead, I was being used as an excuse to get drunk and gamble.

Yay.

Vegas was not for the under twenty-one crowd, at least by

myself, and at eighteen, I was a few years shy of being able to do all of the stuff I had little to no interest in doing anyway.

I wanted to visit the aquarium in Mandalay Bay, the wax museum, ride the coaster at New York New York, see the fountains at the Bellagio, and go see a Cirque du Soleil show.

I was really wishing my best friend had been able to come.

Closing out of my Kindle app, I decided to head over to Starbucks for a pick-me-up and a chance to stretch. Checking my phone, I found a new text message. *Five more minutes*, she said. More like five more hours.

I was stuck in limbo. I should have just abandoned her and gone out on my own, but we were there together, so I resigned myself to wait.

Grabbing a coffee, I found a comfy chair and opened my phone back up to my book.

"You have me curious," a voice said as I moved to put my earbuds back in.

I blinked and looked up at a man sitting across from me, his blue eyes locked on mine. He had a coffee cup in one hand, his phone in the other. He was handsome. Very handsome. Medium length brown hair, striking blue eyes, and a strong jaw. A slim and fit physique was noticeable under his crisp suit.

And he was talking to me.

"What's so curious about me?"

Normally, I didn't stick out in a crowd.

Overall, I was pretty average—at least in a class of over a thousand. I didn't go out of my way, spending an hour to get ready with full hair and makeup in the morning, all in an attempt to look older. I liked sleep.

I didn't have the time, nor did I care that much about that stuff. My black hair was long with a slight wave, and the same colored eyelashes framing my sea blue eyes. Ninety percent of the time, I was a jeans and T-shirt girl, or shorts and a tank top. Plain vanilla with no flashy decorations.

"Why that"—he pointed to my phone—"has so much more of your attention than everything out there." He hooked his thumb over his shoulder.

He seemed to think that I was an exception, because I was sitting in a gigantic hotel lobby and I was the only person reading a book instead of gambling in the huge attached casino.

I glanced back down to my book, and the play button my thumb was hovering over and shrugged my shoulders. "Reading and music are good ways to pass the time."

His fingers stopped typing, and he quirked his brow at me. "You're in Vegas to pass the time?"

"My mom's in the casino."

"Ah, not a gambler?"

I shook my head. "No, for a few reasons."

"Well, I'm curious again," he said with a smile, and leaned forward.

"I don't see you in the casino." I tried to deflect because it was nice to talk with someone, but I knew when my age came out, he would be long gone.

He smirked, and I wondered if he knew how good he looked when he did that. "I play a little, but I'd rather put my money toward a bigger gamble. So, why aren't you in there or out and about like everyone else? Why here?"

I sighed. "Various reasons, including lack of funds and . . . I'm not allowed."

"They kicked you out? Are you the counting cards type?" He narrowed his gaze on me, but he was still smiling.

"Do I scream MIT?" I shot back, and attempted not to fawn over his sexy smile. How did one smile sexy? I had no idea, but the man in front of me was a sexy smile master.

He laughed. "No, but I'd put you at above average."

"Now, I don't know how to take that. Either you're insulting my intelligence when you find out I actually do go to MIT." I scooted to the edge of my seat. "Or I'm flattered that I don't come off as average."

He held his hands up: coffee, phone, and all. "I believe I need to apologize. I didn't mean to insinuate you had below-average intelligence . . . as smarter than average is below for MIT standards."

"Well, you're off the hook. MIT didn't want me," I said and leaned back into the chair. Even if I'd applied, chances were high that I wouldn't get in. Good grades, but not good enough for them.

He smiled and shook his head. "Okay. Harvard? You seem Ivy League."

"Too pretentious."

"All right, so where do you go?"

I grimaced. "Umm, I go to Zionsville High School just outside of Indianapolis. Next fall I'll go to USC."

He stared at me, stunned. "Wow, I honestly thought you were in college . . . Over eighteen."

"Eighteen exactly," I said, for some reason, wanting him to know I was of legal age. Who was I kidding? I was still in high school, a virgin, and in Vegas with my mom, while he looked like he had expensive taste, was very intelligent, and was obviously placating me.

"USC's a good school. I live not too far from the campus. It's expensive," he said with a nod.

"Yeah, I think my mom is trying to win my tuition, but knowing her luck, I'll still be paying off student loans when I'm dead."

He nodded, his fingers tapping on the side of his cup. "Yeah, loans are brutal," he replied, before moving to stand. "Well, I need to get to a meeting."

My stomach dropped, and I attempted to smile up at him. "Yep, I knew I lost you. Even though I'm only eighteen, we can still talk, you know?" *And I can stare at you a little bit longer.*

His eyebrows shot up and he shook his head as he smiled. "You didn't scare me away, but I have an eleven o'clock meeting to get to. Promise," he assured me.

"Oh." I felt heat rush to my cheeks.

"I forgot the introductions. My name is Weston," he said, stuffing his phone in his pocket before holding out his hand.

"Wren."

There was a humming that moved up my arm when I took his hand, a vibration I felt down to my bones. Odd, but I chalked it up to nerves.

"Good luck, Wren." He smiled and placed a light kiss on the back of my hand.

Heat flooded my face at the romantic gesture. I didn't know guys still did that. "You too, Weston. Have a fun meeting."

Laughing, he released my hand. "Oh, these meetings are never fun. Merely a necessity."

With a wink, he left and I returned to my book and tried to forget about the good-looking man who I would probably never see again. Which sucked, because I think we could have talked for hours. He could have saved me from my torment.

"Wren! There you are!" Mom's voice called from the Starbucks entrance a few minutes later.

"Hi, Mom," I said as I watched her walk over with a glass in her hand.

Her eyes, the same color as mine, were bright and wide. At only thirty-seven years old, she looked more like twenty-eight with barely a wrinkle on her face. Her long brown hair was up in a ponytail, and she was wearing my hoodie.

"I've been looking everywhere for you." She help up a small stack of bills and I understood what her excitement was about. "Are you ready for some lunch?"

I wanted to roll my eyes. I was ready to do anything that involved leaving the hotel.

"How much did you win?" I asked as she set the stack in my hand.

Her smile grew as she held her arms out wide. "Enough to have lunch wherever you want to go."

"Nice. Can we do some sightseeing after?" I asked, practically begging. I hoped her doing well in the casino could get her out of it for a little while.

"Sounds like a good idea. What do you want to see?"

We talked about how to spend our afternoon, but I knew no matter what we saw, the only thing I would remember from the day was Weston.

Chapter Two

OUR FIRST OUTING

I T WAS THE SAME AS THE DAY BEFORE—RINSE AND THEN repeat. It wasn't even ten and Mom was already in the casino, while I was in the lobby reading. We only had one more night left before heading home, and there was still so much I wanted to see.

Sadly, it looked like I would be going home unfulfilled. It was a complete waste of a trip for me.

"Did she leave you alone again?" a familiar, smooth voice called, coaxing me to look up from my book.

I quirked my brow. "That obvious?"

My jaw wanted to drop at that sight of him, but that would be too conspicuous. If I thought he looked good in the suit from the day before, it was nothing compared to how sexy he was standing in from of me in the low-rise jeans and fitted button-down shirt with the sleeves rolled up that he was sporting.

What God did I need to thank for seeing him again?

"Fairly." He chuckled and took the seat next to me.

"Dang, and here I was trying to look all important and above it all, instead of the lonely girl waiting to be rescued from her boredom," I said and let out a high-pitched sigh for emphasis.

It got him to smile and let out a little laugh, so I found my attempt at humor successful.

"Did you get to see all the sights you wanted to see yesterday?"

"A few," I said with a real sigh this time. "But everywhere we went, she spent time in the casino. Overall, we didn't see nearly as much as I'd hoped."

"Is she spending all day in the casino again?" He looked toward the entrance.

"Possibly." My gaze also moved toward the entrance. There was no sign of her.

"Could you leave her behind?" he asked, turning his attention back to me.

I shrugged. "I don't think she'd notice either way." *Where is he going with that?*

"Then why not go out with me?"

I stared at him in shock. So much so, it took my brain a second to light up and compute his questions. "W-what?"

He turned to face me and began his explanation. "You want to see the sights, and I want to see the sights. I've spent the last three days in meetings, and I only get one day off. I want to go out, but it's boring on my own."

"You could be a serial killer." I narrowed my gaze on him in a teasing fashion.

He pursed his lips. "This is true. I suppose you wouldn't go traipsing about with a strange serial killer. No, that just won't do."

Turning off my screen, I stuffed my phone back in my purse and stood up. "So, where are we going first before you kill me?"

He smirked and let out a laugh. "Well, we could start across the street and work our way down the strip."

"The wax museum?" I asked, my lips curling up into a smile and my widening eyes giving away my excitement. It was near the top of my list, I'd always been curious how the celebrities looked in person.

"Perfect."

"You won't turn me into a wax doll or anything, will you?" I joked as we headed out of Starbucks and toward the casino front door.

He laughed. "No. You're much better looking when you move than when you're standing still."

"But if I was still, you could do all sorts of sordid things to me," I said. *Did I just flirt?* I think I did.

He stopped, and I turned to look at him. He was smirking and I swallowed hard, my body heating up. What was I doing going around Vegas with a guy that attractive?

"I'm fairly confident I wouldn't need to dip you in wax to accomplish that."

"So sure of yourself?" I tried to sound confident, but my voice wavered. Yeah, I'd probably let him do anything to me. Virgin or not. What I lacked in experience, he was helping me make up in desire.

"Yes. Now, I want to check out some creepy, realistic looking bits of wax." He slid his fingers around my hand and pulled us out the door and across the street.

I was going to have some stories to tell my best friend when I got home.

Weston paid for the tickets, and while he was doing that I sent a text to my mom, which included an on-the-sly picture of Weston.

Met a tourist buddy and we're checking out the museum across the street.

It took less time to peel her vision away from the spinning wheels than I thought.

Have fun! Don't get in too much trouble. Keep me updated. xo

I think she was happy not to have to entertain me, and was all for it, even though I'd told her I was going out with a stranger. At least I sent her a photo in case I went missing. My mom wasn't irresponsible or anything, otherwise I wouldn't have made it as long as I had, but she did have an open mind. Plus, she knew I was smart, and at the first sign of trouble she knew my ass would be running and screaming bloody murder.

"Ready?" he asked, his hand outstretched.

The sight of him like that basically told me that I had nothing to worry about. He looked excited, happy to have an adventurer at his side as excited to see the sights as he was.

The wax museum was a trip. We moved through each room, looking at some of the biggest stars in my lifetime and before. Weston kept saying how so-and-so didn't really look that good without her makeup, or how another actress we'd stopped to admire was a bitch, or how an actor that I ogled was a poser. He seemed to speak from experience, though, not as a hater.

"Where do you get all this knowledge? Or are you just spiteful?"

His head tipped back in laughter. "It's experience. I live in L.A. and I've met a lot of them."

Once we'd left the wax museum, we decided to grab a quick bite to eat and figure out where we wanted to go next.

An hour later, I was gawking out of the taxi window as we made our way down the strip to the Shark Reef at Mandalay Bay.

"Oooh, the High Roller!" I pointed, my arm stretching in front of Weston as I leaned into him.

"I bet the view is best at night when the strip is lit up," he said, his breath blowing against my neck.

I turned my head up to look at him and noticed just how close we were. How close his lips were to mine. There was a shift, the mood getting heavier than the lightness of the day.

My lips pulled up into a smile as I sat back in my seat, suddenly very conscious of the beautiful man next to me whose thumb was making light circles against my own.

The aquarium was fun, watching the sea life swim all around us. Next on our tour was the Luxor; we stopped not only to see the inside of the pyramid, but to also hit the artifact tour.

He held my hand in his the entire time. When I shivered from the cold of the air conditioning, he pulled me to him and wrapped his arm around my shoulder. I didn't know what to think about his actions, but I liked it. It felt . . . natural. It was as if we'd known each other for years, instead of being two complete strangers who'd only met twice.

I even overheard people talking about us, saying how cute we looked together. Some called us newlyweds, others were jealous that I was wrapped up in him. I smiled, because for one day, I felt special, loved, and taken care of. It was a day lived in a fantasy land where princes really did exist.

We continued down the strip to New York New York and boarded the Manhattan Express. I wrapped my arm around his as the roller coaster climbed the hill, clicking and clacking as we moved, our anticipation rising.

Screams erupted from both of us as we crested the hill and dropped back to the earth. With each twist and turn, my grip tightened and I was frozen, glued to him, as we pulled back into the hotel.

We took it easy after that, both of us a bit queasy after riding. Walking down to the Bellagio, more people whispered about us and pointed, but I dismissed it. We stood in front of the fountains, listening to the music and watching the water dance in time.

I'd never had as much fun as I did with Weston. We'd done nearly everything on my mental list of things to do in Vegas. And I hated that with every passing minute our time together was growing shorter.

"It's even better when it's dark and the lights are on," he said as he leaned farther into me.

"Maybe we should come back after dark, then." My comment was a bit forward, but the sun was starting to set and I really wasn't ready for our day to end.

He looked down at his watch. "Do you have a dress with you?"

I scrunched my brow and thought about it. The only nice dress I owned sat in my hotel room, never worn. My mom made me bring it so we could have a semi-elegant night out, but that hadn't happened, so it was still hanging in the hotel closet. It was sleeveless with a white top, black sash, and black lace over a white skirt. Not as nice or formal as his suits, but it was all I had.

"Sorta. It's nothing special, but it's a decent dress." It felt like a thousand butterflies suddenly erupted in my stomach when I answered him. Anticipation filling me that maybe he also didn't want to leave me.

"Wren, would you join me for dinner tonight?" He brushed a lock of hair from my face. "May I take you on a date?"

I stared up at him, stunned.

A date? With him? I'd never been on a date before.

"Yes," I said. As if there would be any other answer.

Chapter Three

OUR FIRST DATE

WAS A BALL OF NERVES AS WE STEPPED INTO THE ELEVATOR. His hand hadn't left mine, and we were headed on a date. My first outing alone with a man.

"What room are you in?" he asked, his other hand hovering over the elevator buttons.

"21030. You?"

He pressed the button for the twenty-first floor, then pulled his room key from his pocket and inserted it into the slot before punching twenty-eight.

"28014."

"Let me guess—you're on the suite level?"

He smirked at me. "Yes."

"So, why didn't you stay at one of the more expensive hotels on the strip? Why the Mirage?"

He shrugged. "I've always liked it here, and the added bonus was that many of my meetings this week were in the hotel's confer-ence rooms."

The elevator slowed, then doors spread open. My gaze moved to him as I stepped forward, our hands still locked.

"See you in an hour?"

For a split second, he stared at me, but then his body was right up against me. His hand cupped my cheek and his lips pressed lightly against mine.

Shock and heat flared through me from the spark of his kiss. Then he stepped back. Our eyes were locked as he made space between us, his intense gaze fanning some internal fire inside me. Holding the door with the hand that had been on my cheek, he released my fingers, allowing me to leave.

But I didn't want to.

I wanted to be with him. To have his lips on mine for more than the brief second. A hunger for him started to grow inside me, begging me to pull him down for another.

"One hour. 21030, right?" he confirmed.

I managed to nod, my foot catching slightly as I backed up. "21030." I turned, and tried to remember which way my room was.

It wasn't my first kiss, but I was sure to remember it over all the kisses that had come before.

"Wren." I glanced back to find a smiling Weston. "I'll see you soon."

The doors closed, and it took me a few beats too long to turn down the hall.

Somehow, in my Weston-induced haze, I found my room and immediately stripped out of my clothes to jump in the shower. Once out, I blew my hair dry and attempted to style it with little success. Mascara and eyeshadow were all the makeup I had on me, along with a tube of lip gloss.

Opening the closet, I pulled out the dress and swatted it with my hand, attempting to pull out any of the leftover wrinkles from the suitcase. The peep-toe heels my mom bought me to go with the dress sat on the tile floor. They weren't really my style, but I was very happy to have them at that moment.

As I was putting on my bra, I heard the door click and open.

"Wren, I'm back!" Mom called, stopping in her tracks when she saw me. "Are you going out to dinner?" She wasn't upset, just curious, and then a grin spread on her face. "Is it with the man you spent all day with?"

"Yes, Mom. I'm going to dinner with Weston. He'll be here in about five minutes, so I need to finish getting ready."

I pulled the dress over my head, and she walked over to help me straighten it out.

"Aren't you glad I bought you those fancy shoes now?" she asked, her smile reflecting in the mirror as she zipped me up. "I'm so happy you met someone! Tell me about him."

"Well, he's older than I am. I'm not quite sure what he does for a living, but I can tell he makes a lot of money. Not that it matters. Just stating a fact." A smile grew on my face as the memories of our day together ran through my mind again. "I had a lot of fun with him today. The most fun I've ever had with anyone."

"Wow." There was more than a twinge of awe in her voice as she sat down on the edge of the bed.

"What?" I blinked at her.

"I've just never seen you smile like that. He must be special."

I let out a nervous laugh and brushed my hair behind my ears just in time to hear a knock on the door.

"That must be him!" She clapped her hands as she jumped up and ran to open the door despite my protests.

After opening the door, I noticed there was silence from her.

"You must be Wren's mother," Weston said from the other side of the door.

"Uh-huh," was all that my mother managed to squeak out at first. "Hi, I'm Karen." She held out her hand.

"Weston."

"Oh, I know." I rolled my eyes at my mother's fawning. I'd only said his name once. "You're really taking my daughter out?"

"If it's all right with you? I have flowers here to bribe you, if need be."

Slipping on my shoes, I grabbed my clutch and headed to the door to free him from the awkwardness of my mother ogling him. Weston handed the flowers to Mom and held his hand out to me.

"You look beautiful," he said as his gaze slowly slid down my body and back up again.

"Thank you." I ogled him just the same. "You look very handsome."

He smiled and shrugged his shoulders. "This is everyday wear for me, but thank you."

Mom grabbed on to my arm and held a finger up to Weston. "Give us a quick sec." She pulled me into the bathroom and shut the door. "Do you have your mace on you?"

"Mom."

"I'm just saying, be careful."

"He can hear you, you know. This room echoes."

She shook her hand in my face. "Just check in, okay?"

I nodded and reached for the door, pulling it open and smiling up at a Weston, who was wearing the sexiest amused grin.

"I'll see you later, Mom," I said, crossing the threshold and taking his arm.

"Have a great time! I'll see you later!" She waved.

We walked arm in arm. The elevator ride was silent, but I was just happy to be with him. The day had definitely sealed in his status as a crush.

"Where are we going?" I asked when we reached the lobby.

He gave me that sexy smirk again, and I couldn't help but think of our kiss from earlier. "Off the strip."

"Off the strip?" Did people go off the strip?

He smiled devilishly and took my hand as we crossed the lobby and exited out the front doors. I thought we were headed toward the taxi stand, but he pulled me toward a limo that was sitting in front of the door. The driver was standing there, holding the door for us.

"Good evening, Mr. Lockwood," he greeted, and then looked at me curiously.

"Good evening, Dan." Weston shook his hand and we climbed in.

His eyes were on me, studying something, but I couldn't figure out what.

"This is slightly overkill, don't you think?" It wasn't like we were going to prom or something.

Weston laughed and relaxed back onto the seat, leaving me once again wondering what he did for a living. "I like to do things with a bit of flare. That, and do you know how many germs are in those cabs?"

"Are you a germaphobe, Weston?" I teased.

"Hardly, but I wouldn't want to sully your pretty dress with that grimy cab."

"Flattery will . . . yeah, flattery will get you somewhere." We both laughed, mine with a bit of a nervous edge.

He reached out and ran the back of his fingers down my cheek. Our eyes locked again, intensifying the want to be closer to him. "I'm not sure where I'm trying to get with you, but I'll let you know, okay?"

"Okay," I said in little more than a whisper.

Why did we just have one night? And why did we have to live so far apart?

His "off the strip" wasn't far, just off the main drag to the Rio Las Vegas Hotel and Casino. We rode the elevator almost to the top, up to the Voodoo Lounge.

The waiting area was packed, being that it was Saturday night, but it was almost like the seas parted when Weston entered the room. The hostess showed us right to a private, reserved table that was hidden from prying eyes. No waiting for . . . what did the driver call him? Mr. Lockwood?

"Just who are you?" I asked with squinted eyes as we sat down.

Weston laughed, smiling as he remained silent. I remembered seeing people staring and practically bending over backward for him all throughout the day, but I just thought it was because of his good looks. I was beginning to suspect it was something more than that.

"I don't want to say. It's very refreshing to be with someone who hasn't heard of me. I'm liking this way too much to ruin it," he said, taking my hand in his and kissing it. "Right now we are two strangers getting to know each other."

Heat flooded my cheeks, which I hoped he didn't notice in the low lighting.

We were looking over the menu when the waitress came in to get our drink order. Before I could speak, Weston ordered a bottle of champagne.

After she left, I leaned forward and whispered, "You do remember how old I am, right?"

He chuckled. "I thought we could just enjoy the evening. Celebrate a little."

"What are we celebrating?"

His fingers linked with mine, that warm vibration spreading up my arm again. "The end of a fantastic day."

The smile dropped from my face. "That makes me sad, though." I didn't want to leave him. But come morning, I would have to and our time together would be just a memory.

His smile faltered as well, nodding in agreement. Our champagne arrived and was poured before the waitress took our order and left.

"To a wonderful day, with a wonderful woman," Weston said, raising his glass.

"To a wonderful day that I hate to see end."

We toasted and I had my first taste of champagne. The bubbles tickled my throat as I took a sip before setting the glass down. Weston's fingers entwined with mine again, and then he put his lips to my fingers. I stared at him, watching intently, while his gaze moved over to me. He leaned forward, and gently pressed his lips against mine.

It was an epiphany-type moment when I reacted and kissed him back. I could almost hear the "click," like we belonged together. It was perfect. Or maybe just perfect in my teenage, hormone-ridden mind.

Whatever it was, I didn't care. I just knew I wanted it and more.

It was more intense than in the elevator. There was what I could only describe as desire taking over as our lips parted, his tongue brushing against mine before his lips closed again.

He retreated, and I was left staring at him, my lips tingling, and crying out for more. Fire burned, searing me to the core, heat pooling between my legs.

"Don't tell me that was your first kiss?" His eyes were wide in amused shock as he pulled back.

I shook my head. "No, you kissed me in the elevator." His eyes went wide, and my lip twitched. "And there were a few fumbling guys at my school. It was also just . . . so much better than I imagined a kiss *could* be."

"I'm glad I'm not the only one," he said and took another sip of champagne.

I followed his example, my mind wondering so many things. I didn't know a lot about him—I hadn't learned much through the day—I just knew that we had a lot of fun together. That we had an attraction.

"All right, Mr. Mysterious, tell me something about yourself."

"Hmm." His lips twitched up and he tapped his fingers on the table. "Well, I had an unconventional childhood."

"Okay . . ." Something about the way he started made me think getting anything out of him was going to be difficult. Then again, he seemed to like that I didn't know who he was.

He chuckled. "It's not something I talk about, really, but it led me to where I am today." He took another sip. "Oh, I'm a USC graduate."

"Maybe you can give me a tour when I come back out in the summer." A hint that I'd be returning soon and that I'd like to see him again. Even though it was far away, just the possibility of being near him again gave me hope.

He smiled at me, his thumb caressing my fingers. "I'd love to."

The intensity in his eyes combined with his words left me a little mesmerized. He wasn't just blowing me off with a "sure" or "that sounds like fun." He sounded genuinely excited about seeing me again.

I broke away from his stare, taking another sip of champagne to calm myself down. "Okay, your teens or before was somehow messed up. What about brothers or sisters?"

He cleared his throat and leaned back into his chair. "I have an older brother. He's my best friend, and even with our hectic lives, we make sure to get together at least every other week, if not more."

"Sounds like you work a lot."

He nodded. "Days like this don't happen very often." He let out a sigh and brushed the back of his fingers across my cheek. "I would love more days like today."

His blue eyes were dark and looking at me with so much intensity, there was hardly any volume to my response. "Me too."

"What about you? Any siblings?"

I shook my head, using my "no" to clear my head a little and loosen his hypnotizing grip on me. "I'm an only child, but I do have a stepsister. She lives with her mom in Georgia, so I don't see her very often."

"Your parents are divorced?"

I nodded. "Mom's been remarried for about five years. What about yours?"

"They're still married." The tone of his voice dropped.

It seemed that his parents were not his favorite topic.

"How old are you?" I asked as I raised my glass to take a sip.

His gaze locked on mine. "Thirty-one."

The little champagne that had slipped into my mouth shot back out into the glass.

Thirty-one? Seriously. What was a hot guy like him doing hanging out with a girl thirteen years younger than him?

I chugged the rest of my glass, tipping the bottom up until every last drop was warming my veins.

"How old did you think I was?" he asked as he took the bottle out of the ice bucket and refilled my glass.

I shook my head and took another long sip. "No clue. It didn't really matter."

Leaning forward, he tangled our fingers together. "Then I kissed you."

I couldn't help but lean forward until we were only a few inches apart. "And I wondered, why?"

"Because you're beautiful, and I had the best day that I've probably had in a decade with you. Because it felt right." He pressed his lips against mine. Soft and light, and it made my brain foggy. "Have I scared you off?"

If anything, he was drawing me closer with his allure. Never had I ever been so physically affected by a boy, but Weston was no boy; he was a man.

I shook my head. "No, but I really do feel like I'm in some strange fairy tale."

"Fairy tales are good," he said as he leaned back again.

I stayed leaning forward. "But they're usually just tales."

He quirked his brow. "Won't this be a tale when you go home?"

"True." He was right. When I returned home, it would just be a fantastical story of a night that I spent with a prince.

"Tell me about your home." The change of subject made me wonder if he was trying to cool it down between us.

"Well, you met my Mom."

He nodded. "She's a character."

"She's married to Mike. My dad lives in Chicago, and I get to see him about once a month and for a couple weeks in the summer."

"How far is that from where you live?" he asked.

"It's just over three hours."

I lost track of how many glasses of champagne I'd consumed, but before our meal had even come, the bottle was empty. Another bottle quickly took its place, and Weston refilled our glasses.

The second bottle was half gone by the time our dinner arrived, and I was feeling a bit loopy. Weston ordered yet another bottle, and we dove in to our food—and even more champagne.

"You know," I started, waving my fork loosely in the air. "My mom and dad got married when they were my age. My age! They made it last waaaay longer than it should've, but I can't even imagine it!"

"Yeah? My parents have been married for thirty-seven years."

"My mom has all these warped ideas on marriage, especially about getting married at a young age. She has just beaten them into my head," I said, my hand making the hammering motion I was trying to describe.

"How long were they married?" he asked curiously, stealing the bite of food from my fork.

My mouth dropped open, unable to believe he stole my bite. He was grinning and looking like a sexy little demon. Grabbing his hand, I pulled his fork to my mouth and stole his bite, my eyes daring him to object. Turnabout was fair play.

He didn't object, but he did wet his lips and bite his lower lip when my mouth wrapped around his fork.

"So, how long?"

I knew I was getting drunk when all I could think of with his question was how long *he* was.

"Mmm, eight years, I think," I replied, taking another sip and giggling.

Weston leaned forward and placed a kiss on my neck, sending chills down my body, and I took in a shuddering breath.

"I think we could beat that," he whispered in my ear.

"Yeah?" Excitement coursed through me.

"Yeah. Come on," he said, standing and throwing a string of hundred dollar bills down, then taking my hand.

I stumbled a bit, but he caught me, drawing me in.

"Where are we going?" I asked as he wrapped his arm around my waist, holding me to him as we made our way to the elevator.

It arrived in less than a minute, and as we entered, he pressed his lips to mine. He kissed me, hard, pushing me into the elevator wall as it descended. I was buzzing, high from his lips, and probably all the champagne I had consumed.

"Let's get married," he said, grinning like a kid on Christmas, his eyes sparkling.

"Okay," I replied, and pulled his lips back down to mine. I'd do whatever he wanted, as long as he didn't stop kissing me. Maybe getting married was how I could stay with him. Maybe forever.

I was giggling when the elevator reached the lobby. We climbed back into the limo and Weston directed the driver to head to the mall at Caesar's Palace.

"Why there? They have a chapel? Are we going to the Little White Chapel? That would be so cliché!" I giggled, loving the idea.

His lips found my neck, his arms pulling me onto his lap. "We need rings, baby girl."

"Oh . . . yeah," I said, distracted by his hand caressing my thigh under the hem of my dress and his mouth on my skin.

Things seemed to blur, and time moved faster after that. I remembered sparkling diamonds, heavenly kisses, and a very excited "I do."

Chapter Four

OUR MESS

THE NEXT MORNING I AWOKE TO SOMETHING HARD slamming into my forehead. Opening my eyes, cringing against the harsh light streaming in from the window, I found the offending item. Sitting on the ring finger of my left hand was a very large, pear shaped diamond ring.

My eyes widened and I sat straight up. A bad idea as my head began to pound, and it suddenly felt very heavy. Unable to hold it up, I fell to the side to lie back down and burrow into my pillow. I was stopped before reaching the mattress by a warm, moving, soft body. The person I landed on groaned, his arms swinging to wrap around me.

I froze, and so did the body, both of us halting our breath. Large hands roamed down my sides, then over the swell of my hips and butt.

A deep groan escaped the chest beneath my head. How did this happen? My gaze flitted around, realizing that I was not in my hotel room. My eyes shot down, and I sighed when I found my dress was still on, and so was most of his suit, though his shirt was unbuttoned enough to reveal the sculpted chest beneath.

One of his hands moved up and brushed the hair from my face before tilting my head back. Weston's eyes widened when they met mine.

"Jesus-fucking-Christ!" he cursed.

His eyes squeezed shut, and he pinched the bridge of his nose between his thumb and forefinger. I don't know why, but his reaction made my chest tighten. I needed to leave, get away. Now.

Using the hand on his chest, I pushed up, lifting my body from the bed and his warmth.

"I . . . have to go," I whispered.

He opened his eyes at my movement and his hand reached out, grabbing mine as I tried to remove it from his chest. "Wait . . . What the hell is that?"

My gaze followed his down to the large diamond ring I was sporting.

"I don't know. It was there when I woke up."

Quickly, he jerked his other arm out from underneath my body, his eyes widening when a white-gold band reflected in the light.

"Oh my God!" I gasped. "Did we . . . I . . . how . . ."

"I don't know, but I think so," he said in reply to my incomplete and incoherent questions. The same thoughts probably running through his own mind.

Jumping up, he staggered and grabbed his head, quickly stumbling back to the bed. Trying again, slowly, he walked out of the bedroom to the large dining room table and picked something up from the glass top.

He picked up another item, and then began mumbling and chanting "fuck" over and over.

"What is it?" I asked from the doorway, though, I had a feeling I knew what it was already.

"Well, Mrs. Lockwood, it's our marriage certificate."

Fuck. Me.

My stomach turned as I stared down at the tile floor that seemed to be disappearing from beneath me.

The night returned in bits. Fuzzy images, but I remembered fun. I remembered Weston and how good his body felt pressed against me. His lips on mine, his hands roaming and lighting up my skin.

I reached up to my rat's nest of hair and remembered the feeling of his fingers tangling, knotting it up as we made out. Probably from dry humping and on the cusp of sex.

"I asked you to marry me, in the elevator after dinner," he recounted as he stared down at the items on the table. "We went and bought rings, and we found a chapel on the strip."

He was right. Vague memories surfaced, filling my mind with images of diamonds sparkling and walking down a short aisle to him. Though, I mostly remembered his body pushing mine against the wall inside that elevator. I stared down at the ring on my finger, entranced as I watched it sparkle under the light.

I lived in the dream for the smallest of minutes, wondering what life would be like with him. Because I knew that I wouldn't be wearing it much longer. Soon, he would be returning it to wherever we picked it up.

And then we would go our separate ways, our next contact in the form of papers to annul our drunken decision. Nothing left but memories of the beautiful being, his magical lips, and the most wonderful day of my life.

A quiet sigh slipped from my lips.

"Annulment is probably best," I said, taking one last gaze at the ring before looking up to where he was standing across the room.

His gaze shifted to mine, and I was shocked to see surprise in his features.

"Annulment?" He glanced back down to the table. "Yes, I suppose you're right. Best."

He appeared saddened, not quite the reaction I was expecting. Turning, he moved past me and into the bathroom. I moved from my support and went to get a look at the certificate. It wasn't the only thing lying on the table. There were a few photos of Weston and I, looking happy, excited, and in love as we said "I do."

Did I just think we looked in love? No, it wasn't possible, but sure enough . . . it showed in the pictures.

Oh God, my head was spinning, along with the light pounding.

Weston came out a few minutes later and stood next to me as I stared at the photos.

"Can I have one?" I asked, my voice almost a whisper.

"As many as you want, as long as I get one," he replied.

"Whichever one you want," I said.

I watched him grab the one of us smiling like fools for the camera. The rings sat on our fingers, and I was holding a small bouquet of white roses. It was the best one.

The room was quiet, neither one of us knowing what to say or do. It was suffocating, something I'd never felt with him . . . not that I'd known him that long.

"I should get back. Mom's probably worried," I said, turning and looking up at him.

He looked pained, a heavy sigh escaping his lips. His arm reached out and pulled me to him, and I was once again—probably for the last time—pressed into his warmth. He kissed the top of my head, hard, his hand cupping the back of my head, as if trying to embed his being into me.

"I should go with you, let her know what's going on. Give me a second to change," he said, releasing me and moving back.

I stayed where I was to give him some privacy. That's when I noticed just how large of a suite we were in. It was easily bigger than my house. It was lavishly decorated, and a vast contrast to the room my mom and I had floors below. Moving to the window, I looked out at the spectacular view of the strip in awe.

"Nice, isn't it?" Weston's voice came from behind me.

"Beautiful," I said as I turned to walk back to him.

"Here." He held out his hands. Looking down at them, I found my purse, shoes, and the pictures.

"Thank you," I said solemnly, taking them from him.

I removed the ring from my finger and placed it in his hand.

"You probably want to return this."

"Yeah," he replied, his voice almost sounding sad, and placed it in his pocket.

The atmosphere was awkward between us, and I didn't like it. I wanted what we'd had the previous day. But between our hangovers and what we'd done, I wasn't sure there was a way to go back.

"We should go." Reaching out, he laced his fingers with mine, and we headed out the door to tell my mother the grave news.

Chapter Five

OUR PREDICAMENT

I COULD ALMOST HEAR THE SNARE DRUM IN MY HEAD BEATING a march like we were walking to the gallows, its beat picking up in pace as my hand reached out to slide my key into the slot.

My heart stopped as the door flung open, my mother standing there with wide eyes, worry etched into her features.

"There you are! Thank God!" She pulled me in for a hug, then stepped back to let us in. "I tried to call, but it went to voicemail. I didn't think you'd be out *all* night."

"Sorry, Mom."

She glanced at Weston and looked to me, her worry melting away.

"Did you two have fun?" she asked with a smile and a wink.

I wanted to facepalm myself from her one-eighty change in reaction. My mom was actually hoping I had sex with him? I hoped that wasn't it.

"I'm surprised to see you, Weston," she said, smiling at him. "Well, hurry up. Checkout is in two hours, and I want to get another few minutes in at the casino before we head out."

"Actually, Karen, we have something to tell you before that," Weston started before announcing, "We got married last night."

The smile fell from her face, and she looked at us with eyes what were almost bugging out of her head.

"Don't worry, Mom, we're going to get an annulment," I said hurriedly.

"Why?" my mother asked. Her brow was scrunched, and she seemed genuinely confused.

What the hell?!

Only my mother. Rational people knew why.

Weston stepped forward. "Because, this was a mistake. We just drank too much champagne. She's only eighteen, Karen."

"So. You're married now. Why not give it a try?" Her tone implying it was the most obvious answer.

I couldn't even form words. Be married, become a wife, to a stranger?

Weston stared at her, his jaw slack, his brain unable to comprehend my mother's words. "She's eighteen and still in high school! We live in different states."

Mom put her hand on her hip. "Weston, do you like her?"

He held up his hands to stop her. "That's irrelevant."

She quirked her brow at him. "Just answer, please."

Weston's eyes widened. "Well . . . yes."

"Good. She'll go home with you, and I'll send her things."

"What?" Weston and I cried at the same time.

"Mom?" Tears stung my eyes as I stared at her, my chest tightening. Was she trying to get rid of me?

"Oh, Wren, sweetheart," she said and wrapped her arms around me.

"Why?" I asked softly, my voice quivering.

"I see your why and raise you a how. How do you two know this wasn't meant to be? Maybe this was destiny hitting you both over the head," she said, then turned to Weston. "Is that really your only concern, Weston, her age?"

"I . . . ummm . . . she's in her senior year."

"It's only the fall semester. She can easily enroll in classes where you live." She looked between us, then let out a sigh. "Look, Weston, there must have been something about her that interested you, otherwise, you wouldn't have asked her to marry you. You bought a ring and said 'I do.'"

"I meant it."

I snapped up to stare at him. *Meant it?*

There was a knot in my chest. We were both a bit hungover, but that's not what I saw in his eyes.

"It was a drunken mistake." *Wasn't it?* We were practically strangers with an attraction. Nothing more, right?

"It doesn't matter how much you had to drink, that was what you did. Drinking is not an excuse to wipe everything away in the morning."

Mom and her lessons—drinking doesn't absolve actions. Though, the situation was a little extreme for a lesson, in my view.

"This . . . Mom, I've known him for two days." Did she really want me to go with an unknown man?

"You two are married. Deal with it."

"Mom!" I cried, choking back the tears I felt pricking my eyes. I couldn't believe this was happening. Weston and I had decided to wipe the slate clean, and here my mother was trying to push us back together.

"Oh, no. You said 'I do,' young lady. You're the same age I was when I married your father. These things happen for a reason. You have a connection, explore it. Don't end this, because you can't have a re-do. You'll be left with 'what ifs.'"

"Weston?" my voice beseeched him, but achingly, while his expression remained deep in thought.

He rubbed his hands across his face.

"You do realize I'm closer to your age than hers."

"As much as I realize she is closer to your maturity level than I'll ever be. Physical age isn't always relevant. Age is just a number. Wren will always be more mature than me. Much more responsible."

Why did it suddenly feel like ancient times and I was just traded for two sheep?

A drunken conversation flooded back to me.

"You!" I shrieked, my heart pounding in my chest. "You're the one who bet we could stay married longer than my parents!"

He grimaced and actually hung his head.

Was that it? Just a bet?

I sunk down to sit on the edge of the bed, my arms wrapped around my waist. My stomach dropped.

"I'm not a gamble." The words that came were soft and as filled with crushed emotions as I felt.

His eyes widened in disbelief before he stepped forward and crouched down in front of me. Reaching out, he took my hands in his. "I didn't propose because I thought you were a gamble . . . well, not in that sense."

"Was it a sense of pride? To see if you could get the girl to say 'yes'?" My anger rose again, and I pulled away from him. "Did you bet with yourself?"

I knew I was getting ahead of myself, but it hurt, in an unbelievable way, to even think that was all the previous night was about.

"Of course not!" he yelled. "I asked you to marry me because I wanted you to marry me!"

My mom lit up, her smile taking up most of her face, while I just stared at him, guilt flooding in that I was getting so upset.

"See!" Mom stood and clapped her hands together. "Oh, this is so exciting!"

Moving to the closet, she pulled out her suitcase to begin packing up, leaving Weston and me there, wondering how our lives were just flipped upside down in five minutes.

"Are you sure?" I asked as I looked up at Weston.

Weston tentatively placed his hands on my knees. "Wren, I'm not going to force you to do anything, but I want to try."

I swallowed hard and stared into his eyes, somewhat hoping they held all the answers. My stomach turned with the fear of what was about to happen. Going home with Weston, remaining his wife. We were married.

I was married to a man I didn't even know. People didn't get married to strangers, at least not in modern day society.

Were we to return to his home, where he would bed me and hang the sheet out the window to prove my innocence and that I was his property?

My innocence … crap. I hadn't told him yet, not that we really had reached that conversation anyway. He didn't know I was untouched goods, that I remained intact. I'd fooled around with guys, sure, but it had never gone that far. Now, I was going to be shacked up with an older man who was sure to be much more oriented in that area, and might very well be expecting me to be as well once we were alone.

"Are you okay?" Weston asked, shaking me from my inner turmoil.

"I think I was just sold to you for two sheep," I replied with a sigh.

He tried not to laugh, but a chuckle came out anyway.

"You'll need this back, Mrs. Lockwood," he said with a smile. It was shy, but full of joy. He pulled the ring out from his pocket. "Not quite two sheep. Actually, quite a bit more."

He took my hand in his, much like I was certain he did the night before, and slid the ring onto my finger.

Weston left a moment later to give us time to talk and pack, but we agreed to meet up at eleven in the lobby.

"Mom, are you sure this is a good idea?" I asked once he was gone.

My nerves were shot, and I wasn't sure I could leave. Could I really go with a stranger, to a strange place, thousands of miles away from the only home I've ever known? Leave everything behind from my life?

Just thinking about it put me on the edge of a panic attack.

"Yes and no. If you had come to me and said you wanted to get married, I would have tried to talk you out of it. But this spur of the moment behavior is so unlike you that I have to believe it's fate!" Her face lit up again as she spoke.

"But I don't even know him!" A tear leaked out and slid down my cheek.

"Oh, baby. You'll get to know him. I see the spark between you two."

"I can't believe we let you talk us into this." I shook my head as another tear trickled slowly down my cheek.

Her arms wrapped around me and hugged me tight. "Wren, it was only too easy, because you both want it. If you didn't, you'd be coming home with me. Give it a try, an honest try, and if things don't work out, you can be on the first flight back to Indianapolis. You'll always have a home with me. Please know that, sweetheart."

"Okay." I was shaking with fear, scared out of my mind of the unknown.

Pulling back, I looked into my mother's pretty face. She saw the tears running down my cheeks and smiled softly before wiping them away with a gentle brush of her fingers like she always did.

Leaving my mom, my school, my friends, and my home. It was all too much.

"Aw, honey, it will be okay, you'll see. Just remember, I love you."

I packed up my suitcase and backpack after taking a much-needed, calming shower, and we headed down to the lobby to meet my . . . husband. Weston was waiting for us, suitcases in tow, smiling as we approached. I hugged my mother tight, whispering that I loved her and to make sure Mike fed my beta fish.

"Call me for anything," she said as she cupped my face in her hands. I nodded and gave her a small smile.

We waved goodbye as she headed down to the casino before leaving for home. I could tell she was trying not to cry as she walked away.

We stood there for a moment watching her go, realizing this was it. We were going to his home together, leaving Vegas as husband and wife. What the hell was I going to tell my friends?

"So . . ." He reached out and slid his hand into mine. "Are we ready?"

I turned and smiled up at him as best I could. "As we'll ever be."

He linked his fingers with mine as our bags were loaded onto a luggage cart. Pulling me to him, he wrapped his arm around my waist.

"Let's go home," he said, placing a kiss on the top of my head.

Leaving the hotel, we headed out to embark on our new life together.

Chapter Six

OUR TRIP HOME

THE ELECTRICITY FROM THE EXCITEMENT MY MOTHER stirred up had waned, and we were left with silence as we left Las Vegas and headed down the highway to Los Angeles, where Weston lived, in his car. The music was on low, and it lightened the mood a bit.

"Am I the only one who thinks this is the most awkward moment?" Weston's smooth voice spoke, breaking the heavy silence and my deep thoughts.

"Nope," I said, popping the "p" at the end.

"Which is strange, because we were both so comfortable with each other yesterday."

"That was yesterday . . . before we got married," I reminded him.

His head hung and he let out a sigh, looking at me cautiously out of the corner of his eye.

"Never, in a million years, did I ever expect to come home from a business trip in Vegas as a married man." He shook his head. "Fuck."

"Why am I going with you?" I asked, yet again.

"Because your mom has some serious voodoo," he noted with a humorless chuckle.

I nodded. "I still can't believe she convinced us this was a good idea."

"Hmm . . . part of me says this is the stupidest idea ever," he said. My body slumped further into the plush leather seats. "But, then part of me wonders if she's right."

A part of me wondered as well, but it didn't quell the twisting in my stomach and the vibration in my veins. Leaving for college was supposed to be my big moment of independence, but suddenly I was completely dependent on a man I didn't even know. That alone scared the shit out of me.

"I don't . . . I don't want to be a burden to anyone. Especially to you, a person I barely know."

"You're not a burden, Wren. Please, don't say that. I really, really enjoyed yesterday." His hand reached out to take mine.

It was warm, and its heat spread through my whole body, comforting me.

"But this is not how you saw your drive home."

"No, it's not. It is what it is, however. So, we'll make do. I'm willing to . . . try," he reassured me.

"So, what now?" I asked as we relaxed a bit.

"Well . . ." He sighed. "I honestly don't know."

"I was supposed to return to school tomorrow."

"Fuck . . . school," he groaned.

"How . . . how long should I wait to change my name?" I asked, realizing we didn't fully understand everything that went into staying married. "I don't even know how we do this."

He pinched the bridge of his nose between his forefinger and thumb. "I . . . it probably would be best to do that as soon as possible. Tomorrow. If anything were to happen to you, they would need to contact me. So, you'll need a new social security card, a license. We'll need to enroll you in school . . ."

"What about just getting my GED?"

"It's best to have a diploma. I know USC already accepted you, but it really is best," he said and began mumbling to himself before he pressed a button on the steering wheel. "Call Julia."

"Calling Julia," an automated voice said through the speakers.

A ring of the phone was followed by a feminine voice. "Hi, Wes. Enjoy your trip?"

He let out a little chuckle and glanced at me. "Yes, I did. In fact, I'm going to be home in just over an hour, and I need you to be there. We'll talk then."

"Aye aye, captain. I'll be there."

There was a click of the call ending, and the music resumed. "Who was that?"

"My assistant."

"You have an assistant?"

He turned and smirked at me. "I have three, and Julia, my head assistant, also has an assistant."

The blood drained from my face. What had I gotten myself into?

"I suddenly feel ill," I said and leaned over. "What do you do? I don't even know what line of work my husband is in!"

He eyed me and grimaced. "I'm a movie producer."

I stared at him in a wide-eyed mixture of surprise and horror. "What?"

"I'm in the movie industry."

It all started to make some sense. From the money, to people practically tripping over themselves to help him. I thought it was just his good looks, but it was more.

"Oh my God. Just . . . take me straight to the airport. Do whatever you need to do and send me the papers. I'll sign them," I rambled. A movie producer? There was just no way it was going to work.

"What? Why?"

"That is a high profile life . . ." I shook my head and my shoulders drew up, my body reacting as my brain tried to form words. "I'm just an Indiana girl, Weston. I'm not cut out for that kind of life."

"You don't even know what kind of life I have or what yours will be like," he said, trying to defuse me.

"It involves lots of money and possibly fame, I can tell that much."

"And you have an aversion to those?" he asked, his brow hitching up. It was one of those looks like he was expecting to see that I had two heads.

I nodded my head vigorously. "Yes."

"You're a strange girl. Aren't you supposed to be wanting to be Kim Kardashian?" he asked.

"I'd rather be the barista at Starbucks," I grumbled with a roll of my eyes.

"Huh." He tapped his fingers on the steering wheel. "Okay, so I think it's best that we don't share a bedroom right away. Agreed?" I turned to stare at him with wide eyes. "Temporary, of course."

I shook my head again. "Airport."

He continued on, ignoring me. "I have a very nice bedroom next to mine you could use. It's fully furnished, but if you don't like it, we can get whatever you want."

"I don't want you spending money on me, and I thought we were headed to the airport."

"Nope. Wren Lockwood, we're going to give this a go," he said, grinning like a fool and ignoring my aversions.

I glared at him. "I don't like you so much right now. Can we go back to five minutes ago when you were almost agreeing with me?"

He continued on as if he hadn't heard me, yet again. "You'll need a car. We can shop for one of those this weekend."

"No." Going to USC was supposed to be the big change in my life. Something I could plan and prepare for mentally. A spur-of-the-moment wedding, tied to someone I didn't know, sent the adrenaline running through me into a nervous humming. My knee began to bounce.

"And, we can change any of the furniture you don't like."

I sighed, finally giving in. "The furniture will be perfectly fine. And I don't need a car."

"You'll need a car to get around."

"I'll need a job . . ." I grumbled, then sat straight up in my seat. "My job!" I was scheduled for a shift the next night.

"You don't need a job. I can set you up an account to use."

His money? I didn't know much about cars, but I knew that the one we were in probably cost more than the house I lived in. Which meant he had more than I could even imagine.

But I'd been working part time since I was sixteen, using my own money to pay for things I wanted.

I shook my head. "I'm not spending your money."

"Yes, you are, Wren."

"We don't even know each other! How are you making these types of financial decisions?" Frustrated tears filled my eyes as the bouncing of my leg sped up.

He smiled softly and reached out to place his hand on mine, which was fisted on my thigh. "Because you're my wife, and I'm going to take care of you."

"Even though, you haven't had any of the . . . benefits of a wife?" I asked quietly, averting my eyes from him to look out the window.

He cleared his throat and shifted in his seat. "We'll get to that."

I tilted my head back against the headrest, then turned to look at him. "We can just have this annulled, is what we can do."

"Dorothy, you're not in Kansas anymore. Follow my yellow brick road, and you'll be fine." His eyes were bright, amusement dancing in them as he smiled at me.

I narrowed my gaze on him. "I'm not sure I like the *Wizard of Oz* analogy." Though I definitely wasn't in Kansas—or Indiana—anymore.

"Like it or not, it's you and me, baby girl. We're in this mess together. No running back to Indianapolis. Your mom was right, I asked you to marry me. I may have been drunk, but I meant it. I spent nearly fifty grand on your ring, so I know I meant it."

"What?" My voice came out in a shrill screech, my gaze moving down to the diamond situated on my left ring finger. It was big, huge, maybe even enormous by diamond standards, but fifty grand?

"That ring is from Tiffany's. The name alone costs."

I shifted in my seat to face him. "I can't wear it in school!"

"We can get you a chain, if you like, and you can wear it around your neck."

"Why are you doing all this?" I asked, defeat filling me.

"Because, as much as I do agree with you, and as much as I know how ludicrous this is, my gut wants to agree with your mom. Don't you feel the same? I won't force you, Wren. You do have free will . . . with the exception of the money acceptance. I guess . . . I just got caught up in the idea," he explained, deflating near the end. "In my fantasy."

"It's not that," I spoke softly, "I . . . I'm caught up in the idea, but I'm scared shitless." I swallowed thickly, fighting back the fear and uncertainty. "A stranger, in a strange land, with no inkling of home?" My heart was aching, chest tight, thinking about all of the things I took for granted.

"How about we just take it one day at a time?" he said. His fingers laced into mine and he began rubbing gentle circles on my thumb.

I took a deep, settling breath. "I think I can handle that."

"Good, because . . . welcome home, Mrs. Lockwood," he said with a smirk.

I didn't realize we'd stopped, and my gaze moved to the vision in front of us. My eyes widened as I looked incredulously at the sight before me.

It didn't matter how much I made over my lifetime, one glance told me I'd never make enough money to pay for the home that lay in front of us.

Holy shit.

I was in way over my head.

WALKING INTO WESTON'S . . . OUR . . . HOME WAS LIKE walking into a different world. The place was huge. And spotless. It reminded me of the display homes in the new neighborhoods that Mom always liked to look at, or a magazine portraying homes of the rich and famous. There was no clutter, not a speck of dust, nothing. It was hard to find personal items, just a few pictures hanging on the wall. Otherwise, it held a museum-like feel to it. I almost wondered where the film crew for MTV's *Cribs* was hiding.

"Kitchen is here, living room is through that way," he said, pointing toward the large arched hole in the wall. We walked through, Weston mapping out the layout with hand gestures. It was a lot to take in, and I knew it would just take some exploring on my own to really understand it all.

He halted when we neared the stairway, and I almost ran into him.

"I didn't think you were here yet," he said.

I looked around him to find a very pretty woman wearing a pencil skirt, a short sleeved sweater, and heels.

I felt very underdressed for my surroundings.

"I snuck in through the front just to scare you," she said with a smile. Her gaze was soft, and she looked friendly.

"Hmm, nice try. I did jump, just a tiny bit. Imperceptible with the human eye," he teased back.

"Bring back a souvenir, Wes?" she asked with a hint of amusement in her voice, her gaze flickering to me.

He let out a nervous laugh. I knew he hadn't thought about how we were going to handle telling people what we were, and neither had I. Hell, I spent the entire car ride from Vegas trying to convince him to take me to the airport. Scared and overwhelmed were just two aspects of my upheaved mental state.

"Julia, I need you to make a list, and have a seat while you do it," he said.

He grabbed on to my hand as we moved into what I assumed was more of a formal living room.

I expected Julia to have a questioning look on her face, speculation clear in her features, but there was nothing but compliance and a soft smile. I watched her gaze at where our hands were connected and, surprisingly, she seemed to like it.

Settling on the couch, she opened up her laptop and waited for Weston to begin. Releasing my hand, he began to pace a bit, stopping every few feet to look at Julia.

"First off, I need you to make an appointment with Reggy as soon as possible." Weston tugged at his hair. "I can't stand this anymore. It's way too long."

I was a bit sad when I realized he was talking about a haircut. It was just so inviting, and I hadn't gotten to really tug on it. Not that I thought that might happen anytime soon. Well, I supposed it could happen. We were already married, after all.

"I also need a credit card on one of my accounts, as soon as possible, in the name of Wren Lockwood," he said, his eyes never leaving Julia.

Her hands stopped typing and she looked up at him, then to me, before moving down to her phone and back up to Weston. They stared at one another for a moment before Julia suddenly dove for the phone that lay between them, her hand wrapping around the plastic and glass. But Weston had also gone after it, his hand occupying the other end.

"No!" he cried vehemently, trying to pull the phone from her hand.

"I can't lie to him, Weston!" Julia protested.

I watched as the two wrestled for it, both trying to pry it away. It was an odd exchange, one that I was not expecting. Words poured forth as they struggled for control: *it's mine, no, don't, he's my fiancé*, etc. Weston eventually won out and stuffed it in his pocket, away from Julia's grasp.

"I live with him. How am I supposed to keep this from him?" she asked.

"I'll tell him, really, I just . . . have to figure out what to say," Weston said, his hand tugging at his locks in what I was now noticing to be a nervous fidget.

"I'll give you till the end of the day to explain this to him. I will not crawl into bed with your brother tonight with *this*"—her hands gestured between Weston and me—"hanging over my head."

"Julia, I'll call him when we're done here and I get Wren settled. Okay?"

She sighed and nodded, returning her attention to the computer on her lap.

"So, more on that, we'll need to get Wren's name changed as soon as possible, tomorrow would be best. Social security card, license . . ."

"I'll get Graham on printing up anything we need Wren to fill out. Not all of that can be accomplished so soon, but I'll see what we can expedite and what favors I have up my sleeve." She looked at me. "I'll need some basic information from you as well." Her gaze turned back to Weston. "Passport?"

Weston turned toward me.

"I have one in Indy . . ." The whole interaction left me standing awkwardly in the middle of the room and sounding just as awkward.

Julia nodded. "We'll get the necessary information to update it and send it in when it arrives. How long do you think it will take? To get everything here?"

Months knowing my mom, but with Mike keeping her in line and out of memory lane, faster.

"Umm, I don't know. Maybe a week or two. I can call and ask my mom later."

Weston turned his attention back to Julia. "Set up an appointment for Wren with Sophie tomorrow. Tell her she has free rein. That should get her off my back for a few weeks."

"Who's Sophie?" I asked, almost getting lost with how fast he was firing things off.

"My personal shopper," he responded without missing a beat.

"No," I said, interrupting him from his next chain of thought. I was putting my foot down. A personal shopper? Too much.

His brow shot up. "No?"

"I can manage just fine for now."

He ignored my comment and turned back to Julia, continuing to talk about me like I wasn't there. "I also need you to call Scott. Wren needs a car. Tell him we'll be in on Saturday."

"Do I have to stomp my foot and act like a child?"

He turned and quirked his brow. "Do I have to act like an overbearing husband? This is all stuff you need, Wren."

"Fine, then give me a couple hundred bucks and point me in the direction of the nearest Old Navy." Seriously, I didn't need that much. "I'll just go there. Oh, and a used car lot."

"No Old Navy if you want to keep the clothes. Sophie will set them on fire. And no wife of mine will be driving a used car," he said. Julia was watching us closely, a smile lighting up her features. "We also need a list of the best private schools in the area."

What was wrong with Old Navy? I loved their clothes. They were my go-to store.

"What kind of school?" Julia asked, her fingers typing more notes than what Weston actually said.

"High school," I chimed in.

Julia's typing halted again.

"H-high school?" she asked, blinking up at us and then staring at me. "Weston . . . the press . . ."

"Doesn't have to know."

She shook her head. "We have to, at least, do a press release. If not, they'll have a field day when they find out about her."

"No press release." He stressed the words, so adamant on the subject that Julia dropped it.

"Press release? W-why would you have a press release about me?" I asked, visions of the airport dancing through my head. It was too much to take in. The room started to spin, and I had to sit in one of the chairs while taking a deep breath to calm myself.

"No press release. Not yet."

"People are going to notice that ring on your finger. You can't hide that."

"Then I'll take it off for now." He looked down at it, spinning it around his finger before relaxing his hands to his side. "Which reminds me . . . when you talk to Sophie, have her bring some white-gold chains so Wren can wear hers around her neck while at school."

Weston's list calmed down after that, and soon they began talking business. He had a busy schedule for the week, but he had Julia redirect some things in order to be with me and help get me settled.

While they were talking, I shot my mom a text.

Arrived safe to my new home in LA. What have I gotten into?

An hour later she hadn't responded, probably still on the plane.

A few minutes later, we parted from Julia. She headed to Weston's office, and we went up the stairs. The hallway he led me to was long as I peered down it, but we didn't go far.

"This will be your bedroom . . . for now," he said, his demeanor a bit nervous as he turned the handle.

The room behind the door was larger than any room in my mother's house, and over twice the size of my tiny bedroom. Rich gold, tan, and red fabrics adorned the bed and windows. Cream and black painted dressers and end tables, a chaise lounge and chair by the window, and an adjoining bathroom finished off the space.

"It's beautiful," I said softly as I entered.

"You like? If not, there are other rooms, or we can get new furniture."

I shook my head. "No, I love it."

"Good," he said with a smile and leaned in to kiss my forehead.

I tilted my head up so that his lips met mine instead. It was light, sweet, and helped calm me. He grinned down at me and cupped my face, bringing it to him for a real kiss.

His lips were soft at first, then his tongue slipped across, coaxing my mouth open. It was our first kiss all day, and it helped to relax the awkward air around us.

His hands flattened out on my back, pulling me closer. My own hands reached up and wrapped around his neck, keeping him close as the depth and strength of our kiss increased until I was completely mashed against his strong chest.

My whole body tingled. Needs I wasn't used to crawled in, taking control of my muscles.

"I really should stop." His breath was hard, lips ghosting across mine.

A desperation took hold, pushing me closer. "Yeah?"

"This close to a bed? Oh, yeah." He let out a sigh and drew his hands back, forcing me to do the same. He cleared his throat and reached down and pulled on his waistband. "I have to make a few calls. Why don't you take a look around? Make yourself comfortable, unpack, whatever."

"Okay."

He nodded and turned to leave, but stopped at the doorway. "Wren?"

"Yes?"

"I'm glad you're here," he said with a shy smile before disappearing down the hall.

My bottom lip ended up between my teeth. He could be so adorable. Very different from his sexy side, which was turning me into someone I didn't recognize. I liked that I would, in time, get to know all of his sides.

Turning, I threw my suitcase on the bed and opened it up. The items in my bag stared back at me, and we began a Mexican standoff. I wasn't quite ready to unpack, especially considering I felt more like I was a guest at a fancy hotel, not wanting to bother unpacking, than my new home. I sighed. It was like I didn't know how long I would be staying. I knew, in my head, I was my new home, but in my heart . . . not so much.

My new reality was a stark contrast to the old, and the learning curve was daunting.

Deciding to get my bearings of the monstrous mansion, I headed out to get the lay of the land. Walking down the hall, in the opposite direction in which we came, I found various bedrooms, some furnished, some not. Artwork hung from the wide hallway, all the way to the end where I happened upon a second staircase. There were more stairs than I was used to, thanks to the tall ceilings, and as I descended the stairs I was surprised to end up just outside the kitchen.

Walking through the kitchen, I explored all the rooms we passed on our way to where we'd found Julia. Soon, I found myself in a large, windowed room overlooking the side garden, with a beautiful baby grand piano in the middle. I walked up to it, lifted the lid a bit, and let my fingers lightly tap on the partially exposed ivory keys. The sound bounced off the walls, a tinkling much like bells. It was literal music to my ears.

I looked around, and, seeing no one, I gingerly sat down on the piano bench and slowly lifted the lid all the way back to unveil all of the keys. I stared for a moment, swallowing thickly. I'd always loved playing the piano, but due to various reasons—money and work—I hadn't played in over a year.

I let my fingers softly ghost over the ivories and sighed as I began to play a soft, soothing melody. It wasn't a tune I recognized, just whatever came to me. I closed my eyes, feeling the music, letting my fingers gracefully move over the keys to form the beautiful melody. My eyes opened and reality took hold, pulling me from the light, happy place I spent mere moments in. With a sigh, I stood and closed the piano before continuing on my way.

Passing through another door, I found myself in a fancy porch-like area containing slate tile flooring, a water fountain, and lounge chairs. It looked like a wonderful place to spend time with a book and a cup of tea. It overlooked a sculpted rock pool, which was a paradise all on its own, complete with a waterfall, slide, and shallow lounge area, not to mention the plants and the circle I was pretty sure was a hot tub.

Another door led to a formal living room that opened up into the large entryway. As I headed down the hall, I heard Weston's muffled voice coming from behind one of the doors that I suspected was his home office.

"No, Miles, it's not like that . . . She had no idea who I was . . . Yes, I'm certain of it . . . She's . . . Wren is wonderful."

My heart leapt from my chest at his words. Was there such a thing as love at first sight? Had I found it in Weston? There was something between us, for sure.

"I know she's young, I just couldn't . . . I wanted to spend more time with her, we had a bit to drink . . . I know that isn't a valid reason . . . yes, I know. Miles . . . Miles . . . Miles! I'm married! I'm staying married! We'll get to know each other in time."

Not wanting to eavesdrop any longer, I headed up to my new bedroom, mulling over his other statements . . . Who was I married to? With everything, it was obvious my prince charming was more than he'd let on. I needed to find out, and soon.

My suitcase was lying open, still staring at me, so I decided to just do it and unpack. It was weird not to have all of my belongings, to be starting from scratch in a way. I puzzled over where I wanted to put my clothes, laying out a mental plan of what went where. Not that there was much—it was only enough for a long weekend, and half of it was dirty.

Thankfully I was an over packer, so I had a few days of wiggle room before I needed to figure out where in the behemoth of a house the laundry room was.

My phone went off, and I picked it up to find a text from Mom.

Long flight. Home safe. Mike says Hi. Talk to you after work tomorrow. Love you!

And that was it.

It was a life-changing event for me, but I was happy to know she got home okay. Unfortunately, she left her daughter over two thousand miles away.

I had to admit, I could get used to it all. It was just difficult for me to accept such generosity from someone I didn't even know. It felt awkward.

My parents never made a lot of money, so Weston dropping more on me in one night than my mom made in a year was a bit staggering. From the time I was little, Dad used to tell me that nothing would ever be handed to me, and to rely on myself and hard word to get anywhere. It was his way of prepping me to make my mark on the world.

"Wren?" Weston called from the doorway. He found me in the bathroom, organizing. "Wow, you settled in pretty fast."

I shrugged my shoulders. "There wasn't really that much to settle."

He leaned against the wall and smiled at me in the mirror. "Did you take a look around?"

I turned to face him. "Yeah, it's big and beautiful, and the pool is ... I love the pool." I didn't know why, but that nervous awkwardness had returned. We stood there, neither sure of what to say or what to do.

"Well ... we should think about dinner."

"Yeah, dinner," I agreed.

"What do you like?" he asked.

It was then I realized I didn't even know any food he liked. There was so much that we didn't know about each other.

"Are you allergic to any foods?" I blurted out.

"Umm . . . I have a dill allergy," he admitted with a sheepish look.

"Oh, I don't cook much with dill, so that's good." Silence set in again. "Well, we could check out what you have, and I can see what I can whip up."

"What?" he asked, seemingly very confused by the prospect of me cooking.

"Food. Cook. Dinner?"

"Menu. Order. Delivered."

I quirked a brow at him. "You have no food?"

"I . . . don't cook, and I gave my chef time off until tomorrow."

He had a personal chef.

There was a strong feeling in my gut that said the surprises weren't going to stop for a while.

"Weston, I can cook. I've had to almost every day for the past eight years."

"Why?"

"My mom is a terrible cook, so I learned from my grandmother. Once I got some basics, I became the cook of the house," I explained. "Mike's pretty good, but he works second shift."

"Well, the cook has been off for the last four days, so I don't think whatever food is left is any good. But, we do have a vast assortment of delivery."

"Chinese? Pizza?" That was all we had where I came from. Surely that was something that couldn't be vastly different, right?

He chuckled. "Not quite. How do you feel about some Chicken Marsalis, salad, and maybe soufflé for dessert?"

I stared at him. "They deliver that?"

He smiled and grabbed for my hand. "Yes. Now come, let's go order and get to know each other a bit better."

After heading down the stairs to the kitchen, we found the menus tucked in a drawer. Out of curiosity, I opened up the refrigerator to find that Weston was correct—the shelves were pretty much empty.

Weston watched me out of the corner of his eye, smirking, and I walked over, leaning on the counter next to him.

We laughed as we went through the menus. It was unbelievable what some places would deliver. His body was touching mine, and I felt sparks move between us. I knew he did as well. Leaning down, he placed his lips on mine. It was soft and sweet, hinting at things to come. I couldn't help but blush when he held my face in his hand, his thumb caressing my cheek as his eyes stared intently down into mine.

I felt so safe and secure in his presence. So cared for, which was a change from what I was used to.

Maybe this could be the beginning of a beautiful relationship. Maybe Mom wasn't so crazy after all.

Maybe love at first sight wasn't a myth.

Chapter Eight

OUR FIRST NIGHT

INNER WAS ENJOYABLE, THE ATMOSPHERE FROM THE previous night returning. Weston was sexy, playful, funny, and sweet. A deadly combination. Afterwards, we curled up in front of the TV and channel surfed, catching a few minutes of some reality show and a bit of a comedy movie. It was very relaxing, lying nestled into his side, his arm around me. I felt warm, safe, and cherished.

That night, it didn't feel like we'd only known each other for a few short days. Instead, it felt like years had passed and we were an average couple hunkered down for the evening. Two people just enjoying being together. I hoped that even after some time passed that feeling would continue, never to fade.

When it was time for bed, he walked me upstairs and stopped in front of my bedroom door.

"Goodnight," he said as he leaned down and pressed his lips to mine.

I didn't want him to pull back. I wanted to continue feeling his body against mine and the comfort he provided. He looked between his bedroom door and me, then with a long sigh, pulled away.

"Night," I said. It was delayed, and my voice faded off at the end.

It took a few minutes to get ready for bed, but once my phone was plugged in, I turned off the light.

But sleep didn't come.

It was silent. Still. And a foreign environment. Nothing felt right, and I had the weirdest feeling of being off topped with sadness.

While the bed beneath me was soft, it wasn't my bed.

Not my blankets or pillows.

To top it off, the whole reason I was here was lying in the bedroom next to the one I was in.

I couldn't shut my brain off for hours, going over and over the last two days. Suddenly, I was hit with a desire to tell him I was sorry for seeming like an ungrateful brat. That I was happy he wanted me. To let him know I recognized how sweet, kind, and generous he was to me, and how much I appreciated him trying to make me feel comfortable.

I rose from my bed, deciding to see if he was still awake, so I could tell him my nonsensical, sleep deprived, blabbering speech. The door was open, and I wondered if it always was, or if it was just because I was there and he wanted to be able to hear me. Standing in the doorway, I looked in to find him in the middle of a king sized bed, lying on his side with his arms wrapped around a pillow. He looked so adorable, and I couldn't help but stare. He must have heard me, though I knew I barely made a sound, and his gaze lifted to find mine.

"Can't sleep?" he asked softly. I nodded in response. "Me neither."

I hung my head and shrugged. "It's just a little hard, strange place and all."

He moved the pillow back to its rightful place and pulled back the covers, opening his arms up. "Come on in, baby girl."

I smiled shyly at his pet name for me, then walked toward him and the inviting vibe he was projecting. Climbing in to face him, I pulled the light blanket up and lowered my head to the pillow. His right arm moved to rest on my hip and he pulled me in closer.

"Why can't you sleep?" I asked, relaxing in the warmth and smell of him.

"I have a lot on my mind," he replied, his fingers reaching out to smooth a lock of hair behind my ear.

"It's mostly about me."

Weston gave a rueful smile. "Yes. This is new and strange to us both. I hadn't even thought about anyone outside of us knowing, and after evaluating it, there is so much more to this than just you and me being married. Julia was right. The press and paparazzi will go nuts when they find out about you." He let out a sigh. "I think it's in both of our best interests to let our marriage lay low for the time being. Then we can give thought about when and where to announce it. I can tell you, though, if they found out right now, it wouldn't be good for either of us."

"Wow, paparazzi. I never in a million years thought I'd ever have to worry about them."

A low chuckle rumbled from his chest. "Unfortunately, they are always around. That's why I think it's best we lay low. If they don't understand who you are, you'll be okay. The problem is, the moment they grasp what you are to me, all hell will break loose."

"Really?" I asked. My stomach turned at the thought of being followed and hounded.

"Really. Welcome to the movie business. You'll be hot news for a few minutes, and then it will die down."

"I didn't see any in Vegas."

"Because there wasn't anything interesting going on. Meetings about a possible new movie usually don't attract paparazzi unless a high roller, or wild star, is in the mix. This weekend was just a bunch of guys in suits talking business."

"You look good in a suit," I whispered, and he grinned.

"Thank you. I prefer a pair of jeans, but suits are sometimes necessary."

"You look great in jeans too." I giggled then pursed my lips and narrowed my gaze on him. "You weren't in a cloud of adoring fans. I'm not sure I buy all this."

Another chuckle, louder than the first. He was enjoying my ignorance of his identity way too much. I should have known— he was familiar in some ways, but I just couldn't put my finger on it. Then again, he could just be familiar from awards shows. Mom was an Oscars nut, and it was only in the past few years that I had been spared from her madness come February.

"I'm not high on people's radars anymore. And I may have made sure you didn't notice the few autographs I signed while we were out. You were also somewhat oblivious to people staring and pointing."

My mouth went slack. "Well, you know, you're kinda attention grabbing without the whole Hollywood aspect."

His hand caressed up and down my arm. "What's keeping you awake?"

"What isn't? The absolute silence for one. Do you have bugs out here?"

He laughed. "Yes, though I had them turn the volume down."

"Smartass." I laughed and swatted at him. He grabbed hold of my hand and brought it to his lips, placing light kisses on my fingers. "The . . . strangeness of the situation is probably the biggest reason I can't sleep." I blew out a breath. "Suddenly thrust into a new life without closing my old one? I mean, I knew I was moving to California, but I had time to prepare before because it was ten months away. Now? Now I'm in California, married, and without a school or friends. I just kinda feel like I'm in the Twilight Zone."

"It will get better over time, I promise. I know we both have a lot to adjust to," he said, the back of his hand lightly caressing my cheek.

Scooting forward, I buried my head in his chest, my body lining up with his. His arms wrapped around me, an almost purring-like sound coming from his chest as he pulled me close. He slipped a leg between mine and I hitched my left leg up his thigh.

"Thank you for everything today. I didn't mean to come off as rude, it's just . . . I'm very much off balance with you."

"Does this mean you will accept my money without griping about it?" he asked. I could almost hear the smile I was certain he was wearing in his tone.

"I can't guarantee that, because I'm not used to being showered with money, but I'll try. It'll just take time."

"That we have," he said as his hands moved up and down my side in a soothing motion, his touch heating my body every time he reached bare skin.

Wanting to be closer, I wiggled one arm between us to his waist. His shirt had risen and my fingers were graced with the bare skin on his hip.

"It feels so good right here," I said, snuggling deeper into him.

"I couldn't agree more." His voice sounded softer and lower than before.

"Shouldn't we be resisting or something? Trying to be guardedly polite with one another until we become comfortable together?" I asked, my head tilting up to look at him. "Or am I just naïve?"

He shook his head. "Sometimes chemistry is undeniable. I think that is a definite with us."

"I'd say we have it in spades," I whispered.

He leaned forward and pressed his lips to mine. It was soft, tentative, our eyes locked as if he was asking for my permission. I didn't understand his apprehension compared to the previous day, but I needed to make him understand that it was okay. Craning my neck toward him, I deepened the kiss, my eyes fluttering closed. His tongue swept against my lips, and I opened them to let him in.

His arm pulled me closer as he began to devour my mouth. Sparks emitted from where he touched me, bringing my body to life. I moaned into his mouth, my hands reaching up into his hair. I pulled him closer while my fingers tangled in the silky strands, tugging back.

He must have liked that, because he growled deep in his chest. I think I squeaked at the sound as a fire spread through me. He felt so good, so unbelievably good. It was the most erotic, sensual experience I had to date. If it was any indication of things to come, the future was looking very nice indeed.

Hands flexed against my skin, and I pulled back. I could tell my lids were heavy with the lust that coursed through me for this man. My hips and thighs were moving of their own accord, seeking some form of friction.

Leaning down, he began licking, kissing, and sucking on my neck. His teeth nipped at my skin, and I let out a shuddering breath.

"Weston."

Shifting his weight, he rolled me onto my back, arms wrapping tighter around my body. Everything suddenly became more urgent and not enough, desperation for him racing through me. My legs spread open and his hips settled between them, allowing his hard cock to press against my aching heat.

Detaching his lips from my skin, he peeled off my tank top, exposing my chest to him.

"Fuck, baby girl," he growled, his hips flexing against mine.

He devoured me with eyes that had become so dark they almost didn't appear blue any longer. The expression on his face was pure desire, causing a shiver to run down my spine and my nipples to harden. His hands moved to my breasts, weighing them in each hand, pressing my sensitive nipples between his thumb and forefinger. I cried out, my hips bucking up against him. His tongue swept across his lips, hips pressing forward.

"So fucking beautiful. You're perfect," he whispered before leaning down and pressing a hot, open-mouthed kiss to each nipple and suckling lightly.

His fingers moved up my sides, skimming the sides of my breasts. Switching to suck on my other nipple, one hand traveled down, massaging and caressing as he went. A moan escaped my lips when he reached my hip, tickling me and setting me on fire at the same time. His hand slid further down and cupped my sex, massaging me, forcing small cries of pleasure from my lips.

Moving my shorts and panties to the side, his fingers met my burning flesh.

"Damn, damn, fuck!" he cried. "You're fucking soaked." His hand brushed up and down, moving the moisture around a bit. He found my clit and began playing with it: pinching, pulling, flicking, massaging.

I bit down on my bottom lip, my hips rocking up into his hand, begging for more.

"W-Weston, I need to . . . mmm . . . tell you something," I struggled to say, but I needed to get it out before he was surprised, even more than he was bound to be. He needed to know . . .

Leaning back down, ignoring my plea, he resumed sucking on one of my nipples, making me cry out while his hand continued its assault on my clit. He pressed his fingers at the opening of my pussy.

"Oh, oh God!"

He chuckled. "No, baby girl, I'm your husband."

He continued suckling and rubbing until I was a nearly unintelligible mess.

"Ah . . . W-Weston," I tried again. "I'm a . . . ung . . . a v-virgin."

Weston's movements stopped immediately. An audible groan, part pleasure, part pain, erupted from him as he slumped against my body.

"Fuck!"

He pushed off in an attempt to get up, but I stopped him by wrapping my legs around his waist, pulling him back down, and trapping him. A guttural noise escaped from his chest, his eyes rolling back as his clothed cock pressed against my heat.

"Fuck, Wren!" An almost animalistic groan left him as his hips flexed against mine. "No one? Ever? Touched even?"

"Touched over clothes, that's it," I said.

He hissed as his fingers dug into my skin.

He was breathing a bit harder, a shudder running through his body. Leaning down, his mouth was next to me as he whispered into my ear.

"Untouched by any other man? Only my hands, tongue, lips,

teeth, and cock marking you as mine? That is so unbelievably fucking hot. To claim your body as mine, to take you . . . Fuck!" he cried as he abruptly sat up and tried to push away again.

"Don't. I'm your wife," I pleaded. I could see the turmoil in his eyes. He wanted this, wanted me . . . possibly more than anything in that moment.

"Wren . . . I can't . . . do this . . . right now," he said and moved his hands behind him to untangle my legs.

Rejection filled me, and I felt the tears prick my eyes. I turned my head, not wanting him to see them fall.

"Wren, it isn't you," he tried to assure me, his fingers bringing my gaze back to his. "I just . . . losing your virginity is a big deal. It's a once-in-a-lifetime moment and . . ."

"Weston, we're married, and that, to me, should be once-in-a-lifetime," I said as a tear escaped and slid down my cheek. "You're my husband. If we're going to give this an honest go, this has to happen at some point, so why not now? Why wait?"

I was so turned on from his touch that I wanted it, wanted him. Why wait? I wasn't going anywhere, and by all rights, my virginity was his to take. And I wanted it to be him.

His head dropped until his forehead rested on mine. "That's a powerful argument, but I don't . . . are you sure? Right now? I want you so badly I don't know if I can control myself. It will hurt."

I reached between us and began stroking him through the fabric of his shorts. His eyes, that had been locked on my own, rolled back into his head, his body shaking.

"I'm *your* wife," I said as I slid my hand between his waistband and skin, taking his bare cock into my hand. "Take me. Make me yours and only yours."

I watched him tremble at my words. "Say it again."

"Take me."

There was a rumbling in his chest just before he hooked his thumbs into my shorts and panties and pulled them down my legs. Then a hard, rushed kiss before his lips were creating a hot, wet trail down to the apex of my thighs. I watched as he stared down at my pussy that was now unveiled before him.

"So, nobody has ever done this before?" he asked, his hand reaching out to cup my sex, his thumb grazing against my clit.

"N-no!" I stammered, my hips rotating for more.

His fingers continued to explore, expertly touching me in places he knew would have a reaction.

"How about this?" he asked and leaned forward, licking from my opening to my clit.

I nearly launched out of the bed, and probably would have if Weston hadn't wrapped an arm around my thigh. My back arched as he began licking and sucking on my clit, his finger teasing my entrance before slowly pushing in. It was too much and not enough at the same time. I was writhing on the bed as he devoured me with his mouth. Weston was pushing me to the brink, and I sat on the precipice of my first oral orgasm.

He sat up, his hand replacing his lips and tongue, rubbing furiously against my sensitive nub. "You're so close, baby girl, just let go. Come for me."

I wanted to do it, so badly, but I just couldn't fall. His hand put more pressure as he leaned forward to take one of my nipples between his teeth. Unintelligible, pleasure-filled noises fell from my lips, hips bucking into his, but it was the feel of the burning hot and dripping head of his cock against my thigh that sent me spiraling into ecstasy.

My muscles, coiled tight, froze as my back arched, and a scream erupted as my pussy pulsed.

I collapsed, my breath coming out in hard pants from the most intense orgasm I'd ever had. The first one not given by my own hand.

Weston wore a triumphant smile while he leaned down to capture my lips. I could taste myself on him, but I didn't care about that. He was kissing me, hips rocking against my still-dripping core. That was all I cared about. It was all that mattered in that moment.

"Baby girl, I want you so badly," he whispered, groaning, his hot breath against my skin. "Are you ready?"

"Yes."

He moved to settle squarely between my thighs, parting them further. The hot head of his cock twitched against my skin, causing a shudder to run through me. Leaning down, he ghosted his lips against mine as he pressed the head against my wet entrance.

I tensed and stopped kissing him. Suddenly, I wasn't sure I was prepared for the pain I knew was to come.

"It will only hurt today. After that, I promise to make you feel so good you won't even remember the pain," he reassured, taking a nipple between his teeth.

I gasped in pleasure, my body relaxing as he kissed his way back up to my lips.

There was pressure, then he pushed past the proof of my innocence in one quick thrust, as far as he could, and stilled. I cried out in pain, my nails dug into his back, and my face scrunched up, a tear sliding down my cheek and a small sob escaping from my chest.

"Mine," he growled into my ear, his body trembling.

Hip lips moved up my neck to my cheek, and kissed away my tears. Patiently, though I knew with great struggle, he waited, his body vibrating with the need to move.

I nodded at him, giving him the okay, knowing the worst was over but that my first time wouldn't get any better. His hips slowly began to move, pushing him in and pulling him out.

"So tight, baby girl," he murmured breathlessly.

I gasped, one hand clenching the sheets, the other pushing against him, grabbing at his arm, side, anywhere. Not in an effort to get him off, just my mind trying to find a way to stop the pain. It was burning and it hurt, but it was not unbearable, just uncomfortable. That didn't stop the whimpers from escaping.

He began moving at a steady rhythm in and out. I hoped he would be done soon, and prayed that the next time it would be pleasurable as he claimed. Because he was right; our chemistry was undeniable. My body craved him. Even with the pain, I wanted to consume him and be consumed *by* him.

His pace quickened, hips slamming into me, and I watched his expression turn to one of pain before he cried out. It felt like he got even larger inside me before I felt him twitching. Hot streams began pulsing into me until he collapsed on top of me.

His chest expanded with each labored breath. Hot, hard pants against my neck. When he pulled back, I could see beads of sweat dripping from his brow. Slowly, he pushed against the bed, relieving me of his weight. His forehead rested on mine, lips kissing, fingers caressing.

After only for a few short moments, he sat up and gazed down at where we were joined. I winced as he slowly pulled out, while he held a wild almost animalistic look in his eyes. "Mine," he whispered and looked up into my eyes.

"Yours," I agreed softly.

Our eyes locked for a moment, one of his hands reaching up to cup my face. I could see adoration gleaming in his eyes, and I smiled back.

"Stay right there," he said as he climbed off the bed and walked over to the bathroom.

The water began running, and he returned a few minutes later with a towel in hand. He pressed the warm, wet rag between my spread legs, and a small hiss escaped as he moved it around, cleaning me off as gently as possible.

Returning, he climbed back under the covers and pulled me to him so that my head was lying on his chest, his arm around my shoulders, his fingers caressing up and down my arm. I snuggled in deep, relaxing in his warmth. I was a little sore, but there was no way I was leaving that heaven.

"Oh, what you do to me, Mrs. Lockwood," he whispered with a sigh, placing a kiss to the top of my head.

"Ditto, Mr. Lockwood," I replied, kissing his chest.

It was in that moment I truly began to believe it was possible, that maybe we did belong together. I didn't know what the morning held, but I hoped we would make it through whatever was to come our way, together. It wasn't long before we were both asleep, wrapped up in the safety and security of each other.

Chapter Nine

OUR NAME

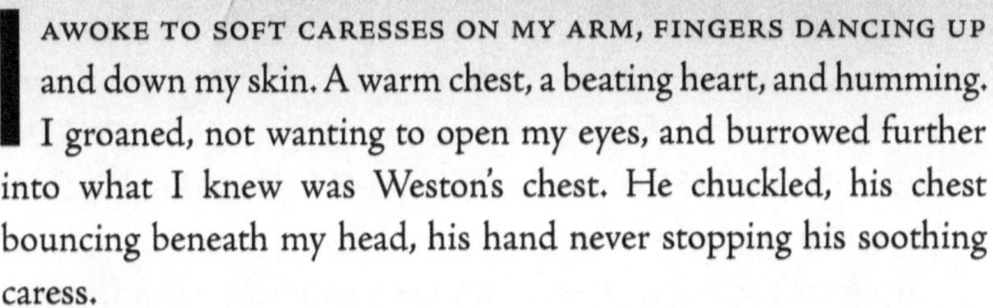

I AWOKE TO SOFT CARESSES ON MY ARM, FINGERS DANCING UP and down my skin. A warm chest, a beating heart, and humming. I groaned, not wanting to open my eyes, and burrowed further into what I knew was Weston's chest. He chuckled, his chest bouncing beneath my head, his hand never stopping his soothing caress.

"Too early," I said as I nuzzled against his skin.

"Good morning to you, too."

I pulled back, tilting my head up, and Weston did the same, his eyes dancing with amusement.

"Morning."

"How did you sleep?" he asked, his hand moving to brush the hair from my face.

"Extremely well. You?"

"Ditto."

I burrowed back down, loving his spicy scent that filled my senses. My eyes drifted closed again as I lay in his warmth when he sighed.

"I don't want to get out of bed. It feels so good here with you." His arm wrapped tight around me, pulling me as close to him as he could.

"But?"

"But, I need to get the day going. You stay and sleep for a while longer. I'm going to go workout," he said as he gave me a kiss on the forehead and climbed out of bed.

The sound of the splashing water filled my ears, and I felt another soft kiss before all was silent again.

I awoke a little while later and Weston's side of the bed was cold. I rolled over, soreness from the night before making itself known via pain in my abdomen. Everything was so silent as I lay there, and after a few minutes staring at the ceiling, I was ready to get up. Rolling to the edge of the bed, I expertly tumbled off and onto the hardwood below, a slight twinge catching me. It was then that a small, dark red stain on the sheets caught my eye.

Blood. My blood.

I stood there, staring at it, asking myself if I felt any different ... besides the pain. Wasn't there some switch to make you feel like a woman afterwards? If there was, I didn't feel it. What I did feel was lonely and in need of Weston.

Running back to my room, I tossed on some clothes and headed down the stairs. As I searched from room to room, I was left wishing the house had a paging system ... or a tracking device. There were a lot of places to hide in a house that large, but my sleepy brain vaguely remembered something about working out.

A light tapping drew my attention, and I found Julia sitting on a stool at the kitchen counter, typing away on her laptop.

"Oh, hi," I said, startled to see her. It wasn't even seven in the morning.

"Good morning, Wren," she greeted with a pleasant smile, before her attention returned to her computer. "I've got yours and Weston's schedules done for the day. You have one hour left to eat, shower, and get dressed before we head to get your name changed with the social security office and then your license before heading to see Sophie."

"S-schedule? I have a schedule? W-why?" I stammered.

Julia smiled sweetly. "Because you're not in Kansas anymore."

"I'm not sure I like these *Wizard of Oz* analogies I keep hearing," I grumbled, frowning.

Julia blinked at me before breaking out into laughter. "Well, you might as well get used to it because it is one of Weston's favorite musicals. He tends to quote it without really knowing he's doing it. I'm sure I've picked it up from him."

A memory of something he'd said about an actress popped into my head. "So, that's why he said 'if she only had a brain' at the wax museum!"

Julia giggled. "Oh, yes, he has a strong opinion of some actresses, or those claiming to be. Did he happen to do a little jig after? You can sometimes catch him doing that just like the Scarecrow would."

I leaned against the counter. "I need to see that."

"It's been a long time since I last saw it."

"How long have you worked for him?" I asked. Based on their conversations and their relationship, which seemed to hold a lot of friendship and a sibling-like aspect, I guessed quite a while.

"I started working for him about seven years ago."

"Wow, that's a long time."

She nodded. "Tell me about it. I spend more time with him than anyone else."

"No wonder you picked it up."

She let out a little laugh. "We have to be in sync or things fall apart, which is probably how Oz references weaseled their way into my vocabulary. When I told him I didn't like the movie because the monkeys freaked me out, I thought the interview was over, but he hired me."

"And that's how you met his brother?"

A blush spread on her cheeks, and she nodded. "About a week in, Miles bumped into me, spilling the stack of papers in my arms all over the floor. He was so apologetic and helped me clean up, but he didn't ask me out for over two years."

The story she painted was so cute, but based on the conversation I overheard, my first meeting wasn't going to be as nice.

"Miles also doesn't understand Weston's Oz obsession."

I shook my head. "So odd for a man like him to love *The Wizard of Oz.*"

"Well, I think it stems from when he was in junior high and played the cowardly lion. He was so cute!"

"How do you know that?" I asked, my brow scrunching up.

"His mother had it on video. I stole it when . . . well, let's just say Weston and his parents aren't on the greatest of terms right now." Julia pursed her lips, seeming hesitant to say more. But I didn't know if it was more about his parents, or more about him.

"They don't talk? That's a shame. I hate that I don't get to see my dad all the time . . ." I trailed off, my mind wandering to the fact that I was going to have to tell my dad, and what his reaction would be.

"Wren?"

"Sorry," I said, waving the thought away. "I was just wondering what my dad was going to think about all of this. My mom was all for it, but they're pretty different."

"Do I need to be concerned about security?" she asked half-jokingly.

I nodded. "Possibly. Before he moved to Chicago, he had a full gun safe."

"Hmm, that actually does sound like it could be a security issue." She pursed her lips and typed frantically away. "Please just let me know when your father is informed and if we might expect a visit."

"Will do." While I don't think she was brushing me off, I could tell her mind was on a million things and I didn't want to disturb her any longer. "Do you know where I can find Weston?"

"Oh!" Her eyes popped open wide. "He's in the gym. Just go down that hall, take a left at the end, then a right, and it's the glass door on the right."

"There really needs to be a map of this place," I said with a shake of my head. I didn't even know there was a gym. Apparently, I hadn't been thorough enough in my exploration the previous day.

After a few twist and turns, I finally arrived at a glass doorway and spotted Weston jogging at a steady pace on the treadmill. His head turned in my direction when the click of the door sounded my entrance. He smiled and hit a few buttons, the belt of the treadmill quickly slowed down to a crawl and then stopped.

"Hi," he said, breathing hard.

Stepping down, he grabbed the base of his shirt and pulled it up to wipe the sweat from his face. As it lifted, his tight abdomen was exposed, and I fought the urge to lick my lips. He was so enticing, and though I felt him the previous night, I hadn't really seen him.

"How are you feeling?" he asked with genuine concern.

"Umm . . . a little sore, but nothing too bad." My weight shifted as silence fell over us and Weston's gaze moved over my body.

His hand moved up to my face, the back of his fingers caressing my cheek.

"J-Julia said we don't have much time to get ready," I stuttered, his eyes burning into me.

Leaning forward, he pressed his lips against mine, one arm pulling my body in line with his and wrapping around my waist. My fingers clenched in his damp shirt, and I rose to stand on my toes.

His lips released mine with a groan. "We should go find her."

Grabbing my hand, we walked out of the room and back down the hall. Julia no longer sat perched on the bar stool at the counter and after calling out for her, we located her in Weston's office.

"Busy day?" he asked as we stepped through the doorway.

"Not terribly, but you are quite packed while Wren is with Sophie. I managed for you and Carson to meet with the cast just after you drop her off, and then quickly shuttle off to meet with the guys at Universal, followed by another pitch meeting with Fox."

"What about Summit?"

"They're booked until next week."

Weston's eyebrows rose in surprise. "Guess they're going to miss out on it."

I looked around as they talked more business, noticing all the movie posters that lined the walls. His whole office was filled with various movie memorabilia.

"Okay, I'm going to go grab a bite before I jump in the shower. Have you eaten yet?" he asked, his question directed at me. I shook my head. "Come on, baby girl. Breakfast is the most important meal of the day."

Following him out of the office, I stopped at the movie poster by the door. I remembered the movie. A young angel fighting against the demons of hell to stop the apocalypse. The angel in the poster was dirty, beaten, bloody, his wings broken. He looked tired and defeated, but his blue eyes were bright and shone with inner strength, brown hair blowing in the breeze. I remembered the movie, but had only seen it on cable. A blockbuster hit that summer, breaking opening weekend records at a time before Harry Potter. Its CGI was beyond the time, making everything incredibly lifelike—so much so that even fifteen years later it was unbelievably realistic.

I stopped at that thought and looked closer at the young man. He was thinner, and younger, not as filled out, but there was no doubt about it.

It was Weston.

My eyes scanned down to the bottom and, sure enough, his name appeared.

Holy shit.

I didn't marry a movie producer. I married a *movie star*.

I didn't know whether to laugh or cry or vomit. How did I not see it before? Was it because he was filled out now and much more manly than back then?

Everything made sense. His conversations with Julia. Talk about press releases and worrying about paparazzi. My wonderful night in Las Vegas with a beautiful man had landed me right in the middle of a Hollywood life.

"Everything all right, Wren?" Julia asked from behind me.

I turned to look at her, my mouth opening and closing repeatedly, unable to speak. Pointing to the picture, she seemed to understand.

"You didn't know," she said with a nod. "I had a feeling."

I shook my head violently. "No. I didn't recognize him." My eyes scanned around to the other posters that adorned the walls; more of Weston's movie posters. "Julia, I don't think I can do this." My voice came out barely above a whisper.

"Do what?"

"Be married to a movie star."

She gave me a gentle smile. "He doesn't act anymore, Wren."

That didn't matter. The things they talked about already freaked me out, but I'd thought I could adapt. I wasn't so sure anymore.

"It's still not a life I'm cut out for. I'm just a simple Indiana girl. We have a single story, three bedroom home on half an acre with a horse ranch behind us. There is an actual rooster that crows all day nearby."

Julia stepped around the desk and walked over to me.

"Look, Wren, I've been Weston's assistant for seven years, and I've never seen him as happy with anyone as I've seen him with you in the past twenty hours. He's a good guy, and I think you two could really have a shot. It's not going to be easy. I won't lie to you. This business is cutthroat. But if you have each other for support, nothing can stop you." She took hold of my hand and squeezed. "You're in for quite a ride, but don't worry, you have a large support system here. Starting with Weston. It's obvious how much he adores you."

"Thank you, Julia. That means a lot," I said with a smile and headed to the kitchen where my husband was calling my name.

My stomach rolled, and I wondered if I'd be able to even eat breakfast. My heart was beating so fast it actually worried me, and I struggled to take a full breath.

Weston blinked at me when I entered, his eyes widening as he stepped forward and wrapped his hands around my face.

"What's wrong?"

I just stared at him, trying to take in a deeper breath. "You're a freaking movie star!"

He pursed his lips and glanced behind me before looking back. "I was."

I shook my head. "Weston, you weren't just a guy who appeared in movies. You were the *star*. The leading man in huge hits!"

"You're really upset by this?" he asked, confusion etched into his features.

"Yes!"

"Would it have changed your mind about marrying me?"

The way his tone dropped made my chest clench. *Would it have?* If I'd realized earlier, when we first met?

"I don't know," I answered honestly. "But, fuck." I shook my head back and forth. "I don't know if I can do this."

He ran his hands up and down my arms and led me over to the table. After sitting on one of the chairs, he pulled me down to his lap.

"Shh, calm down, baby girl." His arms wrapped around me, and I leaned my face into his neck.

It wasn't until he spoke that I realized how worked up I'd become.

"So, yeah, that's my unconventional childhood."

My brows rose. "It's more than unconventional."

He nodded. "It's not like I didn't know this was going to come out, but I was worried about how you'd react."

I knotted my fingers into his shirt. "Not good."

His hand continued moving up and down my arm. "Not how I was expecting either."

"I'm not going to fangirl you," I said against his neck.

He chuckled. "I think I like this reaction better."

"Better than fangirling you? Why?" I asked, my brow scrunching.

"Because it just confirms even more that you're not with me for the fame. You're with me because of me."

My chest clenched. "It's been about you since we met."

He pressed his lips against the top of my head. "I know the feeling."

"I do like your movies, though," I said to let him know I was a fan.

He chuckled. "That's good. Do you feel better now?"

I craned my head back to look up at him and cupped his cheek. "As long as you're with me."

"I can do that."

"All the time."

He pursed his lips. "That might present a few problems."

"Like what?" I asked, my lips twitching.

"Well, I can't exactly have my wife following me into the men's room, can I?" His lips slowly drew up, his eyes brightening. "Wait, let me change that."

I couldn't hold my smile back any longer. "You were thinking something pervy, weren't you?"

He leaned down and pressed his lips to mine. "See, you're getting to know me already."

"Are there anymore secrets I need to know about?" I asked.

It was just a flicker, but I could swear I saw the amusement fall from his eyes into something darker, but it was gone before I could dwell on it more.

"Nothing you need to worry about."

My stomach clenched. "That means yes." Oh, God, did I hope it wasn't something big. I couldn't handle any more big reveals.

He swallowed hard. "Some things from my past are just hard to talk about, but I promise I'll tell you. After all, we have so much to learn about each other."

Past. Now that was a pass I could give him, but I hoped one day we'd know everything about each other. Time would tell.

After a bite and a quick shower, we were dressed and ready for the day. Weston took my breath away with the gray suit he wore, no tie, the top buttons undone. He chuckled as he approached.

"Enough of that," he said, kissing me hard before heading down the stairs.

I must have been a little too obvious in my ogling.

The three of us loaded into Weston's Bentley and sped off. I felt like I was in a foreign country as we zipped through the lush green hills of California. Julia handed me a whole file worth of paperwork to fill out for my new social security card, license, and various other things, including medical history for insurance. I'd never even considered all of the red tape that went along with a marriage, let alone the added name change. It was all a bit staggering.

Half an hour later we arrived at our first stop. It didn't take long since I had all of the paperwork with me, and there wasn't a line yet. I wasn't sure if the lack of people was normal or set up using his connections, but we were off again a few minutes later.

Upon arriving at the DMV, Weston stayed in the car, while Julia and I entered. It was there I met another of Weston's assistants, Amy. She'd arrived when they opened and had been holding a spot in the packed office. It took about forty-five more minutes until I walked out with a new driver's license with my brand new name: Wren Alexis Lockwood.

It was official, more so than before. A strange feeling, almost like sadness, washed over me as I said goodbye to Wren Bradford. Something inside told me I might miss the days of being a Bradford. That being a Lockwood was going to be so much more than I ever imagined.

I wasn't sure if that *more* was good or bad, but I had the feeling that highs and lows would be part of my new life.

Two hours after leaving the house, Weston and I pulled up to a large building; with a sign reading Brooks Fashions out front. Julia had gone ahead with Amy to meet up with Mallory, Weston's third assistant, to prepare for the day while he dropped me off.

Inside the large warehouse was a bustling mess of fabric and people. They were running around with their arms full of clothing, each and every one greeting Weston with a smile, and I was sur-prised he knew them all by name.

"Oh, Weston!" a small woman cried out, bounding over to him, her long aqua hair with purple accents trailing behind her. "I'm so glad you're here! I've been thinking about the Oscars."

"Sophie, the Oscars are over four months away!" Weston pro-tested, a smile lighting up his face as he shook his head.

"Yes! We're almost out of time."

I almost laughed, but didn't because her stern face showed her utter seriousness.

"Strange, strange, creature. It's only a tux. How many ways can one be made?"

She rolled her eyes. "Says the man who hasn't bought his own clothes since the nineties. And it's not about the style—it's all about the name on it."

Weston's eyes narrowed at her. "I bought some clothes at Old Navy in college. On sale."

Sophie's eyes widened, a loud gasp coming from her small frame. "Weston! No! I thought I taught you better."

Weston turned to me. "See, I told you."

"I'll forgive you that blasphemous act, but you have to come see what I've found you first. Oh, I'm so happy you came in today!" She clapped her hands together in excitement.

Weston let out a sigh, his hands wrapping around my biceps, lifting me up before setting me down right in front of him. My eyes were wide in surprise as I stood, stunned, in between the two.

"This is why I'm here. Wren needs clothes. No ball gowns, just everyday wear for now. Whole new wardrobe."

Sophie's head tilted to the side, then to the other, as she ob-served me. "Who is this?"

"Remember those chains Julia asked you to bring?"

"Yeeesss." Sophie drew out the word, caution lacing her tone.

Weston grabbed my left arm, bringing my hand, and my ring, up to her view.

"Oh my God!" she cried.

Weston shushed her, while Sophie's face was almost a mask of horror. "Sophie, calm down and meet Wren, my wife."

Her movements stopped, eyes bulging. "Your what? Weston, please tell me you didn't do what I think you did."

"Long story, and I have a meeting. Wren will tell you all about it. Free reign," he said, kissing me lightly before heading out.

"Yeah, I see why now," she said, looking to me before turning to watch Weston scurry out the door.

"Love the new color!" He waved.

"Suck-up!"

Then he was gone. My safety net. The only person in the state who I knew, besides Julia. And they were the only two that accepted me and the predicament that landed me in front of a gorgeous, chic woman.

I swallowed thickly while Sophie scanned over me. She circled me, making little noises, her brow scrunching more than once before she grabbed my hand and dragged me off.

"So, what the hell happened here?" she asked.

I gave a nervous laugh. "What happens in Vegas doesn't always stay there."

She put her hand on her hip, the other on the table next to her. "Oh, *this* I have to hear."

I heaved a sigh before going into our sordid story, starting at the Mirage Starbucks. Sophie simply stared at me when I was done, before stepping away and between some of the clothing racks.

She was silent, but the slamming of hangers against each other said everything I needed to know. Pushing her way out of the clothes jungle a few minutes later, her arms were stuffed with different articles.

"You're still very young, so we will need a youthful sophistication. That way, people won't suspect you are quite as young as you actually are."

"That's it?" I asked, staring at her skeptically.

"Honestly, I'm still processing it all," she said, then slammed a hanger down on the counter. "Damn him!"

"Sophie?" Her outburst confused me.

"Did he even think about how hard all of this would be on you before he wrangled you into his life? Or on me, having to now find you a gown for the Oscars?"

I had to blink, her two questions so vastly different. I felt like my head was spinning. "I . . . I won't be going to the Oscars."

"Of course you will." It was blunt and not open for debate.

"But we're keeping our marriage secret for a while," I said in protest.

"You can still go as his date," she said as she held various articles up in front of me. It was interesting to watch the different expressions pass over her face before she threw a piece to one side or the other. She let out a huff before delving back into the racks. "Don't get me wrong, Wren. I'm happy he's met someone that makes him feel something he has never felt before, but couldn't he have dated you first?" Another load of clothing was dumped out onto the table, Sophie resuming her search. "I mean, you're still in high school! What the hell was he thinking?"

"He wasn't."

"No, he wasn't." She popped her head out and nodded. "That's exactly it. He was living in that fantasy of his." Frustration laced every word, along with a little growl. "I'm sorry, Wren, it's not you. I'm just kind of shocked. Weston's like a brother to me and this is very much an unexpected development in his life. And what's worse is I can only hope he did it for the right reasons. The last thing I want is for him to hurt you because he wasn't thinking."

"He's had the best intentions since we met, so I believe he did do it for the right reasons."

She blinked at me. "You do?"

"Yes, because every fiber of my being answers his call. Do you believe in love at first sight? Soul mates?" I asked. Sophie nodded. "So do I." I couldn't keep the smile from my face.

She smiled and pulled me into a hug. "Then I'm happy for you both." Releasing me, she looked me over again. "So, you really didn't recognize him?"

I let out a laugh, my cheeks heating. "I don't think I'm ever going to live that down."

She shook her head. "Not when we're talking about Weston Lockwood."

After over two hours, I was equipped with enough clothes to fill the walk-in closet in the room where the rest of my possessions resided. I convinced her I was a casual girl, and eventually she relented, but still added some of her favorite dresses. She also included undergarments and swimwear. It was still a few hours until Weston was due to return, so Sophie asked me to lunch.

We were sitting at an outside seating area after ordering when Sophie began to tell me about Weston.

"I want to tell you about my best friend," she started. "But I'm also hesitant. After being burned, we all kinda protect each other, and especially Weston. He . . . didn't have it easy growing up after his first movie."

"You knew Weston then?"

"He was my next door neighbor. He, Carson, Lance, and I were thick as thieves growing up. Miles, Weston's brother, is three years older than Weston, and six years older than me, thus was too old to play with 'babies' like us."

Drinks arrived, and I downed half the glass of tea in a few gulps.

"Carson? Lance?" I already had learned so many names, and those were just his assistants. Now Sophie had named off three more names. I was going to need some of those "Hello, my name is" tags.

A huge smile broke out on her face. "Carson is my husband. We've been married for eight years now. We were those high school sweethearts that were voted most likely to get married, even though people didn't think we'd last past college. Well, we did. It helped that we grew up in love and knew that there wouldn't be anyone else, so we got married after my first year in college."

"Oh, wow. That's sweet."

She smiled at me. "Thank you. Carson and Weston do a lot of work together, producing and such. He used to be a talent scout, but when Weston left acting, Carson decided to join him in his new venture. Lance is Carson's younger brother . . . well, stepbrother actually. He's a stunt performer and provides action services. He just opened up his own stunt company. It's still small, but growing, and he's still the leading man."

"Wow, that's amazing that he's had your support for so long. You and Julia both speak so reverently of him."

The loyalty they showed was envy worthy.

"He's a really great guy, Wren," Sophie said.

I smiled at her. "I can tell already."

She took a sip of her drink, seeming to stall. "In a way, he's still a thirteen-year-old boy. Fame ripped him from his childhood innocence," she said, sadness in her eyes. "While you were playing around, carefree, in your backyard, Weston was being hounded by paparazzi. He would have given anything to have that again. To have people see him as just a boy, just a guy, and not as Weston Lockwood, hottest teen on the big screen. It was very rough on him."

The waiter arrived, setting our salads in front of us. Very different than what I would be eating at school.

"I can't even imagine. This is already so much bigger than I ever expected out of my life, and it's only day two." My mind whirled around our day on the strip. "I was just a girl who saw a handsome man. I still feel like I'm in some sort of dream and I'll wake up any second."

She looked at me and set her fork down. "Please don't think you not recognizing him was the only reason he married you. Weston is used to women falling at his feet to get a taste of his fame, to use it for their own agenda, but not really caring about him. It hardened him a lot, causing him to lock himself away. I can see your appeal, why he couldn't let you go."

"Why is that?" I asked as I took a bite of what was probably the best salad I'd ever had in my life.

"You're not Hollywood. He always said he wanted the girl next door. Natural beauty with a brain. That's you. You also seem to have some aversion to material goods."

"It's just . . . weird to accept things from an essential stranger. Especially with the price tags he's talking about."

"Well, it's something you're just going to have to get used to. He'll spoil the hell out of you, because he believes you're his chance."

"His chance?"

"Of finding meaningful happiness. It was the biggest reason he stopped acting and moved to the other side of the camera. To get away from the spotlight and find a real love. Which is a shame, because he loved acting. He just hated the price."

Everything Sophie told me gave me the aching need to hug Weston. To reassure him I was there for him, that I didn't want anything but him. It was a long two hours, and when he did finally arrive I jumped into his arms, holding him tight. He was surprised for a short moment before his arms wrapped around my waist and his head came to rest at the crook of my neck, breathing me in.

"What was that for?" he asked softly, brushing my hair back, his eyes sparkling.

"For being so highly regarded by everyone around you. It just shows how wonderful of a man my husband is," I said as I stretched my neck to kiss him on the cheek.

He smiled down at me. "You had doubts?"

I pursed my lips. "Not really, but confirmation from outside parties just solidifies it."

He squeezed me tight. "Ready to go home?"

"Oh, Wren, wait!" Sophie called, halting me in my tracks. Taking my hand, she placed the chain I had chosen into my palm. "I didn't want to put it with everything else." She grabbed my hand

and ran her thumb over the diamond. "It really is a beautiful ring. I'll deliver everything tomorrow and help you get it all situated. Okay?"

I nodded and wrapped her into a hug.

"Thank you, Sophie. For everything."

We headed home, Julia in the back seat again. He didn't say anything about his meetings, but I was certain in time I would learn more about his world. The phone rang, and my attention turned to the scenery that was flying by.

Upon arrival, Weston introduced me to Kelly, his personal cook. She was a friendly woman, in her mid-thirties, with a husband and two kids. The three of us went over the meal for the evening, and that was when I learned Miles, Weston's brother, was coming over for dinner.

We moved to his office, and he took a seat at the desk while I perched on the edge, my mouth still salivating over the wonderful menu planned for the evening.

"So, what did you think of Sophie?" he asked, curiosity written all over his face, letting me know he'd been dying to ask.

I thought about it for a moment, laughing a little as I remembered her running around with her arms full. "A bit clothes crazy, and at first she was very friendly but very curt at the same time. So, for a while I couldn't tell if we were okay or if she couldn't stand me."

That made Weston laugh out loud. "Sophie is very friendly, but I'm afraid after all the drama with my ex, she's a bit more reserved with that now when it comes to new people."

I didn't get to tell him it was because of him, because of her love for him, but one small word caught my attention. "Ex?"

"I was in an on-and-off relationship with a woman who hated Sophie," he admitted.

"For how long?" I asked. It was the first time I'd heard about the previous women in his life. Then again, I really knew little about him.

"For about six years."

"Wow," I whispered, stunned. "That's a long time. You never got married?"

He smirked. "Nope, just you," he answered, placing a kiss on the back of my hand.

"Why not?"

He squirmed, and I could tell he wasn't all that comfortable. "Well, I guess the best answer is that I never felt one inkling of the feeling with her that I have felt with you in the past few days."

"And yet you stayed with her? Why?"

He sighed and shook his head. "I don't know. Because we knew each other and were comfortable? Because I had never met anyone that really grabbed me? Because me being taken kept some women away? Because I was waiting for you?"

I smiled. "How do you know you were waiting for me?"

"You are quite inquisitive today," he said with a chuckle.

I shrugged my shoulders. "Just trying to get to know my husband."

"As you have every right to." He took a deep breath, his hand caressing mine. "To answer your question, I couldn't stop myself from asking you to dinner that night, even if I'd wanted to. Because I asked you to marry me."

I leaned forward and pressed my lips to his.

"So, we have a lofty goal, don't we?"

He smirked up at me. "How about we start with that on our way to forever, Mrs. Lockwood?"

"I think I like that a lot, Mr. Lockwood."

A name. Something so small, but so definitive. It wasn't just mine now—it was ours.

And I loved our name.

Chapter Ten

OUR FAMILY

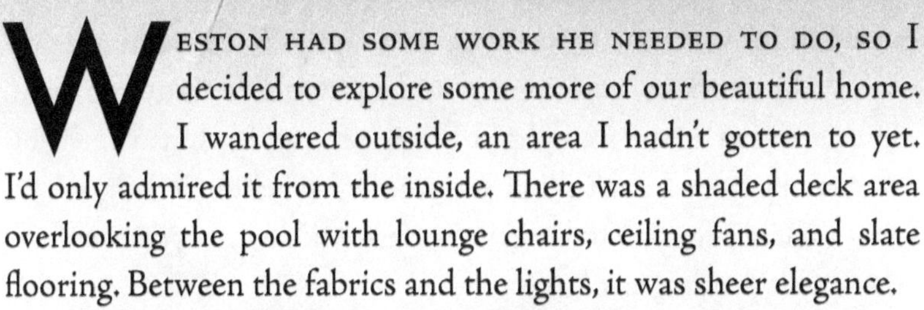

ESTON HAD SOME WORK HE NEEDED TO DO, SO I decided to explore some more of our beautiful home. I wandered outside, an area I hadn't gotten to yet. I'd only admired it from the inside. There was a shaded deck area overlooking the pool with lounge chairs, ceiling fans, and slate flooring. Between the fabrics and the lights, it was sheer elegance.

Sitting down on one of the two-person loungers, I looked over the beautiful grounds. It was paradise, pure and simple. I could see myself spending many hours out here reading, or swimming in the pool. Sophie said she set me up with about ten swimsuits, but I never did get to see one. Maybe in the morning I could take a swim.

While dreaming, my phone rang from the pocket of my jeans. Pulling it out, I saw "Mom" flashing on the screen.

"Hi, Mom," I said after hitting accept.

"Wren! Oh, honey, I miss you so much! How is California? How's Weston?"

After seeing the movie posters, I was certain my mother knew who Weston was when she first met him.

"California is great so far, and Weston is wonderful. Did you know he used to be a movie star?" I asked, trying to sound as innocent as possible.

"Oh, really? I knew he looked familiar," she said, but I could tell by her tone she knew.

I let out a sigh. "Mom, why didn't you tell me?"

"What good would it have done? You two were already married."

I threw my arms up in the air. "Is that why you were so adamant about me going with him? Because he was a movie star? Because he has money?" I accused and immediately felt bad. I knew my mother wasn't that kind of person.

"No! God, Wren, no! Of course not. You know me better than that. I did it because, well, you couldn't see it, but I could."

"See what?"

"The way you two looked at each other. I pushed you to go because I didn't want you to lose what I thought was something beautiful. His intentions were sincere, and I saw his adoration for you. He was so sad at the thought of losing you, and I don't think you saw that, because I don't think you wanted to believe it. But, Wren, I saw a chance for you to have a wonderful life with a great man."

"He is pretty great."

"So, tell me, what's happened? Have you lost your virginity?"

"Mom!" I cried out in embarrassment.

"Well, it's better you did it now instead of waiting. You'll probably want to get on birth control, so I'd make an appointment as soon as possible."

Crap. How had I forgotten about something so important? That would just be the icing on our complicated cake for me to have become pregnant on our first night together.

"I'll talk to Weston about it." For the first time ever, I hoped my period arrived ahead of schedule.

"So, what have you two done since you arrived?"

I blew out a breath. "Well, as soon as we walked into the house, one of Weston's assistants was here waiting for us. Her name is Julia, and she is very nice and soon to be Weston's sister-in-law."

"Have you met his brother yet?"

"No, he's coming over for dinner tonight, and I'm a bit anxious." I glanced down at my watch to check the time. "I overheard

Weston talking to him on the phone last night, and I think Miles has the wrong idea about me."

"When he meets you, I'm sure it'll be okay. He's probably just being overprotective. Don't worry about it."

Don't worry about it . . .

How could I not worry about it? With each new person I met, I braced myself for their reaction. Everyone in his life seemed protective of him, and being who he was, I could understand. So me, a wife he suddenly brought home, who's thirteen years younger than him, probably put the hackles up. Unfortunately, that left me on the receiving end of the negativity.

"I also met one of Weston's friends today, Sophie. She's his personal shopper. I'm now stocked with clothes. Which reminds me . . . when do you think you'll get my stuff sent out?"

"Mike and I are working on it. Probably by the end of next week it should reach you."

"Good. I need my stuff. Weston keeps trying to spend loads of money on me. I don't even want to think about today's total." I was pretty sure the total was easily more than all of the money I'd made over the last few years at my part-time job.

"I know it's not what you're used to, but having money is something you're going to have to adapt to. Oh, by the way, Daniel called looking for you. I didn't say anything. I thought you would want to talk to him and explain things yourself."

Fuck. Daniel.

I'd ignored his texts the last few days because I was so overwhelmed that I just couldn't handle him. We were going to graduate high school and go to USC together. How was I going to tell him I wasn't coming back to him? How was I going to explain that I was now living in California with my *husband?*

"I'll call him in the next day or two. I have to figure out what to say."

"Good. He sounded so sad." And it was only going to get worse.

We continued to talk for another hour, about how my life was going to change, about school, about Weston and all that I had learned about him. By the end of the conversation I felt more at ease knowing my mom was just a phone call away. Knowing that she would drop everything to talk to me. Add that to all of the support I was feeling from Julia and Sophie and maybe, just maybe, things would work out. Maybe this Hollywood life wouldn't be so bad.

After hanging up with Mom, I stared out into the sky, the sun setting on the horizon. It was beautiful. I still felt like I was on a vacation, though. Perhaps when my stuff arrived it wouldn't feel like that.

When the rainbow that was the sky had faded, I decided to head in. Navigating my way around was still a pain, but I was finally getting an understanding of the general layout. Once I discovered all of the rooms, I was certain it would be easier. Which then reminded me that there was still the basement to discover and explore.

Walking down the main hall toward the kitchen, I smelled the delicious meal that Weston's chef, Kelly, had prepared. It had my mouth watering and my mind dreaming of roast beef and root vegetables. The smell had me so distracted that I didn't hear the voices until I was right outside Weston's office.

"I just don't understand why you didn't get it annulled," a strange man's voice said as I approached the door. "You didn't even get a fucking prenup!"

Prenup?

Oh my God. I hadn't even thought about that, which I was certain only painted our situation in an even worse light.

"I know, Miles. There wasn't time, and to be honest, I wasn't thinking."

"At least we both agree on that," the voice, I assumed was Miles, grumbled.

The sinking feeling that Miles wasn't going to like me

increased with each word from his mouth, and I began fidgeting with the broken belt loop on my jeans.

"Stop, Miles. There's something about her. I can't describe it," Weston said.

Miles. Weston's brother was in there, talking about me.

"*Something* doesn't save you when she plays you for half of your net worth."

"Miles . . ."

"Never in your life have I ever heard of you doing something so impulsive."

Miles didn't sound happy, and the nervousness kicked in. Winning him over was going to be a fight.

"Do you believe in love at first sight?" Weston asked.

There was a silence and then Miles spoke, his voice so low I barely heard him. "Weston, how can you even believe in such a fairy tale after all you've been through? And being so reckless. A stranger? Really?"

"Fairy tale? Absolutely. Reckless? Maybe." There was the sound of something being thrown down on the desk. "But have you ever seen me with *that* look?" I could just imagine Weston pointing to the pictures of us in Vegas.

"Jesus." Miles's voice came out in a whisper.

"She did that. I told you—she's special. You'll understand when you meet her."

Footsteps headed in my direction, and before I could move Weston was coming out of the door. My eyes grew wide as I stared up at him. Once he registered me, he glanced back into the office and gave me a bashful smile, making me melt.

"Wren."

"I-I'm sorry, I didn't mean to eavesdrop. I w-was just walking by," I stuttered, internally facepalming myself for being that nervous to meet his brother.

And then he was there, behind Weston; blond hair, same blue eyes, tall like Weston, and he was staring at me. Weston gave a small chuckle and leaned down to kiss my forehead. Slipping his arm around my waist, he turned so that we were both facing his brother.

"Miles, I'd like you to meet my wife, Wren. Wren, this is my older brother, Miles."

"Pleased to meet you," I said. I held out my left hand as my right was behind Weston's back, gripping his shirt.

Miles continued to stare at me, his expression blank. "I'm sorry," he apologized and took my hand, his face unfreezing and a smile forming. "Miles Lockwood."

It was an awkward shake, stiff and jerky. He moved in an almost mechanical way, his shock coming through in his movements. His words might have been fluid, but his body was anything but. Even the smile on his face seemed guarded and disingenuous. It was evident that Miles had not inherited the acting gene.

My grip on Weston's shirt did not lessen as we headed into the kitchen. He ran his hand up and down my arm soothingly, but I wasn't sure if it was me or himself he was trying to soothe. Upon entering the dining room, Julia's face lit up in a smile from the table but quickly faded when she saw our expressions. Her gaze lingered on Miles, who I could see had clenched his jaw.

We sat down at the table opposite Miles and Julia, and the tension began to crawl in like a thick cloud. At that moment Kelly entered and began setting dishes full of spinach salad down in front of us.

"Oh, Kelly, you should have called me. I would have been happy to help you set the table," I said, smiling up at her as I thanked her.

Kelly smiled at me. "So sweet of you to offer. Don't worry about it, Wren, it's part of my job."

I nodded. "Sorry. I'm just used to doing the serving, and not being served."

That simple comment seemed to catch Miles's attention, and he began staring at me once again.

Silence descended again. Forced conversation, started by Julia and Weston, to lighten the mood did not help. Miles was stewing, and we could all feel it. The tension was palpable.

After our salads were finished, the main course was delivered. I couldn't believe how good everything was. Kelly was a truly gifted cook. Maybe she could teach me some tricks.

"So, Wren, how old are you?" Miles asked about halfway through the meal.

There was a pregnant pause, everyone halting what they were doing, holding their breath for my response and his reaction.

"I'm eighteen," I said.

Weston and Julia's eyes flickered to Miles to see his reaction.

Hadn't Weston already told him? He knew I was young, but perhaps, like Weston, had guesstimated very early twenties. I glanced over to Weston to see him give Miles an almost pleading look. It didn't help. Miles's fork became lax, tapping down on the ceramic of his plate with a loud clang.

"W-what?" he asked in shock, and I knew he was hoping he'd heard me wrong.

It was a naïve thought that everyone would be as accepting as Julia and Sophie, but I suppose I was not expecting the first negative reaction to come from Weston's best friend and brother. Therefore, I was not prepared for the maelstrom that was Miles Lockwood.

"Eighteen? Are you fucking kidding me?" Miles asked Weston, ignoring me. "You said she was young, not a teenager!"

"She's perfectly legal," Weston said in a calm voice.

"And that means what, exactly? She can vote? Buy cigarettes? Is she even in college?" Miles's voice rose as he vented.

Weston tensed beside me, the calm slipping away. "What's the problem?"

"It's a fucking scandal! You've worked so hard to get out of the public eye, to be able to live a semi-normal life."

Weston gritted his teeth, his jaw jutting as they clenched. "It's my life, Miles."

"And I'm not disagreeing on that." Miles held up his hands.

"God knows I've heard that enough with Mom and Dad, but the fact here is that you've essentially married a child. You know that's how the media will see it."

A child. I supposed he was right, being that Weston was in his thirties.

"And for right now, we plan to keep it quiet."

"If you wanted to do that, you shouldn't have changed her name yet," Miles argued. "Where was your brain? I'm just astounded that you would make that kind of decision. Fuck, Wes, how do you know she isn't playing you?"

I'd taken the beating, because they were all points I'd also thought of. However, the last comment was a direct hit at me, calling into question my character.

Before I could even defend myself, Weston leaned forward, his words laced with venom. "Shut the hell up! You don't know her. You don't know anything about her."

"Neither do you! That's what I'm getting at. You're risking your career, your reputation, and your finances. To throw it all away for some girl."

"She's . . ."

"Special. Or so you say." Miles's lip curled up. "Tell me, what is so damn special? Is her pussy that good?"

Julia gasped, and I turned to find her mouth agape and a horrified expression on her face as she looked at her fiancé.

Weston choked on his wine, and I could tell by the immediate shift in his demeanor that he couldn't believe what his brother had just said. He narrowed his eyes, and in a low, ominous voice that made me shiver, he said, "Miles, don't you *ever* fucking say something so crass about my wife again, or you and I are going to have a serious fucking problem."

I had reached my boiling point. I was completely insulted, and Weston was shaking with fury. Slamming my hands down on the table, I stood from my chair. The wooden legs screeched against the floor, and all heads turned to look at me.

"Can't you just be the least bit supportive of your brother?" I glared at Miles. "Yes, what we did was reckless. We were going to get an annulment, thus negating all of your complaints about me, but we changed our minds." I wasn't going to bring my mom into it. He didn't need a new target to spew his hate at. "There's something strong between us. It may be new, but it is too strong to be denied. Scandalous? For this day and age, yes. Hence, why we are keeping it on the down-low for now, but the bottom line is that Weston is being a decent man and taking responsibility for his actions, as am I. Is it too much to ask for the person he is closest to, the person he respects the most, to stand by him? Is your prejudice that blind?"

Fingers touching my hand caught my attention, and I flinched involuntarily until I realized it was Weston. I relaxed as our fingers intertwined, his lips placing a soft kiss on the back of my hand. My glare moved from Miles, softening as I turned to Weston, a small smile spreading.

"Thank you, baby girl," he said, smiling up at me and pulling me onto his lap, his arms wrapping around me before placing a kiss on my neck.

I looked back up at Miles, who was now slumped against the back of his chair, staring at me with his mouth open.

"You're my brother, and I love you, but stop being such as asshole to Wren and about our situation," Weston said as he stared directly at Miles. "She's your sister now. A Lockwood. Part of our family, so you're going to be seeing her a lot. Get over it. We're married, staying married, and I don't need your approval, but I'd like your support."

Miles shook his head. "I just can't help but think what a huge mistake you are making. And while I may have some respect for you after your speech, Wren, I just don't trust you with him."

With that, Miles stood, threw his napkin down on the table, and walked out of the room. The hurt was evident on Weston's face as he watched his closest confidant walk out. I pulled him closer, and he buried his head into my neck, his arms wrapping tightly around my waist.

Upon hearing a chair move, I looked up to find Julia standing. With everything going on, I'd forgotten she was there. She looked so sad and despondent as she gazed at us.

"I'll talk to him. You know he won't be the last to be opposed. I'm just sad and disappointed that he was the first."

"He's my brother, Julia. He of all people should support me, even if he doesn't agree with it," Weston replied, standing as well and putting me back on my feet. Leaning forward, he kissed my forehead. "I have a lot of work to do tonight, baby girl, so I may be up late."

He was distant, lost in his own mind as he turned to leave, his hand slipping from mine. I stared after him, watching as he disappeared around the corner, the door to the office clicking closed behind him, leaving me standing there in silence.

"It'll be okay, Wren," Julia said, squeezing my hand. "Please don't let Miles upset you. He really is a nice man. I wouldn't be marrying him otherwise. He just wants what's best and to look out for Weston. Though, I will be giving him a stern talking to. That's no way to talk about any woman."

"Thank you, Julia," I said in kind, forcing a small smile that didn't reach my eyes.

She squeezed my hand one last time before heading for the door. "I'll see you in the morning."

"Good night."

The house was eerily silent with everyone gone and Weston locked up in his office. I attempted to help Kelly clean up, but she refused, sending me on my way to the great room where I channel surfed. Shortly before she left, Kelly dropped off a chocolate soufflé that she had made for dessert, and I devoured its chocolaty goodness, asking for the recipe between bites.

I didn't think I'd be hungry, thanks to what went down at dinner, but the smell alone changed my stomach's mind.

Kelly left soon after and I was all alone. After a few hours of the television, bored and a bit tired from the long day, I trudged up the stairs and stared at the two doors—Weston's room and my room.

I wasn't certain what to do. Yes, I'd slept with Weston the night before, but I had no clue what that meant. He hadn't said anything about me *not* keeping my own room now. He had just said he'd be up late, and I was really tired, confused, and emotionally drained. Listening down the stairs, I found no indication that he was headed up any time soon. I didn't feel right climbing into his empty bed, so I opened the door to my room and walked in. After changing my clothes and brushing my teeth, I pulled back the covers and settled in, turning the TV on for some noise and a bit of entertainment to help me drift off as I snuggled in. A while later my eyes began to flutter shut, and I soon began walking in dream land.

Unfortunately, it wasn't one of rainbows and sunshine, but of families breaking apart.

Chapter Eleven

OUR DESIRE

IT WAS SO WARM AND COMFY ALL SNUGGLED DOWN IN MY BED the next morning that I didn't want to wake up. I was dreaming of Weston: his warmth, his scent, his touch, his body. And I didn't want to leave it. I wanted to indulge in every heavenly ounce of it. The comfort of his body pressed against mine was all I needed.

It was when I felt the hairs tickle the back of my neck that I realized the warmth wasn't solely from my covers. As I surfaced into consciousness, I felt the weight of Weston's arms across my waist, legs tangled in mine, the warmth of his body pressed behind me, and his breath as it swept across my neck. Turning to look back at him, he groaned, his grip tightening on my waist, his face nuzzling into my neck.

The feeling that coursed through me from such a small, simple action was indescribable. Warmth, need, want . . . love.

I tried to turn around again, and a frown formed on his face. He reminded me of a little kid who didn't want to wake up. A giggle escaped me, and that seemed to rouse him. His eyes fluttered open, a smile lighting his face upon seeing me before nuzzling my neck again.

"Baby girl," he murmured.

"Good morning, sleepy boy."

"Good morning, beautiful," he responded, placing a kiss on my neck.

"Honey pie."

He smirked. "Sugar bear."

"Snuggle muffin."

"Mmm, snuggle bunny," he said with a smile that quickly turned into another frown, and I knew this time he was finally awake. "Why did you sleep in here? I was worried when I came up to bed last night and couldn't find you."

"Well, you never said anything about moving into your room . . ." I trailed off. He nodded in understanding. "And then after the dinner fiasco, you disappeared."

"Yes, I suppose you're right. I guess I just thought . . . but then with all that crap last night, I forgot to talk to you about it," he said, his hand brushing a strand of hair behind my ear. I loved when he did that. "I'm sorry about Miles and for not staying with you. I just couldn't believe . . . I still can't believe he said that. I was in shock. Complete shock. I've *never* heard him say something like that before. It's just not his style." His voice dropped to just above a whisper, body slumping back down into the bed as sadness took over. "I knew he didn't take it well, but I never had an inkling that was what he really thought. He's been with me through thick and thin, so his rejection of you, of us, hit me really hard."

He drew in a shuddered breath, sighed, and closed his eyes. I reached out to smooth the lines from his face that his sadness had created. He leaned into my hand, kissing my palm before opening his eyes to gaze into mine.

"He really was an ass. I mean, a lot of what he said made sense and I agreed with him on many of the points, but then he just became downright crude. He really didn't like me, and the only reason I can come up with is because I'm young and unknown to him."

Weston nodded. "He's not very trusting of new people in my life. He's also very unhappy with me and took it out on you. Not to excuse his behavior, because I'm still angry that he would say that, but it was really directed at me. It's not easy being who I am and doing what I do . . . or used to do. Everyone wants a piece of you.

I've had women claim that their kids were mine, men tell me how much they wanted to beat the crap out of me, and a few saying how I should just die for no reason, just because of who I was. People want a piece of the money and the fame and will stop at nothing to accomplish it, including making outrageously false accusations. All of it beats you down over time, and becomes a huge scandal when there are no grounds for it."

"All of that just means he has become closed-minded when it comes to you, and we are very much an open-minded situation in this day and age."

"Society is closed-minded in general. That's why people will be against us, Wren."

"How do *you* feel about this?" I asked. I knew my feelings, and even with my nerves and fear, I really liked Weston.

"Do you think I regret this? I thought I'd been pretty obvious regarding how I feel about you."

"But your brother . . ."

"He hasn't seen what I see every day when I'm with you. An intelligent, strong, caring, beautiful woman. That's what you are, and as you get older I can only see those qualities getting better. They're reasons I didn't want to let you go."

Conversations with Sophie and Julia surfaced, and I couldn't stop myself. "That, and I'm a normal, average girl?"

His gaze didn't waver, didn't falter. "That's one of my favorite parts about you."

"I'm not a Hollywood girl."

"And I don't want a Hollywood girl. I want happiness. For once I want to be truly happy. I want something real." His mouth opened wide, a yawn taking over, his body stretching out until he settled back down. "I think that's one thing that has thrown Miles off. I've been unhappy with a woman I would never marry, on and off for the last six years. Then suddenly I meet you and marry you in less than thirty-six hours? Yeah, he's probably wondering when the invasion of the body snatchers came along."

"Well, as insulted as I was by his comments, it seems maybe he's just shocked at your one-eighty on life and relationships. He's probably also wondering when the hell you're going to come to your senses."

"I am one hundred percent in my senses, and he needs to come to his senses and realize that."

"What about the fairy tale?" I asked as I laid my chin on my hands, looking up at him as I rested on his chest.

"Oh, fairy tales are real. Didn't you hear that part?" His lips twitched up into a smirk.

"Do fairy godmothers exist, then?"

"Oh, yes. They're named Karen." He let out a laugh.

My mouth dropped open as I stared at him, then moved into attack mode. I tickled his side, causing him to squirm. "Oh, you think you're funny now, huh, Mr. Lockwood?"

"Oh, yes, Mrs. Lockwood. It's one of my many good qualities."

"Many?"

"Many," he stressed, and the mood shifted as he pulled me closer. "I have a very nice, large quality I'd like to show you." His lips descended upon my neck, kissing and nibbling down to my shoulder while his hand moved up my side, thumb grazing the side of my breast.

"Y-you do?" I stuttered.

"Mm-hmm."

His hand slid between my thighs, gently pushing them apart, and lightly trailed up until he was exactly where he wanted to be. Gently, his fingers danced over the cotton of my panties, passing over my clit more than once and making me draw in a sharp breath each time, much to his delight.

"How's my girl feel down here?" he asked.

I knew what he was referring to, and I began to rock my hips against his hand, begging for the friction, burning with desire. "Needy," I breathed out.

"Fuck," he groaned and rocked his hips into my thigh, letting me feel how hard he was for me.

The pressure he was placing on my rapidly wetting pussy increased, sending what felt like a jolt of lightning through me. It was no longer the gentle yet needy feel of our first encounter, creating a slow, building fire, it was desire unleashed. My body was lighting up, fire raging everywhere he touched. An uncontrollable need to feel him took over, and I moved one hand between us. He drew in a sharp breath when my fingers reached his waistband, moaning as his hips pushed his cock against me. That earned me greater pressure, causing me to cry out.

My hand made its way past his waistband and grazed the hot head of his cock. Weston was cursing as my fingers wrapped around him and slowly made a path up and down his length.

"Fuck, baby girl, that feels so unbelievably good," he said between pants.

His fingers pushed aside my panties and began caressing the swollen flesh beneath. One finger was placed at my opening and he pushed it in. I drew in a shuddering breath, my back arching and my hand grasping a little bit tighter on his cock. His hips began to rock him into my hand, the silky skin seeming to grow hotter and the flesh harder. My mind was clouded when he entered me with a second finger, and I knew then that everything was all right. I wanted him inside me.

No, I needed him.

"Weston," I panted, pushing my hips harder into his hand.

"Wren, oh, Wren," he moaned as he adjusted to settle between my thighs. "Baby, I need you."

"Please!" I begged.

He growled in response, and then a voice began to shout, breaking us out of our lust-induced haze.

"Weston! Get your ass out of bed and off Wren! Burning daylight, Lockwood!" I heard Sophie's voice close to my ear, but she was nowhere in the room.

"Fucking cock-blocking little . . ." he grumbled and looked over at the clock. "Damn! I'm late!" Propping his body up and leaning over me, he picked up his phone from the bedside table, tapped a few buttons, and spoke into the receiver. "Overslept, give me ten minutes." I heard his voice ring out and realized that there *was* an intercom system.

"I'm sorry," I apologized as he set the phone down.

He winked at me. "Don't be. I'll just let you stew all day long, waiting for me to come home and take you with all my pent-up frustration." My face flushed and my pulse raced, both of which he noticed. "Then it will be so much better. And, you'll come harder."

He kissed me then, despite the morning breath, before hopping out of bed and rushing to his room. I also got out of bed, quickly moving to wash my face and brush my teeth. Once complete, I threw on some shorts and a T-shirt and walked out.

I didn't think I'd taken that long, but when Weston came out of his bedroom and was obviously showered and dressed, I wondered if he had super speed. He was wearing low-riding jeans, and they hung perfectly on his hips, which just made me want to grab him and throw him on the bed so we could finish what we started.

He shot me a sexy smile as he wrapped his arm around my waist, pulling me close and kissing me hard. "Sophie has brought your clothes. You two can spend the day rearranging the closet and moving your stuff into *our* bedroom."

I liked the way he said *our*.

We moved down the steps hand in hand and found Sophie, Julia, and a few other people milling around the kitchen. There was a squealing sound, followed by clapping.

A beautiful little blonde-haired girl waddled out from behind the kitchen island and headed straight for Weston, her curls bouncing with each step.

"Wehtun, Wehtun, Wehtun!" she repeated over and over upon seeing Weston.

A huge smile lit up his face and he bent down to catch her, lifting her high in the air and twirling her around. The little girl giggled in delight and shortly after was settled in his arms.

"Hello, my beautiful Princess Ari. I've missed you," he said, his face aglow as he gave her Eskimo kisses. I was stunned, staring wide-eyed as he played with the small child. "Your mommy and daddy are mean. They don't bring you around nearly enough for my liking."

"Mean Mommy!" she repeated, her chubby little fingers tapping against his cheeks.

"Hey! That's not nice!" Sophie protested and attempted to snatch her child back, but the little girl just cried out and clung to Weston, burying her adorable face in the crook of his neck.

"Go make your own, Lockwood. Word has it you have a wife now. Knock her up!" an unfamiliar blond man said. It was then he seemed to notice me in the doorway, his eyebrows rising in surprise. "Oh, you must be said wife. Sorry for interrupting your activities this morning. My wife is an early riser." My face flooded in embarrassment. Crossing the room, he held out his hand, and I stepped forward to take it. "Carson Brooks, pleasure to meet the woman who has captured our fair Weston's heart."

He was handsome, with light brown eyes and a cut jaw. Was everyone in Weston's life beautiful? Talk about giving a girl a complex.

"Ass," Weston snorted, earning a smack on the arm from Julia.

"Language!" she chastised, then promptly returned her attention back to her laptop.

"Ass!" Ari imitated, and Weston groaned.

Weston shook his head. "No, Ari, that's a bad word. You shouldn't say that word or Mommy might spank you."

Sophie let out an exasperated sigh. "Why do you always make me out to be the villain?"

"Because thanks to you, he has blue balls," Carson said with a snort before he turned his attention back to me and smiled. "Anyway, welcome to our kooky family, Wren. Now, if you wouldn't mind, could you pry my child out of your husband's arms so I can steal him away for business?"

I smiled up at him. "I think I might be able to do that."

I walked over to Weston, who was deep in conversation with Ari about her teddy bear . . . at least, I think it was about a teddy bear—most of it was gibberish. Weston was hanging on her every word. It was so endearing, and I hoped he would be the same with our children someday.

Our children. It sounded strange and right to my ears at the same time. The word "our" was working its way into both of our vocabularies.

"Weston, can you introduce me?" I asked.

His smile was so big and bright. "This, baby girl, is Princess Arianna. Otherwise known as just Arianna or Ari," he said, turning her in his arms. "Ari, can you say hello to Wren?"

I smiled up at her, but she still gave me a leery eye. Almost as if she was daring me to try and take away her precious Wehtun's attentions. Clinging tighter to him, she shook her head and shied away from me.

"Oh, come on, my princess. Wren is really nice, and I bet she can hunt you down a cookie if you're a good girl."

"Briber!" Sophie cried out, and Weston ignored her.

At the thought of a cookie, Ari smiled and stretched her arms out to me. I picked her up, moving her to my hip.

"You are so pretty," I said, and she looked at me shyly from under her lashes.

"So are you," Weston said, giving me a kiss. "I'm off to work."

"Have a good day!" I watched as he and Carson headed out the door with Julia in tow.

Making good on my cookie promise, I walked to the pantry in a hopeful search for something, but came out disappointed.

"There's a cookie jar on the counter. Kelly usually keeps a small stockpile there," Sophie said, not even looking up from her phone.

"Thanks."

We headed over to the ceramic container that was clearly labeled cookies. Upon closer inspection, the smaller writing beneath read "AKA Weston's drops of sugary goodness. Eat at your own risk." I laughed, knowing it was probably Sophie herself who had purchased it. Reaching in, I brought out two cookies, one for me and Sophie to split, and one for Ari.

"I heard about Miles," she said as she set the phone down and took the cookie from Ari's hand before she broke it up into smaller pieces and handed it back. She earned a most evil glare for her snatching. "We don't all think that way. I just want you to know."

"It was kinda hard to swallow. I know not everyone is going to welcome me or our marriage with open arms, but what he said . . ."

Sophie leaned against the counter and sighed. "I know I was upset yesterday, though less so than Miles, so here's the bottom line after I cooled down. Weston is one of my dearest and closest friends, and I don't want him to get hurt. I'm kind of torn because I get your perspective as well. Here you've been dropped into an unknown situation and life, so at the same time I'm very protective of you."

She took a bite of her cookie before turning and opening the fridge. Reaching in, she pulled out two bottles of water and set one down in front of me.

"Thank you."

She was silent for a few gulps before continuing. "Julia told me what Miles said. You need to know that on some level we all feel the same . . . with the exception of the comment he made about your kitty. I see a scared little girl who I want to protect. Miles sees a gold digging actress trying to get a step up. So, right now I'm at 'hurt our Weston and I will kill you,' and 'if Weston hurts you, I'll junk punch him.' Unfair, I know, but I'm sure you understand."

I nodded. "I understand completely. Weston comes first."

"Rationality." She smiled and nodded. "That's a very good trait to have with Weston and this Hollywood life. I hope you keep it."

Ari chose that moment to interject her displeasure of being cookie-less and Sophie handed her another piece.

"Come on. Let's go rearrange the closet so there is room for everything. We have less than two hours," she said, pulling Ari's bag up from the ground along with her purse, before we headed upstairs.

Being with Sophie in her element was an adventure. Sometime during the "let's rearrange the closet" mission, it became "let's get rid of all the clothes Sophie doesn't like." Needless to say, when the clothes did arrive, we still had no concrete plan. The closet was huge. Easily larger than my bedroom back home. There was no need for dressers because the closet walls were lined with drawers, along with hanging areas. An island in the middle of the room also had drawer storage. There were shoe racks and benches. Weston still had more clothes than I did, even if you combined what Sophie had picked out and all of my clothes in Indianapolis. Ari enjoyed playing with the clothing as well—pulling things down from the racks.

Sophie and Ari left sometime after lunch, and I spent the remainder of the afternoon moving the rest of my belongings into our room and bathroom.

The bathroom was another room larger than my former bedroom, complete with a jetted tub, a large multi-shower-head shower, and two large sinks along with a vanity. Fantasies began to spin through my head of what we could do in that tub and shower, and I soon found myself overheated. My body still buzzed from our morning activities, and I couldn't wait until he returned home.

There was a fantastic view of the backyard from the bedroom, and the beautiful sparkling pool out there stared back at me.

I now had a new afternoon activity.

Moving to the closet, I began to search for the bathing suits Sophie had sent with me. I found them in one of the drawers in the center of the closet. Unfortunately, what I had thought were bathing suits were more like lingerie. Not a bikini and not a one piece, and they were definitely sexy.

Picking out what I deemed the least provocative of the nearly dozen, I pulled it on and headed down to the pool.

It was a beautiful day, hot and sunny, making the cool water feel that much better against my skin. Sinking down into the water was refreshing, and I dove the rest of the way in. The pool was wonderful. I always loved swimming and the sense of freedom that came with gliding through the water.

I lost track of the time, but I hadn't reached the prune-like state when I heard my name being called. Swimming to the edge, I found Weston walking toward the pool.

"Having fun?" he asked from the edge.

"So much."

"Well, I want to get a quick workout in before dinner, so why don't you keep swimming and I'll be right in there enjoying the view," he said with a smirk.

I peered over to the glass wall that he pointed to. There was an exterior door, and through the glass I could see right in to all of the equipment.

"Sounds like a plan."

Leaning down, he placed a kiss on my lips and headed back inside. A few minutes later, I watched him enter the workout room, now wearing his running shorts and shirt. His run on the treadmill began, and I ogled him before deciding to float around for a few more minutes.

When the pruning stage began to show, I decided enough was enough and made my way over to the steps.

Rising out of the water of the pool, I squeezed the water from my hair. It was then I heard a crash and looked over to the workout room to find Weston no longer on the treadmill, but lying against the wall.

Panicked, I quickly ran in through the door that led from the pool area and into the workout room.

I was still dripping wet when I found him lying on his side, clutching his head, the treadmill still running.

"Weston, oh my God. Are you okay?" I asked, rushing to his side.

His eyes opened, meeting mine. I didn't even have time to process the look before he grabbed the back of my head and crashed his lips to mine. He pounced on me, sending me tumbling to the ground, his body pinning me to the floor. He devoured my lips with his mouth while pulling my body flush to his and nestling his hips between my thighs.

The passion, the need, was rolling off of him, and I soon found my mind clouded with lust and desire. In the back of my head I wondered if it was going to hurt again, but with the way my body was aching, craving him, I doubted it.

His lips released mine, and I groaned in displeasure, but that quickly turned to a moan as he kissed his way down my neck. My hips rose, pressing against him, brushing my pussy up and down his length.

"So sinful," he moaned before swiftly pulling my bathing suit straps down, his hips undulating into mine.

His mouth descended on my newly exposed breasts, licking, biting, and sucking on my nipple.

My pussy, my whole body, was on fire. I needed him in me. Otherwise, I was going to combust. His name escaped my lips in a guttural moan, and he growled in response. His hand worked between our bodies and after some fumbling, I felt the heat of the head of his cock against the apex of my thighs. Deftly, his fingers pushed my bathing suit aside, he lined himself up, and thrust his cock into me.

My eyes widened, then rolled back, a cry of pleasure ripping from my chest.

"Fuck, baby girl. So sexy, so fucking sexy," he murmured against my skin, his cock not even halting, sliding in and out.

There was no pain. Instead, I clawed my way closer to him. I needed all of him as close and deep as possible. His pace was fast, almost rough with need. My body was tingling, jolts of electricity shooting through me with every thrust. He felt so good inside me, so un-fucking-believably good that I never wanted him to stop. I was begging him to go faster and he sped up, his fingers digging into my hips as he pistoned furiously until I exploded in pleasure.

Tearless sobs wracked my body, my back arching off of the floor as the most intense orgasm ripped through me. He was unrelenting as I came down, my sanity not even given the chance to return. He was grunting and growling above me, his noises lighting my body again. His teeth scraped against my neck while he changed his angle, unexpectedly sending me spiraling into a second orgasm.

His thrusts became erratic, slamming into me, and he cried out. I felt him pulsing deep inside me as he twitched with each stream. Dropping his head to my shoulder, his body soon followed, slumping against mine. I tried to caress his skin, but my body felt more like Jell-O than anything else.

"Fuck, baby girl. Fuck, fuck, fuck. I haven't come that hard in years," he said between pants.

"I believe you now."

He chuckled. "About what?"

"It does only hurt the first time. After that, the only pain is caused from the aching need," I said in amazement. Even though I'd just come, I wanted him to make me come again.

"Mmm, I plan to make you ache for days after," he said against my neck, giving me a little nip. "Force you to remember what my cock did to you."

I turned to look him in the eye. "My husband is a dirty, dirty man."

He chuckled. "And I plan to make my wife just as dirty as I am."

"Oh, you are well on your way, then," I said with a smirk before slapping his ass. "So, what happened?"

He propped up on one elbow and smiled down at me. "A sexy goddess rose out of the water. I was completely floored that she's mine."

I blinked up at him. *Goddess? Is he talking about* me?

Chapter Twelve

OUR FIRST ARGUMENT

T WAS AMAZING THAT WESTON WASN'T MORE INJURED THAN he was after his tumble from the treadmill. I helped to patch up a burn from the belt on his arm, along with a bleeding gash on his knee, but could do nothing for the bump on his head except kiss it. He said it made it better, but I think he was just placating me. It was sweet nonetheless.

I kissed his boo-boos one last time before we curled up in bed together that night. Our first night with my belongings combined with his; my clothes in his closet, toothbrush touching his, the other vanity no longer empty. I fell asleep easily wrapped in his arms, fingers caressing me into dreamland.

All too soon the alarm was blaring and his body left mine. Weston had unfortunately left for work early with the promise of returning in the early afternoon.

"I'm sorry I keep leaving you alone all day," he'd said with a heavy breath, looking into the mirror as he looped his tie around his neck.

"This wasn't planned, and you still have work. I know you can't drop everything to stay with me. I understand. Just . . . hurry back?"

His arm had swept behind my back and pulled me flush to his chest, lips pressed to mine. "As fast as I can, baby girl."

I pried myself from the bed a few hours later and searched for signs of life, while at the same time searching for some brunch.

Nobody was around, at least from what I could tell, but there was some yummy leftover chicken and pasta in the fridge.

Left to my own devices, I found my way into the piano room and began playing. I played some classical pieces, and pieces of my own. Something new struck me, and I began working it out on the keys until it was flowing freely, the beautiful medley unfolding. Before I knew it, almost two hours had passed.

Closing the lid, I headed out to the back patio and pulled out my phone. I knew Daniel's schedule by heart, and I knew he was in study period. It was time I called him, time I told him about Weston, and that I wasn't coming home.

Finding his number, I hit send and put the phone up to my ear.

Then promptly pulled it away when Daniel's high-pitched scream came through the speaker.

"Wren!" he screeched. "Oh, sweetie, I've missed you! Please, please, *please* tell me you're home now! There is so much to talk about. I'm on my way over. We have to talk! Trevor is a fucking slut. We broke up again, he was eye fucking Steve Diller, and I told him he wanted him more than me. He tried to deny it, but I know it's true. Ugh! He's just a pig. Oh, I've missed you!"

I took a deep breath and sighed. "I miss you so, so much."

"So, where are you?" he asked, and I hated to crush the excitement in his voice.

"I . . . am at home." The vice around my chest tightened.

"Oh, thank God! 'Cause I need a Wren hug, like seriously."

"I'd love to give you one, because you have no idea how much I need one right now, Daniel," I said, my voice wavering.

"Wren?" His voice dropped, worry creeping in.

My fingers played with the hem of my shirt as I took a few seconds to steady myself. "I say I'm home, but . . . see, the thing is . . . Indianapolis is no longer my home."

"W-what? What are you talking about? Your mom came home, and I know there is no fucking way you would suddenly move to Chicago."

"No, not Chicago. Los Angeles area or thereabouts. I'm not exactly sure, not too familiar with the layout yet."

There was silence on the other end of the line before a sharp intake of breath, combined with an almost sob. "Wren, please tell me you're joking. Please tell me you're in the house you've lived in since we were eight."

"I can't," I whispered. "My"—I cleared my throat—"husband's house is much larger than my mom's."

"Your *what?* You got *married?*" His voice rose in volume with each word, the pitch angling up to an almost shriek. "Are you fucking serious?"

"Yes."

"To who? I need to know. And, I can't believe anti-young-marriage Karen was cool with it. If you say she was, I really will think I'm dreaming, hang up, and when I wake up, all the shit that has come from your mouth will just be a bad dream."

"I married Weston Lockwood in a drunken night in Vegas," I said in a rush, letting out a sigh of relief at having it out and off my chest.

There was complete silence for a short moment before laughter took over. "Oh, now I *know* I'm dreaming! Weston Lockwood married you in a cliché Vegas way? Gorgeous, fuck-hot, Weston Lockwood from *Genesis, The Last Hero,* and so many more? Girl, my dream gave you a winner!"

"I didn't even recognize him at the time, Daniel. It wasn't until I saw the movie posters in his office the other day that it all clicked," I admitted bashfully.

"Wait . . . you're serious?" he asked, his voice wavering. "And you're just now telling me?"

"Yes, to both." I cringed at the hurt in his voice, then tried to explain. "I didn't know how to tell you. It was all so weird."

"You really aren't coming home?" he asked again, no life left in the voice streaming into my ear.

"I am home," I whispered.

"You don't even know him!" Daniel finally yelled, his tone changing to near frantic. "He could be some deranged psychopath! I can't believe Karen let you go with him."

Tears filled my eyes. I hated doing it, hated being so far from my best friend. "He is a really wonderful person, Daniel. And when you come out to visit, you'll see."

"Visit? No. You come home. You come home right now, Wren. Please . . . please, I need my best friend, please come home to me," he begged, desperation in his voice.

The tears began to slide down my cheeks. "Daniel, you know I love you." My nose began to run, causing me to sniffle.

"Who the fuck is Daniel?" I heard Weston demand through clenched teeth. I turned, just as the lounge chair beside me flipped over forcefully and crashed to the slate deck. His eyes were wide, his jaw set and he was vibrating with anger.

"What the fuck was that?" Daniel asked in surprise, before his voice lowered to a whisper, "It sounded hot and angry, which I gotta say made me twitch a bit."

I let out a little forced laugh at his comment and put my finger up to Weston, the universal sign for hold on, and that seemed to upset him further.

"Daniel, everything will be okay. We can still text and send pictures."

"Like hell you will," Weston said with a sneer.

"Jesus Christ, Wren, are you sure you're okay? He sounds fucking pissed!"

"Yes, I'm fine. *Weston* is just being an ass." I glared at my husband.

"Fine, but you have to get back to me ASAP so I know you're doing okay, and I will need to talk to you a lot so I can feel like you're actually here with me, sorta."

"You can visit, and I can visit, and before we know it you'll be here and we'll be at USC," I said to reassure him as I swiped at my tears.

"I'm holding you to that, Bradford . . . or should I say, Lockwood." I heard Daniel sniffling too.

A minute later, and another I love you, I ended my call. Weston was fuming, arms crossed over his chest, and I could almost see the flames surrounding him. He was seriously pissed, and the chair looked mangled.

"What the fuck was that about, Wren? Who the hell is Daniel? Is there something I need to know? Please tell me if I'm wasting my fucking time here. You could have fucking told me you had a boyfriend!" He laid into me, but I wasn't going to be intimidated.

"Whoa! Hold on, Weston." I jumped up from the lounger and stood in front of him, my finger poking into his chest. "You don't get to judge and fly off the handle based on what tiny bit of my conversation you overheard."

He had no right to accuse me of anything. Especially, since he knew so little about me and where I came from.

"You just told some guy you love him," he seethed. "I'm your fucking *husband*! Those words are reserved for *me*!"

"Oh, and you think your behavior right now is acceptable? Will make me love you? Because I can tell you right now, Mr. Lockwood, that you are currently not being endearing at all. Jealousy is *not* a lovable quality."

"I just don't like that my *wife* is talking with another man and telling him she loves him, something she hasn't even told me!" He clenched his fists tightly together at his sides.

"Oh, fuck off, Weston!" I screamed back at him. "Daniel is my best friend! My very close, very dear, very *gay*, best friend. And now, because I'm here with you, I've lost him in my life on a daily basis. The only person I have ever been able to count on in my life." The tears rolled down my face, my bottom lip trembling. "So excuse me for being upset and for loving him!" I wiped the tears from my cheeks, but Weston remained silent. I looked back up at him and squared my shoulders, turning to leave. "Oh, and Weston? Thank you for putting so much trust in me, your wife."

I turned and stormed off, my chest tight as I held everything in. I didn't know where to go, but I just wanted to be alone, and with such a huge house there had to be a few good hiding spots. There was a living room with chaise couches laid out before a large TV. I threw my body down on one and sobbed into the white corduroy fabric.

It had been harder to tell Daniel I wasn't coming home than I thought. He was hurt that I hadn't called him immediately. He was upset, and rightfully so. We talked daily, and I had ignored him for days. I missed him so much. I missed Indiana, I missed my mom, and really anything that had been my life before Vegas. I missed the home I'd always known.

Homesickness sunk in, enveloping everything.

I wanted to be home, in my comfort zone, not stuck in a foreign place.

Now Weston and I were fighting, and I was reminded of how very alone I was in my *new* home. We were bonding, but we still had a long road ahead of us.

I heard footsteps coming close before the warmth of his hand laid on my shoulder. It only made me cry more. He slid down behind me, wrapping his arms around me.

"Wren, I'm sorry. I overreacted and shouldn't have gone off like that," he said softly as he pressed light kisses against my skin.

"No, you fucking shouldn't have," I replied, trying hard to ignore his touch.

"I was just dumbstruck listening to you tell some guy that you love him. Because those are words I want you to eventually say to me."

"There's still a long way to go until then." The words were spoken mostly out of anger. Truth was, I was falling for him. The connection we had was too strong not to. That, and he was a wonderful man . . . he'd just not used his head and stuck his foot in his mouth.

"I know, but I can't wait until you say them to me. And I can't wait until I can say them to you," he admitted.

I relaxed back into him. "You seem pretty certain that we'll fall in love."

He made a humming sound against my shoulder. "It's a feeling I have. Don't you feel it too?"

"I wouldn't be here if I didn't. You know that."

"Please say you forgive me," he whispered as he placed a kiss on my shoulder.

I turned in his arms until I was on my back, able to look up at him. "Just . . . use your head next time? Think before you speak."

"Promise."

"And, Weston, if we are going to have a *real* chance at a life together, at making this work, you are going to have to *trust* me, and ask questions *before* you yell and curse at me."

"Okay, I know, and again, I'm sorry, baby girl. This is all so new to me, these feelings and emotions coursing through me. And, I want to trust you. I do trust you."

"Thank you," I said softly, pulling his arms tighter around me.

We lay there snuggling as my tears dried up. It felt good just to have him near. I already craved him so much. Any and all affection he would give, I would gladly receive.

My head was thumping a bit from the crying, and I turned more to nuzzle into his chest.

"Better?" he asked, brushing my hair over my ear.

I nodded in response and tilted my head up to place my lips against his.

"So, foot in mouth is a Lockwood family trait, huh?"

Weston let out a low chuckle, a smile forming on his face. "I guess it must be. It's from my father's side, and I will try and quell this awful genetic inheritance of mine. Because the last thing I want to do is hurt you."

"That would be nice." Silence took over, and after a moment I decided it was time to get moving again. "I think I want to take a shower," I said and sat up. I turned to look at Weston. "Want to come?"

He smiled and kissed me. "I would love to join you, beautiful."

We walked upstairs, hand in hand, to the master bathroom. With gentle hands and a slow pace, he removed my shirt and helped me out of my shorts.

"Mmm, you are so alluring," he whispered in my ear while his hands reached around my back to unclasp my bra.

My hands fumbled with the buttons on his shirt. "Says the most alluring man on the planet."

"The planet? Really?" he teased.

"Well, at least on planet Wren, but I'm pretty sure you're near the top on Earth."

He chuckled as he turned the water on and set the temperature. There were two showerheads along with multiple side sprayers. It was a dream shower. Taking my hand, we stepped through the glass door and under the warm spray.

Closing my eyes, I let the warm water run over my body. My muscles relaxed and the remainder of the tension faded, washing away with the water down the drain.

"Fuck," Weston whispered.

I opened my eyes to find him staring at me. "What?"

"You."

"What about me?"

"The sight of you naked beneath me is one of my favorites, but the sight of you naked standing in front of me . . . wet? Perfection."

I blushed, taking my bottom lip between my teeth, my eyes turning to appraise his form. Attraction was definitely not a problem.

Weston had a fantastic body. He was fit, the six-pack he sported making that obvious, but he wouldn't be described as ripped. He was toned, probably from all of the running he did. Strong arms and pecs, a toned abdomen, and a big strong . . . cock.

"Holy shit!" I yelled out as I looked down, finally getting a good look at Weston's goods. And boy were they good.

"What?" he asked with a teasing smirk, fully aware of what had caught my appraising eyes' attention.

"This is what you've been thrusting in me?" I asked in awe, my hand lightly stroking up and down his hardened length.

He twitched in my hand at my words, a shudder running through him as he hardened further. "You never looked?"

"Maybe a glance, just not this up close and personal." I couldn't even touch my fingers to my thumb.

"Feel free to take a real close look whenever you want, baby girl. You can get a great view from your knees," he teased with a wink.

"Why, Mr. Lockwood, are you suggesting I put this huge thing in my mouth?" I tried to sound as provocative as I could, adding in looking at him from under my lashes, which caused him to groan.

He pulled my head to his, lips crashing to mine. "I am definitely suggesting that."

"Mmm, maybe I should inspect, to make sure everything is in working order. After all, I am your wife, and as such it is my duty to make sure that my husband is properly taken care of," I said as I lowered down to the tile floor.

"Fuck, yes," he panted.

I finally got to lay eyes on the beast up close and personal. Weston was bigger in both length and girth to the only other specimen I'd touched before. It was also straight, but curved up ever so slightly at the tip.

"Perfect," I whispered before leaning forward and placing a kiss to the hot red head. It really was the only word I had to describe his physical appearance. Because to me, he was.

"Have you ever sucked a cock?" he asked.

I shook my head as my mouth opened, looking at him from under my lashes, my tongue sneaking out and rubbing against the underside of his head.

"Fuck!" he cried as his lust-filled eyes closed, his head tilting back, and one hand moving to rest on my cheek.

Opening my mouth, I tentatively wrapped my lips around the

tip, earning another moan and a thrust of his hips. The skin was warm and smooth, the flesh beneath rigid yet pliable.

"Damn, baby girl, your lips feel so good," he said in praise before grabbing a fistful of my wet hair.

I took him deeper into my mouth and looked up. The expression on his face caused heat to pool between my thighs. It was pure bliss; heavy-lidded eyes, open mouth, harsh breaths, and flushed skin.

I did that to him.

I smiled internally and focused on my task, my tongue stroking down, then back up, before taking as much of him in my mouth as I could. I gagged more than once, not used to something so big in my mouth.

There was a bit of fumbling, but Weston didn't seem to mind. He was trying his best not to thrust into my mouth, but I noticed every time he did, and I gagged, he released a low, throaty moan. I knew then, he liked the sound.

Having enough of my teasing, Weston shut off the shower and picked me up, which was a difficult task with wet skin. Walking over to the bed, he tossed me down before jumping on top of me with a playful growl. I squealed in delight and feigned fear. He seemed to like this, his tongue running up the length of my neck, nipping at my ear.

"Turn around, baby girl. I'm going to show you how the animals do it."

"Mmm, like they do on the Discovery Channel?" I asked with a giggle as I turned around.

Weston's hand smacked playfully down on my right butt cheek before gripping it hard.

"Are you laughing at me? Not a wise idea."

"No?"

"No," he stated before slamming his hips forward, burying himself hard and deep.

I cried out, my hands fisting in the sheets, a tearless sob

erupting as I clenched around him. His fingers found my clit, teasing it as his hips rotated, slamming his cock in and out in a delicious motion. Bliss. Pure, erotic bliss.

His free hand gathered my hair, and he leaned forward.

"You have to tell me if you don't like something, baby girl. Okay? I want you to get as much pleasure as I do," he said.

I wondered what he meant, and I found out when he straightened up and pulled on the hair he had fisted. It was painful, but at the same time sent tingles through my body. The action lifted my torso, allowing him to hit a different angle. He released my clit and pushed down on my lower back while pulling me back to him.

"Oh fuck!" I sobbed, my muscles tightening, and I knew I was close.

He was relentless. His breath was coming out in pants, but he wouldn't slow down, wouldn't stop, until he pushed me over the edge.

"Baby girl, you feel so good wrapped around me. Do you like it like this? Do you like me fucking you like an animal?"

"Yes! Oh, yes!"

"Good, because I fucking love it!"

It was intense, but Weston was showing me a side of myself I had an inkling was buried deep below. I wanted him to dirty me in every way possible.

With one nip of his teeth at my neck, I was pushed over the edge, free-falling into orgasmic bliss.

His strokes began to falter while my walls milked him, and he let out a strangled cry. His hips bounced against my ass as he flexed, trying to get his cock deep into me as he emptied inside me.

There was no strength left in him when he was done, causing him to collapse on top of me. He didn't stay there long before he rolled on to his side so he was spooning me while we caught our breath.

"The animals know how to do it," I said between breaths, sending Weston into a fit of laughter.

"I would have to agree."

After our breathing regulated, I turned in his arms to face him. We needed to talk before I forgot again, and before we found ourselves pregnant before we were ready . . . if we weren't already.

"Weston, I know this is a little late, but I'm not on birth control," I said and braced myself for the backlash.

But there wasn't any. He wasn't shocked, just pressed his lips to mine.

"Would it be weird if I said that was okay? That I liked this Russian Roulette? It's fucking hot as hell." His tongue slipped out and across his lips, his teeth biting into his bottom lip as he stared at me with heavy lidded eyes.

"I'm not here to be a baby factory." I probably looked at him like he was crazy. "This is an awfully big gamble, Weston. And usually when a girl gets pregnant, guys think it's to trap them."

He shook his head and chuckled. "Wren, you're already my wife. And, as strange as it may sound, I trust you more than anyone I've ever dated, and I've known you for a week. I know I may not have acted like it today, but it's the truth. And the baby factory thing . . ." He leaned back and held up his hands. "I only meant that . . . I've always had a vision, a dream, of having a family, and I've been excited to find someone to do that with."

"Someone or anyone?" I asked. My stomach swirled with uncertainty.

His hand cupped my cheek and he tilted my head up to meet his gaze. "*The* one."

The *one*? Yeah, he could be my one. I could totally feel it.

He let out a sigh before continuing, our faces inches apart. "Girls always want to marry the movie star, while I always wanted the girl next door. To have two point five kids and a white picket fence. Because, to me, even if it's outdated, that's normalcy, and that's something I haven't had since I was a pre-teen." I brushed my fingers through his hair, earning a moan. He leaned closer, his nose ghosting against mine. "I can see that dream happening with you

. . . well, the happy family part. You're so down to earth that I feel grounded. With you, I'm just a man."

Just a man. *My man.*

I loved him showing me more of who he was at his core. It made me fall for him more.

"Because I didn't know who you were?" I asked, my brow quirking.

He chuckled and rubbed his hand up and down my arm. "That does have something to do with it."

Even with his emotional confession, it didn't dampen my concern. "I'm only eighteen, still in high school. Are you the one trying to trap me?"

His eyes bored into mine, fingers caressing my cheek. "Wren, I would never trap you. If you want to get on birth control, we'll have Julia find a doctor and make an appointment. But, if you want to know what I honestly think? I'm all for letting fate give us what it wants to. It brought us together, after all."

"You are way too charming and persuasive, Mr. Lockwood."

"And I haven't even fully unleashed it on you yet," he said with a smirk. "So?"

I swallowed hard. "It's pretty much a given I'm going to end up pregnant if we keep this up. I'm starting college in the fall. Do we really want to give the press more ammo?"

"What, you think 'Weston Lockwood married to pregnant teenage high school senior' is so much worse than 'Weston Lockwood married to teenage high school senior'?" he asked.

I cringed. "I don't know . . . I've never really thought about having kids."

"You had Karen," he said jokingly.

I swatted his arm. "You're bad, and she wasn't in diapers."

"Yet."

I rolled my eyes. "Yet."

I groaned, my head falling against his chest and my arms wrapping around him. Breathing in his scent, I felt a warmth rush over me. There, in Weston's arms, I knew where I was meant to be. I wanted to give him his dream. I wanted to have a family with him, with this man I barely knew. Did it really matter when we started? We were already married. Sure, we were still essentially strangers, but I knew deep down I was falling in love with him, and at a lightning-fast pace.

"What if I'm already pregnant?" I asked him nervously. The unknown, the possibility, was unnerving.

"Then this whole conversation is kind of moot."

"I don't know if I'm ready to be a mommy, but I do somewhat agree with you on the whole fate argument."

It scared the shit out of me, but I could also see the appeal. But, I still had things I wanted to do independently, including getting to know my husband before we became parents.

"We'll do whatever you want to, Wren, but once you're pregnant, there's no going back. No undoing it."

The thought hadn't even entered my mind. "Well, I need to have an appointment anyway, so why don't we have Julia find a doctor and by the time it comes around, I'll decide."

"All right," he agreed, kissing my forehead and rolling me onto my back. "Have I told you how much I love coming inside you?"

I bit down on my bottom lip, my eyes lighting up. "No, but perhaps you could demonstrate it for me again?"

"Oh, I'll demo it as many times as you want," he teased before attacking my lips, hands grabbing my hips.

The next day Julia called the same doctor she went to and made an appointment. I had three weeks left of Russian Roulette. Three weeks to make a decision that could alter my life forever.

Chapter Thirteen

OUR FULL GARAGE

FRIDAY.

The end of the work and school week.

The marking of my first full week of knowing Weston Lockwood, and the last day I would be stuck at home while he was away at work. The good news was, during all my free time, I got to spend hours playing the piano, which was something I'd always loved doing. The bad news was, my hands ached. Muscle memory served me well, but I'd obviously lost some dexterity and stamina.

With a piano in the house, it wouldn't be long before I was back up to where I was.

Amy, one of Weston's assistants, showed up at the house mid-morning with bags in her hands.

"Good morning," I said, trying to be friendly. So far, the only interaction I'd had with her was when she held our place at the DMV.

She smiled at me, a genuine one that made it to her pretty blue eyes. "Good morning, Mrs. Lockwood."

"You don't have to call me that. Just Wren."

"Oh, I know," she said with a grin and a giggle. "It's just fun to call you that."

She made me laugh a little with that, and I sighed with relief. It was the first time I got to look at her. She wore the same kind of business casual clothes as Julia—skirt, nice shirt, and sometimes a sweater or blazer. Maybe in her mid-twenties, she looked like any girl at my old school. She was pretty, with shoulder-length brown hair that had a small wave.

"I have, for your viewing pleasure, your new school uniform."

"Really?" School had barely come up, with the exception of a brief mention that I was starting on Monday. Then it hit me. "Uniform?"

"Yes. Olympus Academy. It's an elite private high school. A lot of teen actors and Hollywood kids go there. With your transcript, Julia thought it would be a perfect fit. They are very strict on privacy, seeing who their students are, as well as the professional status of the parents."

I pulled the top items out of the bag; a crisp white short sleeved button down, navy sweater vest, and blue plaid skirt. My eyes were wide in shock as I looked at the skirt. I thought uniforms were supposed to be modest. Apparently not the case in California. There was another matching skirt beneath, long sleeved button down, cardigan, and two ties. Julia had also thrown in some knee high socks.

"I have to say again . . . uniform?" I grumbled. "And what kind of uniform is this?"

Amy smiled at me. "Welcome to California!"

I grimaced and rolled my eyes. "Yay."

"It's not so bad. You'll get used to it. And I'm sure you'll make some friends, so it won't be so lonely."

"Lonely?" I asked. It was our longest conversation. How could she know how I was feeling?

"Wren, I may not be around here much, but I can't even imagine how lonely this all must be for you. To still be in high school and leave everything you know without any warning? That takes a strong person."

"Or a stupid one," I said with a sigh. Though, what she said made me think that she knew what I was going through. I had a feeling Amy wasn't a California native.

"I really think going to school will be a good idea for you. We looked into so many options, trying to find what was best for you. With Weston's schedule, it will be good to have something of your own to do."

I nodded. Honestly, I hadn't thought of any other option than the brief idea of getting my GED. But Amy was right. If I thought I was lonely this week when Weston was away at work, it would be worse if I didn't go to school. And while I missed Daniel and his friendship something awful, I knew I could make friends here as well. I'd always been well-liked and friendly.

"Knock, knock," a male voice called out.

A tall blond guy in khakis and a button down with the sleeves rolled up stood in the doorway with a file in his hand. He stared at me with a smirk on his face, brown eyes sparkling.

"You must be the infamous Wren," he said as he walked forward. He held out his hand. "Hi, I'm Graham."

"Hi."

He had a firm shake. "Julia asked me to bring these by. It's paperwork from the school we need you to fill out."

"Graham is Julia's assistant," Amy said, probably seeing my confusion.

"Weston's assistant has an assistant?" I asked. They both nodded. "Is there a reason why work wouldn't just be passed down to you or the other assistant?"

They looked at each other and then back to me.

"We all have different responsibilities. Julia is like Weston's sidekick, she's the one that delegates things, but we all have our own roles as well. And Mallory . . . well, let us just say I'm really hoping Graham gets a promotion."

His mouth popped open wide. "And leave my goddess?"

Amy rolled her eyes. "You want to continue working under Julia?"

"I'd love to work under her for the rest of my life." His eyes went wide, and he stared at me. "Please don't tell her I said that."

"He's got a huge crush on Julia."

"Amy! Jesus." He looked back to me, his cheeks pink. "It's not something I'd ever admit to her. I mean, she's got the perfect relationship with Miles."

Graham's face was beet red. "Can you just . . . fill those out so I can get away from my embarrassment?"

"Sure."

It took only a few minutes, and a reminder from Amy of what my last name was. When I was done, I signed my name, the lettering still a little bit shaky as I'd only done it a few times.

"So when do I get to meet . . . what did you say her name was?"

"Mallory," Amy grumbled. "And hopefully never."

"Why is that?" I asked.

"Mallory is in time out," Graham said. "She's on the edge of being fired and isn't allowed to do a whole lot of things that involve Weston, especially since you arrived."

"Why?"

Amy glanced at Graham. "Mallory has been doing some suspicious things."

"Ah." I'd heard a little about Mallory before, and it worried me. "Why does he keep her around then?"

"We're not really sure," Amy said. "But I'm sure it's on advice from his legal team."

Legal *team?*

Once they were gone, I decided to get everything ready for Monday so I could spend the whole weekend with Weston uninterrupted. I had taken my backpack with me to Las Vegas, so luckily I didn't need that new as well. I found a pair of shoes in the boatload worth that Sophie had delivered, and washed and ironed my new uniform.

It was the perfect time to catch up with Daniel as school was just letting out in his time zone. I slipped my bluetooth in my ear and hit dial. It didn't take two rings before his voice came through.

"Wren, my angel love," Daniel said into the phone as I ran the iron over the short-sleeved shirt.

"Hey, hot stuff. How's it hanging?"

He made a hmm'ing sound. "To the left today. Tell me, what's happening over two thousand miles away? Are you getting a tan?"

I chuckled and rolled my eyes. "Nothing that relaxing. In fact, I'm ironing my school uniform."

"Ew . . . school uniform? Seriously? That sucks."

"It's actually not bad looking. I start Monday at some elite private school." After closer inspection and a quick fit check, it actually was pretty nice as far as uniforms went.

"You could be hanging with me, but nooo. Had to go and marry some big-time Hollywood actor."

I let out a little laugh. "Yeah. All fun and games over here."

"How did it go the other night?" he asked.

"He apologized." I sighed. "There's still so much we don't know about each other."

"You do know I will keep my word and not tell anyone, but the second it's announced, I'm going to yell it from the rooftop of the school."

"When that happens, you should come out and we'll celebrate."

"Oh, I'm sure you're having lots of fun celebrating with Weston." If he was in front of me, I was sure he'd be wagging his eyebrows.

"Oh, my God. Not you, too." My face flooded with heat.

"Lost your V-card to a celebrity. Can't freaking believe it."

I let out a chuckle. "You're just jealous."

"Totally." There was noise in the background and people talking. "Damn, I have to let you go, buttercup."

"Okay. Give me a call later."

"Will do. Love you!"

"Love you, too," I said before hitting the button and ending the call.

The rest of the afternoon seemed to drag, and I was beginning to feel happy school started for me on Monday. I didn't know how many more days of sitting around I could handle with nothing to do. It was really starting to get to me, but at least I got to spend some time at the piano composing. That had always filled a void in my life.

I was hanging out in the living room, cleaning out my backpack, when I heard his voice.

"Baby girl?" Weston called out, and I hopped up from the couch, running to the kitchen.

"You're home!" I skidded to a halt, my eyes widening when I saw him.

He looked nervous. "Like it? Reggy cut it a little bit shorter than I like . . . Wren?"

"I can't fist my hands into it," I said as I stared at Weston's shorn head. I knew he was headed to get a trim, his unruly hair too long for his liking.

I agreed it was too long, but now I thought it was too short, and he seemed to agree with me. At least on the sides. The top thankfully still had some length.

Weston chuckled and grabbed my hand, pulling it up to the back of his head. There were no longer strands of hair, but a fuzzy, soft sheen. My fingers danced around, loving the feel of it as I moved them up and down.

He let out a contented sigh, a smile forming on his face as he leaned into my hand.

"You like that, don't you?"

He moaned in response.

"Keep that up, baby girl, and I might be forced to take you right here on the kitchen floor," he growled and nipped at my arm.

"Mr. Lockwood, I thought you knew by now that you can take me anywhere you want."

He grinned at me before heading up to change out of his suit.

I couldn't wait until he came back down. I needed time with him, a sense of grounding to my new reality to help prepare me for the next week.

The next morning, we loaded into Weston's car and headed out for some car shopping. I wasn't particularly happy with Weston insisting on buying me a brand new car, but I had to admit I was excited about it. My car in Indiana was over a decade old and had close to two hundred thousand miles. It was always on the constant edge of dying. I never knew if it was going to start or not.

We arrived at the car lot just after ten, but as we drove through I was having trouble recognizing most of them. It wasn't your run-of-the-mill US dealership. No, because I was able to identify one as a Ferrari, and a few Bentleys like Weston's.

We were greeted by a man named Scott. I remembered his name from when Weston was talking to Julia about cars a few days' prior.

Scott was an outgoing man in his mid-thirties, and he wore a huge smile on his face. No doubt in correlation with the commission he would get from the pending sale. He and Weston talked, and I overheard some of the numbers being thrown out and began freaking out as I looked at the dealer's inventory.

How could I drive something that cost as much and probably more than my mom's house? I was becoming more nervous that I couldn't deal with that pressure.

It was then that Scott brought it around, the car that met the specifications Weston had given to him.

Beautiful and sleek, and apparently pretty safe. All things Weston wanted in a car for me. It was a sporty, Audi R8 in a stunning maroon color.

I slid into the seat, my hands caressing the steering wheel as I looked around. It was an exquisite car.

"Thoughts?"

"Can I drive it home?" I said, which made Weston let out a chuckle. "It's beautiful."

We took it for a test drive, and I fell further in love with it. It was more car than I needed, in price, style, and power, but I didn't want to argue with him about it because I wanted it. Weston asked if I would throw a fit if he bought it for me, and I surprised him by kissing and thanking him.

"You aren't going to protest?" he asked in surprise.

"Is it going to do any good? Or are we just going to get into an argument that I'm going to lose in the end anyway? If that's the case, I don't want to fight, baby."

"You love it, don't you?" A smile of triumph grew on his face.

"I do," I admitted in defeat, looking up at him sheepishly.

He groaned, pulling me to him, whispering in my ear. "I really wish I could remember you saying those words to me."

His lips traced kisses down my neck.

"I do . . . too." My eyes began to flutter at his touch, my tongue darting out to wet my lips.

"But it's a bit blurry. Maybe after you graduate we can have a redo with our friends and family," he said, pulling away to meet my eyes.

"I'd like that." I reached up to cup his face.

Scott came back with the paperwork, and shortly afterwards, I was following Weston home in my new car. It really handled like a dream and filled our four car garage up—the last empty space.

Weston was going to have Graham input directions into the GPS sometime during the weekend so that I could get to school, his office, and many other places. It was a necessity, as I didn't know anything about L.A. or its layout.

"Okay, bad news," he started after dinner while we were curled up on the couch.

"Uh-oh."

He sighed. "You've entered my life at a very busy time. I have one movie in production, one in pre-production, and two in the works. Unfortunately, this means I'm not going to be around as much as I have since we got back from Vegas. I hate to leave you alone so much, but I promise when things calm down, you and I will run away together."

I scrunched my brow as I looked at him. "Run away?"

"Yes. I can't plan very far ahead, so I always refer to vacations as running away from home."

I giggled a bit at his running away description, but my smile fell into a frown. "Well, I . . . that just really . . . sucks."

"The good news is you start school on Monday, and we can text throughout the day. I'm sorry. I really don't want to be away from you right now," he said, his hand stroking my cheek, his lips leaving small kisses on my shoulder.

"But duty calls. You have a very strong work ethic."

A grimace spread on his face. "I guess I have my father to thank for that."

"Where are your parents, Weston?" I asked. They'd been alluded to multiple times by multiple people, but that was all it ever was.

"I haven't spoken to them in over four years," he said with a sigh.

"Why? What happened?"

He groaned and shifted his position. It seemed to be a subject he didn't like. "A lot happened, but it boils down to pushing me to the breaking point and being overly controlling of my life and career. I'll tell you all about it, but can we put it off a little? I just want to enjoy my weekend with you, not think about them. Just thinking about my family that is right here in my arms. You're my family now, Wren."

I smiled up at him, placing a kiss to his neck before wrapping my arms around his waist. "Okay. Let's go to bed."

The next morning my eyes fluttered open, the room still dim but starting to fill with the morning sun. The clock beside me read shortly before seven, which was way too early for a Sunday. I couldn't keep my eyes open and tried to go back to sleep, but a pestering fullness kept me from doing so. Throwing the blanket off, I pulled myself out of Weston's arms and headed into the bathroom.

There was relief as I used the restroom, but pain remained. Forcing my eyes open, I looked down to find red—my period had arrived.

Great.

Sleepily, I reached for the cabinet next to me, stopping when I noticed it looked wrong. My mind cleared a bit, and I remember just where I was and that I did not have what I was reaching for. Standing up, I stumbled back to the bedroom, my hand covering my abdomen.

"Baby girl, you okay?" Weston's groggy voiced asked from the bed.

I lay back down with a groan, pulling my legs up into the fetal position. "No."

He hadn't been expecting my answer and sat straight up, leaning over me. His hands rubbed up and down my arm. "What's wrong? What can I do?"

I groaned. What could he do? I couldn't exactly ask Weston freaking Lockwood to run to the local grocer or pharmacy to pick up tampons, could I? No, I couldn't. Plus, he was a man, and this was a matter for women.

"Call Julia."

"W-what?" he stuttered, confused.

"Call Julia," I repeated, and burrowed further into my pillow.

He shook his head. "We don't need to bother her."

"Then call Sophie."

He let out a huffing breath. "Wren, just tell me what to do, and I'll do it."

"Then fucking call Julia or Sophie!" I yelled and slipped deeper into the fetal position as a particularly bad cramp took hold. A small sob broke out. It was going to be a bad week.

"Wren . . ."

"Weston, I can't exactly send you out to buy tampons!" I hated how I was acting toward him, but I was just so uncomfortable and there was no way for him to understand.

"Oh!" His eyes popped wide as he finally got it and turned to the bedside table where his phone rested.

Julia picked up quickly, and Weston handed the phone to me. I explained to her what I needed, and she was thankfully understanding with a promise to be right over. I hung up, setting the phone on the bed beside me. Weston got up and walked around to my side, settling in behind me. His arms wrapped around me as we spooned. Grabbing his hand, I brought it to my lips for a kiss.

"I'm sorry," I said.

"Sorry for what?"

"For snapping at you. I just hurt so much."

"It's okay, baby girl," he said with a kiss to my temple.

He stayed wrapped around me, which was wonderfully soothing, while we waited for Julia to arrive. Soft kisses, gentle touches. He was a truly affectionate person.

Julia arrived and solidified herself in my mind as one of the most wonderfully caring people I'd ever met. With her she brought a heat pad, tampons and pads, and some Midol. She also whispered something about chocolate in the kitchen as she brushed some hair from my face and left with a soft smile.

Weston helped me out of bed, and I took care of things, my mind wandering to Julia.

"How is someone that sweet marrying your brother?" I asked in wonder as I climbed back into Weston's comforting arms.

Weston grimaced. We hadn't talked about Miles in the last few days, but I knew he hadn't spoken to him since that night. "Let's just not talk about him right now. Okay?"

I nodded and laid my head on his chest, his arms wrapping

around my shoulders. We settled back in bed and began drifting in and out of sleep. After an hour or so, the Midol kicked in enough that it wasn't too bad to move, and we headed downstairs.

We found some pancake batter in the fridge from Kelly, and a bag of mixed chocolate candies from Julia. I think she bought one of each item at the store. Weston was able to work the griddle, with some guidance from me at my stool perch, to cook the batter up. One time, he tried to flip a little early and ended up with a mess all over the place.

Once breakfast was done, we headed to find a TV and settled on the room with the chaise couches.

Pulling a blanket out of a cabinet, Weston covered us up, and I curled into a little ball in his arms. We watched a comedy, and when that was done he handed me the remote, showing me all the buttons and letting me decide what was next.

I appreciated that he understood I wasn't feeling well and not up to doing anything. The first day was always like that for me, but it usually got better.

I scanned through the guide, trying to find something that struck me.

That was when I saw it—*Midnight Horizon*.

"Oh, my God, I love this movie!" My thumb pressed the select button repeatedly until it changed channels.

Weston turned beside me and looked at me as if I'd grown a second head or like he was wondering who the girl beside him was. He then burst out into a fit of full-out laughter.

"What?" I asked, which only caused his laughter to increase and made him unable to answer me.

I returned my attention back to the screen with a huff. The narration started up, and a white light filled the frame. The light began to fade, and a pair of bright blue eyes took over, followed by a strong jaw and some wild brown hair.

My mouth dropped open as I stared in disbelief at the much younger version of my husband that filled the large screen.

"Baby girl, you should see your face right now!" He was laughing so hard he shook me as he pulled me closer and kissed my hair.

How did I not recognize him before? I had seen this movie numerous times. I turned to look at him as he was wiping tears from his eyes. "You think this is funny, huh?"

"Well, now I'm wondering if you would like my autograph." He barely finished his sentence before I smacked him with a pillow and moved to the far corner of the chaise to watch the movie.

Chapter Fourteen

MY FIRST DAY

I T WAS MY FIRST DAY AT MY NEW SCHOOL, OLYMPUS ACADEMY. Thankfully, my cramps had calmed down and I was more uncomfortable than in pain. I was a bit worried about wearing a skirt, especially since it was not really my kind of normal dress code. As I pulled into the parking lot, I wondered if my car would stand out, but when I found an empty spot between a Bentley and a Mercedes, I knew I'd blend right in. I was also armed with four hundred dollars in cash and Weston's Black American Express card until mine came in.

In cash alone I was carrying more than I made on a paycheck.

Yeah, at least parts of me were going to blend in, but I wasn't so sure about the rest of me. The *me* parts, and not the props.

My eyes scanned the courtyard, and a tiny bit of dread fell over me. If I thought I felt out of place at my old school, it could never compare to the barrage of L.A. girls done up to look like movie stars and the boys who were ripped and ready for the next action movie.

It looked more like a movie set than a high school. I began to wonder just what type of school Julia had found for me.

I looked ghostly pale and plain in comparison to the socialites around me with their contoured makeup and false eyelashes. I adjusted my skirt, feeling oddly exposed. I wanted my jeans back, or shorts, it didn't matter, just as long as it wasn't a skirt. Making sure that my ring was tucked into my shirt, I headed up the steps and into my new school.

I received a few strange looks as I navigated my way around, weaving in, out, and around other students, to find the office. Standing at the counter was a frazzled-looking redheaded woman.

"Excuse me," I said, trying to gain her attention.

"Oh, hello!" she replied and stepped over. "How can I help you?"

"I'm new and was told I needed to come here to pick up my schedule."

Her eyes widened. "A mid-semester add?" she asked, not necessarily to me. "What's your name?"

"Wren Bradford," I said, and realized my mistake, internally cursing at myself for the slip. "I mean Lockwood. Wren Lockwood."

"Oh! Yes, that's right, I remember now. Let me get that for you."

I breathed out as she walked away. My new name was going to be a difficult thing to get used to. More and more, I was missing Indiana, missing my school. After a moment of staring at the ceiling and clicking my heels together unsuccessfully, Mrs. Rochester, as her name plate stated, returned with a handful of papers.

"All right, here is your schedule, a map of the school, and your class outlines. You need to head to the bookstore to pick up your assigned texts before heading to class," she said with a smile. "Have a wonderful first day!"

I tried to smile back at her, but I had a feeling it came across as a grimace. After retrieving my books, I located my locker, dumping my extra books, before turning in the direction my map said my first class was located and headed that way. The bell rang overhead, and the halls began to scatter. I barely made it through the door of my first class by the time the second bell had rung.

I stopped as soon as I entered, twenty pairs of eyes turning to stare at me.

"Can I help you?" the teacher, a pretty woman probably in her forties, asked.

"Um, is this room 1412?" I asked, glancing down at my schedule.

"Yes . . . are you the new transfer student?"

I stepped forward and smiled awkwardly. "Yes, Wren Lockwood."

As soon as my last name was in the air, whispering picked up, causing the teacher to call them to order. Her eyes scanned the room and found what she was looking for.

"There is an empty seat over there you can take." She pointed to an empty seat near the back corner, and I headed toward it. "Class, this is our new student, Wren. Please make her feel welcome."

"Hi, I'm Charlotte," a brunette girl to my left said as I sat down.

I took her offered hand and gave her a small smile. "Wren."

"Wren, you don't look so happy to be here."

I shrugged my shoulders. "New school during senior year? Yeah, I miss my old school."

Her nose wrinkled. "I can't imagine that. Can I see your schedule?" I nodded and handed her the slip of paper. "Hmm, well, we have two classes and lunch together today, and three classes tomorrow. Good."

She smiled up at me, and I relaxed a bit when I saw that it was genuine. She had beautiful, kind green eyes.

Charlotte helped me to find my next class and said she'd find me at lunch. I was happy to have found someone so nice to help me out. I hoped maybe I'd found my first friend.

I shared a desk in my next class with a guy named Aaron. He had the jock mentality and the smirk to go with it. He was also a little too friendly for my taste. His attentions caused me to get the stink eye from a few of his admirers.

The day seemed to drag by, and I was happy when lunch arrived. Aaron escorted me to the cafeteria, and I had to step back when he tried to kiss me on the cheek. I smiled and waved and was thankful when Charlotte grabbed my hand and dragged me away.

"Thanks," I whispered as we walked away.

She smiled. "He's the resident playboy. Thinks he's God's gift to women and that they should all . . . submit to his advances. Preferably from their knees."

"Not going to happen," I said, and whispered "asshole" under my breath. "I'm taken."

"You have a boyfriend?"

I grimaced. "Something like that."

She cocked her brow at me, but I didn't expand and she didn't pry.

We made our way through the lunch line and headed out to the courtyard, which she said was her regular spot. There was a group of people sitting under a large tree, and we joined them.

"Everyone, this is Wren Lockwood. Wren, this is my boyfriend, Liam, and our friends Kandace and Spencer, Travis, Bianca, and Cloe." She pointed to each one as she said their names, but I knew it would be a while before I remembered them all.

"So, Wren, where are you joining us from?" Travis asked, and all attention turned to me.

"Indianapolis area."

"Why the move?" Kandace asked before taking a bite of sushi.

"It was a . . . sudden move by my . . . family," I forced out, and could tell nobody really believed me by the questionable looks on all their faces.

"Are you in witness protection?" Liam asked with a laugh.

"No, no, nothing like that," I assured and smiled. "Sometimes life just throws a wrench in your plans. And you have to go with the flow."

"Oh, hell, yes. Most of us understand that!" Spencer yelled, and the group broke out into laughter.

It was then that I noticed Cloe staring at me, and when I returned her stare, she looked away but not before asking, "Lockwood? As in Weston and Miles Lockwood?"

I sighed. Shit. We really hadn't hashed out how I would handle questions about our similarity of last name.

I decided simple honesty might be the best policy and answered, "Yes." I wasn't going to offer any more detail at that moment.

"So, what kind of school is this?" I asked in an attempt to change the subject and get the focus off me and my past. It worked as they all went into who they were and what they did.

Bianca was a foreign diplomat's child. Liam and Kandace were siblings, children of two of Hollywood's biggest names. Charlotte was also the child of a big actor. Travis was an actor himself, as were Cloe and Spencer. The school was known for its powerful, rich, and famous students.

My phone buzzed as we talked, and I pulled it out to find a message from Weston.

How's it going, baby girl?

My lips formed a straight line as I typed back.

Fabulous -_- So out of place it's not even funny, but have met some nice people.

I'll make sure tonight you feel in place. Right in my arms. I bit my lip and smiled down at his text.

"Look at that genuine smile," Charlotte teased. "Your boyfriend? Is he back in Indiana and that's why you're so thrilled to be here?"

I felt the blush rise on my cheeks before telling them to fuck off, which caused the group to erupt into more laughter.

After lunch, Charlotte and I headed to our next class. It was some musical composition class. It took me a couple of times of looking at the name to understand what exactly it was, and I still couldn't figure out why Julia would put me in a music class.

"You'll love this teacher. Not only is he very easy on the eyes, but he is a musical genius!" Charlotte gushed as we entered. There was something else she wasn't telling me. I could tell by the almost twinkle in her eye and her smile.

The teacher stood at the head of the class, his back to me as I approached to introduce myself. Then he turned around.

"Ah!" I squeaked, my eyes wide as I stared at my blond-haired music composition instructor.

His eyes met mine and his movements stopped, the smile fading from his face. "Wren, what are you doing here?" he asked, his tone harsh and low.

"I'm going to school, Miles. I'm the new transfer. Although, if I'd known I was going to be in your class, I would have gladly enrolled in another school, but I don't think your meddling fiancée would've gone for that."

He stepped forward, his lip twitching as he glared at me. "Watch what you say about her."

"Meddling is not a bad word, Miles, and Julia is a wonderful woman. I'm honestly in shock she would want to marry someone like you," I spat.

"You know nothing about me," he growled.

"You know nothing about me. Your words the other night were inexcusable and you deeply hurt . . . him," I whispered harshly, noticing that we'd garnered an audience.

"Take a seat," he said through clenched teeth, having noticed the same thing.

I turned to find Charlotte had saved me a seat next to her. Miles took roll and began the lesson. Apparently, they were working on original compositions. This wasn't the music appreciation class I was expecting. It was Music Composition, with emphasis on the Composition.

Why would Julia put me in something like that? Did she know I played piano? Had she heard me playing at the house one day? Or was it simply to throw us together?

Thoughts for another time, because Miles was speaking and saying my name.

"Wren is new to our class, and as such, I think she should play something for us. That way we know where her skills are and what level pianist she is."

I glared up at him and plastered on a fake smile before

standing and walking to the piano. Taking a seat, I began to play a piece to warm up, but ended up being interrupted.

"That's all good and well, Wren, but don't you have anything of your own? This is a *composition* class, after all."

I clenched my jaw, took a deep breath, and let my fingers glide across the keys, morphing into the melody that had been flowing through me all week. I became engrossed, feeling the music, the emotions. I don't know how much time passed, but at some point I realized it was enough and ended it.

There was silence, except the chords that still echoed throughout the stillness. I looked up to find every student in the room staring at me. Most of all, I noticed Miles's look of absolute shock. I blinked out at them in confusion before standing and returning to my chair in the middle of the room.

It was then the enthusiastic clapping began, started by a smiling Charlotte and quickly moving to envelop the entire room. Even Miles.

I sat back down in my chair, staring defiantly at Miles who merely grimaced back before turning his attention to the class and picking on the next student.

I whipped out my phone as soon as the bell rang and stormed out into the hall to text Weston.

Remember all those nice things I said about Julia?

I hit the send button and headed for the bathroom before going to my last class. My phone buzzed within seconds.

Yeah?

Oh, yeah, Weston. Oh, yeah. My fingers flew across the letters. **I take them all back.**

Uh-oh. Why?

Betrayal! I'm in Miles's class. I was able to type out that one last message and send it before walking into my class. With a sigh, I headed to teacher number four and found my new seat, which was next to Aaron again.

After the last bell rang, I ran out of the room and headed to my locker to swap out my books, trying to avoid Aaron. The guy was just kind of creepy and an asshole.

On my way out, Charlotte nearly ran into me, her arm wrapping around mine.

"Soooo, what was that about in music comp?" Charlotte asked as we walked down the hall. "You and Mr. Lockwood . . ."

"Ugh, don't call him that!" Calling Weston "Mr. Lockwood" in flirtation was one thing, but associating that name to Miles was ruining it for me.

"Okay, what was going on between you and Miles?" she asked, planting her feet and halting me, my arm nearly wrenching out of the socket. "I know we acknowledged the famous Lockwood link with your last name at lunch, but what's the story?"

My eyes darted around for onlookers, or eavesdroppers, but everyone at this school seemed to be too absorbed in themselves.

"Miles is my . . . estranged brother," I said cautiously, giving an accurate but vague description.

"Your *brother*?" she asked. "Wait, so that means you're directly related to Weston Lockwood?"

I breathed a sigh of relief that she said *related*. "We're practically strangers."

Her mouth dropped open. "Wow, I mean, the gossip rags said years ago that there was a falling out."

"Yeah, well, I didn't expect to end up in the same school as Miles. We don't get along very well."

"The whole room caught that, believe me."

My head fell back. "Great."

"Don't worry about it, your kick-ass performance kind of took away from the worst of the drama and the rest, we'll take care of it," she assured me.

"We?"

She gave me a smile. "It's high school, Wren. The rumor mill is vicious, and I know how important it is to keep a secret. We'll just make up a reason."

"Why would you do that for me? You don't even know me."

"Because, I know what it's like being related to Hollywood," she said, leaning in. "Not only is my father a big actor, but, he's the same as Cloe's."

"Same as Cloe's?" I asked, clearly confused as to the direction our conversation had turned.

"Our dad is Damien Clark," she said, waiting for me to bug out.

I did, my mouth dropping. Damien Clark was a huge star. Rivaling Weston a decade ago.

"Cloe is my sister. I know, I know . . . we look nothing alike." She shook her head. "She got our dad's exotic look, while I look like our mom. I also go by my mom's maiden name, while Cloe uses our dad's. Very few people know we're sisters. Can I count on you to keep it that way?"

I quirked my brow at her. "I'll scratch your back if you scratch mine?"

She smiled and took my arm in hers, directing us out the front door to the parking lot.

"You know, Wren Lockwood, I think I like you."

Turns out, Charlotte's car was the Mercedes I parked next to. She complimented my car, and I couldn't keep the cheesy grin from my face at thinking about Weston and his generosity.

Yeah, I loved the car. More than I needed and over the top? No doubt. Completely Weston's style? For sure.

After exchanging numbers, we got into our cars and headed out. Thank God for the GPS instructions Graham had installed or there was no way I would have found my way around.

The phone rang on my way home, Weston's name popping up on the screen.

"Hello?" I answered.

"Everything okay, baby girl?" he asked. I could hear the concern in his voice as it rang out through the car's speakers. "I'm sorry. I never thought Julia would do that, and I never would have subjected you to Miles with his current attitude."

"Yeah, that was not a happy surprise."

"Did he say anything?"

I told him about our little tiff before class and him trying to embarrass me and me winning that little game.

"You play the piano?" He sounded very surprised.

I smiled, not that he could see. It was another reminder we still had so much to learn about each other.

"Yes."

"You really are amazing and will have to share that with me soon," he said, and I hummed in agreement. "I wish I could take you in my arms right now."

"Mmm, me too."

"But it's going to be a late night. I'm sorry."

My heart sank, but we had talked about it, and I knew it was going to be happening.

"How late is late?" I really did miss him and had looked forward to his comforting arms after my first emotional school day.

"Past dinner, probably after you're asleep."

I sighed, not liking it, but there was nothing I could do. He had taken a lot of time off the week before to be with me. "Make sure you eat a good dinner."

"I will."

"I miss you," I whispered.

"I miss you too. So much."

We hung up and I continued my drive home, the loneliness beginning to creep in. With him I was okay. Without him there was silent nothingness. The music thumping in my car helped to drown it out some, but nothing except Weston could take it away.

Well, nothing in L.A.

Upon entering the house, I found Kelly in the kitchen and let her know it was dinner for one. It was still strange having a cook, but with Weston's job, I understood why he needed one.

I changed my clothes, did my homework, and called up

Daniel to give him the four-one-one on my first day of high school in California. All was done before my solitary dinner.

I spent the remainder of the evening watching television curled up on the couch, having a brief conversation with my mom, and finally turned in for bed early out of boredom. Sometime around midnight I felt arms wrap around me and warmth surround me. He placed kisses on my temple, neck, and shoulder while whispering that he was home and how much he'd missed me. Only then, with Weston beside me, was I truly home and able to fall into a deep slumber.

Chapter Fifteen

OUR BINDING REUNION

OVER THE NEXT FEW DAYS I HARDLY SAW WESTON. IT was just me and a big, empty house. At least the piano was there to keep me company. And an entire library's catalog of movies to watch. Then there was the homework, which I was struggling a bit to catch up on.

Weston wasn't kidding when he said he'd be working a lot. A few text messages passed throughout the day, but otherwise it was mostly silence. He would hug and kiss me goodbye in the morning, but had only been home in time for a late dinner one night. When he did come home, he encased my body with his, and I felt whole. By the time he left on Friday morning, I could see the exhaustion etched into his features, leaving with a promise to be home for dinner and the hopes for earlier than that.

I spent the morning before school playing with my new phone. Weston had gotten me an iPhone, which Julia then uploaded Weston's schedule into. Being the smart woman that she was, she knew it would make our lives easier if I knew when he had meetings and stuff.

She also uploaded mine, which didn't include much, but did remind me of my upcoming appointment with my new gynecologist. It was only two weeks away now, and I had made my decision. If in two weeks all was good, I would go forth with the plan.

I was still mad at Julia for putting me in Miles's class. Apparently she'd fought with him about it as well, because the next time I saw her she threw her hands up in defeat and simply said, "Yes, yes. I know."

With classes every other day, I'd only seen Miles one other time. We didn't speak much, though when we did, he sounded almost civil. I thought I saw a flicker of remorse in his eyes, but time would tell. I wasn't about to back down and beg for him to like me. He not only insulted me to my face, he upset Weston, putting strain on our already awkward and precarious relationship.

Charlotte was becoming a very good and loyal friend. She had kept her word. No one knew about my link to Miles, and therefore, my link to Weston. Our group knew a little, thinking they were my brothers just like Charlotte, but the rest of the school thought something totally different.

Apparently, a few in the rumor mill were saying Miles and I had a lovers' spat, insinuating that we were once together. Some even saying I transferred to this school to stalk him. The other, more popular and more believable theory in my eyes, was that Miles was my estranged father, and that I inherited his musical talent. That one was even possible, given our age difference.

Musical talent. Yes. Miles was not, in fact, a high school instructor. He was a composer, and a fairly well known one as well. Focused mostly on film scores.

Imagine that.

He apparently liked to help shape young talent, and when the prestigious Olympus Academy contacted him to teach one music composition course, he agreed. He was well loved by all his students, except me.

"Hey, Charlotte?"

"What's up?" she asked, our arms linked as we walked down the hall.

"What are you doing tomorrow morning?" I asked. I was a bit nervous. I wanted to tell her who Weston really was to me. I needed to confide in someone before I went insane. I'd checked his schedule, and he had a meeting from ten to noon, and was due home after that to spend the day with me.

She made a humming sound as she thought about it. "I'm free. Want to do something?"

"Want to come over?"

Just then someone slammed into my shoulder, knocking my backpack off and nearly sending me to the ground.

"Watch where you're going, jerk!" Charlotte yelled down the hall. The guy kept running, but at least he did call out that he was sorry. "You okay?"

"Yeah, I think so," I said, leaning over to pick up my bag and the few contents that had spilled out.

"Wren, what's that?"

"What's what?" I asked as I stood up straight.

She pulled me closer, placing her hand on my chest, and whispered in my ear. "The huge-ass diamond ring that's hanging around your neck."

I stepped back, wide eyed, and looked down to find that under Charlotte's hand hung my wedding ring. It must have fallen out when I bent over, escaping from its hiding place inside my shirt. Frantically, I stuffed it back in, cursing as I did so.

"So, wanting me to come over better have something to do with that," she said, raising an eyebrow.

"It does," I said. "Ten tomorrow? I'll text you the address."

"All right. Tomorrow." She gave me a hug before heading down to her car.

I'd planned to tell her the truth in the morning, so her seeing my wedding ring didn't change anything. I was ready for someone else to know, tired of lying to everyone. Our group didn't ask questions, because they, like me, favored privacy, all having their own celebrity background of sorts, as well as secrets.

When I got home, I threw my bag on the island counter along with my keys. Even though I might have been against Weston spending so much money on a car, I had to admit, I absolutely *loved* it. I could drive it around for hours and not tire of it.

In search of a snack, I moved to the fridge, opening it and gazing over the contents. Finding nothing, I closed the door and moved over to the fruit basket. I really needed to find a grocery store and stock up on some snacks to munch on. I chose a nice-looking apple and was about to head upstairs to change when I heard the garage door open.

"Baby girl, I'm home!" Weston called out.

I stopped in my tracks. "You're home?" I was in shock but held back my excitement in case he was headed back out for some reason.

"Yes, thank fucking God, yes," he said, smiling before throwing his keys next to mine.

He was wearing a steel gray suit that seemed to make his eyes pop, even more so with as wide as they were. It felt odd that he was looking at me with such a stunned expression. He stopped advancing, his hand frozen on his tie that he was in the process of loosening.

"Baby?" My brow furrowed at him while I wondered what made him stop.

"W-what the hell are you wearing?" Weston stuttered, his tongue peeking out and licking his lips.

"My school uniform?" I replied, though it came out more like a question.

He walked toward me, his eyes growing heavy as his body started moving like an animal stalking its prey. Deftly, his fingers pulled the knot in his tie free.

"You've been flaunting those luscious legs all week and I didn't know? Those boys in your school are probably fantasizing about having them wrapped around their waist as they thrust their teen-age cocks into you." His voice had the hairs on the back of my neck standing up in a strange cross between fear and excitement. "They're probably hoping you'll flash them your panties. Get an outline of your plump little pussy."

He stopped in front of me, appraising me from head to toe, his thumb running against his bottom lip. I was suddenly hyper aware of him.

"Do you tease them? Flip your skirt up and put on a show for all those little boys at the academy?"

I shook my head as I instinctually backed up. He reached down, his fingers trailing up the inside of my thigh and underneath my skirt. I was struck unable to respond or do anything other than feel my heart race and my pussy clench.

"Oh, I bet you do. Naughty girls do that, and you are becoming a very naughty girl. I think you need reminding who owns that pussy of yours, baby girl. A man owns it. I own it." He pressed his fingers against my clit, and my mouth popped open. "You're off your period, right?"

I bit my bottom lip and nodded, excitement running through me. "Oh, yeah."

"Take your vest off, and unbutton your shirt," he instructed as he shrugged out of his suit jacket.

Excited, I did as he told me, quickly shedding the vest while my fingers fumbled with the buttons. I looked up to find his gaze locked at my breasts, a growl coming from him. Leaning forward, his warm breath set my skin on fire.

"Put your ring on," he growled into my ear.

Unclasping the necklace, I freed my ring and slipped it on my finger.

"Mine," he practically moaned, staring at my hand. His eyes snapped up to mine, burning into me with crippling intensity. "Tell me."

"Yours."

"What's mine?" he asked, his hand resting on my collarbone and slowly trailing down to the valley between my breasts.

His voice was so low and seductive. I'd never heard anything like it, and my body responded by heating up at his touch.

"I am," I said in an almost whisper as his hand swept into my bra and against my sensitive nipple.

"What of you is mine?" he asked as his hand slid slowly down my body.

"Everything," I panted, his hand pressing into my abdomen over my skirt. Fuck, he was turning me on so much.

"I know that, but specifically, Wren. I'm trying to teach you a lesson here." His fingers moved up my inner thigh, under my skirt again, and trailed my slit. Slipping under the edge of my panties, his fingers lightly teased, moving down farther.

"M-my pussy is yours."

Two fingers suddenly plunged into me, his palm pushing against my clit, and he pulled me toward him by the part he owned, lips crashing to mine. His free hand fisted into my hair as his lips parted, tongue searching out mine. I moaned, loud and deep, clutching his shirt as his hand that had ahold of my pussy was gyrating in a wave-like motion, pushing his fingers in and out while his palm showed my clit no mercy.

His lips released mine and he was breathing so hard, he was panting into my ear.

"It's been almost a week, and this isn't going to be gentle. I need you too fucking much. This is going to be hard and rough, and you will fucking love the pleasure I give you."

"Oh, God," I whimpered.

"I'm going to wreck you, baby girl," he whispered harshly into my ear.

My knees went weak at his words, and I had to grab hold of the table ledge to keep from falling.

He stepped back, removing his hand and bringing it to his lips. I whimpered at the loss, but watched as his tongue darted out to lap up my juices. I never knew how erotic an image like that could be, and Weston's lust filled eyes locked on mine made it even more so.

He pulled his tie from around his neck and motioned to the table. "Bend over."

Following his orders, I bent over until my face was level with his crotch, wetting my lips in anticipation.

"Fuck," he snarled, one hand pulling my head toward him while his hips pushed forward, rubbing his cloth covered, hard length up and down my face.

Stepping toward me, he forced me to stand as he advanced, until I was pressed into the kitchen table.

He cupped my cheek, lips teasing mine. "See how worked up you have me? I meant bend over the table, but you had me so distracted. You were such a good girl and did as I said. So, once more, bend over the table, baby girl."

I bit my bottom lip to keep my amusement in. It was wonderful to know I had that kind of power over him.

He grabbed my wrists and pulled them to the table edge, his free hand wrapping the tie around them.

"W-what are you doing?" I asked with wide eyes, my voice wavering as a bit of panic settled in.

"Tying you up so you can't run away," he said, his hand releasing my wrists and moving down beneath the ledge. When he was done securing my hands to the leg, he reached out and caressed my cheek. "Do you trust me?"

I nodded and watched as he stood and walked back around behind me. I pulled at the tie, but it wouldn't budge. I was trapped with my torso spread over the wooden top, while my ass stood out at the other edge.

"R-run away from what?" I stuttered. There was a sudden breeze when he lifted my skirt up over my ass, exposing my wet panties to him.

"Your punishment."

Grabbing hold of the thin cotton, he slid the fabric down my legs. I felt my cheeks flush, realizing I was now very much exposed and tied to a table. People were always coming in and out of the house. What if someone came in right then?

The thought of someone seeing us, watching as he ravaged me, surprisingly turned me on. I had no idea what punishment awaited me, but I was excited and nervous to find out. My gaze flickered from Weston and then to the door and back again.

"Don't worry. No one is coming today. I told them I needed time with my wife," he said as he ran his hand over my right cheek.

Then I felt it; the harsh sting of his palm against the flesh of my backside. I cried out, tears burning my eyes. His hand rubbed soothingly over the area while my mind spun, trying to figure out the last time I'd been spanked and wondering how it was supposed to be erotic or pleasurable. He repeated it on the other side. A tear fell, not from pain so much as surprise, though it did sting.

His hand came down again, this time slapping hard against my pussy, the tip of his middle finger tapping my clit. The sharp sting on my nub made me gasp and I moaned, my body arching.

Oh, so that was how.

"You like that, baby girl?" I looked back at him, at the devilish grin on his face, and shook my hips, asking for him to do it again. His finger slid down the crack of my ass, dipping slightly into my slit, but stopping just short of my clit. "I asked you a question, and you will answer me."

He had me panting with that one sentence. So much domination in his tone, and I realized I was falling in love with his game.

"Yes," I hissed and was rewarded with another slap to my pussy, another tap to my clit.

He repeated the pattern—one hit to each cheek, two smacks to my pussy. The strikes to my swollen lips were doing me in, making my whole body scorching hot.

He groaned, his hands grabbing hard onto my butt cheeks, fingers digging in. It was painful, but also a turn on knowing he wanted me so much.

His hot breath moved down to my aching center, his tongue flicking my clit before taking a long lick all the way back up. My pussy quivered, and my hips began moving, trying to ride his face. All movement was stopped by the hard grip he had on my ass. I only received what he gave and no more, whimpering as his mouth attacked. I was on the edge, at his mercy, only for him to back off when my body began to tighten.

Standing, he pushed his hips against my ass, and I could swear I heard him growl. Leaning down, he nipped at my neck, his hands reaching under and pulling the cups on my bra down before his fingers began pinching my rapidly hardening nipples.

"I'm going to fuck you so hard, baby girl," he whispered before pushing his body off and away.

I whimpered from the loss of contact. I had been so close to coming, and he stopped. Torturing me with the promise of pleasure and then denying me.

The excitement in me rose as I heard the jingle of his belt buckle, then the sound of his zipper as it moved down. There was a little shuffle of clothing before I felt it—the head of his cock pressed against my entrance.

But he didn't fully enter. Instead, he pushed in slightly and pulled out. Then slid down my lips to my clit and back up before pushing in, only to pull back out.

"Please!" I begged, his teasing driving me insane.

His cock smacked against my ass before repeating the torturous action. In, just the tip, and out.

"What do you want, Wren? Tell me what you want." His voice was raw, hungry, and it made me whimper.

"Fuck me, please. Fuck my pussy."

"I thought we talked about this. I thought you understood. It's not your pussy."

He was going to have me coming in no time at that rate, and he still hadn't even entered me fully.

"Please, fuck your pussy."

He pushed forward in one jarring motion, making my thighs slam into the table ledge. A scream tore through me as a white light covered my vision for a split second before clearing.

And again.

There was no pause, just the unrelenting pounding. His cock thrusting hard and fast. I couldn't form words, only sounds, as he abused my pussy in the most delicious way. Thought left my mind, fading in and out, along with the blinding white light that flashed in my eyes every time he bottomed out. My hands clenched around the edge of the table as he mercilessly slammed into me, hands gripping my hips tight.

It was by no means gentle, he was right, but I couldn't deny how fantastically painful and pleasurable it was at the same time. He had me so worked up from all his teasing that him filling me repeatedly had me teetering on the edge, and I lost it.

Sobs erupted from my chest, pussy clenching him tight, my body tense as I pulsed around him. I thought I was going to pass out from the intensity. His movements didn't falter, they became harder. Not even giving me the chance to come down before building me back up.

Bending over me, his hand slammed down on the table next to me. He panted above me, cursing.

"Fuck, baby girl. That's it, milk me. Tighten around me like a naughty girl and make me come."

It was a good thing the table was holding me up as my legs had given out long ago. His cock was relentlessly pounding into my pussy, and I cried out in a soundless scream as I came again with nearly the same overwhelming force as the first.

"We-Weston . . . I . . . I . . . can't . . ." I trailed off, unable to speak, but trying to tell him I couldn't take anymore. My body was exhausted, and he was spurring me quickly on to another orgasm.

"You can and you will take everything I give," he growled, standing back up and grabbing my hips to pull me toward him as his hips pushed forward. This caused the restraints on my wrists to tighten even more.

There was no silent scream when he forced a third orgasm from me, the walls ringing out with my cries. My head collapsed down on the table, eyes in slits, panting and moaning.

There was a change in him. He began grunting louder and it felt like he had grown bigger inside me, his movements no longer as fluid, and then he was gone.

Hot liquid droplets landed all over my skin, first on my lower back, then on the cheeks of my ass as he grunted and groaned. The last spurts coated the outside of my pussy while he chanted "mine" behind me.

I shuddered, never understanding before how it was hot to have a guy come on you. Before it just sounded gross, but living it, having him mark me with his come, was unbelievably erotic.

He stood behind me, hips pressed together, cock nestled between my ass cheeks, while his breathing settled.

After a few minutes, he stepped away and I heard the water running, then the clicking of his shoes on the tile floor before a warm cloth moved around my skin. There was a tug on my wrists as he freed them, but my hands continued to dangle off the edge. Weston gently took hold of my hands and softly rubbed then kissed each of my unbound wrists.

I was spent, a pile of goo, unable to move. He had accomplished what he set out to do; wreck me. No man would ever compare to him, no man would ever be able to satisfy me like him. I was young, naïve, and had no idea what I liked sexually before I met him. Since then, every fantasy that I never knew lurked deep inside of me had been replaced with a reality that was better than anything my imagination could have ever created.

Strong arms lifted me from the table and carried me through the house to the family room that was nice and dark. He sat on a sofa chair, propping his legs up on an ottoman, while he cradled me in his arms and turned on the stereo. Soft music filtered through the room as his hands gently swept my hair from my face, eyes meeting his.

"Are you okay?" he asked, his tone and eyes full of concern. I merely nodded, my head leaning onto his shoulder. "I'm sorry. That was really . . ." He let out a hard breath, then chuckled. "So, you've probably guessed that I can be . . . quite dominating, when the mood strikes."

"I'll say," I managed to squeak out, my voice rough.

"Not being with you in almost a week and seeing you in this outfit made me snap," he said with a sigh, his hand trailing up my thigh as he spoke. "I hope I didn't hurt you. The last thing I want to do is scare you away right now. I shouldn't have let go like that yet."

"I liked it," I said, my hand managing to rise to cup his face, while my eyes fought the heaviness of my lids. "I like the soft love-making too. We haven't done anything that I haven't liked. It's all new to me, and to be honest, a little scary at times, but, wow. How you were today? I never thought I would end up a limp noodle, or that a man could make me come that many times in a row. I also never knew I would like being restrained, but you showed me how fantastic it can be to let someone I trust take me and have their way with my body."

"Not someone, baby girl. Me, your husband," he practically growled, sending a shiver through me.

"Just using it as description, baby," I said, soothing him, my eyes fluttering closed. "Now I need to nap. You wore me and your pussy out."

He smirked and looked at me sheepishly. "And I'd do it again."

"You better."

"I will, but Wren, you know that I adore you, right?" he asked, and I heard the trepidation in his voice as his fingers gently caressed my skin. "And that I would never intentionally hurt you, sexually or otherwise."

I looked up at him and smiled. "Yes, Weston, I do know that. And believe me, I would tell you if it was too much. Don't worry. I'm fine."

"Good." He breathed a sigh of what I thought was relief.

He then leaned down and kissed me, lips soft, as his fingers caressed my skin. Pulling a blanket over us, I quickly fell asleep snuggled in the warmth of my kinky husband's arms.

I AWOKE THE NEXT MORNING TO SOFT CARESSES AS WESTON'S fingers gently traced up and down my spine. The previous night came flooding back when I tried to scoot closer and received a small twinge in my abdomen.

Jesus, his large cock could pound hard and deep, but it seemed that sometimes there was a flip side the next morning.

"How do you feel, baby girl?" his low, sleepy voice asked.

My head tilted up, and I stared into his lapis blue eyes as his fingers ghosted over my cheek.

"No worse for wear," I reassured him.

After Weston's dominant display, I'd fallen asleep in his arms as he placed soft loving kisses and touches all over me. I awoke a few hours later, still in his arms; he hadn't moved.

He'd been nothing but gentle with me last night after our tryst on the kitchen table, a trait that continued into the morning. I think he was trying to make up for going overboard like he did. Assuaging his fears and insecurities helped, and calmed his obsessive need to make certain that I was all right. I meant it when I told him I liked it, but he was still worried that he'd pushed it too far.

Admitting to him that I liked it and was looking forward to the next time was a little bit odd, and I found myself blushing, something he liked quite a bit. One night when we were in bed, he did say he had the desire to tie me to the bed and flog me. It didn't sound appealing to me, but as I told him, I was up for trying new things. Although, I did tell him I would like to know more about it, and he said he'd be more than happy to educate me beforehand, when and if the time came. Though, I was pretty sure it was more when than if.

But that morning, lying in his arms, was nothing but sweet, tender touches and kisses. He'd gotten the overruling lust out of his system the night before, and the only thing that remained was the absolute adoration I knew he had for me.

"Good," he said with a sigh of relief, his lips pressing against the top of my head.

"So, are you . . . into that, umm, a-all the time?"

A low chuckle rumbled in his chest. "No need to worry, baby girl. I'm not into that lifestyle, but I am a kinky bastard sometimes. If it bothers you . . ."

"Oh, no. Trust me, I liked it. I was just a bit . . . overwhelmed with it all."

"I have to admit that last night was a fantasy that came true."

"Really?" I gazed up at him.

"Really," he said, assuring me with a smile and a stroke of my cheek.

Eventually, unfortunately, we both crawled out of bed. Weston headed toward the shower, dragging me in with him. It was mostly down to business, but then there were times he would wrap his arms around me, fingers trailing down my wet skin as he told me how delectable I looked between kisses to my shoulder and neck.

After we were out, I quickly brushed my teeth and headed down for some breakfast, leaving Weston to get ready for his meeting. I didn't realize quite how stiff and sore I was until I started moving, especially down the stairs. Weston had said he wanted me to remember he'd been inside me every time I moved, and it was one of those days his mission was accomplished.

It was strange living in a house with people coming and going at almost all hours of the day. The doors didn't have the conventional key, more like an office with pads you swiped a card across before the locks turned. Doors locked and unlocked on their own, no need to remember after you'd let someone in. The only doors that weren't like that were the ones that lead to the pool because the grounds gate had the same security pad.

Julia was already in the kitchen, typing away, which seemed odd for a Saturday, but not so much when I remembered they were leaving soon. She'd brought with her some muffins, holding them out to me as a sign of peace.

"Forgive me?"

"Julia, why?" I asked with a bit of a whine in my tone.

"It's a really great school, perfect for you. I swear that picking it had nothing to do with him."

"But why *his* class? What if I didn't play any instruments?"

"I heard you," she confessed quietly.

I pulled out a chair and sat next to her. "What?"

"I heard you playing. You're very talented, Wren. It was so beautiful, and I took it as an opportunity to maybe bring the two of you together as well."

"Oh, it brought us together all right, and he's lucky he didn't get my fist in his face," I said, the memory making me fume.

"He's very impressed by you," she said. I snorted. "It's true. You really blew him away. He admitted he was being a prick, putting you on the spot like that. He was hoping to defraud you, but boy was he the one that ended up with tomato on his face." She chuckled, smiling brightly.

"Good," I said childishly, my eyes hard. "Maybe it will teach him not to judge people he's just met."

"I think he understands that now, but he's a very proud man, just like his father, and I'm afraid it will probably be a while before he apologizes. He's still not keen on the idea of Weston marrying a stranger, but what I think rocks him the most is that he can see what the rest of us do. The way you both light up when you look at each other," she said in all seriousness.

"Too bad he had to be a shit about it. I don't think Weston has talked to him since, and I can tell he misses him," I said with a sigh as I broke a chunk off of my muffin.

"He's doing it to protect you. The last thing Weston wants is for you to be upset. Especially right now with all the changes you've endured, and if that means staying away from his brother, he'll do it. You and Miles are both so stuck in this image you've built up of each other. I hope one day you'll be able to get past it."

My heart swelled with the sadness of Weston's sacrifice for me, but it wasn't enough to hold out an olive branch to Miles. At least, not yet.

I popped another bite of muffin into my mouth. "Well, I think it will be a long road for us."

Julia's gaze was curious as she looked down, and my eyes attempted to follow but were blocked by the edge of table.

"By the way, why is Weston's tie wrapped around the table leg?" she asked with a quirked brow, her fingers bringing the other end up on the tabletop. My eyes widened in horror, not knowing how to respond. When she looked back to me, recognition dawned. "Oh, I see. Well . . . as long as you had fun, but if you didn't . . ." My face turned beet red, and her lip twitched up into a smirk. "Do I need to have the table disinfected?"

"Julia!" I cried out, groaning as my head dropped to the wooded top.

Her laughter filled the room, and I couldn't help but join in, happy we were back on good terms. Even though I still didn't like Miles.

Weston came down a few minutes later, and I could see in his face how happy he was that Julia and I had made up. His smile was so bright I almost didn't recognize him. That's when something Sophie said came back to me, saying that she and his ex didn't get along, and I wondered if that extended to the rest of his camp. Everyone was so welcoming to me, with the exception of dickhead Miles, that I wondered if the same wasn't true for her. Had they all tried to include her and she shut them out? Sophie didn't paint a very good image of her. Maybe at dinner I could ask about her, and maybe then I would get some answers to my burning questions.

Weston gave me a long, hard, sensual kiss before he left, promising to be back early in the afternoon, and even talked about going out together. He was apprehensive as he left, but wished me luck. I almost didn't want him to go because I knew as soon as he left, Charlotte would be arriving.

Nervousness coursed through me, my heart beating against my ribs, and I found myself biting my nails while I waited for her to arrive. Not ten minutes after he left, her Mercedes pulled up into the drive. I hit the button to open the gate to let her in, and began questioning my decision.

Weston was reluctant at best when I told him I wanted to confide in Charlotte, especially since I hadn't even had an opportunity to tell him about her. I just wanted someone, outside of his circle, in the same state, to know what I was going through. Tit for tat, I told him who her father was because I could see how agitated and nervous it was making him. That calmed him greatly because he knew her, or rather, he knew her father and sister, and he had met her on more than one occasion.

I twirled my ring on my finger as I waited by the door, flinging it open as soon as she reached it.

"Hi," she said, slightly startled.

I attempted to smile at her. "Hi."

"Is it that bad?"

I gave her a nervous laugh. "You have no idea."

I ushered her in, and she looked around in awe. "Wow, nice place. I knew you had money, but this may be bigger than my house."

"I swear I need a map to navigate around."

She let out a little laugh, and I gave her a roundabout tour, ending up at my favorite spot—the patio. Well, if you could even call it that. It was equipped with a fireplace, TV, as well as lounge chairs and couches. But I loved that it was outside. L.A. had such amazing weather.

"So," she began, looking at me expectantly.

"It's a little bit difficult. I trust you, I do, but this is huge, and I need your reassurance that you will not tell a soul."

"I promise, Wren. You're my friend, and you know my situation. I would never tell anyone because I know what it's like to live this kind of life being related to someone famous." She looked at me, waiting, but I didn't move. "But I have a feeling it's more than being related, isn't it?"

I took a deep breath and did exactly what Weston did to Sophie; I reluctantly raised my left hand and showed her my ring's true home.

"Wow, just . . . wow. I mean, I suspected things weren't what you led me to believe. But this!" She shook her head. "You're really married to a Lockwood?"

"Yes."

"Holy shit!" She jumped up and started walking around. "I mean, all the Lockwoods are hot. It's like you have to be for that family."

"Yeah. Funny part is, I didn't even recognize who he was when we met, when we . . . got married in Vegas . . . two weeks ago."

Charlotte stared at me with wide eyes, her mouth hanging open as she sat back down. Her eyes scanned the house, and I could see the wheels turning. "You didn't just marry any old Lockwood, did you?"

"Weston thought it was hilarious. He teases me constantly about it."

"You married Weston-fucking-Lockwood?" she asked in disbelief, standing again from her seat. "Weston Lockwood, one of the most eligible bachelors in L.A.? Weston Lockwood, *People* magazine's Sexiest Man Alive?"

I nodded. "Wow, I didn't know that one. He definitely earned that label."

"*You* are Mrs. Weston Lockwood?"

I nodded again.

Charlotte flopped back down in her chair, staring at me in disbelief. "Lucky bitch!" She laughed, and she sat back. Then her eyes suddenly shot wide and she leaned toward me, her face turning serious. "The press doesn't know?"

I shook my head. "We're keeping it private until I graduate."

"Wren, that's almost eight months away! How is it going to stay hidden? You live in his house, you have his name. Are you just going to stay a dirty little secret until then? Locked up in the tower? Never to go on a date with your *husband*." Charlotte's brow was scrunched up, worry written all over her face.

She genuinely seemed worried about me, which warmed me more than I expected. For the first time in weeks, I didn't feel quite so much like a fish out of water.

"It's better this way for now." My voice was low, betraying how I really felt. I wanted to go out with him, as his wife and not his sister. But I understood and could wait, for a while.

She nodded. "Oh, I agree. As soon as the press finds out, you'll have paps lining the block to get a glimpse of you. Especially with how you married!"

I groaned at that. Being a spectacle, a person on display, was not what I wanted in life, but by being married to Weston, I was becoming increasingly aware it was bound to happen.

"Look, Wren, I get how new and strange all of this is to you, and I want you to know that I'm here for you. I'm not a fame seeker, which is obvious by the path I chose with the family I'm from."

I nodded. "I know you aren't, Charlotte. That's why I trust you, and I need someone to confide in, someone I can trust, and someone who understands what's really going on in my life."

Charlotte smiled, then blew out a big breath. "Interesting situation you've gotten yourself into, though. I'm actually surprised your parents went along with it."

I groaned again.

"Your parents didn't go along with it?"

"It's not that, because my mom was for it," I said, and ran my hands through my hair.

"But?"

"My dad doesn't know yet. And in my defense, he lives three hours away from my mom, and it's not like we talk all the time."

"My advice is that you tell him before he finds out from the press. No father wants to find out their daughter married a Hollywood big-wig from the nightly news."

I agreed, and we both sat back, lost in thought.

"So . . . this turned out to be a much more interesting day than I thought it would be," Charlotte said and looked over to me, trying to appear serious. I could see the tenderness in her eyes, though, and the gleam of amusement.

We both broke out into laughter, my hand grabbing a pillow and chucking it at her.

"Yeah, well, then you can imagine what it's been like for me!"

Charlotte turned to me, her expression more serious. "Don't worry, Wren Lockwood, I've got your back. And now I get why you and Mr. Lock—" She shook her head. "Miles . . . don't seem to get along. He doesn't like your situation, and possibly you, right?"

I let out a sigh before going into the details of my estrangement with Miles. She agreed with me that he was an ass, but was quite surprised that he'd been so vulgar in his comments about me, though in the end she agreed with Julia that maybe something good would come out of it.

A few hours later, there was a buzzing at the gate and someone unknown to me let them through. I'd have to ask Weston about it later, because I thought I was the only one home, but if I didn't let them up, who did?

It was only the UPS guy, and he had a total of six boxes for me. That was all it took for my mom to pack up my life. I was pretty sure I already had three boxes worth of clothes in the two weeks I'd been in L.A.

Charlotte said goodbye, wishing me luck in unpacking after helping me haul the boxes up to my bedroom. She gave me a hug and told me to call her if I needed anything. It felt good to confide in someone, and I felt like a weight had been lifted from my shoulders.

"When is Karen sending the rest of your stuff?" Weston asked an hour later, after arriving back home.

I was in the bedroom, going through my clothes and deciding where to put them, when I heard his footsteps in the hall.

"This is all of my stuff," I said quietly. "All but the furniture."

"You're joking, right?" he asked as he stripped off his suit. It was one of those kind of meetings.

"No. I'm a simple girl, remember?"

"Wow. I'm sorry. I'm just shocked you didn't have more to unpack."

I couldn't help but lick my lips as I watched him undress, the way his muscles flexed and stretched when he pulled each piece of clothing from his gorgeous, taut body. My tongue swept across my lips, an action that did not go unnoticed.

It was his turn to ogle me, his eyes sweeping up and down my body, and a familiar tingle crept in. Standing before me in nothing but his tight boxer briefs, he cocked a brow at me, his lips moving up into the sexy smile I'd become accustomed to.

"See something you like, Mrs. Lockwood?" he asked as he sauntered toward me.

Yes, the man had swagger, and I couldn't keep my eyes off the prize that was the last bit of him hidden from my view. He pulled me into his arms, and pressed his lips to mine.

"Mmm, yes, I think I do," I said as he released me.

"How are you feeling?" He reached down to adjust himself, which didn't do much good because he was only wearing the sexiest pair of underwear I'd ever seen. "I know I was a bit ruthless with you last night."

"Nothing I can't handle." I smiled up at him before turning back to the box I was going through.

Ah, Old Navy shirts and jeans, how I've missed you! I thought, a smile forming as I hugged the garments, earning a chuckle from Weston.

Moving to the closet, I hid them away in a drawer in hopes that Sophie didn't show up one day, see them, and make them disappear. Weston smiled at me as I exited.

"Wren." I heard Weston make a coughing sound as I reentered the room. "Is that a vibe?" There was a playful twinkle in his eye.

I froze before diving forward to grab it before him, but he pulled it from my reach. Mom had bought the silver bullet for me for my seventeenth birthday, saying I was a woman and all women needed a good vibrator.

Weston smirked at me, hitting the buttons of the remote, and an evil glint overtook the playful twinkle in his eye.

He stepped toward me, and I stepped back like a frightened rabbit. My favorite part of our games: anticipation and domination.

I ran around the room, but I was tackled to the bed in just a few strides. After a bit of a struggle, I ended up lying across his lap and fighting to get away.

"Don't make me get out the handcuffs," he threatened, as his hands worked to pull my pants down.

I fought, laughing as I did so, but lost when his strong hands wrapped around my wrists, pulling them above my head. The action brought my nipples to life, and they strained against the thin cotton of my tank top.

The movement of my hips trying to shake him off me only seemed to make it easier for him to get my pants over my ass and hips, but maybe that was what I wanted. As soon as the fabric was just past my pussy, his hand moved swiftly, setting the vibe against my clit and turning the power on.

I nearly shot out of his grip, my back arching, screaming pants of "Oh, God" falling from my lips. The heels of my feet dug into the bed, pushing off, but it only pressed the vibe harder against my clit.

It was torture—sweet, delicious, harsh torture. My moans and cries were proof of it.

His hand moved so that his palm was pressing the bullet against my clit, and his fingers teased my entrance before sliding in.

The suddenness, the unexpectedness, coupled with everything else he was doing, had me rocketing toward the edge.

It was too much, painful almost, as my orgasm built up. He was unrelenting, turning the power to high while his fingers were thrusting in and out as fast as they could. Determined to make me come, and quickly.

"W-Weston," I whimpered as my eyes rolled back, my muscles tightening.

"Come for me, baby girl." He was panting into my ear, his hips rocking against me. "I want you to come. You're so close to soaking my fingers."

He dug in harder, fingers moving faster, his head bending down to my breast. Using his nose and teeth, he moved my tank top over before licking, then biting down on my nipple.

The combination was overwhelming and my body tensed until it snapped, sending me screaming as I fell. Each pulsing wave of pleasure rocking me.

I still felt the bullet pressed against me as I came down, creating an almost painful sensation, but before I could protest Weston dumped me onto the bed face down. He climbed on top of me, straddled my legs and lifted my hips slightly, then slid all the way in.

I almost came again, his cock filling me entirely.

"Yes, baby girl, you're so fucking wet. Makes it so easy for me to slide right in," he said, his voice low and rough.

He found purchase on my ass, grabbing it, pushing and pulling as he thrust hard.

I was quickly climbing higher and higher, my whimpers muted by the pillow.

"Feels so good. Making me come so fast. Damn, baby girl," he moaned, his pace increasing.

I loved the sounds leading up to him coming, and even more so when he did. The arousal they created moved straight down between my thighs and pushed me over the edge again, tightening around him.

"Oh, fuck!" he cried out, thrusting a few more times before pulling out.

With each jerky thrust of his hips, I felt the heat pumping out of him and landing onto my gaping pussy lips as well as my tight puckered ass. He groaned at the sight of marking me, and I wished I could see it too. Calming down, he pushed the head of his cock against my pussy, before dragging his warm come to my tight hole and pushing in lightly.

"One day I'll take you here," he promised before sliding his length up and down the crack of my ass, spreading his seed around.

The thought of anal was more than a bit unnerving, and honestly, sounded down right painful. But I knew whenever we did decide to go that route, Weston would be gentle and caring as always. He would never do something that I asked him not to.

He collapsed onto the bed next to me a moment later and began laughing.

"What?" I asked.

"Nothing," he said, shaking his head. "Just, I think I may have beaten a record or something."

"Why do you say that?"

He pointed to the clock. "We both came in less than five minutes."

"A true quickie."

His arms wrapped around me, head dipping down to the crook of my neck, as his body relaxed around me.

"We should get cleaned up."

He nodded before burying his head further into my neck. "In a minute," he said with a deep sigh.

A minute later he was dead weight, half on top of me, his breath lightly tickling the hairs on my neck. Realizing we weren't going anywhere, I closed my eyes and joined him in a nice afternoon nap. He needed it with the schedule he'd been working, and after all, there were no meetings scheduled on Sunday. It would be just me and my Mr. Lockwood.

Chapter Seventeen

OUR CHEESY QUOTES

WAS HAPPY THAT WESTON HAD TAKEN ALL OF SUNDAY OFF. I looked forward to spending some much needed time with him. It was still early when we woke, Weston getting his first full night of sleep in a week, and neither of us wanted to move from our cuddlefest. My head was resting on his chest, rising and falling with each breath he took. His fingers trailed up and down my back, the sensation so soothing I almost drifted back to sleep.

In that moment between wakefulness and sleep, I remembered the gate and how I hadn't had a chance to ask him about it the previous evening.

"Weston?" I waited for him to look my way.

"Hmm?"

"I meant to ask you . . . When UPS came by with my boxes, I didn't let them in, so who did?"

He shook his head, unfazed. "Joe did."

"Joe?"

"I haven't been able to introduce you to him yet. Joe is head of security. He supervises the house, oversees security at the company, and is my personal bodyguard when I attend major events. He works down at my office."

"Wow, that's a lot. But how does he supervise the house?" I asked, still confused.

"All security access points run through his phone and

computer. So, if there's a delivery and someone presses the button he can see who it is and let them in."

"That's a lot of power for one phone."

"Joe's got a whole security team to help with the company, but my security is his job," he said. I stared at him, stunned. Another reminder of the man I married and how different our lives were. "Don't think too much on it, Wren. You'll get used to it in time. That's just how my life is, and has been for a very long time."

"Well, your life is so over the top, I'm not sure I'll ever get used to it."

He broke out into laughter then. "Just keep not recognizing stars and you'll be fine."

There was a good chance his teasing would never end. In my defense, it had been a few years since I'd seen *The Last Hero*, and he spent half of it covered in blood.

Nagging thoughts of not only having a security team, but one that was constantly watching out for him worried me. "Is it really that dangerous for you?"

"No, no, baby girl." He ran his hand up and down my arm. "Don't worry. It's just, with my career, I guess I've become a bit paranoid with my space. I don't really like invaders."

"I invaded."

"Yes, you did." He narrowed his gaze on me, before shrugging and grunting. "Eh, you're beautiful, I'll let you stay."

"Charmer."

He tilted my chin up. "You know, you should swing by the office sometime this week."

"Really?" I questioned, becoming excited to see where he worked when not at home.

He nodded. "You're on the list, so just pick a day and come by. I think Graham already put my office in your GPS."

The phone went off, breaking us out of our nice bubble.

Reaching over, he grabbed his phone and swiped it before bringing it up to his ear. "Hey, Carson, what's up?" His smile faded, and he closed his eyes as his head tilted back. "Yeah. No, I get it . . . Right . . . See you soon."

He dropped his arm to the bed and he blew out a breath. "One day off is too much, I guess." He looked down at me, sadness etched into his features. "Sorry, baby girl."

Well, there went our day alone.

We pried ourselves out of bed and got ready for the day and Carson's arrival. Apparently, there was trouble with one of the many projects Weston currently had a hand in, and he and Carson needed to have an emergency meeting.

I decided to busy myself making cookies, since I learned Weston's penchant for them the week before. Luckily, I found all the ingredients I'd need stockpiled in the pantry. Kelly must have made cookies weekly, because there was enough bags of chocolate chips for at least a hundred batches of cookies and brownies.

As I worked, I thought back to my text conversation with Daniel, when I told him I was going to confide in Charlotte. He sounded down, and I knew it was a combination of me not being near and the fact that I made a new friend, one I was going to trust with our secret. We'd also worked out trying to map a time for him to visit. Weston even offered to pay for the ticket. I think he was trying to make up for his behavior the night he found out about my best friend—and his gender.

Weston decided to take a run before Carson arrived, to work off some of the frustration that was building at whatever new catastrophe had occurred. I spent that time measuring out all of the ingredients, and munching on a few of the chocolate chips. I had Pandora piping through the speakers, loving the music system I'd discovered was throughout the whole house.

My brow furrowed when I heard the garage door in the small silence between songs.

"Hey, sweet cheeks, what you got cooking?" Carson asked, coming up behind me and taking a chocolate chip from the measuring cup.

"Hey!" I cried out in indignation, smacking his hand away.

"It's only one," he said with a sly smirk.

I rolled my eyes and went back to the recipe, measuring out the salt.

"Step away from the cookies," Weston ordered from the door, his face dripping with sweat, and I smiled, but my expression quickly turned into a frown.

"Oh, so the girl's fair game? Alrighty. You know, Sophie and I have talked about a threesome," Carson said with a wag of his eyebrows.

"Ugh, leave her alone, and step away from the whole cookie making process, which includes my baby girl."

"But everything over here is just so sweet," Carson said as his hand moved to my hip, over my shorts, and down my thigh.

If I could see his face, I was certain there would be a challenging smirk for Weston. That thought didn't keep the blush from spreading on my cheeks, or the growl from Weston's chest.

"That's *my* sweet. Don't go dirtying it with your crude thoughts."

Carson let out a loud laugh. "Don't even go there, man. I know you."

"Shut your mouth. That's my wife," Weston growled as he stepped closer to Carson.

"I know." Carson moved as well. "So why the fuck are you standing here arguing with me about cookies?"

I snickered, knowing that Carson was just baiting him, and it was working. They were face to face, eye to eye, Carson smirking, both waiting for the other to crack. It took me a moment to realize what was going on.

They were having a staring contest.

Really? They were in their thirties!

Then again, being in your thirties didn't mean you couldn't have childish fun.

Carson must have broken it, because in a flash Weston had his head in a bind and was messing his hair.

"All right, you won that one, but I'm getting a damn cookie when they're done."

"Nope, they're all mine. You know that."

"Fucking cookie obsessed bastard. You're gonna get fat, and no one will want to cast you anymore."

He shrugged his shoulders and smiled. "I don't act anymore, so it doesn't matter."

"You may not act, but that doesn't mean you don't get offers. I know. Besides, you need to stay trim and fit so that sweet little thing doesn't up and leave your fat ass."

Weston walked over to me and wrapped his arms around my waist. I ignored him and continued on with my baking.

"Baby girl, you wouldn't leave me if I gained a few cookie pounds, would you?"

"Nope. Your sexy ass is stuck with me," I replied and turned for a kiss.

My gaze moved up just in time to see Weston's tongue peek out in Carson's direction. I could just hear the nana-nana-boo-boo.

Carson clapped his hands together. "All right, time to get down to business."

"Fuck, why business? It's Sunday, and I took the whole day off for my girl," Weston said with a pout.

"Don't worry, pussy. You'll be able to hit that in about an hour."

"Why didn't you bring my baby?" Weston asked. His gaze moved about the room, looking for signs of his princess.

Carson rolled his eyes. "*My* baby is spending a girls' day out with her mommy. Like I said, make your own."

"Get the fuck out of here, then," Weston said as he popped a few of the chocolate morsels, earning a smack with my spoon.

"Not until we talk. There's an issue."

Weston groaned. "An issue? Don't tell me that diva has already fucking started in."

"Okay, I won't. So, I'll just tell you that production is almost to the point of halted."

"Fuck!" All humor left him, his hand running through his

hair in agitation. "Okay, let me grab a quick shower and meet me in my office in ten."

The boys left me to my cookie making, and I let the music take back over. I hated that someone had soured Weston's mood on his only day off this week. I'd hoped we'd have the weekend to spend some real quality time together. Some t

ime to get to know one another a little more, since I'd barely seen him the week before. We'd been married for two weeks, and while I was getting to know him more physically, we still knew very little about one another on a personal level.

After adding all of the ingredients, I mixed everything up, stealing a few bites of dough from the sticky concoction. It was so good I had to stop myself from eating it all. I pulled out two cookie sheets, which took me a little while to find, and a smaller spoon than the large plastic one in my hand.

I had just placed a few dollops onto the tray when I heard the garage door again over the music. It was odd for Carson to leave and not say goodbye, so I didn't think anything of it until large arms wrapped around my body and pulled me back.

"Gotcha!" a man's voice said.

I emitted a scream so loud and high-pitched I had trouble believing it came from me. I thrashed in his arms, my vocal protests unrelenting, so panicked I couldn't catch my breath.

The sound of heavy footsteps pounded toward the kitchen, and relief washed through me.

Weston's face filled my vision, and I watched it morph from terror to anger in a fraction of a second.

"Goddamn it, Lance! Put her down!" Weston yelled, and the arms complied, dropping me down on my now shaky legs.

I gulped in a deep ragged breath as Weston rushed to me, wrapping me in his arms, and checking me over with worried eyes to make certain I was okay. "You all right?"

"Yeah, as soon as my heart rate is back to normal," I said between breaths, and turned to look at my assailant.

Light hair and green eyes, along with a cheesy grin. He was a little bit taller than Weston and definitely more cut. Whoever he was, he was fit. He reminded me of some of the posters Daniel had hanging on his walls.

He quirked a brow at me and turned to Weston. "Since when did you get rid of Kelly?"

It was Carson attempting *not* to laugh that caught my attention near the doorway. He had an interesting reaction to the situation.

"Tell her you're sorry," Weston said as he pulled me away from him.

"I'm sorry," he said sincerely with a bit of a pout.

"It's all right, just don't do that to people you don't know," I said, letting him off the hook because he really looked like such a softie and I had a strange urge to hug him.

He looked down to the floor, thoroughly chastised.

"Lance Evans," he said, holding out his hand.

Tentatively, I placed my hand in his. "Wren Lockwood."

"Damn, Weston, I didn't know you had such a fine little sister," he said, grinning down at me and winking.

Carson snickered, and Weston looked like he was about to explode.

"Lockwood is my married name," I said, thinking that if he knew Weston, he would get it.

"Married? Wait, when did Miles leave Julia? I'll kick his ass!"

Carson was gasping for breath, his laughter filling the room, while he leaned on the center island for support.

"Not Miles. She's *my* wife," Weston growled, his jaw tense.

"Shut up. Is it April Fool's day? Fucker, you did not get married. Stop fucking with me."

Carson was now on his knees, gripping the counter ledge to keep him from rolling on the floor.

"Damn, man, you practically lived in my house when we were kids. How the hell did you come up with sister?" Weston asked as he gave an exasperated shake of his head.

"Well, if she was related to you, that would mean I might have a shot," he said with a grin.

"Unbelievable." Weston rolled his eyes.

"Pretty thing, if you ever want to ditch him, you give me a call, okay?"

I stared up at him in shock. Was he really flirting with me in front of my husband?

"Lance, what are you doing here?" Weston asked.

Lance's brows shot up. "Oh, yeah. I tried to call you, but I was headed this way so I thought I'd stop by. What's this about me and my guys not being able to work with the actors this week for *Trap Door?*"

Weston sighed, and Carson frowned.

"We're having issues with the lead actress," Carson said with a grumble.

"You're warning me now she's going to be a bitch during training? Fantastic." Lance blew out a hard breath, but his mood swiftly changed. "Well, can we at least work with the male lead? We're all ready to go. It does us no good to sit around until some diva gets off her high horse."

"Wow, that was a mood swing," Weston said with a chuckle.

Lance shrugged his shoulders. "Me and my guys have been working on choreographing the fight scenes for two months, turning down other offers, because you know I play favorites when it comes to you, Wes."

"I know, man, we're going to talk to her and get her back on track. I promise," Weston assured. "So for now, why don't you come to my office, and we'll give the male lead a call and see if we can start the training for him? And by then, Wren's cookies will be done, and I'll let you have one."

I heard Carson protest before mumbling about it being unfair, while Lance's sullen mood disappeared and an adorable smile lit up his face again.

The boys retreated to talk business, and I finished up the cookies, sticking them in the oven. An hour later, Lance and Carson were walking out the door with a few cookies in their hands, Carson also carrying a small bag for Ari.

Weston was still on the phone, so I moved to the piano room, an itch to play overtaking me. I sat down at the bench and began playing the melody that had been going through my head since the table incident. It was full of hard, deep, low notes, with a seductive overtone. Lost in my little musical world, I didn't hear Weston enter the room.

"That's beautiful, baby girl. Did you compose it?" he asked from the doorway.

"Hmm, I think it's more *we* composed it," I said as my fingers continued to flow across the ivory.

"Yeah?" A grin spread on his face, and he walked toward me.

"This was the kitchen the other night," I said, finally knowing where it came from.

His eyes darkened, and he licked his lips. "I can hear it now. It's hard and beautiful at the same time."

"Yes, it was," I agreed as he slipped down next to me.

He leaned over and placed a kiss to my temple. "You're so good at that, baby girl."

"Thank you. It's something that has always just flowed naturally from somewhere within me."

Weston's fingers fell on the keys as well, adding to the piece. His side was lighter, more fantastical, but no less representative. We played together for a few more minutes, Weston adding in when the melody changed. It changed because he was near me, turning lighter, happier, until coming to an end.

While the last chords still rang out around us, his hands cupped my face, his lips pressed lightly against mine. He deepened the kiss, pulling me onto his lap, his lips moving slowly down my neck, his arms holding me close. There was no rush, no need to devour. Just soft touches and light, reverent kisses that held so much meaning behind them. It was sweet, sensual, and so different from the dominating side that had been present lately.

"Do you have any idea how happy I am that I found you?" he asked as he kissed down my jaw.

"No," I said in a whisper, my hands running through his hair, still enjoying the fuzzy buzz near the nape of his neck.

"I feel like we connect on so many levels . . . I never thought I'd have that. I never thought I *could* have it. I wanted it, so badly." He reached up and gently brushed the hair from my face. "And then I met you and now I feel . . ."

"Complete? Are you trying to say that I complete you?" I asked, my lips turning up in a smirk.

He leaned forward, resting his forehead on mine. "Yeah, I guess that is the best way to describe it."

"I'm sure I could think of one or two more."

"Oh really?"

"Let's see," I said, thinking, but distracted for a moment by the hypnotic beautiful blue of his eyes. "I'm just a girl, sitting on a man's lap, and asking him to love her."

His fingers reached up to caress my cheek, an unknown emotion crossing his face, his eyes somewhere between pain and something more than the adoration that was usually present. "I like that one very much," he whispered against my lips, "but now it's my turn." He regarded me reverently for a moment. "You make me feel different, more like myself, like the man I was meant to be."

I smiled at him, placing a kiss on his nose, which made him smile back at me. "You know, I'm not perfect and you're not perfect, but I think we could be perfect together."

"Perfect for each other," he echoed, his head resting at the crook of my neck, his arms wrapped tightly around me.

We stayed that way for a few minutes, just soaking each other in. It felt good to connect that way. Times like that were rare, and we took advantage of it. Life was still new for us as a couple, and for me in California. The sweet moments were a reminder of how good it could be, hopefully for many years to come.

Chapter Eighteen

HIS LIFE

TIME SEEMED TO SPEED BY OVER THE NEXT FEW DAYS. I went to school during the day, talked to Daniel, hung out with Charlotte, did my homework, played the piano, and then waited for Weston to arrive. On Wednesday he got home at eight, and as soon as he was in the door, he grabbed my hand, undressed us, threw me on the bed, wrapped his arms around me . . .

And fell asleep.

Things were also getting worse with the diva. There was a photo shoot that she didn't show up to and didn't have a reason or excuse. Weston spent a lot of time with the punching bag that night. Something needed to give soon. Otherwise, I was afraid about the toll it would take on him.

It was a nice, sunny afternoon that Friday when I left school to visit Weston's office. Then again, it was always a nice, sunny day every day in California. I changed into a Sophie-approved dress, complete with heels, bangles, and some designer purse that had arrived with five others earlier in the week. I felt much like Wonder Woman, or some other female superhero; schoolgirl by day, wife of Hollywood superstar by night.

I checked my makeup before settling into my car for the drive. Graham had put the directions into the car's GPS, thankfully, so I let it guide me to where I needed to go. It would be a while before I got the hang of the layout and could navigate myself. I was bouncing in my seat the whole drive, excited to see Weston outside of the house for the first time since we got married. Hence the dressing up. There was a parking garage across the street, and I found a spot before walking in to the impressive, twenty-plus-story building.

The lobby was bustling with people, elevator bays lined up, each with security of their own. Some of the people walking around had cameras in their hands. I didn't think much of it until my eyes found the placards on the wall. It was then I noticed the multiple Hollywood names plastered behind the security desks. My eyes zeroed in on Lockwood, and I made my way over toward that elevator bay. It didn't escape my notice that most of the people were down by the other two bays. Security seemed to be holding them back, and arguing with others.

"Excuse me, miss, can I help you?" the portly security officer inquired.

"Umm, yes, I'm here to see Weston Lockwood," I said, looking back at the man who was scrutinizing me.

"I'm sorry. Mr. Lockwood isn't expecting any visitors today."

"Well, he's expecting me," I said.

"Is that right?" he asked sarcastically, turning to the other guard who was chuckling.

"Yes, he is. My name is Wren Lockwood."

"Oh, Wren Lockwood, you say?" He chuckled, knocking elbows with the other guard.

"Are you going to let me up?" I asked, my ire beginning to rise.

"Umm, let me think . . ." He tapped his chin for dramatics. "No," he said with a shake of his head. "I don't think so. You'll have to be a bit more creative than to just use his last name as yours."

"I am not lying," I said, putting my hands on my hips. "You're not going to at least call up and ask?"

"Nope," he said, smiling, seemingly happy that he was diverting me.

"I'm on the list, are you at least going to check that?"

"Honey, I know all the names on all the lists, and yours isn't there." He looked me up and down, settling on my face. "I'm certain of it."

"So you won't check it?" It was to the point of ridiculous. Yes, they were doing a good job of keeping people out that didn't need to be there, but they were pissing me off by refusing to do something as basic as check. I didn't want to pull a hissy fit and act like the diva that had been causing Weston such a headache, but I wasn't above it either.

"Sorry, sweetheart, better find another excuse."

"Fine, have it your way," I said, and pulled out my phone.

Weston answered almost immediately. "Baby girl, I'm glad you called, I was missing you. Where are you?"

"I'm down in the lobby, actually," I said as I glared at the security guards who were having fun at my expense.

"Come on up," Weston said. I could hear Julia in the background. "I've got a call on the other line, but I'll be off by the time you get up here."

"I can't get up."

There was a pause. "What do you mean you can't get up?" His voice was lower, irritation lacing his tone.

"The security guards refuse to check the list and won't let me up or call your office." I continued to glare at the guards, but as I continued talking to Weston, a smirk grew on my lips. "They even accused me of lying about my name."

"I'll be right there," he hissed into the phone before hanging up.

"Is that supposed to intimidate us?" the guard asked, laughing.

"No, it's supposed to scare you," I answered boldly, taking advantage of my new status for the first time. Weston was going to be furious.

A moment later, Weston stepped out of the elevator, Julia in tow, and stormed over to where I was standing. He glared over at the guards as he passed. Leaning down, he gave me a soft kiss on the cheek in greeting before turning to the men that were staring at us with stunned expressions on their faces.

"Explain!" he snapped at them, causing them to panic and stutter.

"Please explain to Mr. Lockwood why you did not let Wren Lockwood up," Julia demanded in a harsh tone. "She is on the list—did you even check it? Her photo is there as well."

"W-we just thought she was a-another fangirl," he stuttered under her scrutiny. Julia was quite a force when she needed to be.

"There is a reason we give such detailed lists of approved visitors," Weston seethed, stepping toward them.

"Your ineptitude is insinuating that I did not do my job properly, so you will show Mr. Lockwood the list," Julia commanded. "And then you will make damn sure you know it better than you do now!"

The guards fumbled over each other as they flipped through a booklet containing Weston's list. Sure enough, on the front page, which even indicated priority access, was my name and photo.

"Apparently, you aren't as fluent with the list as you claimed," I said with a smug smile.

"Terribly sorry, sir, it won't happen again," he apologized.

"It better not, because if it does, if you do not check that list with every person who comes forward, you will find yourself without a job. Do I make myself clear?" Weston growled.

"Crystal, Mr. Lockwood, sir."

Weston cursed under his breath as he looked around the lobby. We'd caught the attention of the people milling in the lobby, some even moving closer, calling out his name. His jaw locked, one of his arms rested loosely on my waist, ushering me to the elevator.

"Who were they?" Weston asked Julia as soon as the doors closed.

"Couple of trash mags, and a few I couldn't identify," she answered. "I don't think we have anything to worry about, her back was to them, and they were across the lobby waiting for a big name.

By the time they became interested in what was going on, it was over."

"Good."

"I'm actually surprised security even let them in the building. Something must be going on," Julia said.

Weston nodded. "I agree. Have Mallory keep a lookout."

"Mallory?" Julia's eyes were wide as she looked at him. "Are you sure?"

"If they saw nothing, there is nothing for her to find, and it will keep her busy," Weston said, then shook his head, his grip unconsciously tightening around me. "I want her gone, Julia. I wish we could just get rid of her."

"She can't say anything, Weston," Julia said, trying to reassure him.

"No, but an anonymous source can, just like before," he said bitterly.

Julia's eyes dropped to the ground. It made me wonder if she felt responsible for whatever happened.

"I'm not letting her go until our marriage has been revealed. I'm not taking the risk," Weston said with a sigh. "Just keep her on odd jobs for now, and make sure she has no access to any files. Also keep a tab on her phone. It's company property, so tell Joe I want her phone monitored; texts and calls."

"What's going on?" I asked, but the opening of the elevator doors halted conversation.

Weston guided me through a door that read Lockwood Entertainment on it. On the other side I saw some familiar faces, like Graham and Amy, along with new ones. It was decorated in fairly modern furniture in an assortment of grays and oranges.

We moved into a large office that I assumed to be his, and as soon as the door was closed, his arms were around me, lips pressed to mine.

"Hi, baby girl," he said, smiling down at me. "Welcome to my world."

"Nice office," I said, my eyes scanning the room, noticing the huge windows that wrapped around the corner office. "Wow."

"Nice view, isn't it?" He wrapped his arms around my waist, his chest to my back.

I turned in his arms and smiled up at him. "It's impressive, but I prefer this one."

Standing on the tips of my toes, I pulled his lips down to mine. He moaned at the contact, a sound I loved. We were interrupted by the door opening and Mallory stepping in. Her gaze was not friendly. In fact, I was certain she was glaring at me.

"Here are the items you requested, sir," she said, walking in and placing something on the table.

"Thank you," he said, not even looking at her. She stood in her spot, staring at us. It was a bit unnerving, and I could see Weston's jaw tense. "Back to work, Mallory," Weston commanded, his voice cool. "Oh, and don't forget to knock next time. I've warned you about that."

She huffed and left, closing the door behind her.

"What is her problem?" I asked, still stunned by her reaction to me.

Weston glared at the door and sighed. "She's pissed off and knows she's about to be fired. I don't trust her at this point."

"Then why don't you fire her?"

He let out a sigh. "If only it was that easy. She had to sign an NDA when she was hired on, one that packs a pretty big penalty if she breaks it. But I still don't feel safe letting her go."

"So, that's what you were talking about in the elevator?"

He nodded and took a seat in the chair behind a large wooden desk. "Proprietary information was leaked on a film two months ago. We know it came from our office, and based off of what went out, all signs point to Mallory."

"That should be grounds for firing her!" My blood began to boil, outraged that one of his own assistants would do something to jeopardize his company.

He shook his head. "Not since we got married. Now the age old adage is very fitting; keep your friends close, and keep your enemies closer."

I could tell how stressed he was, and determined to make it better, I decided to change the direction of the conversation.

"What about wives?" I asked, walking up to him.

His brow quirked up at me, a sly smile forming on his lips. "Oh, wives you keep the closest of all. Very close."

"This close?" I asked, standing in front of him, a small gap between us.

"Closer."

"This close?" I asked again, stepping forward and straddling his legs with my own.

His hands reached out and grabbed my waist, pulling me down hard onto his lap. I let out a gasp, followed by a moan when his hips flexed up, pushing his hardening cock against my pussy.

"Closer," he whispered, his head dipping to lick and nibble on my neck.

My hands wound around his head, hips pushing down. "How do we get closer than this?" I asked, making my voice as innocent sounding as possible.

He chuckled into my neck, kissing the sensitive skin below my ear.

"We get closer by me laying you down on the desk, pushing your dress up, pulling your panties down, and plowing my cock deep inside that sweet little pussy of yours."

I could feel a gush of wetness from his words and let out a little moan. His hands roamed around my body, squeezing, groping, and making me want more. His lips attacked mine and he stood, placing me on the edge of his desk and tilting me onto my back.

"You know," he said, trying to kiss and talk at the same time, "I've had many fantasies about sex on this desk since I bought it years ago."

I giggled, my teeth biting down on his bottom lip. He stood back up, undoing his belt buckle and freeing his cock. I licked my lips, my hips moving on their own, hands squeezing my breasts to give him a show.

"Fuck, baby girl, you look so good spread out on my desk like that," he said in a low, husky tone.

His fingers moved beneath the fabric of my panties, his other hand pushing my dress up to my waist. My body shuddered as his knuckles moved up and down over my clit and wet opening. He removed his hand, bringing the same knuckles that had been touching me up to his mouth, moaning as he sucked my juices off.

"My wife is so delicious. I wish I had time to eat her out right now, but I need to be buried inside her," he said seductively, pushing my panties aside, not wanting to take the time to actually pull them off, and sliding in.

My head fell back, a guttural moan slipping past my lips. His hands gripped my waist and he began thrusting in and out, pulling me to him with each flex of his hips. Needing him closer, I grabbed his tie and pulled him down on top of me. He took the hint and pressed his lips to mine, our tongues mingling while one hand wrapped around my back, resting at the nape of my neck.

"Oh, baby girl, I've missed you, missed this," he whispered against my lips.

I was lost in the feeling of him filling me, making me feel whole. The motion of his hips increased in speed, and I was panting against his lips.

"Weston . . . oh, Wes!" I gasped.

The situation, the knowledge that there was an entire office of employees on the other side of the door, was revving me up faster than normal.

"Are you getting close, baby girl?" He groaned as I squeezed down around him. "That's it. I want to feel you come undone around me."

My body tensed, gearing up to give him what he wanted. He changed the angle slightly, pushed harder and faster. My eyes lost focus, back arching as my legs locked around his waist.

Then I shattered, my teeth sinking into his neck to stifle my screams as wave after wave of mind numbing pleasure ripped through me.

Weston groaned, his body jerking, pulsing inside me. I released his neck, licking and kissing where my teeth had been. His lips pressed against my temple as we lay there, catching our breath.

"That was . . ." Weston trailed off, a knocking on the door springing him into action, pulling us back down on his chair.

"Weston, I need you to . . ." Julia stopped speaking. I was certain she was staring at us, but my head was buried in the crook of his neck. "I'll be back in a few minutes."

With that, the door closed and we were alone again, panting against each other.

Weston chuckled into my hair.

"It's not funny," I grumbled.

"Yes, yes, it is," he said, still laughing. "You didn't see her face."

"Oh, my God." I burrowed my face against his neck. "I don't think I can look at her again."

"It's fine," he said as he ran his hand up and down my back. "She's an expert at 'I didn't see anything.'"

I pulled back and rolled my eyes at him. "That doesn't make it any less embarrassing."

He reached over and grabbed some tissue. "I think we should get cleaned up and grab an early dinner."

I beamed down at him. "I think that's a great idea."

The next morning, I found Kelly making breakfast in the kitchen: pancakes and bacon.

"Morning," I said as I reached out to sneak a piece of bacon.

Kelly glared at me before slapping me on the wrist with her spatula. "Bad girl."

I stared up at her in shock, but backed down. She pointed with the spatula toward the kitchen table. "Go sit with your husband."

I turned to find Weston sitting at the table with a smirk on his face, still chuckling as he read the paper and sipped on a cup of coffee.

"Are you laughing at me?"

"Maybe." He leaned over and kissed my cheek before taking another sip.

There was a strange normality with the situation, and I began to wonder if things were starting to *feel* normal to me.

It was only another minute before a plate heaping with pancakes was set on the table between us, followed by a pound of bacon.

"Now, you can have some bacon," she said with a smile and a wink.

I picked one up and bit into it to find it perfectly cooked and crunchy.

Weston chuckled at me as he passed out pancakes.

They were so good I planned to beg her for the recipe the next time I saw her. She'd headed out the door less than five minutes after she set the plates down. Such strange hours she worked, and it left me wondering if she was a personal chef to anyone else.

"What's your schedule look like today?" I asked before taking one of my last bites, already mourning the loss, but my stomach couldn't handle any more.

Pulling out my phone and reviewing his schedule would tell me, but that just seemed so impersonal.

"Absolutely nothing," he replied, licking the last of the syrup from his fork.

My clit twitched as I watched his tongue lick up the tines, making sure to collect all of the sticky, sugary concoction.

"So, you're all mine today?" I asked as I popped the last bite into my mouth.

He grinned. "All yours."

I scooted back and stood from my chair. "No meetings or phone?" I asked, my hands on his shoulders as my legs straddled his.

He shook his head. "Just you and me, baby," he said, pulling me down onto his lap, his lips attacking my neck.

"Wow, I'm such a lucky girl. Whatever shall we do?" I asked, my mind already beginning to cloud.

"Anything. Everything," he whispered before his lips hungrily found mine. "Fuck, you taste good."

I was moaning against his mouth, my lips never leaving his. His hands wrapped around my waist, pulling me down on his growing erection while he thrust his hips up. We rocked on the chair, and the need to be naked so that he could slide right in was growing.

In my lust-clouded mind I thought I heard a throat clearing, but I didn't care enough to remove myself from him.

"Hello!" a female voice yelled, breaking through our lust-filled haze.

We both pulled back and turned to find a woman with long brown hair and expensive looking clothes standing in the doorway. She was sporting a bitch brow, her arms crossed over her chest, and her four-inch heel tapped on the hardwood.

"Natalie? What the hell are you doing here?" Weston asked, his brow scrunched and obviously annoyed that someone had disturbed us right before the good part.

"Oh, I'm so sorry, was I interrupting, you asshole?" Her lip twitched up into a sneer, and I suddenly felt like I was in the middle of a lovers' spat. Which was odd, because I was the wife.

"Asshole?" his voice boomed out in indignant anger, and he lifted me from his lap so we were both standing.

"I've been gone for a few months filming and you are fucking around on me!" Her hands were waving wildly in the air.

My head snapped in her direction. *What the hell?*

"I can't fuck around on someone I'm not even in a

relationship with," he said calmly, his eyes regarding her coolly, and it all clicked. She was the ex. "You wanted to be free before filming, so you could fuck your love interest in the movie without feeling guilty per usual. We haven't been together in over six months."

"Well, I'm back. So, send the little trollop home," she spat, her eyes shooting her bitch death glare in my direction as she walked toward him.

My jaw dropped, my eyes wide, my blood boiling. "Excuse me, bitch?"

Weston stepped forward, his body partially blocking me.

"She is home," he said, shocking me that he said it so freely to her, but also making me happy he did because it would put her in her place. "And you need to watch what you say about my wife."

Her eyes shot open, giving her a crazed expression. "W-what?"

"Wren, this is my ex, Natalie Larson. Natalie, this is my wife, Wren."

Her eyes remained wide as she processed what he said, and I waited for the coming explosion.

"*What?!*" a shill scream escaped, a murderous gleam in her eyes.

"I'm sorry, I didn't realize you had gone deaf," he replied in a condescending tone. "This is my *wife.*"

"Six years, six fucking years you throw down the drain for some *girl?*" she raged, pointing in my direction.

Weston wasn't fazed by her outbursts, probably used to and tired of them. "Six fucking years of never falling in love with you, and I started falling in love with her on day one."

My head snapped to him and I couldn't stop the smile as I looked up at him. I felt the same.

"You think you're in love with her?" Natalie chuckled evilly. "Do you even know her?"

"I feel more for her than I ever did for you," he answered honestly.

Her face was red with anger, her finger poking into his chest. "That's a lie. We talked about marriage."

"*You* talked about marriage," Weston said, making sure he stressed it was all her. "Almost since the day I met you, I might add. To me, it seemed like all we were was business with sex on the side. You never wanted *me*, as a person and a friend, you only wanted what my name and status could bring your way."

"That's not true, Weston. How can you even say that? All I ever wanted was you! I wanted to get married, have babies, and you threw it all away!" she seethed, tears springing to her eyes.

Weston rolled his eyes. "Oh, please, Nat. You can stop quoting your own movies," he said. I couldn't stop the snicker that popped out. "Get over yourself. You're not that good of an actress."

Almost faster than I could blink, her hand whipped out and across his face. He grunted, jaw clenched, his face turning back to her. I tried to lunge at her and scratch her fucking eyes out, but I was trapped by Weston's arms as they wrapped around my waist. I was left unable to do much other than watch the carnage.

"You fucking asshole!" she shrieked.

"Don't you touch him, bitch!" I spat, still trying to get to her. "You need to get out of our house, and now!"

Natalie looked more annoyed than threatened by my presence, but if Weston let go of me, I'd show her how to slap.

"You have exactly two minutes to turn your bitchy ass around and leave, or so help me, you will not like what comes next," Weston said as he pointed toward the door.

"Are you threatening me? Going to hit me?"

Weston's spine straightened. "While it might feel good, I don't hit women."

"I wouldn't have a problem with it," I chimed in, still pissed that she had the gall to attack him.

Weston glanced at me before giving his attention back to Natalie. "Also, I'm not threatening your person, but we both know what your career would be without my support."

"You wouldn't!" she gasped, her hand flying to her chest.

"I would, and I can. That's a promise."

She looked between the two of us. Calculating, looking at her options, and then turned and stomped off.

"I'll see you on Monday!" she called.

"Make an appointment, or I won't see you," Weston yelled back.

We both heard the front door slam, and Natalie let out a shriek of frustration. I found Weston's shunning of her and her exit somewhat hysterical. Her wake, unfortunately, left an unsettling mood in the room. Weston was fuming, and I was stumped at what to do to calm him. There was one thing I knew that would bring him back, and hopefully it worked because I did not want her presence to ruin our day.

Taking his face in my hands, I kissed him hard. He froze, stunned, but soon melted into it, moaning as his arms wrapped around me.

"Sorry about that," he said, leaning forward so his forehead rested against mine.

"Answer me this—how many people have access to this house?"

He chuckled. "Obviously too many!"

"Seriously. I feel like we're always being interrupted."

"Well, there's us, Joe's team, obviously." He pursed his lips, eyes unfocused. "Then Carson and Sophie, Lance, Miles, Julia, Kelly, Amy, Graham, and Natalie."

"And why does Natalie still have access if you two are no longer together and haven't been for six months?" I asked, somewhat annoyed, as I rubbed his face gently where she slapped him.

"Because, if I hadn't met you and she just arrived, I probably would have gotten back together with her again," he admitted, albeit a bit sheepishly.

It stung a bit, but I saw their interaction. He was immediately on the defensive as soon as venomous words were directed at me. It was *me* that had a hold on him, not her.

"But I do have you," he said, then took my hand in his and placed his lips on my palm. "And therefore, no reason to go back to her. I'll have Joe deactivate her card today."

"She ruined the mood, so that makes me dislike her." I kissed his reddened cheek several times.

He chuckled. "*Everyone* somehow always manages to ruin the mood barging into this house."

I laughed at that. "Yeah, you're right."

"So why don't we rewind to five minutes ago," he said as he moved back to sitting in his chair. "I was sitting here, and you . . ." he grabbed my hands, pulling me to straddle his lap ". . . you were right here."

"Mmm, yes, and your lips were right here," I said, pressing my lips to his.

We quickly found our way back to where we'd been. Soon thereafter, he was stripping me of my clothes and I was riding his cock.

Chapter Nineteen

OUR FAMILY EXPANDED?

Time. It was time to find out where fate would take us. Time to see the doctor.

It was hard to believe three weeks had passed so quickly. That meant Weston and I were coming up on the one month anniversary of our marriage in a few short days.

The blaring of the alarm went off, waking us both. Weston's hand slammed down on the clock before he snuggled back down into the bed. His arms wrapped around my waist and pulled my back to his chest.

"Good morning, baby girl," he whispered into my ear, holding me close.

I smiled and sighed in contentment. Weston's arms were my special place. A place filled with safety and security, and the love that was blooming between us.

"Morning," I murmured, turning toward him, my face burrowing into his chest, breathing him in.

His hands trailed up and down my back, making me hum in appreciation.

"Today's the big day, huh?"

"Yeah," I replied.

His hand cupped my face, tilting it up to look at him. Our eyes met before he spoke. "Whatever you decide, I'm with you."

I smiled and leaned forward to place a chaste kiss on his lips. "I know."

The alarm went off again a few minutes later, forcing us out of bed and to start the day.

After showering and changing, I headed downstairs for some breakfast while Weston finished getting ready. In the kitchen I found Julia working away, early as usual.

"Morning, Wren," she said with a warm smile.

I didn't know how the woman was always so bright and cheerful all of the time, especially living with Miles, but Julia had to be one of the most wonderful people I'd ever met.

"Morning," I said with a yawn, moving to the fridge in search of something to eat.

"I was looking at the schedule for today, and I know you have your appointment after school, so I'll make sure Weston is home by the time you get home."

"Thanks, I appreciate that, Julia."

Julia stared at me, the smile gone, and replaced with pursed lips. "Wren, do you want me to go with you?" she asked, concern written all over her face, and I was very much tempted to say yes.

"Thank you for offering, but I'll be all right," I replied, picking up an apple and then putting it back down.

My nerves kicked in, and I found I wasn't hungry any longer. My appointment wasn't until the afternoon, and Julia had made sure Weston's schedule was clear and that he would be home early. Just in case it did turn out that our young marriage was going to be tried by more than a pissed off Hollywood actress.

I couldn't even think about what happened with Natalie the other day, or how my insecurity was creeping up. Weston had assured me she never technically lived with him. That it was more business than emotions.

We didn't see Natalie at the house again in the days following her explosion. She did go to see Weston, and I think she tried to play him, but then again he might have known her agenda. She was on her best behavior, all sweet and flirtatious when she visited, he'd said. Even going so far as congratulating him. It was obvious she was trying to get back on his good side, and I knew it wasn't the last we'd see of her. Unfortunately.

I'd rather it was, but I knew from past incidents that she was clingy and possessive. When I pictured Weston's ex, a bitchy Hollywood actress with attitude to match her ego was not what I had envisioned. Then again, from what I'd learned from his camp, my entering his life had changed him. Reverting him back to the guy they used to know, versus the one with that bitch Natalie.

Weston came down after a few minutes, kissed me hard with a promise to see me soon, and whisked away with Julia in tow. I left then as well, heading to what was bound to be a day filled with nerves. I couldn't wait for the afternoon to come, just so I'd know either way. Not knowing was most of the problem for my anxiety; I was so torn on whether I'd be happy regardless of the outcome.

The day moved on, and I honestly had no recollection of what went on at school. Charlotte was concerned, but I assured her it was nothing, just a lot on my mind. At three, I was on my way to the doctor, my leg bouncing.

As I sat in the waiting room, my nerves had progressed from just a leg bounce to all out fidgeting—fingers tapping, leg bouncing, biting my lip. The nurse called my name, and I followed her back to the standard sterile exam room, though, this one was high end compared to my doctor in Indianapolis. Just like all offices, it was cold, and I was glad I'd grabbed my sweater. I was in my school uniform, which probably wasn't the best, considering the situation.

"Hello, Wren, my name is Dr. Chambers," a blonde woman said as she entered a few minutes later, holding her hand out.

"Hello," I replied, slipping my hand in hers.

"So, what brings you in today?" she asked with a standard smile.

"Well, I just moved here, and I need to have an annual and I wanted to talk about birth control."

"Well, welcome to L.A., and we can do all of that today. I'll just need to get a little information from you, and then we can do the exam and have a little talk. Sound good?" she asked. I nodded. "When was your last period?"

"Thirteen days ago," I answered.

She noted it in her computer. "And is there any chance you could be pregnant?"

"Yes."

She looked up. "Have you and your boyfriend been using any protection?"

"No, my . . . husband and I have not," I replied carefully.

"Husband?" Her eyes were wide, blinking at me before she glanced down at the computer, her mouth dropping open when she saw Weston's name as the emergency contact and his relation. "Oh . . . wow . . . I'm sorry, I didn't realize."

I shook my head. "It's not publicly known yet."

She closed the laptop and addressed me. "I'm sure Julia told you we value our patients' privacy and safeguard our patients' protected health information, so you have nothing to worry about."

I let out a breath. "Thank you."

She stood up. "All right, so we'll need to do a test to make certain you aren't pregnant before we begin. Okay?"

"Okay."

It was forty-five minutes later when I was putting my clothes back on after the examination, and I was lost in my thoughts. The pregnancy test came back negative, and I didn't know which emotion was strongest about the results.

There was a huge rush of relief, but also a pang of sadness. Weston seemed so excited to have kids, but I was still in high school. I'd already made my decision, but still I warred, two sides forming: one pointing out how short of time we'd known one another, the other stating that time didn't matter because every fiber of my being knew that he was it, no other man would do. One side reminded me I was still in school and was registered to attend college the following fall, the flip side pointing out the no-limit credit card burning up my wallet; I didn't need to work. I didn't need to do anything . . . but I wanted to.

I wanted a career of my own. Something I acquired on my own, with my own power, and not something given to me.

It was true that I didn't know what I wanted to major in. I didn't know what I wanted to do for a career, but I did know I wanted to do *something*. I wanted to go to college. I didn't want to be some plastic piece, or a trophy, and I knew Weston didn't want that either. That was one thing he loved about me, even with all the expensive stuff he threw at me. It was really a show, like a hunter catching the biggest, most fierce animal to show he was a good provider. He wanted me to have the best.

Dr. Chambers came back in and went over all of the different birth control options, and there were many, but one stood out: the Depo-Provera shot. It would give me three months of protection and no periods, and in three months I could make the decision to renew the shot or go off of it. It would give me more time to get to know Weston and decide what I wanted to do about my future, as well as ours.

So, protected for three months, I headed home to tell my husband the news.

"Not pregnant? Huh," Weston said, slumping down on the couch after I told him the news. "I'm actually kind of sad. I don't know . . . I was excited. I just didn't realize I'd become so attached to the prospect of having a baby with you."

I wrapped my arms around him, his expression making my chest clench. But it was the right decision. One of us had to have a level head about it.

"I got the birth control shot. It lasts for three months. With all the changes . . . I'm just not ready for that yet. I got wrapped up in the idea with you, the fantasy, but realistically . . ."

He nodded and kissed my neck. "You're totally right with that. I told you that I was fine with whatever you decided, and I meant it. I just got caught up in my dreams. You do that to me a lot."

"Yeah, I noticed," I replied, stretching up to kiss his lips.

"One day, Mrs. Lockwood, I'll knock you up. When the time is right," he said with a genuine smile.

"I think that is a fabulous plan, Mr. Lockwood."

"However, I think we'll need a lot of practice between now and then," he said, kissing down my neck as he leaned forward, pushing me onto my back. "Practice does make perfect, I've heard." His hands crept under my shirt, warm against my skin.

"Oh, yeah? Well, if that's what they say . . ." I trailed off, smirking as I ran my hands between us and to his belt.

He sucked in a breath when my fingers wiggled in between his waistband and the tip of his cock, moaning when I wrapped my hand around his hardening length.

"Baby girl, I love when you touch me. You have no idea how good it feels. How warm and exciting."

I smiled at him and kissed his lips. "Oh, Mr. Lockwood, I do. You do the same to me."

We took our time making out, stripping each other of clothing. Touching, tasting each other's flesh. With a slow, teasing movement he slid inside me.

"Fuck, Wren, you feel so good," he groaned.

His hips rocked a slow and steady rhythm. My legs wrapped around his waist, drawing him closer with each thrust of his hips. His mouth lavished attention on my neck, fingers tweaking my nipples.

My Mr. Lockwood had about as many sides to his personality as characters he'd portrayed, and each one of them loved me physically in a different way. I felt like I was seeing a teenage Weston, going at it on his parents' couch, trying not to get caught. He was my age in that short time, the businessman long forgotten.

"Oh, baby," I moaned, wrapping my arms around his neck, pulling him closer.

"I want to fill your sweet little pussy, baby girl," he moaned into my neck.

His hips picked up the pace, pushing me over the edge, my walls squeezing around him. As I came down, he stilled on top of me, filling me, just like he wanted. Branding me, just like he desired.

I stopped by the grocery store on the way home to pick up some Sprite that I'd been craving for days and a few snacks that Kelly wouldn't buy. As I was standing in line, I was shocked when I saw the trash magazines at the counter. There, in a corner of one of them, was a picture of my backside with Weston's arm around me. The clip read "Look out, Natalie! Weston Lockwood lays claim to mystery woman."

I groaned and vowed to be more careful the next time I visited. It wouldn't have even happened if the security guards had done their damn job in the first place.

After leaving, I pulled out my phone and dialed my best friend.

"Hey, babe, just calling to clarify our plans. You are still coming in next week, right?" I asked, hopeful that there'd been no change; I really needed my best friend.

"Wouldn't miss it for the world! I miss you, Wreny!" Daniel whined from the other end.

"I miss you, too. You'll be here soon and we can have lots of fun."

"We better. I'm getting too much crap from my mom about why you suddenly moved to California," he said with a sigh, and then began laughing. "Girl, your mom's telling everyone that you met a handsome foreign stranger and eloped like in some Harlequin novel. She even has the creepy, dreamy eyes."

"Oh, don't tell me that!" I groaned. Once we hung up, I needed to call my mom and talk her down from the grand fantasy she was spreading.

"It's true! My mom doesn't want me to go because of that, but when I explained to her I was eighteen and you already bought my ticket, she finally let it go."

"Good, 'cause I've missed my best friend."

"Shit, you're making new best friends, I know it," he said.

I could almost hear his pout through the phone.

"No one will ever take your place," I reassured him.

"Shit, Mom's calling," he hissed. "I'll call you later, and we can iron out the details for next week."

I chuckled. "Sounds good. Love you!"

"Love you, too! Bye!"

I hung up the phone and opened up my text messages, asking Graham if he could put in directions to the airport for me. It was one of the rare moments I was happy Julia put everyone's contact information into my phone.

A few days later, and I wasn't doing so hot. I hadn't felt well all morning, but I didn't think I was that bad off until the words on the chalk board became difficult to see and the letters swirled around. I needed to go home, but I also knew I couldn't drive. I needed Weston.

As soon as my class ended, I gathered up my stuff and slowly made my way into the hall and to my locker. I stood there quietly and leaned against the wall, while the students milled around and the hallway emptied again as the next class started. My vision was blurring and I couldn't see the screen of my phone very well—my hand was also shaking. My head was pounding and I felt like my brain was mush, so much so I couldn't even dial the numbers.

"Wren?" a voice called, and I tried to look up.

It sounded like I was hearing through water. In front of me, I could tell whoever it was had blond hair, and was not a student.

Miles?

"Wren, are you all right?" he asked.

I looked down at my phone. "Weston," I croaked.

"Wren, let me help you to the nurse," he said. It was Miles, but why was he being nice? Things had gotten better, the hostility gone, but the dislike still remained. At least on my end. Maybe I was holding a grudge, but he owed me an apology.

He grabbed my arm and I tried to step forward, but as soon as I did, my knees collapsed out from under me. I didn't hit the ground, strong arms wrapping around me, catching me. They were Miles's. I could hear him mumbling something, saying I was burning up. It didn't matter, because after that the world turned black.

Angry words filtered through my unconsciousness, but I could hear the worried tone behind them. My eyes wouldn't open, but every word bounced around the space.

Weston. He was there, the rich tone of his voice rousing me.

" . . . don't have anything to say to you at the moment, Miles." Their words filtered through, all muffled like I had cotton in my ears, but I could still make out most of what they were saying. Weston had a sharp tone in his voice. "I thought you hated her. You were such an ass the last time we were all together."

Miles must have agreed, but all I heard was, "I don't hate her . . ."

Then Weston gathered me up in his arms, lifting me from where I was lying. I could tell it was him from his scent, and the care in which he picked me up.

"It's okay, baby girl, I've got you," he whispered, placing a kiss on my forehead.

"Don't get too close. You don't want to get whatever she has," Miles said as Weston carried me out of wherever I had been.

"Wren needs me. We can have our family showdown later. Until then, can you do me a favor and help me get her in the car?"

"Okay."

The bell rang, and they both cursed as the sounds grew louder, the halls filling with students again. Girls gasped seeing Weston, only a few noticing me in his arms. Having Miles with us only made it worse. Based on the lies I'd told the student body, it probably looked like a twisted Lockwood family reunion.

My brain was too foggy to really hear much of anything, but by the breeze, Weston had picked up the pace. Before I knew it, I was in a car and drifting back into the dark.

The next time I surfaced, Weston was beside me, moving a cool cloth around my face.

"Weston, what are you doing?" I asked. My voice was scratchy, and it hurt to talk.

"I'm taking care of you," he said, placing the towel on my forehead.

"What about work?" I tried to sit up, but fell back down. "Go, I'll be fine."

"Wren, you're my wife. I'm going to take care of you."

Trying again, I managed to get propped up on my elbows. "But . . . you're so busy."

"Stop arguing with me, Mrs. Lockwood, or I'll bring out my other personality, Dr. Brighton, and he'll put you in your place."

My eyes widened, and I lay back down to comply. I closed my eyes and stopped trying to get him to go back to work. I didn't want Dr. Brighton from *Thorntown* to come out. I was slowly becoming well versed in all his movies and characters.

It was only a few minutes before I was drifting off to sleep.

I was stirred from sleep, my brain fuzzy from my fever, but I could hear two voices arguing nearby. Weston was angry. Not shouting, but his tone was cold.

"What are you doing here, Natalie?"

"Weston, darling, we need to go over some things for the upcoming movie. Pre-production starts just after the new year, and there still isn't a full cast."

I wanted to gag at her attempts to sweet talk him, but I couldn't move or open my eyes, so I listened on.

"Once again, why are you here? This is clearly something that we can talk about at my office."

"I'm here because you weren't at your office, and we usually talk about business here anyway. I will say I was quite offended you revoked my keycard access."

"You need to go. I don't have time to deal with you right now," Weston hissed, in a forceful tone.

I smiled a little at Weston's attempts at trying to get rid of her.

"Why? Little missus giving you trouble?"

"My *wife* is sick."

Natalie made a strange huffing sound, making her displeasure of my role in his life evident.

"I know you still want me, baby. We were so good together. I could fuck you so good. Much better than that child of a wife you have."

My eyes popped open, and I shot daggers in the direction of her voice. He was *my* husband, and I would be the only one to fuck him.

"You just can't accept that I'm happy, can you?" Weston said, his exasperation evident before turning to anger. "Get out, Natalie. Come by the office tomorrow, and we'll talk about business then. Leave. Now."

Weston dismissed her, and I could hear the anger in the shrill of her voice, even through the door. My eyes were open, but just barely. Enough that I could see Weston's silhouette walking toward me. His fingers gently brushed a stray strand of hair from my face before he leaned down to press a kiss to my forehead.

"Don't like her," I mumbled.

He chuckled and pulled the covers up higher. "Don't worry about her. I'll take care of her. You just sleep, baby. I need my wife to get better."

My lids fluttered closed again, and I drifted off.

The sound of the alarm jolted me from a dead sleep, my body heavy and unwilling to move. It also jolted Weston, who'd apparently fallen asleep while working, because papers and his phone went flying as he scrambled to shut off the alarm. His hands rubbed his tired face before gathering up the sheets and setting them on the nightstand. He turned to look at me and smiled when he found I was looking back.

"How are you feeling?" he asked, voice just above a whisper, his hand reaching out to feel my forehead.

"Like I weigh a million pounds and am stuck to the bed. I ache all over."

He chuckled. "Well, the flu can do that to you."

"The flu? That sucks," I grumbled.

"Yep. So, no school today and probably not for the rest of the week. I have to go to work, but Kelly's going to come by and make you some lunch," he said before going into my list of babysitters. At least that's what it sounded like to me. "Also, Julia's going to check up on you periodically. Charlotte called last night, and she is going to stop by after school with your assignments. If you need anything today, just call me. Before I go, I'll bring up some drinks . . . or do you want to set up camp downstairs?"

I thought about it, weighing out the pros and cons, and decided I'd stay put for the day. The bed was just too cozy, and I didn't want to move. After telling him my decision he disappeared, returning a little while later with a large bottle of water, a glass, and an ice bucket. He also brought up a bag of snacks and a bottle of aspirin.

I smiled at him for his thoughtfulness as he handed me the remotes and kissed me on the forehead.

"Get better, baby girl."

"I'll try," I replied with a heavy sigh.

I watched as he walked out the door, glancing back at me before making his way down the stairs and then to work.

I spent the day watching television, mostly from Netflix because I was behind on a few of my favorite shows, and sleeping, snuggled down in my blankets and the scent of Weston. Julia popped in twice to check on me, bringing some orange juice with her. Kelly made me the traditional chicken noodle soup, but also a chicken and mozzarella panini. She even made me some pudding for dessert.

I couldn't eat a lot, but what I could was delicious.

Weston called around noon to check on me, waking me from a nap, and a few hours later Charlotte arrived.

"Hey, sicky, I've got your assignments from the last two days!" Charlotte said with fake enthusiasm as she entered the bedroom.

Joe or Julia must have let her in. I tried my best to smile at her, but I ached too much.

"I wouldn't come any closer," I said, holding my hand up in warning.

She stopped just inside the room, sitting on the chair that sat next to the door.

"I'll tell you, you sure know how to make an exit!" Charlotte laughed.

I let out a whine. "Oh, no."

"The whole school is talking about how your 'big brothers' came to the rescue when you were sick," she said, shaking her head. "It was quite entertaining, especially when I know the truth. Needless to say, the whole school now knows that they are your 'brothers.'"

"Oh, what fun it will be when I return!" I only hoped my sarcasm came through my scratchy voice.

"I'd polish up your backstory since there is quite an age gap. You were adopted or something, and had a disagreement with your parents so your brother offered to let you move in with him."

"That's not bad," I said with a smile.

"I mean, everyone knows Weston is estranged from his parents, with that whole thing years ago when he was acting."

"What thing?" My brow scrunched in confusion.

"I don't remember, but it was about ten or so years ago when it went down. So is the life of a child actor when parents are their manager. Nothing good comes out of it," she said with a sigh. "It happens all the time. We've seen it countless times around here, believe me."

"His parents were his managers?" I asked. It was news to me.

"Well, I think it was just his father," she clarified before asking, "Why don't you know this? You're the one married to him."

"Weston doesn't like to talk about his parents . . . at all."

"Whatever it was, sounds like it was pretty serious. Anyway, I should let you get back to sleep, and douse myself with antibacterial crap," she said, standing and picking her bag up from the floor. "Get better, girl. It's no fun at school without you."

"I just hope to be better by the time my friend Daniel arrives next week."

"Oh, that's right! Get some rest. I'll call you tomorrow." She blew me a kiss and then was gone.

After she left, I switched to the digital movie collection and scrolled down to *The Wizard of Oz*. It was Weston's favorite and it'd been years since I'd seen it. What better time than when I was sick?

"You're awake," Weston said with a smile, stripping off his suit as he walked in hours later.

I smiled up at him, my hand lazily grasping for his. "Were you *frightened* I wouldn't be?" I accentuated the word, hoping it triggered his Oz-wired mind.

"Frightened?" His brow rose, and he smirked before becoming very animated, even dancing toward me. "I was petrified." He leaned down and gave me a quick kiss to my forehead as I giggled. "You watched it today, didn't you?"

I shrugged my shoulders. "I felt I needed to be more versed in my husband's favorite musical."

His shy smile, the one that only came out on rare occasions, crept up on his handsome face. I hoped I'd be able to bring it out more and more. There was nothing as beautiful as my husband when he smiled like that.

Chapter Twenty

MY CONFESSIONS

Never again would I doubt Charlotte and her knowledge. I'd been back to school for three days and found I had a whole lot of new friends.

"Wren! Hey, Wren! Wait up!" a voice called out from across the parking lot of my school.

I shook my head and attempted to run away.

"Hi, Wren!" A random girl popped up in front of me, a frightening smile on her face.

"Hi," I replied, stepping around her.

"I was wondering if you wanted to hang out this afternoon?" she asked, stepping up to walk beside me.

"Who are you?" I asked.

"I'm Kim! We have Physics together."

"Sorry, there are so many people in that class," I said, picking up my pace.

"So, what do you think about tonight? We could hang at your place."

I groaned and rolled my eyes. It'd been like that ever since I got back from the flu. Charlotte wasn't kidding when she said everyone would be talking about my "brothers." As soon as I returned, everyone knew who I was, that I wasn't just any old Lockwood, and I had a sudden influx of fifty new BFFs.

"There you are, Wren!" Charlotte grabbed my hand and

pulled, taking off down the concrete path. "We're going to be late to class!"

I could hear the girl from behind me, saying we'd talk about our plans later, as Charlotte and I sped off. We were both breathing hard by the time we reached our class. I wrapped my arms around Charlotte, thanking her for rescuing me from my newest admirer.

"These girls are crazy," I said as I plopped down in my seat. "Three days of madness!"

"They go to school with movie stars, so you'd think they should know how to act," Charlotte grumbled. "I think it's just because you're Weston's . . . sister."

I heaved a sigh. "I just want to get through school without being harassed."

Charlotte rolled her eyes at me. "Wren, I've told you, it's only going to get worse as the word spreads."

And she knew firsthand. Her father's stardom had left her growing up with paparazzi always following them around. Now that her sister was also a star, it had only grown.

"I thought here was a safe haven, though. I mean, almost everyone is either someone or related to someone. So, shouldn't the starstruck looks be less?"

Charlotte quirked her brow at me. "It was confirmed that you are tied to Miles, and everyone saw proof that you have ties to *Weston* Lockwood. He was carrying you! You know how big Weston was, how famous!"

"*Was* is the keyword there, Charlotte."

"He's still in the biz, and super hot. *People* magazine's top ten hot. Cover hot."

"Okay, yeah, yeah, I get it," I said with a huff, just as the bell rang.

The rest of the day was spent avoiding all of my new "friends" and slipping out before any of them could follow me home. I had hoped that it would all settle down soon. Charlotte was right, though. I needed to get used to it, because it was just the tip of the iceberg of what would happen when the truth came out.

Natalie was in the kitchen a few mornings later, talking scheduling with Julia, who didn't look happy at all. Despite having her card deactivated, she was still getting in. She'd been popping up everywhere. I swear she would just show up and make herself at home. I could tell it was grating on Weston every time he threw her out. She was always interrupting us, or putting herself between us, and I was pissed. The worst was the day she came into our bedroom while we were having sex.

I wasn't quiet when he touched me, I knew that. He could make me scream so loud I was surprised the sound came from me. It was like that the day she came in, and there was no doubt she knew what she was doing. It made me sick.

More than once I just knew I caught some smug smirk on her face, and I was seconds from clawing it off. They were working on some project together, which didn't make me happy, but it was in effect long before we were married. That was why she was around, disturbing our already limited time together, or at least that was her excuse for being there.

She was a deceitful woman, and I couldn't stand her fakeness. Weston double checked with Joe, and her access to even the gate had been revoked, but I had a feeling someone was helping her get in the house.

"Wren, have you thought about Thanksgiving?" Julia asked. She'd asked days prior what the plans were, but I had no clue and hadn't been able to talk to Weston yet.

"I'm pretty sure we're having dinner here, but I'll have to double check," I replied.

I'd almost forgotten about the holiday, one I always spent with my dad. It was nearing Thanksgiving, and I seriously needed to call him and tell him what happened. I'd been procrastinating the phone call and put it off for a lot longer than I should have.

With Weston still at work and me alone, yet again, I found my favorite place on the patio and dialed his number. Mom was going to get an earful once our call was over. There was bound to be a lot of yelling and screaming, another thing I'd been avoiding.

"Hey, Dad," I said into the phone after he picked up.

"Hello, my lovely daughter. Where have you been hiding? I tried to call you a couple of times, but it kept going to voicemail."

I bit down on my lip, then released it. "Sorry, it was probably when I was in school."

"I called after three," he said.

Three in the afternoon in Chicago was one in Los Angeles.

"Well, I was still in school."

"After three?" he asked, and I could hear the skeptical tone in his voice.

"It was earlier than that here."

The line went silent.

"What are you talking about?" he finally asked.

I blew out a breath. *Here goes nothing.* "Dad, I'm living in California now."

"What?" his voice boomed out so loud I had to pull the phone away from my ear. "What the hell are you talking about? Your mother wouldn't move out of the state without letting me know."

"It was very sudden."

"What's that mean?" he asked.

Blood pumped through me in a quickening pulse. "Well, remember how I told you about me and mom going to Vegas?"

"Yes," was his curt response. "And I never got a notification from you that you arrived home safe, just a text from your mom."

"Well, I may have gotten married and am now living with my husband in Los Angeles." I spit the words out as fast as I could.

There was stunned silence before the yelling began. "What do you mean you got married? Wren Alexis Bradford, what in hell were you thinking?"

"I'm eighteen, Dad," I argued.

"And somehow that makes it okay?" he snapped. "You're still in high school."

"It's the same age you and Mom were when you got married."

"Ah . . ." Then silence. "Yes, but your mother and I dated for two years. Do you even know this person? Was he a stranger?"

"He was, but he's a really nice man."

"Nice man? Jesus Christ, Wren. Is he good and kind, too? Are you brainwashed? Do I need to ship you some pepper spray or come rescue you?"

I tried to reassure him, calm him down. "Dad, really, everything is fine."

"Well, who is he?"

"Umm, you remember that movie, *Midnight Horizon?*"

"That sci-fi space movie?" He sounded very confused.

I would be too. It's not every day your child calls and tells you the strange story coming out of my mouth.

"Yeah, that one," I said.

"What does that have to do with anything?" he asked.

I braced myself for the next big surprise. "The lead actor is my husband. I married Weston Lockwood."

Silence again. "You married a movie star?" No yelling, but his voice was low, surprised even.

"He doesn't act anymore. He produces," I reasoned.

"He's from Hollywood, Wren. That's a lot different from you."

Didn't I know it. "It's a good deal different in our case."

"Where are you living? Are you finishing up school?" Dad asked. At least he wasn't yelling anymore, but I could hear the concern in his voice.

I was eighteen, and while he could disapprove, there really was nothing else he could do.

"I'm living in L.A. with him, and I'm going to a really good private school. Then next year, I'll continue my plan to go to USC."

He was happy to learn I wasn't ditching college, but he still wasn't sold on the idea of Weston.

"I want to meet your . . . husband," he said, grumbling the last word.

"Okay, we'll buy you a ticket."

"I can buy my own damn ticket, Wren," he said with a huff. "I work for an airline, remember?"

"Yes, but you are coming to meet Weston, a trip you wouldn't normally take. Let us pay for your ticket so you can get here and not use one of your buddy passes."

"You know, your mother called me a few weeks ago, which was odd. She cryptically said you had some news for me, but this . . . I never in a million years thought it would be finding out you got married," he revealed. I didn't know whether to hug my mom in that moment or strangle her. "She supported it, and I guess I'll find out for myself why. I mean, there's not much else I can do. I don't agree with it, I don't like it, but it's done."

"Mom may have pushed us to stay married, but I think it was a great call on her part. You'll see in a few weeks."

"In a few weeks," he reiterated. "Oh, one more thing."

"Yeah?"

"You two are being safe, right? I mean, having children at eighteen is a tough thing to handle. Take it from me. Especially with a relationship as new as yours."

"Dad!" I cried in protest.

"What? I just want to make sure you two are being sensible here," he argued. I wanted to laugh at the clairvoyance he was having at the moment, though a few weeks late. "You two hardly know each other. Do you really want to have a baby with someone you just met?"

"I'm hanging up now. I'll call you with the flight information."

"Be safe, Wren!"

There was grumbling and arguing, and I realized where my stubborn side came from. We set it up for him to come out in just over two weeks for Thanksgiving. Weston took the visit announcement in stride, and even though he and Miles were still strained, I encouraged Weston to invite him and Julia as well. I didn't want our discord to stop him from spending time with his family for the holiday.

It was the week after when things began to change. I knew Miles was trying to get over it. He'd been civil to me in class and had praised my performances. He even gave me an A for the quarter, which apparently was a difficult thing to get out of him. And we had worked out some of our differences.

"Why did you give me an A?" I asked after school one day.

"Because you earned it, Wren."

"And not because I'm your brother's wife and you're trying to sweeten me up?"

"I don't give out A's lightly. That last composition project you wrote was excellent. Wren, you are talented, and your A reflects your hard work and creativity." He smiled and continued, "Perhaps a part of me was hoping it might help bridge this gap you created as well, and give us a chance to talk."

My eyebrows shot up. "I created? No, you did that all on your own."

"I'm sorry, but your appearance into his life was unexpected, and I reacted poorly to it." He looked down and shook his head. "I'm still not comfortable with the idea that he married someone he doesn't know and who's only eighteen. I've gotten to know you well enough to see that you must understand my side of things."

I crossed my arms over my chest. "I do. What I don't get is your blatant lack of civility the night we met."

"I'm sorry about that. Though it was what I was thinking, I never should have said that out loud, especially that comment about your . . . um . . . well, you know . . . and in front of you."

"Are you apologizing?" I asked, stunned. My eyes were wide as I stared at him.

He looked around and nodded. "Yes, I suppose I am. You're his wife, whether or not I agree with it. At first I thought you were just another star seeking gold digger, but I've seen you here. No one knows, and your ring is hidden."

With that, Miles held out his hand. I stared at it for a moment before slipping mine in and officially calling a truce.

"How's he doing?" he asked, his voice low and filled with genuine concern, and I could see how much the rift had hurt them both. "We only talk about business these days."

"He misses you, I know that much. Other than that, he's . . . stressed."

"When isn't he?"

"Well, production is halted on one project due to a diva, and Natalie's constant presence is grating on us both."

Miles froze. "Natalie's back?"

"Yes. She's been constantly showing up over the last few weeks," I grumbled.

"How did she react to you?" he asked with a stern look on his face.

"Not well."

"I'd be careful about that one," he warned. "If anyone deserved the words I called you, it's Natalie."

"You really don't like her that much?"

"She's poison," he said, his lip curling up. "Another reason I went off on you. I didn't want him to have another Natalie in his life. But I get it now. That isn't what you are at all, and for that much, I'm grateful."

I nodded in acknowledgement of his warning, and in thanks for his newly recognized faith in me.

After school on Friday, I headed to the airport to pick up Daniel. I smiled the whole day, my body vibrating with excitement to see my best friend. When we last parted, it was with a hug and a "See you on Monday." That was well over a month ago, but it felt more like a year.

Daniel had been my everything: friend, confidant, and surrogate brother. As I waited for his flight to arrive, I realized just how much I depended on him. Even though he was thousands of miles away, he'd still been there to help me get through the toughest time of my life.

I couldn't help jumping up and down, like the teenager I was, when I saw his bleached blond hair and bright green eyes come bouncing out of the baggage claim area. We ran to each other, jumping and hugging, huge smiles on our faces.

"Oh, Wren, I missed you so much!" he cried out, kissing my face all over.

"Not as much as I missed you!" I laughed, tears filling my eyes as we squeezed each other.

We let go, our hands entwined, and headed to the parking garage. I hit the remote, unlocking the doors. The flashing lights caught his attention, and his jaw dropped when he saw which car was mine.

"I think I'm in love," he said reverently as he walked up and put his bags in the trunk.

"Baby, you don't even know." I smiled as I climbed behind the wheel.

"Oh God, you've been in L.A. way too long."

I shrugged my shoulders and hit the gas, sending us speeding off toward home.

"He bought this for you?" Daniel asked, his eyes taking in the interior.

"Yep."

"Do you know how expensive this car is, Buttercup?" he asked, using the nickname he'd given me years ago.

It warmed my heart just to hear it.

"No, and I don't want to. I love this car, and I know it will just make me sick if I know the exact fortune he spent on it. I'm betting it comes close to his Bentley, though."

"He has a Bentley?"

I nodded. "And a Range Rover."

"Holy shit! Buttercup, you are way out of your league here."

"It's been interesting, I'll say that much," I said as I turned the wheel, my eyes focused on the roads. L.A. was no navigational joke. "How are things back in Indiana?"

He shrugged. "Shannon thinks you were kidnapped, and Derek Hart says he misses you."

I glanced over at him, my face scrunched up. "Derek Hart?" He wasn't even really in our circle of friends, a jock that crossed high school social boundaries thanks to having a brain.

"Apparently, he had planned to ask you out."

"Shut up."

Daniel turned in his seat. "No, seriously." I glanced over to find his eyes wide and his head nodding furiously. "He comes up to me almost every freaking day asking if I talked to you. And honestly, if you were home, I'd be pushing you toward that fine ass." He fanned his face.

I shook my head. "You're unbelievable."

"I said *if*, as in, if you hadn't married a Hollywood superstar."

"Well, welcome to my new Hollywood home," I said as I pulled into the driveway and waited for the gate to open.

He let out a gasp, his eyes widening at the sight in front of him. "Oh, my God, you live *here?*"

I smirked. "That was my reaction. This place is huge."

We pulled into the garage and got out. Stepping through the door, I heard Weston talking, then saw him sitting on one of the counter bar stools, his cell phone up at his ear.

The sound of Daniel's bag dropping to the floor drew Weston's attention, and he ended his call.

"It's him. Holy shit, it's really Weston Lockwood," Daniel said with dreamy eyes. "Damn, he got hotter."

Weston smirked and headed toward us. He just had to be dressed in those damn jeans I loved and a T-shirt that hugged him just right.

I tried to act all offended. "Hey! That's *my* husband you're talking about!"

"Lucky fucking bitch," Daniel said, still in his dreamy voice. He turned to me and grabbed onto my arms, jumping up and down. "You really did marry Weston-fucking-Lockwood! Holy fuck, holy fuck, holy fuck!"

I burst out laughing, as did Weston, and nodded. "Oh, so *now* you believe me."

"Well, hold on now. I haven't seen him kiss you yet. I think I need proof." He sighed and raked his eyes over Weston's body.

I smirked, and with my pointer finger summoned my husband over. He was chuckling, walking with a little extra swagger in his steps just to fuck with Daniel, and took me into his arms.

"Hi, baby girl," he whispered, running his nose along my neck.

"Hi."

He peppered kisses down the length of my jaw. "I missed you today."

"I missed you too," I managed to say before his lips devoured mine.

It was by no means a chaste kiss; he was out to prove to Daniel I was his. His arms relaxed around me but still remained wrapped around my waist.

Weston looked to Daniel and smiled. "Hi, Daniel, it's nice to finally meet you."

"Hi . . . ugh . . . Weston," Daniel managed to splutter out. It was obvious he was a bit star struck and almost looked like he was going to pass out.

I looked up at Weston and interrupted with our plans. "We're going to camp out tonight in the chaise room, watch some movies, eat some popcorn."

"Camp out? Do I get to join?" Weston asked, his eyes wide with hope.

"No straight boys allowed," Daniel said with a giggle.

A small pout formed on Weston's lips, and I couldn't help but smile.

"It's okay, baby. I think you can survive a couple of days without me."

"A couple? Wait, what? I don't get to see you enough as it is!" Weston shouted in protest, his arms tightening around me.

I let out a little giggle at his antics. "Sorry, but we have company. And I haven't seen Daniel in so long. He's only here for the weekend, and we're going to go sightseeing."

His face dropped at that. Sightseeing in L.A. was something he didn't need to do—he'd lived there long enough. Plus, he didn't need to see his own star on Hollywood Boulevard—he was there when it was placed. That, and there would be a ton of people who would recognize him.

Even after the time I'd been there, I'd hardly seen any of the sights, and was just as excited as Daniel. He looked between Daniel and me and sighed before giving me a soft kiss.

"I've got some work to do anyway. You two have fun."

Reaching up, I pulled his face down and planted another kiss on Weston, then grabbed Daniel's hand, leading him away.

After changing into some pajamas, we were curled up on the chaise, blankets draped around us as we perused the digital movie collection. We'd popped the popcorn and started up *Genesis*; one of Weston's movies.

Daniel filled me in on more gossip from home. Not many at school were missing me, not that I really expected them to, but they did notice the gap at Daniel's side. He'd made up a stretch of the truth, much like the one my mother was apparently spouting, about how I'd run off with some rich guy while in Vegas. No one in school seemed to believe it. I was just barely visible Wren Bradford in a sea of thousands of students, certainly not movie star catching material.

Last laugh was mine.

But I guess what bothered me most was not only did I have

rumors and lies circling at my current school, but my former as well.

"And, oh my God, Trevor was waiting for me at my locker this morning. Can you believe he was trying to get me back?"

"After he cheated on you?"

"Yes!" Daniel waved his hands in the air.

"Babe, you deserve so much better than Trevor. Please tell me there's someone else who's caught your eye."

"Well, last weekend I did go to Karrie's house party and met her cousin, Collin. He's a hottie, and a freshman at IU. We really hit it off, and he asked for my number, so maybe I'll see him when I get home. But we've got all weekend to talk about me and catch up on you. I just want to cuddle with you like old times. Fuck, I've missed you, Buttercup."

I noticed his voice had gotten quieter as he spoke, and when I looked up at his eyes, they were swimming with tears. I pulled him into a hug before settling his head in my lap, just like we used to.

We watched the movie, giggling about Weston's naked ass and how hot the sex scenes were. I may have divulged that the real thing was so much hotter.

After hordes of food and lots of reminiscing, we fell asleep; it was good to have my best friend again.

I didn't even wake when Weston picked me up and took me to bed.

"Come on, Daniel." I rolled my eyes as I watched him trying to get each strand of hair styled just right. "Sheesh, your hair looks fine. Fuck, man, you're worse than a girl!" I giggled, because he really was.

We were heading out to do some sightseeing, and I was excited to get going. I'd actually seen very little since I'd arrived over a month before. With school and settling in keeping me busy, it was fun getting to go see some of Hollywood's sights.

"Okay, I'm ready!" Daniel jumped in front of me wearing tight black jeans and his favorite blue "Yes, I might just be the man for you" T-shirt.

I laughed and shook my head. God, I'd missed him so much. "All right, let's go!"

We ran out of the house holding hands and jumped in my car. Weston had left earlier for a meeting, with a promise to see us later that night so we could all have dinner together, leaving Daniel and me the whole day to explore.

Our first stop was The Grove; it was a mega outdoor mall, and Weston said it was our best bet for locking eyes on some serious stars and getting in some great shopping. Daniel and I had a blast that included one of the largest book stores I'd ever seen. Small markets, big name stores, all of it thrown together and so unlike anything in Indiana.

And the food! It was almost a state fair like smorgasbord of options. A maze of small vendors with treats from meat on a stick, to crushed ice creations. There were stores with tons of Hollywood knick-knacks—all the touristy goods—and we picked out a few.

It was amazing. After dropping what I considered tons of money via my new credit card, courtesy of Weston, we drove toward Hollywood Boulevard. Finding parking was awful, especially with all the people walking around, but we eventually did.

It was quite a walk to Grauman's Chinese Theatre, but the entire sidewalk was covered with the pink stars.

"Holy crap, I didn't know that there were this many," I said in awe as I looked across the street to see the other side had the same pattern.

Daniel glanced at each star we passed. "I wonder where Weston's is."

"I didn't even think to ask."

"Oh! Oh! There's Damien Clark!" Daniel screeched as he bounced up and down.

I laughed and watched as he frantically pulled out his phone to take a picture.

"Didn't realize you were such a fan."

After snapping a few pics, he stuffed his phone back into his pocket.

"He had a new movie come out a few weeks ago and Shannon and I went to see it . . ." he fanned his face. "Wren, that man can not only act, he sets the screen on fire with his hotness."

My jaw dropped. "Hotter than my husband?"

He glanced down at the next star. "Maybe. It's tough. Damien is a bit older and has a more rugged look these days."

"Can I pout that you went with Shannon to go see it?" I pushed my bottom lip out for emphasis.

He tilted his chin up and shook his head. "No, because you left me and I was lonely."

I wrapped my arms around his arm and leaned my head against his shoulder. "So, I probably shouldn't tell you I go to school with Damien's daughters."

He stopped in his tracks, pulling me back. "Are they pretty?"

I nodded. "Very."

He started walking again. "I wish I could transfer to your school."

"For all the pretty girls?" I giggled.

"If there are pretty girls, you know there are pretty boys. So, there's that and, well, I just want to spend my freaking senior year getting into all sorts of trouble with you."

My head dropped and I nodded. "Yeah, I know what you mean. With the exception of this trouble you speak of."

The Asian roof line of Grauman's Chinese Theatre came in to view. It was set back from the street, which surprised me and explained why we couldn't see it.

"There it is!" The smile returned to his face, along with the excitement of being there.

It was infectious, and I was surprised how excited I was to see it as well. Maybe it was just the novelty of it, or the surreal feeling when the slabs of concrete with handprints started showing up. Ghosts of stars from the past century forever etched in the ground. Just knowing they had been there, seeing the evidence and their signature.

"Here he is!" Daniel screeched and waved me over.

Looking down at his name, his hands and feet, was when it really hit me. I, Wren Bradford, now Lockwood, of nowhere, was married to a celebrity.

It was for *Genesis*, the movie we'd watched the night before and one of his highest grossing films.

"God, Buttercup, look, his hands are *huge!*" Daniel smiled at me and winked.

"Yes, they are, and you know what they say about the size of a man's hands being proportional to his . . ." I stopped as Daniel burst out into a full belly laugh.

"Oh, stop bragging, you whore, and get down there so I can take a picture of your hands in . . . his." He managed to stop himself from saying husband, but given our surroundings, I don't think anyone would take it as more than a wish.

I bent down and slowly ran my fingertips through Weston's handprints, and an idea hit me. I pulled my ring out from around my neck and slid it on. Daniel had nearly shit when I showed it to him. I then placed my hands in Weston's, as Daniel took a picture—my ring on full, shiny display. I couldn't wait to show him.

"Selfie time." Daniel turned as I stood and pressed his cheek to mine, both of us smiling like fools as he tapped the button a dozen times just to make sure he got the best angle.

Then we walked into the theatre where we took the most awe inspiring tour. We learned that since 1927 it had been the home of some of the most famous red carpet movie premieres. Weston had also told me once that he'd been there many times, and as Daniel and I wandered around, I wondered if I'd ever get the chance to visit with Weston sometime.

The next day was kind of solemn. We spent the day at the house, goofing off in the pool and trying to keep the evening at bay.

"This was not nearly long enough," Daniel said as we lay on the shallow ledge of the pool, letting the few inches of water cool us down from the sun that was right overhead.

"I know."

"We barely got to see anything."

"We got to see each other," I said.

His bottom lip jutted out. "Not nearly enough."

"Enough to hold us until Christmas."

"Are you coming home then?" he asked.

"I hope so. At least some during the holiday."

"You can't miss our annual cookie baking."

I reached over and squeezed his hand. "I'll do everything I can to not miss that."

"Better."

"Though just think about next year. Did you see all the counter space in that kitchen?" I asked, side-eying him. "The island alone has enough room for a dozen batches."

He pursed his lips. "Stop trying to bribe me. What would we do with that many anyway?"

"We could pass them out to some of Weston's famous friends."

He perked up at that. "Is Damien Clark a friend?"

I laughed and slapped at his chest. "I don't know, but I can find out."

"Just curious."

I rolled my eyes before picking up my phone. Weston helped me set it up to the Bluetooth sound system the house was wired with, which let me play music in whatever room or outside area I was in over some fantastic speakers.

I switched Pandora stations, finding something a little bit happier. Justin Timberlake's "Sexy Back" started up and Daniel started dancing in his chair.

"By the way, girl, *you* are bringing sexy back. I mean, do you even know how hot you are in that . . . is it called a swimsuit?"

I laughed, but could still feel my cheeks heating. "I think Sophie called it a monokini . . . whatever that is. And thank you."

"Seriously. You'd have a dozen guys fawning over you if we were at a public pool."

"I prefer the one falling off the treadmill when he saw me."

"Wait, what?"

I nodded. "I got out of the pool, heard a thump, and found Weston had tripped and been flung across to the wall. All because he got distracted when I got out of the pool."

"He still got in his exercise though, didn't he," Daniel said with a wink.

My mouth popped wide before I hid my face in my hands.

A huge smile formed on his face. "I'm right, aren't I? See, you're smoking hot!"

"Never really felt like that in Indiana."

"Midwestern high school. I mean, you've always been pretty, but all guys at our school stare at the girls dressed like sluts."

"Daniel!"

"It's the truth. Becca Miller had a nip-slip last week her shirt was so low cut. They made her go home early, and I think she got a ride from a bunch of guys from the basketball team."

I shook my head. "You're awful."

"It's the truth."

I let out a laugh, but it was cut short by an alarm going off on my phone. My stomach dropped, all the joy leaving me.

Daniel slipped his hand into mine. "I'm going to need constant updating. Like, annoyingly constant."

I nodded. "Me too. You're the only one I've even talked to."

"Doesn't matter, I'm the most important anyway."

That got a small laugh from me and I squeezed his hand. "I wish you could stay."

"Me too."

The alarm went off again and we got up, finally facing the bitter truth—it was time to take Daniel to the airport.

It was a quiet drive to the airport, Daniel and I both struggling with the loss we already felt from his departure. We'd had an incredible weekend. Spending time with him made me ache for home and the simple but enjoyable life I'd left behind.

"Love you, Wren," he whispered into my ear as he wound his arm around my waist.

"Love you, too," I said, looking up at him as I squeezed him tight.

"Make sure that man of yours takes good care of you," he choked out as we walked toward the security checkpoint.

I couldn't respond. A lump had formed in my throat and the tears began to leak from my eyes.

"It'll be summer before you know it, and we'll be together again." He smiled at me through his own tears and leaned down to kiss my cheek.

Tears dripped from my eyes and my chest ached as I watched Daniel disappear behind the security zone. Once again, I felt alone and suddenly wished Weston had come with us.

Just as I was turning to head home, more than a bit depressed, I heard my name being called.

I turned to find Cloe, Charlotte's sister, coming out of baggage claim with what I assumed was her father behind her. There was a sudden swarm of paparazzi in the area.

Boy, was Daniel going to be bummed when I told him he'd missed Damien Clark by less than five minutes.

"Wren!"

"Cloe! Hi! What are you doing here?"

"Just got back from an audition," she said, beaming.

"How'd it go?" I asked.

"Awesome! They offered me the part. And it was great, because my dad's going to be in it with me!" She gestured to her father, who was being flashed to death by cameras.

Unlike with Weston, I recognized him as soon as I laid eyes on him. He managed to break free for a moment and joined us.

"Dad, come meet my friend," Cloe said, waving him closer.

"Hello, Mr. Clark." I glanced behind him to find the large amount of paparazzi that was headed our way before holding out my hand. "I'm Wren Lockwood."

"Please, call me Damien," he said, giving me his movie star grin. Oh, how Daniel would have swooned. "My daughters tell me you're related to Weston Lockwood."

I nodded, a bit starstruck, before choking out, "Ah . . . y-yes . . . older brother."

He stared at me, deep in thought, before smirking. "Please tell your *brother* that I said hello. Maybe we'll have lunch and catch up."

I began to panic a bit from all of the paparazzi, shying away from the cameras. Damien told us we better get moving, so Cloe grabbed my arm and started walking away. I dropped my head and slipped on my sunglasses.

"Just ignore them," she whispered. "I always do."

I tried, and we raced out the doors. I said goodbye to Cloe and Damien as I hurried to my car, which when I finally climbed in and locked the doors, felt more like a safe haven in that moment.

As I drove away, I could see the flashes still going off in my rearview mirror. I prayed there were no clear pictures of me because somehow I didn't think that would go over well with Weston.

When I was off airport property, I called Daniel.

"Miss me that much already?" he said as he answered.

I let out a laugh. "You are *not* going to believe who I just met."

Chapter Twenty-One

OUR AWKWARD THANKSGIVING

Thanksgiving was only a few days away, and I was happy to have a couple extra days off school beforehand so I could prepare our meal and pick up my dad from the airport. I wanted to cook the meal myself, having done it the past few years, but I forgot the scale of people at this occasion versus the past, and I needed the extra time.

It was going to be an interesting holiday, for sure. My dad was coming in that night and leaving Friday morning, unable to get much time off work on short notice, especially with his job.

I made sure there was no chance Natalie would show up and ruin the day. Weston assured me she always spent it with her family, thousands of miles away. I understood they still had to maintain a working relationship for now, but she didn't need to be coming into our home whenever she felt like it, or at all in my opinion. Maybe I'd become a bitch when it came to her . . . maybe I needed to. Every time he kicked her out, she came back that much sooner.

The whole Natalie situation had become a huge sore point with us, and between us. Weston revoked all of her access, but she was still getting in somehow. He had a feeling it was Mallory helping her in, due to her recent behavior when Natalie came to his office, but with no proof, there wasn't much he could do. Joe was monitoring the entries at the gate, but nothing had come up yet. Even Joe was having trouble figuring it out as only the names with cards he approved were coming up on his access report, and no out of the ordinary access was being granted.

"Has her access really been denied, or is that just what you're telling me?" I asked, frustrated at the situation as he walked back in from making certain Natalie left the property.

Weston sighed and rubbed his face, sitting down on the armrest of the couch. "Joe revoked her card and changed the access codes on all the doors. You heard him say that yourself. I had him change the gate last week."

"Well, someone is helping her in," I said, my anger leaking out. "Someone is violating our security, Weston, and it needs to stop."

"Thank you, Captain Obvious," he said, sarcasm lacing his tone. "We've been rehashing the same conversation for two weeks."

I glared at him, arms crossed over my chest. "You could be a little less accommodating every time she gets in."

"I've thrown her out almost every time," he argued.

"Half of them nearly an hour after she arrived!"

"We have work, Wren!" he snapped, and jumped up from his seat on the couch.

"Then do it at the fucking office!" I jumped up as well. There was no way he was going to run away from what I had to say. "She plays you, Weston. She knows you have trouble putting work off, so she's using that as an excuse to keep close to you. She's up to something."

"I know," he whispered, his hand reaching out for me. "But I only want you, Wren."

With reluctance, because I was still ticked about her arrival, I slipped my hand in his, allowing him to draw me near. His arms wrapped around me, my own slipping around his shoulders, fingers playing with his hair, which had lost its buzzed shortness at the back of his head.

"I just want to get this project with her done, and then I'm never working with her again," he said against my neck before placing a lingering kiss there. "I don't want to fight about her anymore, baby."

"I don't want to fight, period."

He shook his head. "No more."

"I want peace."

"Make love, not war," he whispered into my ear, his hands roaming around my body.

"What are you doing?" I asked, a smirk forming on my face.

His lips kissed down my neck, hand grabbing my ass, pulling me closer. "I was thinking make-up sex. Baby girl, you are fucking sexy when you get feisty."

"You are a horny one, aren't you, Mr. Lockwood?"

"Only for you, Mrs. Lockwood."

I led him to our bedroom, where we continued with the "make love, not war" theme.

The day before Thanksgiving, Weston repeated his desire to go to the airport with me to pick up my dad, but I reminded him it wasn't a good idea, especially after what happened with Damien Clark. Instead, he was forced to wait at home while I went alone. Weston wanted to hire Dad a driver, but I had to reinforce that it wasn't my dad's style and he probably wouldn't appreciate the gesture.

It was great to see my dad's face coming out of baggage claim. I'd forgotten how long it had been since I'd seen him.

"Wren!" he called out, beaming at me. His brown eyes were bright, and his salt and peppered hair was mashed on one side, probably from sleeping on the plane.

"Hey, Dad." I threw my arms around his neck, and he lifted me up off the ground.

He placed a kiss on my temple as he set me down. "How's my girl?" he asked as we waited for his bags.

I laughed, unable to contain the humor from his innocent question. "Wow, that's a loaded question if I've ever heard one."

He chuckled. "Yes, I suppose it is. You've grown."

I scrunched my brow at him. "Grown? Are you trying to say I've gained weight?"

"No, no. Not physically, but maybe, I don't know, emotionally?" he said, though it ended up being more of a question.

"Very possible with all that's going on."

His bag showed up, and we headed out toward the parking garage.

"How's the windy city?" I asked.

"Busy as ever. They bought a hundred planes this year and we've been busy upgrading them."

When we made it to my car, he stared at it with wide eyes for a moment before frowning. Unfortunately, I knew it wasn't going to be as fun of a drive home with my father as it was with my best friend.

"This is your car?" he asked. I nodded in response as I helped load his bag in the trunk. "He bought it for you? Your . . . husband?"

"Yes, Weston bought it for me." I climbed in and turned the ignition on.

The GPS began talking, and he grumbled. "This"—he gestured to the LED screen—"is how you get around?"

"It's a great help, otherwise I'd get lost. Graham put in all the places I need to go and taught me how to use it."

He scrunched his brow. "Graham?"

"Julia's assistant."

"Julia?"

"Weston's assistant."

"So your husband's assistant has an assistant?"

I chuckled. "Weston has a whole camp. There are four assistants in total, plus his pack from growing up, one of them being a partner, the security guys, the cook, and I know there's a housekeeper that comes in, or elves," I joked. "I haven't figured it out yet. The list is endless, and every day it seems I learn of a new one."

Dad shook his head. "How are you coping with all of this, Wren? Sounds like you don't get much time together."

I shrugged my shoulders. "Time is a luxury, but we deal with it."

"So, what are the three of us having for Thanksgiving?" he asked as he watched the scenery fly by. It was obvious he was a little uncomfortable; he'd never been in a car with me driving.

"Three of us?" I scoffed. "Oh, no. Try the nine of us."

"Nine? Are all of his employees coming as well?"

I shook my head and smiled. "Weston's extended family, and one assistant that is his brother's fiancée."

"What about his parents?"

"They're kind of a forbidden topic. Alive, but I don't know anything about them."

He was too stunned to respond, instead changing the topic. He asked how school was going, and I told him about Charlotte and my other friends. When he asked where my wedding ring was, I told him how we were keeping it secret until I graduated. While driving, I pulled the necklace that held my ring over my head and handed it to him. The gasp of shock did not go unnoticed.

We pulled up to the gate and waited for the large iron doors to open.

"This is your home?" he asked in disbelief.

"Yup."

I pulled into the garage, next to Weston's Bentley and the Range Rover. Strange how fluid and normal it had become and I didn't even notice.

We got out and grabbed his bag from the trunk, then walked through the door to the kitchen where Weston was waiting for us. He was sitting on a stool at the island, his foot tapping nervously on the ground, then stood when he saw me come in.

He grabbed for my hand, and I turned to face my father, my arm wrapping around his.

"Dad, this is my husband, Weston Lockwood. Weston, this is

my dad, John Bradford," I said as I introduced them, noticing and realizing for the first time just how close in age they were.

Weston held out his hand for a shake, and my dad stared at him, wide-eyed. I knew then he recognized Weston. Dad cleared his throat and held out his hand.

"Nice to meet you, Weston."

"Likewise, Mr. Bradford."

"John will do," Dad said.

Weston gave him a nod before smiling as he addressed us. "Well, Kelly's prepared us an excellent meal. And don't be mad, but she helped with some of the prep work for tomorrow for you and also left a couple of recipes."

"Thank you, Kelly!" I called out, smiling.

Weston snickered and my dad looked around the room, noticing the blonde woman standing at the sink.

"More than welcome, Wren," she replied, turning and smiling at me, drying her hands on a towel. "I just got the turkey ready for you to put in the oven in the morning and cut up some bread for the dressing so it can dry out. And I may have also peeled a dozen or so potatoes."

I walked around the island and gave her a hug. "You saved me a few valuable hours."

"No problem. I just wanted to help you out with some prep while dinner was cooking."

We left Kelly to finish cleaning up and headed to the dining room. As we took our seats, I could see the look of disbelief and amazement at not only the room, but Kelly's cooking.

"So, Weston, I have to ask . . . why'd you ask my eighteen-year-old daughter to marry you after only a day of knowing her?" My dad, blunt as ever.

Shit. I should have known that was coming.

"I'd say it was the feeling of overwhelming peace and happiness I felt when I was around her and not wanting it to end. The alcohol just helped us make a decision to stay that way."

I wanted to kick him. Drinking wasn't a big deal to Weston, and he had the tendency to forget that according to the law, I wasn't allowed to drink. He never thought about it because he was thirty-one, and I was his wife. My dad, however, wouldn't look at it that way.

"Did you just say the alcohol made 'us'?" my dad asked. "As in, you were both drinking?"

"We ordered a bottle of champagne with dinner, and then a second," Weston replied, confused for a moment, before he caught on to where my dad was going.

"There is no 'we' there. Wren is only eighteen, not of the legal age to drink. You're telling me you took my daughter out, got her drunk, and married her?"

"Dad, stop," I said, my hand on Weston to halt him. "Weston didn't shove it down my throat. I drank it of my own free will. Now, the how doesn't matter anymore. Weston and I are married. The end. This is your new son-in-law, for better or for worse. Done."

My dad pursed his lips and looked at me. "When did you get so mature?" He shoveled another huge bite into his mouth, practically moaning as he chewed. "I wonder how much of this I can stow in my luggage. Talk about fantastic."

I let out a laugh. "Kelly is awesome."

I'd gone to the grocery store days before with my list of ingredients in hand and walked out with a full cart, including a twenty-five-pound turkey. Hopefully, it would be more than enough to feed a crowd of nine . . . well, eight and a half. I didn't expect Arianna to eat much.

Dad spent the morning with me in the kitchen, catching up. I told him more about my school and the friends I'd made there. He shook his head at most of it. It was unreal for me to imagine the life I lived now, and even more so for him.

I had the turkey in the oven, stuffing both in the bird and waiting to be cooked, and had multiple dishes ready and waiting to go into the other oven once the turkey was further along. It was nice to take a break, relaxing out on the porch with my dad, having a snack before I headed back in to change and finish cooking.

An hour or so later, people started to arrive. First, it was Julia and Miles. It was a tense moment, but quickly shifted.

"I missed you," Weston said as he wrapped his arms around Miles, his voice and face full of emotion.

"Missed you, too," Miles replied. He then turned to me and held out his hand, which I took.

Julia, friendly as ever, gave me a hug and asked what she could do to help.

The exchange didn't go unnoticed by my dad, but he didn't ask.

Julia and I put the last of the side items in one of the ovens, while Miles helped pull the turkey out. A few minutes later Lance showed up, giving me a huge hug. He then did the same to my dad before striking up conversation. Dad was a little taken aback by Lance's affectionate welcoming but was won over in seconds by his friendly personality.

Next to arrive were Sophie, Carson, and little Arianna, who made a beeline for Weston. The little munchkin knew where she was going to get some spoiling.

"Wehtun!" Arianna screeched, her little feet pounding up and down on the floor, unable to contain her excitement.

I smiled, my ovaries near combusting at the sight of him bending down and scooping the little toddler up in the air. What was it about a man smiling while holding a baby that made a woman's body react like that? He wasn't doing anything out of the ordinary, just making a tiny little girl laugh and snuggling her close, but it was one of the sexiest things I'd ever seen. Then again, *Weston* was already one of the sexiest things I'd ever seen. I let out an audible sigh at the sight.

Sophie gave me an exuberant hug. It was hard to believe it'd been a few weeks since I'd seen her. I'd seen Carson more often. She even gave my dad a squeeze, surprising him.

"So, who's this little girl?" Dad asked, walking up to Weston.

"This is my little Princess Ari," he said, beaming.

Dad's eye popped open. "*Your* Princess Ari?"

"No, *my* Princess Ari," Carson interjected, pulling Ari from Weston's arms. "He likes to think she's his."

"Wehtun! Wehtun!" Ari protested, her tiny fist balled in Weston's shirt.

Carson shook his head and handed her back with a sigh. "She's my baby, but you wouldn't think so with her attachment to him."

"Hey, she likes him. That's a good sign," my dad said with a grin. "Means he'll be a good dad."

He didn't mean anything by it, not knowing what had been going on, but I could feel my face heat up.

"I keep telling him to go make his own, now that he's married," Carson said, earning an elbow in the ribs from Sophie. "Ouch! What was that for?"

Dad had gone a bit pale, looking back and forth between Weston and me.

"One day," Sophie began, stressing the words and taking Ari from Weston's arms, "he'll make a great dad. When they're ready."

"Which better not be for a long, long time," my dad added.

"How old were you when I was born, Dad?" I asked as I crossed my arms over my chest and leaned against the island.

My dad grumbled under his breath, "Doesn't mean you should have a kid that young."

"No, it doesn't. We'll have one precisely when we're meant to."

Weston smiled and kissed my forehead, gathering me in his arms.

A few minutes later everyone grabbed a bowl or plate and headed to the dining room. We passed the dishes around, taking bits and spoonfuls until they were all back on the table, and began eating.

Conversation was flowing, people had smiles on their faces as they stuffed them, and I received compliment after compliment on my cooking.

"You did good on this, Wren," my dad said, a note of surprise in his tone.

"Mike taught me. We took cooking away from Mom."

He chuckled. "I remember the first time she cooked a pot roast and it was still raw in the center when she served it."

"Time has not improved that." I shook my head, remembering all the awful tasting foods she tried to make over the years. Recipes that sounded good but were way above her skills.

"I can see that of your mom." Weston laughed. "She certainly is . . . unique."

Dad and I agreed, laughing.

"So, tell me about your parents, Weston," Dad prompted.

The whole room went silent with the exception of Ari's giggles.

I knew there was something off regarding Weston's relationship with his parents. Julia had mentioned they were estranged, but the silence my father's question garnered was a response I was not expecting. I turned to Weston, his face a hard mask, eyes sharp.

He looked about to blow when Miles spoke, defusing the situation, "Our parents are well. They're spending the holiday in Aspen with some friends."

Dad was always an observant man, and he *saw* the signs, but he decided to plow right on through, ignoring Miles. "A little unfair, isn't it? You've met your wife's parents, but she hasn't met yours? Kind of shady, if you ask me."

"Weston doesn't talk . . ." Miles tried again, but Dad interrupted him.

"I don't think I was talking to you, was I?" My dad was starting to spoil the meal.

I let out a groan. "Dad, please."

He shook his head. "I want to know why my son-in-law hasn't

introduced his wife to his parents. I mean, you've just said that they are alive, so what's the problem?"

"Dad, please," I begged again, trying to keep the peace. I knew it was a touchy subject, and I felt that it wasn't the time or the place for it.

Weston was practically vibrating next to me.

Dad stared at him, waiting for answers. "Are you ashamed of her?"

"What?" Weston asked incredulously.

"Does anyone outside of this little circle even know you're married? I understand keeping it a secret from the press until she's out of school, which is a great idea, but what about your own family?"

"My family is here. *This* here, these people"—Weston gestured to all of us sitting at the table—"are my family. I have *no* parents to speak about."

Out of the corner of my eye, I could see Julia's head shaking and Miles slump down in his seat. Weston was rigid beside me, and I gathered up his hand in mine. The gesture seemed to relax him, but only a small amount.

"Hmph, you could have just said you don't talk to them, or you don't have a relationship with them," Dad said, shoveling a forkful of turkey into his mouth.

I stared, slack jawed, at my father. He'd probed and then when he finally got his answer, acted like it was nothing.

"Fine, I don't have a relationship with my parents. You probably wouldn't either if your father got you addicted to drugs, just so you could keep up with the hectic schedule he roped you into as your manager," Weston revealed.

I gasped in horror, staring at him, but it didn't deter him. He kept right on with his rant.

"Do you know what it's like to come down off a speed high, John? Do you know what it's like to find out your own father was drugging you? To crave a drug you didn't even know you were taking?" Weston shook beside me before yelling out, "I trusted him! He was my father, and he was supposed to have my best interest at heart. Thank fuck I didn't have any lasting effects, besides the loss of our relationship. Nothing brings family together like the lows of withdrawal."

The whole table looked sullen with the exception of me and my dad, who were staring at Weston in stunned fascination. So much suddenly made sense. Why everyone was so protective of Weston, and why he never wanted to talk about them. Also why he had such a close-knit group. It was more than just being a movie star. My heart ached for him.

Weston's jaw was tense, his gaze still locked on my dad. I held the torrent of emotions and questions at bay for the moment, for Weston's sake. He needed me, the calm in his storm.

My hand moved to cup his cheek and divert his eyes to me. As soon as they met he slumped into his chair, forehead resting against mine. There was pain in his eyes, and a lost little boy I knew well. It was his fantasies that had brought us together, after all. His hand covered mine and he leaned forward, placing a light, reverent kiss on my lips.

"Mmm, Wren, this turkey is great. Hey, why'd you all stop eating?" Dad asked as he looked around.

At that, everyone picked up their utensils and dug back into their plates. Leave it to my dad to restore the peace at the dinner table after being the one to disturb it.

Slowly, the mounds of food on each dish depleted. Plates were emptied while others were refilled with second and third goes.

Weston barely finished his plate before excusing himself. I glanced over to Miles who stared after him, his brow scrunched up.

"Wren didn't know," I heard Julia whisper. "It was going to happen sooner or later."

Miles's jaw ticked as he looked over to my dad.

"I'm not going to apologize," my dad said before taking another bite. "You all have his best interest at heart. Mine? Is with that girl." He pointed his knife in my direction. "She had her life ripped away while very little changed in his. When a suspicious topic comes up, you bet your ass I'm going to find out why. I'll do what I can to protect her, however I can."

I smiled across to my father before standing and walking over to him. "Thank you, Daddy," I said as I kissed his forehead before going to search for Weston.

He hadn't been the same since the conversation about his parents. I found him outside by the pool, a beer in his hand as he gazed out at the city.

"Weston?" I called to him, placing my hand on his arm.

He turned to me with a pained expression.

"Did you ever read the tabloids about starlings having meltdowns and drug problems and how their parents drove them over the edge?" he asked.

I nodded, somewhat surprised he was opening up. Then again, after what he divulged at dinner, I was certain my dad stirred up some painful memories for him.

"I was one of the first. Though I went on to be successful, I still live with it every day." His blue eyes shined with tears he was holding back. "I never want to do that to our kids. I want them to do what they want to do, and not push them into something that is beyond their control."

I smiled and wrapped my arms around his waist, snuggling into his chest. "What if we have a girl and she meets a stranger in Vegas at eighteen and wants to get married to an older man?" I asked, teasing him.

"No way in hell is my little princess going to do such a thing," he replied, his tone lighter, and pulled me closer to kiss the top of my head.

He was so warm, I sighed and snuggled deeper. "We should go back in and join the others. They're probably ready for dessert."

He nodded in response. "Thanks, baby girl. I should have told you before now. It's just . . . difficult for me to talk about."

I cupped his cheek in my hand, drawing his face down to mine. "You can talk to me about anything. I'm here for you. I'm your wife, after all."

He smiled, leaning down to press his lips to mine. Deepening the kiss, our tongues moved together, the tang of his beer overpowering his natural taste. His hands dug into my flesh, pulling me even closer, a moan escaping from deep within him.

A gruff clearing of a throat brought us out of the lustful fog we were falling into. We looked over to find my dad in the doorway watching us.

My cheeks grew hot and I stepped back. "I'll go get the pies."

When everyone had their fill of pie and were entering the food coma stage, people began to head home. Sophie, Carson, and Ari were the first to head out, followed shortly by Lance. Julia and I were cleaning up the table, while my dad, Weston, and Miles were in the basement watching football.

"I think that went pretty well," Julia said as we stacked the dishes on top of each other, walking back to the kitchen.

"Me too," I said with a smile.

"Your dad seemed to take everything pretty well."

I chuckled a little, thinking about the previous night's conversation. "He pushed Weston on purpose."

"That's what fathers do."

"Not all fathers," I said, thinking back about Weston's.

Julia leaned against the counter and let out a sigh. "I was there that day, the last time he saw them."

"You were?"

"Yeah," she whispered. "Miles had taken me home for Christmas to meet his family. We'd only been dating for about six months at that time, but I was already smitten and in love with him."

"What happened, Julia?" I asked. I needed to know more, my stomach still twisting from what I'd learned.

She shook her head. "Nothing good. His mother, Joanna, is

a kind woman, but she left Weston with no choice. Their father, Richard . . ." Julia let out a long sigh ". . . he's a piece of work. He still doesn't see that he did anything wrong. Because of that, Weston's cut off all contact with them."

"I don't blame him. What an awful thing to do to anyone, let alone your own child."

She nodded. "I know he misses his mom often, but he's still so angry with his father. I wasn't working for him back then, but apparently it took years for the effects of withdrawal to subside. He suffered for years. Stephanie, his old assistant, filled me in on it. She and his PR people had done a lot to keep his condition from the tabloids."

I slapped my hand over my mouth as tears filled my eyes. To think he'd been in that kind of pain because of his father, and the permanent damage that could have been done.

Julia wrapped her arms around me, and I felt the tears begin to fall. They were all so protective of him because of all that he'd gone through, not only as an actor, but a recovering drug addict. A drug that was given to him without his knowledge or consent.

A little while later we joined the boys, and I curled into Weston, holding him close.

The next morning I cooked breakfast, giving Kelly the day off again. I hugged my dad tight when he came into the kitchen. Everything I'd learned about Weston's father made me appreciate mine so much more.

I went to dress, hating that I had to take my dad to the airport already. When I was done, I found Weston and my dad sitting outside, the doors wide open, talking.

"You got the shit stick in the form of a father, but he's the only one you got. Part of me wants to encourage you to talk to them, because they won't be around forever, but the other part says screw them for what they did to you. I don't get to see Wren as much as I'd like, but that doesn't mean I don't love her with all my heart."

"She loves you too," Weston said, giving my dad an honest smile.

Dad cleared his throat and nodded. "Yeah, I know. Wren's a good girl."

"One of the things I love about her."

"Do you? Love her, that is."

Weston paused, a small smile on his lips. "We're getting there. I can tell you I feel more for her than I've ever felt for anyone else. I'm . . . afraid to say if it's love or not yet. I can tell you it's very strong, though."

Dad nodded in understanding. "Gotta say, it's kind of weird to have a son-in-law who's only seven years younger than I am. Feels like we should be friends instead of some weird parent/child relationship."

Weston chuckled. "We can have whatever kind of relationship you want, John."

"Take good care of my little girl, Weston, please. Don't make me come back down here to shoot you, and we'll be just fine. Okay?"

"I'll do my best not to get shot," Weston replied with a snicker, slapping my dad's shoulder.

"Ready?" I called from the doorway.

They turned toward me and stood.

"Well, Weston, it was nice meeting you," my dad said, holding out his hand.

Weston smiled at him as they shook. "You too, John."

Weston gave me a kiss goodbye, and then Dad and I headed out, back to the airport.

"Are you happy, Wren?" he asked as we entered the airport. Our drive had been talk about Weston and possibly going out to Chicago with him for a visit.

I smiled at him. "Dad, I'm married to a wonderful man, and while my marriage is unconventional and life is a bit interesting at the moment, I'm very happy."

He smiled and pulled me close. "Good. That's all I want, and remember I'm always here for you." He leaned down and kissed the top of my head. "You'll always be my little girl."

"I know," I replied with a smile. I hugged him tight, relishing in the warmth of my father.

He kissed my hair again and whispered, "Love you, Wren."

"Love you too, Dad."

As I stood in the airport and watched my dad disappear from sight, I realized how thankful I was for him, and all my family.

Chapter Twenty-Two

OUR LANCE AND THE DIVA

I N THE WEEKS FOLLOWING THANKSGIVING THERE WAS A SHIFT. Weston wasn't home much, which wasn't a surprise, but what was a surprise was the change in him. It was barely noticeable at first, but after two weeks of waning affection, I began to feel like a guest who'd overstayed their welcome.

The stress on Weston grew worse with each passing day. One of his project timelines had practically derailed, and others were on the verge. Add in the stress of Natalie's continuous presence, and a rift began to divide us.

His mood soured with each day, leaking into our home life, infecting it. Constantly pissed, he would snap at me for no apparent reason, sometimes apologizing, sometimes not. It seemed like we were barely communicating at all. When I did call him, it either went to voicemail, or a quick "Wren, I can't talk, call you back," and then no call. Texts were answered, but short, three or four words. Loneliness settled in, and I didn't know when or if it would get better.

It came across in my playing, the piano ringing with low, long notes with a dark undercurrent.

We were fighting more and more. One night, I wanted to make up because I needed him close to reenergize my spirit, but when I wrapped my arms around his shoulders and kissed his neck, he removed them.

"I'm trying to work," he snapped.

"Work?" I asked, moving from behind him to in front of him, his eyes still glued to the computer. "You've barely been home in two days. Can't you spend five minutes with me?"

"I *have* to get this done tonight. I promise we'll have time later, but right now . . ." He sighed, his eyes lifting to mine. "I just need you to leave me alone."

It was a gut punch, and I was stuck between burning anger and wanting to cry. "This has been going on for weeks. How much longer is 'later'?"

He let out an annoyed groan. "Later is later. Okay?"

"Not a problem, Mr. Lockwood. Have fun sleeping alone," I spat and turned, walking out the door. Maybe it was childish, but I was going to do what he asked

I slept in one of the extra rooms that night, alone.

After that, I spent a lot of free time with Charlotte shopping for Christmas presents, trying to keep myself busy and away from the huge, empty house that seemed to become colder with each passing day. I had no idea what to get for Weston, but after a trip to an adult store, I at least had one gift for him. Though we hadn't had sex in a week.

There were no plans for the holidays that I knew of, but with how little I'd actually gotten to talk to Weston, it hadn't really had a chance to be brought up. I hoped to see my mom sometime during the break, and that he'd come with me, but I wasn't sure if that was doable.

He didn't make it for dinner most nights, often cancelling last minute, causing a backup of leftovers in the fridge. When he came home earlier one night, I was excited. But then I heard him screaming rooms away, the excitement dropped and so did my stomach. When I got to the kitchen, he was a mess. His hair was disheveled, suit wrinkled, and he looked exhausted.

"Schedule a meeting with the fucking diva. She's not going to put production off any fucking longer!" he screamed into the receiver.

He slammed the phone down on the counter and let out a frustrated yell, making me jump. I waited a moment for him to calm.

"Are you okay?" I asked, but as soon as his eyes snapped to mine, I realized I should have stayed where I was and never spoken.

Nothing good would come from his mood.

"No, Wren, I'm not okay," he snapped, pulling the tie from around his neck and shrugging off his jacket. "I'm losing money by the shitton on this fucking deal. I'm really stressed, and your fucking nagging is really grating right now."

I felt the blood drain from my face and tears sting my eyes, along with the need to get away from him. His words stung, and if I stayed, it could only get worse. Each day his attitude wore me down and made me question why I stayed to take it.

"Nagging?" I nodded with pursed lips. "Dinner's in the fridge," I said flatly before turning and walking out and down the hall.

Whispered words of "fuck" hit my ears as I ran away, followed by what I assumed was the kitchen table overturning and chairs being slammed around.

Tears fell from my eyes that night as I attempted to fall asleep again in a cold and empty bed that wasn't ours.

Nothing was right anymore, and I began to wonder if the void could be filled.

I arrived home late one night after a study session with Charlotte, hoping I was ready for our exam in the morning. The driveway had multiple extra cars, most I recognized as they included Julia and Carson's.

Upon walking in, I heard commotion in the large, open living room where Julia first learned I was Weston's wife. There was a blonde sporting a bitch brow, her arms crossed in front of her, one leg over the other. Just by her demeanor, I wondered if she was the diva that Weston bitched so much about.

Her eyes shot over to me standing in the doorway, still dressed in my uniform, causing the whole room to turn to me. It was just Julia, Carson, Weston, the diva, and who I assumed was her manager, or maybe assistant.

"Can we help you?" the diva asked in a snotty and condescending tone, earning her a glare from Weston.

I was taken aback by her hostility and wondered if *bitch* wasn't a better description of her.

Weston waved me over, which with his past and current mood, I was reluctant to do. I walked to stand next to him. Julia smiled at me and I gave her a small hug as I walked past, then high fived Carson.

"Talia, this is Wren Lockwood. Wren, this is Talia Clark. I believe you've heard me call her the diva."

She scowled at him, glaring, while I held out my hand.

"Pleased to meet you."

"Aw, aren't you cute?" She rolled her eyes and looked at my hand in disgust. "Get that thing away from me. Looks like you just came from school, so who knows what germs you have crawling on that hand. Ugh."

I quirked my brow at her. "Wow, I guess 'bitch' was a good assessment of you, seeing as you can't even be civil to someone you've just met."

Carson was behind me, snickering, and I could see Julia's lips twitching, trying not to laugh. I looked up at Weston to see him smiling down at me, but his eyes were tight.

"Who is this rodent?" Talia demanded.

"Talia, you will watch what you say to her. Did you not hear her last name? Lockwood. She's my family. I'm not bringing your family into this, so don't you fucking dare bring mine," Weston seethed at her. It shut her up, her lips pursed. "Now, back on task.

You have a lot to think about, because I've had enough of your shit. Either you get on board, *now*, or I'm cancelling your contract."

She sat up straight, her eyes wide as she spat, "You can't do that!"

His eyes narrowed on her. "Try me."

"Hey! Is this where the party's at?" Lance's voice called out, echoing around the room. He was grinning like a fool. "Wren!" He swept me up in his arms, holding me high above the ground and making me squeal.

"Lance, put her down!" Weston growled.

"You're no fun." He pouted at Weston as he sat my feet back on the floor.

Then he saw her, the diva, and I swear I could hear some cheesy song playing in the background due to the look on his face.

"Hey," he said, grinning and popping his head in her direction.

I almost fell over when Lance and his antics received a very different reaction to his appearance than I did. Talia's eyes softened, her arms relaxed, and she smiled at him, her gaze taking all of him in. The reaction didn't go unnoticed by anyone, and finally Weston had his way in.

"Oh, Talia, I don't believe you've met the stunt coordinator on the film yet? Lance, this is Talia. Talia, Lance. You two will be working very closely together as soon as she starts to show up to the preproduction training."

Lance grinned at her. "Ah, so you're the pretty little thing that's been causing such a ruckus." Her sudden good mood faltered. "Well, come on, let's see what you've got."

Talia took his challenge, standing with the rest of us, her eyes set on him. "And?"

"Oh, very nice, very nice indeed."

"You're a cocky one," she said, hands moving to her hips.

"And you're a bitch. A very sexy bitch. I like you." Lance nodded, his tongue peeking out to wet his lips. "Very nice, indeed."

I was expecting her to yell, call Lance something nasty, but instead she smiled at him and turned toward Weston. "I'll see you on

Monday." She picked up her purse, signaled to the guy with her, then grabbed hold of Lance's arm as she passed. "See you soon, big boy."

He grinned down at her. "I can't wait to be very close and in your personal space on Monday."

"I bet." She winked at him as she walked off.

We looked between each other for an answer for whatever it was that happened between them while Lance stared at her ass.

"What the fuck was that?" Carson asked in amazement as soon as we heard the door close.

"I like her," Lance said, his grin so wide it was covering half his face. The entire room shook their heads. "What?"

Weston clapped his hand on Lance's shoulder. "Good luck with that one, man." He laughed and walked out of the room, grabbing my hand as he went.

As soon as we were out of the room I pulled my hand away from him.

He blinked back at me. "Wren?"

I crossed my arms over my chest and shook my head. My lip twitched as I glared at him. "No."

His brow scrunched. "No, what?"

"Are you really asking why I might not want you to touch me after what you've done the last few weeks?"

He blew out a breath and nodded. "I'm sorry. I know my mood was terrible, but things will be better now. I promise."

I shook my head. "Not good enough. Not at all."

I turned and walked down the hall, passing by the living room that still housed Julia and Carson. Just from my peripheral view I knew they overheard. Didn't matter. I didn't have the strength to care.

"Wren," Weston called, but I ignored him.

"Ugh, why did I sign up for Business Economics?" Charlotte grumbled, tossing the scissors in her hand onto the table.

We'd spent the last few hours working on a project that detailed a business plan and product.

"Because it was this or Econ 2," I reminded her.

"Oh, right," she replied and then sighed. "I'm so happy they put you in with me."

"Thank God! Otherwise, I might have been teamed up with Aaron!"

She laughed. "That slut has got a thing for you. Normally, he's fickle and the shiny new toy effect wears off, but not with you."

"Don't remind me," I groaned.

"Speaking of sluts, how's the home life?"

I threw a pen at her. "Better since Miss Diva met Lance and actually showed up for production."

"Well, that's good. He was being an ass."

I rolled my eyes. "Tell me about it."

"Did he apologize?"

I shook my head. "I got a half-assed one yesterday when I wouldn't talk to him when he got home."

"The silent treatment? Isn't that kind of childish?" she asked with a wary smile.

I shrugged. "Maybe, but I guess I'm hoping me not talking to him will make him look deeper into his actions."

"You may be waiting a while. He is a man, after all."

I let out a laugh. "Are you saying Liam is just as dim sometimes?"

She laughed as well. "Oh, yeah."

"Well, we'll see how things go, but . . . I don't know." I heaved a sigh and looked down at my phone, which had no missed calls or texts. "Maybe this isn't working out."

"Don't go that far. Not yet."

"Defending him now?"

"No, but you said he was under a lot of stress. Plus, I really don't want you to leave. Who's the diva?" she asked as she tried to paste another piece to the poster board.

"Talia something. I don't remember her last name."

"Clark. Her last name is Clark. And she *is* a pain in the fucking ass, trust me."

My brow scrunched. "You know her?"

Charlotte huffed. "Yeah, she's my other sister."

"What?" I knew about Cloe, who was two years younger than Charlotte, but I thought that was it in the Clark/Younger household.

"She's my half-sister, a product of my dad's younger years in Hollywood with a now no-name actress. Talia makes sure to use our dad's name to its full potential," Charlotte sneered, obviously not a fan of her older sister. "I think we should call it a day."

I looked at our project and nodded in agreement. We would have some more time during the week to finish it up, but I gauged us to be about seventy-five to eighty percent complete. Together, we cleaned up the table, threw away scraps, and packed up all of the materials. Sharing the load, we lugged it all down the hall to our lockers and placed the majority of it inside.

"Don't get me wrong," Charlotte started as we headed out to the parking lot. "I mean, she's my sister and I do love her. We get along for the most part, and she's not a bad actress. She just pisses me off, the way she abuses our last name."

"Our last name?" I'd always known her as Charlotte Younger.

That made her chuckle. "Technically, I'm a Clark too." She pulled out her driver's license, which read Charlotte Amberlee Clark. "I just don't want all the shit that goes with being one, so it's my own stage name in a way, only for real life. My mom of course goes by Clark, but when I got into high school I realized I wanted to distance myself from that name. I didn't want to be known for who I was related to."

I vaguely remembered her telling me she went by her mom's maiden name.

I smiled and wrapped my arm in hers and walked toward the exit. "You know, I'm beginning to understand that a lot."

Charlotte laughed and nodded. "With 'brothers' like yours, I'm sure you are!"

"Oh God. What is going to happen when the truth comes out?"

"Then the truth comes out! Everyone here will understand why you lied. We all do it."

"If you say so."

"Trust me, Wren. Worse things have been revealed."

Charlotte pushed open the door and we headed to the parking lot, only to find most of our group, plus Aaron, gathered near her car.

"You youngins need to disperse," Charlotte teased, pushing her way through and into Liam's arms.

She smiled and relaxed. With only one class together, they didn't get to see each other much during the day. Liam was a lot like her; famous parents but didn't want fame himself. Quite perfect for each other, unlike Weston and me. We were opposites.

Yes, Weston did crave the normal life, but the fact was he was never going to get it. I could try and give it to him as much as possible, but the truth was he was Hollywood through and through. Almost twenty years, thirteen of them acting, most of his movies huge blockbusters.

I still felt like a stupid girl for not seeing it when we were in Vegas, but I wasn't expecting to run into someone like him. All the stares we received were not just because he was handsome, but because he was a movie star. He'd seemed familiar to me, but I couldn't place him at the time.

"So, Wren, you going to the party next week?" Aaron asked as he threw his arm over my shoulder, much to my disdain. The guy couldn't get it through his thick skull that I wasn't interested in him. I tried to shrug him off, but his arm remained slung around me.

Charlotte couldn't help but giggle at my pain.

Retaliation would be swift. I smiled at the thought, which was a bad idea because Aaron took it as a sign I liked his arm around me or something and pulled me closer.

"Um, not sure."

"Oh, you're going, Wren," Charlotte said.

"It is the party of the year! Our own Christmas bash. You have to come," Logan stressed.

"Come on, Wren!" Cloe said, bouncing on the balls of her feet. "I mean, you're a *Lockwood*. You have to come."

I exchanged a look with Charlotte, who turned into Liam's chest, laughing.

"There's a hot tub," Aaron said suggestively, wiggling his eyebrows. I wanted to vomit.

"Aaron, she's been here for two months now. If she hasn't fallen for your charms yet, I don't think it's going to happen," Logan said with a shake of his head. "Plus, she has a boyfriend. And I'm much better looking than you. If anything, she would want me over you."

"Are not!" Aaron protested.

"Dude," Logan scoffed and gestured to his face. "*Teen People's* top twenty-one hottest stars under twenty-one—number four."

We all laughed, and I tried not to stare wide-eyed at that fact. I mean, Logan was good looking, but he just didn't do it for me. I could see why he was so high on the list, though.

"Damn, you beat me again!" Cloe exclaimed, a frown on her face.

Logan grinned at her. "Sorry, Cloe. Four is higher than seventeen."

"I'm only sixteen, and I will beat you before you turn twenty-one," she promised.

We all broke out into laughter over the absurd conversation of who was hotter on some magazine's scale. We talked more about the party, and though I'd already told Charlotte I was going, they all kept trying to convince me to go. It was nice to have so many people, so many friends, to be part of a group that wanted me, especially with how new I still was. They all liked me for me, unlike my newest group of "friends" who liked me because I lived with Weston.

"Wren!" I heard a very familiar, very angry voice call my name. Turning around slowly, I found the source was Weston as he shut the door to his car and stalked over.

I stared at him, confused. Charlotte had picked me up that morning so we could work on the project a little before school, so he knew Charlotte was taking me home. Why was he there?

"Weston?"

His gaze was murderous at Aaron, and I realized his arm was still over my shoulder. I stepped out of it, but Weston's jealousy had already taken over. And combined with whatever drove him to come to my school, it wasn't going to be good.

"Take your damn phone off vibrate. I've been trying to get ahold of you for the last fucking hour," he spat.

Charlotte sent me a sympathetic look and mouthed that it was after six, and I cursed under my breath. He must have done it while we were talking.

Weston had cleared his schedule that evening to make sure he was home for dinner so we could spend some time together. To talk. We'd been working so hard on the project, and I totally forgot. It wouldn't have been an issue, but our group of friends had been in the parking lot and we lost track of time while talking.

"I'm sorry, Weston," I said, and scrambled to pull out my phone. Six missed phone calls and three text messages. Shit. What a difference an hour made.

"Come on," he said, grabbing my wrist and pulling me away.

"See you later." I waved at my friends, trying not to trip as he dragged me across the parking lot. "Jesus, Weston," I hissed, and wrenched my arm away. "I'm not a fucking dog you can pull around on a leash!"

We climbed into his car, and I slammed the door hard before he sped off with all of my friends watching.

"Did you have to be such as ass back there?" I asked.

He turned his head, glaring at me. "I'm sorry. Was I interrupting time with your boyfriend? I'd only cleared my schedule to have dinner with my wife."

"Ugh, there is nothing with Aaron!" I yelled as I crossed my arms. "And I'm sorry, really. Charlotte and I were working hard on our project. When we left, everyone was in the parking lot and we got to talking, and the time slipped away."

"Why was he all over you, then?"

I rolled my eyes. "Because Aaron thinks every girl should want him."

"And he's in your group of friends?"

I sighed. "Not really, he just happened to be there. Why are you so fucking pissed?"

His fingers flexed against the steering wheel. "Because we had plans."

"Oh, and you've never broken plans before?" I spat back. He had no right after cancelling on me three nights in a row.

"I work. A lot. You know this. You only have to worry about school."

I turned toward him, glaring. "What the hell is that supposed to mean?"

"It means you have a lot of free time, and I don't. Therefore, if we make plans, you shouldn't have a problem meeting them."

I couldn't believe him. Did he really expect me to always be available at his whim?

"I'm sorry, Weston, really I am," I apologized yet again. "Time just got away from me. Almost every day I'm home by four, five at the latest."

"You've been home late the last few weeks." He turned into the driveway, and I knew then it wasn't going to be a good night.

"Are you accusing me of something? Because I'd like to remind you that Christmas is less than two weeks away, and I needed to pick up some gifts."

"Who have you been shopping with?" he asked.

"I've told you, multiple times, with Charlotte. Jesus, Weston, get your head out of your ass!" I jumped out of the car as soon as it was in park and stomped into the house.

I threw my bag onto the counter and turned to him, pissed. It didn't escape my gaze that Kelly was still there, finishing up dinner. I'd gotten used to people being around over the last two months, though I still wasn't all that comfortable with our conversations being overheard.

"It's not like I can go shopping with you. Hell, I don't even think you do any shopping on your own unless it's online."

Weston rubbed his temples, jaw clenched tight. "It's not as easy for me to go out as it is for you. You act like I don't want to go out to places with you."

I pursed my lips and tried to hold back the building tears. Sometimes, it felt like it. Was it so awful I wanted to spend time with him outside of the house?

Weston sighed and stepped forward. "Come on, let's sit down and eat. Kelly made us a wonderful meal." He tried to take my hand, but I pulled away.

"You know, Weston, I kind of lost my appetite when you embarrassed me in front of my friends and made me feel like some stupid kid who forgot their curfew."

"Wren," he started, but I cut him off.

"I've had enough of your attitude. I just want to go take a nice warm bath and go to bed."

Multiple emotions crossed his beautiful features before he said, "Look, I'm sorry, okay? I freaked out when I couldn't get ahold of you. I was worried. And then I saw that kid with his arm around you . . . You know I get jealous."

I gave him a small smile, because I knew he meant his apology, but it didn't wash away my feelings. "It's okay, and I'm sorry for losing track of time. But, Weston, you need to get a handle on this jealousy of yours."

He nodded. "I know."

I attempted to give him a small smile, but I just didn't have it in me. "I've got some homework for tomorrow," I said, my voice lower and softer than before. "I'm going to go finish that and go to bed early."

Weston didn't say anything else, but he did come to bed later and cuddle up behind me. I was half asleep when he kissed my shoulder and whispered, "Goodnight, my sweet Wren."

Chapter Twenty-Three

OUR CRACKS

Aᴏᴛᴇʀ Wᴇsᴛᴏɴ's ꜰᴏʀᴄᴇꜰᴜʟ ʀᴇᴍᴏᴠᴀʟ ᴏꜰ ᴍᴇ ɪɴ ꜰʀᴏɴᴛ ᴏꜰ some friends from school, the rumors about me picked up again. Granted, I knew they didn't start them . . . well, maybe Aaron . . . but I also knew other students were milling around from various afterschool activities. What I didn't need in my life was more rumors about me and the Lockwood men. This time, however, people were saying I was in an incestuous relationship with Weston.

I'd thought after getting Talia back on track, his bad mood would dissipate, but then he went off in a jealous rage. It seemed like our "honeymoon" phase had worn off and real life, with all the shit that went along with it, came out tenfold.

Charlotte and I walked into the cafeteria for lunch, and I noticed that an unusual amount of people were looking at me, some pointing and whispering. A shiver ran down my spine as we got in line, wondering if somehow my real relationship with Weston had come out.

No. Weston would have called me immediately, but my phone had been silent.

"Is it true?" Kim, the annoying girl that accosted me everywhere I went, asked.

"Is what true?"

She thrust something at me. "Are Weston and Natalie really back together?"

"W-what?" I looked down at the magazine now in my hands, and my stomach dropped.

On the cover was a paparazzi photo of Weston and Natalie. She was smiling brightly as they entered a fancy restaurant. They looked cozy with Natalie grappled onto his arm, then another shot from behind with his hand on her lower back. The headline, much like Kim's question: *Natalie Larson and Weston Lockwood back together!* The daily rag was dated that day, saying that the pictures were from the day before when they were seen out and about at La Sienna Café.

"So, is it true?" Kim asked again.

I couldn't respond, but I felt the magazine ripped from me and Charlotte toting me away. As we left, I saw Miles across the room, also being accosted, his eyes wide as he looked back at me. Char dragged me down the hall and into the bathroom. I leaned against the counter while she checked to make sure it was empty.

"Okay, look at me," Charlotte commanded. My head rose, eyes meeting hers. "It's a trash mag, paparazzi shit. There's probably a perfectly good explanation for that photo and why they were together. And now that she's back in town, everyone's assuming it's true that they've reconciled 'cause it always happened with them. But he has you now."

"Char, lately I don't know what to think, because I hardly see or talk to him," I said, tears filling my eyes as I held back a sob. "I need to know more."

She nodded, concern written all over her face. "Okay."

"I have to go," I said. "I can't stay here like this. I need to talk to him."

"I agree." She wiped a stray tear from my cheek. "Be careful driving. I really don't think this is anything, Wren. I've seen him with you. It's you he adores."

I nodded in agreement, but at the moment had trouble believing it myself. She walked me out to my car, my footsteps halting when I saw the lawn lined with paps. My eyes widened, and fear overtook me.

Did they know I was a Lockwood? Charlotte noticed them as well, and steered me away. They saw us, but to my relief none approached, and I realized they were waiting for Miles, not me.

I drove toward his office after having checked Weston's schedule on my phone. It indicated that he would be there that day, but I got distracted when I saw a bookstore and couldn't stop myself from going in. The magazine racks were full, having all come out that day, and I was astounded at the sheer volume of pictures of Weston and Natalie. All of the headlines were spouting about how they were back together, some saying engaged, others saying she was pregnant.

There were other photos as well—of me. Well, my backside anyway, from when I visited his office weeks ago, Weston's arm resting on my lower back. "Mysterious meet up at Lockwood Entertainment" and "Weston Lockwood's mistress—Natalie's pissed!" were the words used for the vague photos.

My heart was beating a mile a minute, trying to find a way out of my chest. Was it true? He'd been spending so much time away, and been in such a bad mood toward me . . .

What if he *was* with her?

The building outside his office was crawling with paparazzi when I arrived. This time when I entered his office building the guards gave me no trouble, letting me pass right through to the elevators without delay.

Amy was standing at the front desk with a receptionist who I didn't know when I reached his office.

"Can I help you?" the blonde asked.

"I need to see Weston," I said, directing it toward Amy.

"I'm sorry, Mr. Lockwood is bu—" She was cut off by Amy.

"Come on back, Wren," Amy said with a smile and guided me back to his office.

She tapped on the door before turning the handle and pushing it open. He was on the phone, talking shop to someone. He smiled when he saw me, but it dropped when he took in my expression.

"Hey, Damien, let me call you back," he said into the receiver. "Yeah . . . uh-huh . . . okay, talk to you soon."

Amy headed back out the door, closing it, leaving us to talk.

"Everything all right, baby girl?" he asked as he hung up the phone.

"Your face is all over the tabloids with Natalie," I said in a rush, handing the small stack I'd purchased over to him.

He took them in his hand, glancing over each blurb. "They're nothing." He tossed them down onto his desk. "Don't worry about them."

I stared at him, frozen in stunned silence. He looked beyond tired. The stress that seemed to be tearing us apart was ripping him to shreds.

"But those vultures will be at the house," I said. What were we supposed to do? "They're downstairs right now."

His eyes grew wide, flashing to the window and back to me. "Then what are you doing here? Why did you come in?"

I was shocked, startled by his reaction. "Weston?"

He rubbed his hands on his face, then up through his hair. "You could have called me, or we could have talked about this at home. It was just a lunch meeting, Wren, with ten others about Natalie's project." He gritted his teeth. "You being here just fuels it and gives them an opportunity to snap photos of you."

"You warning me could have helped." A little heads up went a long way, and would have avoided some of the strain.

"I don't have time to tell you every little thing. You have my schedule, know where I am just about every fucking minute of the day. Isn't that enough?" He sighed and rubbed his temples, his eyes screwed tight. "Go home."

"Excuse me?" I asked, hoping I'd heard him wrong.

"Go home and stay inside. Shit! I don't need this shit right now!" he cursed, his temper rising.

His change of mood and words were like a slap in the face. The panic had switched from me to him. "You need to calm down."

"And you need to realize the situation," he snapped. His jaw ticked as he looked away, then his deadened eyes locked on mine. "I have a fuck load going on here, and I don't need our headline on top of all the other trash they're talking about me and Natalie."

"Is it all trash?" The words barely crawled out of my throat. I desperately needed to know, because his mood had changed when she returned from filming and had only gotten worse since then. He'd never looked at me with such disdain, like I was the reason he wasn't with her.

I needed reassurance of why I left everything for him.

"What?"

"According to a recent quote in one of those, Natalie's saying you two are still together and doing fine."

He glared up at me, picking up all the magazines and throwing them in the trash. "Don't fucking read that shit. It's all lies."

"Is it true?" I began shaking, starting with my hands and moving up my arms. He wasn't going to get me to back down until I had an answer.

His jaw jutted forward as he sat back. "I can't believe you're even asking me that."

My stomach dropped. His refusal to say "no" sounded like an admission to me.

"And why is that?" I asked. "You're never home, even less so since she arrived."

Was everything a lie? Were we a fairy tale that didn't have a happy ending?

"Wren, I'm busy. You need to go home, out the back, now. I'll talk to you later, but it won't be about bullshit you read on a trash mag," he said through clenched teeth. "In fact, leave your car here. I'll have someone drive you home."

I blinked at him. "What?"

"You being here is fueling them." His phone rang in the background.

"How is that . . ." I was interrupted by the door opening and Amy walking in.

"Mr. Lockwood, sorry to interrupt, but Talia Clark's manager is on line three."

His jaw ticked, and his eyes were murderous. "Amy, take Wren home. Now."

My eyes widened. "No." I shook my head. I wasn't leaving until I got a straight answer. "I want to know why you went to lunch with her."

"I don't get lunch breaks, Wren, I have lunch meetings. It's all business," he hissed between his teeth. "Now, go home."

I stared at him, completely stunned and hurt and filled with anger. "Thanks for the fucking support, Weston."

I stormed out the door past Amy and didn't stop. When I got to the lobby, I continued on, not caring who saw, only pissed that the one person I could depend on in L.A. dismissed me. Never had I been happier that my car was fast than in that moment as I sped away from his office.

I drove around, meandering through the city with no destination in mind. It was when I came upon the coastal highway that I decided to pull over.

I parked the car at a public beach parking lot, grabbed my backpack, and started walking. There was no destination in mind, I just started walking. I stared out at the ocean, completely in shock. After about an hour, I found a nice spot in the sand and sat down, looking out on the waves crashing along the shore. There were surfers and swimmers, families, couples walking hand in hand.

I was jealous of them, the couples.

Tears sprung to my eyes, and I buried my head in my hands as my body shook with sobs. It was too much, all of it . . . the whole day had just been too much. The tabloids hurt, but not as much as Weston's dismissal. He was my one constant, the one to be by my side in this new madness of a life I'd fallen into. He was my husband, but the man in that office did not act like a husband should act.

I knew he was stressed and busy. I'd tried to help him find peace and normalcy, calm in his hectic life, but I needed his support and he blew me off. It wasn't the first time either, and I was beginning to think this was a one-sided relationship. One in which I provided the emotional support and was financially cared for in return.

I'd needed verification, and he was angry that I'd asked for it. I was the one who had her life uprooted and then was left all alone.

I stared out into the ocean, numb, watching the sun set on the crashing waves until it disappeared over the horizon. It was then I decided it was time to head back to my car, fear for my safety finally kicking in. I unlocked the car and brushed the sand off me as well as I could and climbed in.

I drove around, unknowing, uncaring about the time, where I was . . . nothing. Things were going downhill fast between Weston and me, and it was breaking my heart.

Our period of blissful new love was over.

Fantasy done.

Near ten, I decided to head home. I was tired, and found I was only a few miles from the house. I pulled into the garage minutes later and walked in to find Weston on the phone, pacing in the kitchen. His eyes were wide with relief before narrowing in anger.

"Where the fuck have you been?" He was so loud his voice echoed around the room. "Joe found your car, but you weren't there. You wouldn't answer your phone . . . I've been going out of my mind! What if something happened to you?"

"Oh, so now you're worried about me?" I folded my arms in front of me.

"Why wouldn't I be? I sent my wife home and when I got there, no evidence of her being here could be found." His voice rose in volume. "Then add in an abandoned car . . . I was freaking out that something had happened to you, Wren." He pulled me into his arms, clearly shaken.

I wanted to melt into them, desperately, but I was still too pissed and hurt. So instead, I pulled away, stepping out of his warm embrace.

"I want to go shower. I'm covered in sand and salt water."

"I'll come with you," he said.

"No need," I said, then added, "I'm sure you're busy with work. I'll be fine." Even I could tell how deadened my voice was.

"Wren . . ." he trailed off, and my eyes met his.

They were etched in sadness, but I couldn't help him.

In the shower, I couldn't even gain any kind of warmth or relaxation, no matter how hot the water was beating down on my body.

After I dried off, I stared at our bed, but I just couldn't get in. My favorite place felt foreign, so I grabbed my pillow and headed to my second favorite; the living room with the chaise couches. The light was still on under Weston's office door as I crept by, trying not to make any noise. I really couldn't take talking to or seeing him.

I climbed onto the center chaise couch, pulling a blanket up with me, settling in the middle. I fluffed my pillow and turned on the TV, surfing through channels. More than once Weston's face popped up on the screen, along with Natalie's.

Disgusted, I threw down the remote and curled into the cushion to try and close my eyes, willing it all to just go away.

I felt strong arms wrapping around me, rousing me from my sleep. In my half-awake state I wanted to curl into them, but then memories came crashing down and I began thrashing to get out of them.

"Wren! It's me! Calm down!" Weston cried out, but I just continued until I wiggled free and was back in my spot.

"Go away, Weston."

"Wren . . ."

"Just leave me alone."

There was no movement, no more talking. He just sat there.

My eyes were closed, but I would bet money he was staring at me, wondering what happened to his baby girl. She woke up, no longer in Oz.

The couch moved beneath me and footsteps echoed in the hall. I heard a whispered, "Goodnight," and then all was silent again.

Chapter Twenty-Four

OUR DOWNFALL

LITTLE HAD CHANGED IN THE WEEK SINCE OUR BLOWOUT, but our carefree days were over. I returned to the bedroom the next night, but the following morning he left for a week, out of town on a filming location.

The semester was over, and the Christmas bash that my classmates had been so excited about was upon us. Char had come over the day before, bringing with her about a dozen dresses for me to choose from since I had no idea how to dress up for the occasion. All of my dresses from Sophie were much too elegant for a high school party, and I didn't want to bother her. We ended up choosing one that had a sleeveless top that was filled with silver sequins, a white, flirty skirt below a satin belt, and silver sequined peep-toe heels to match.

I was dressed and waiting, the house empty of all but me, as it had been all week without Weston. It was odd that in all the time I'd been in the house, I'd never been as lonely as I was in that moment, waiting for Charlotte to pick me up. The silence was deafening and oppressive. It had been a quiet week; I'd only spoken to him once and shared a few texts. The gap was evident in the words both said and not. The distance between us, both physically and emotionally, was eating at my heart. I was looking forward to the party, letting loose and hoping to feel better.

"Baby girl, I'm home!" Weston's voice called, the door slamming.

He's home?

His steps slowed, his expression cautious. "You're not excited to see me?"

I blinked at him. "Weston, you've been on set all week. I've barely heard or seen from you," I said. "The last text I received this morning said you'd be home sometime late tomorrow."

"Filming got done early for today due to some technical problems, so I came home. I've missed you."

"*Missed* me?" I rolled my eyes. "I find that hard to believe."

"Wren, look, I'm sorry for the way I behaved when you came to my office. It just . . . wasn't another stress I needed in my life at that moment."

Wow. It was bad enough he thought I was angry for the office incident, but then came the slap of the following sentence.

"Well, Mr. Lockwood, I'm so fucking sorry to have become *another* stress in your life. All this time I thought I was your wife, your calm." The hurt crawled out of me then, finally feeling like it had a chance to be heard.

He sighed and ran his hands through his hair. "Wren, you need to understand, to learn, that in my world there is a time and a place for certain things, and you barging into my office unannounced is not what I need and . . ." He cleared his throat and shook his head. "I need you to call before you come."

I stared at him, promising myself I wouldn't cry. His dismissal of me from that part of his life . . . hurt. Bad. And I realized maybe I didn't belong in his world at all if I was that much of a hindrance.

"Do you want me to leave?" My insides churned, building toward an eruption, all the hurt ready to burst out. "Just say the fucking words and I'll be on the first flight to Indianapolis!"

He shook his head and threw his hands up in the air. "That is your fucking solution to everything! Just run away! Jesus, Wren, since the beginning . . . always so fucking eager to throw in the towel. If you don't want to be here or be with me, then just say it, now, and leave!" He pointed in the direction of the front door.

"Otherwise, fucking suck it up, and stop trying to always make me the fucking bad guy here. Being an adult and in a relationship, especially marriage, is rough and sometimes you have to work very hard at it!" His voice was hard, almost like he was talking to the diva and not me.

"Strong words for a pot. It's hard to make it work if you're never around," I spat back.

He opened his arms, holding them out to his sides. "I'm right here, Wren."

"Until the phone rings, or until someone barges in unannounced."

"You know how busy my life is."

My brow scrunched and I nodded. "Yeah, I get that. I know you're stressed. And I get that you weren't expecting me, and I've excused a lot of your attitude and our time apart for that, but you're the one that needs to man the fuck up and deal with our situation," I argued, and turned to grab my purse from the table. "You can't have a one-sided marriage, Weston, and that's what you've left me with. You're married to your job, not me. I never agreed to be your mistress."

I watched his eyes widen as I walked around him toward the front door.

"Where are you going?"

"Out," I replied with a sigh.

"Running away."

My jaw clenched. I needed to leave before this became worse than it already was. "Charlotte is picking me up. We're going to a party. It's been planned for weeks."

"A party? A high school party?" His eyes moved up and down my body, stopping at my chest that was bare of my ring. "Wearing *that*? Fuck, no!"

"You said you'd still be away." My lip quivered in hurt and anger. "Am I supposed to stay locked up in here and wait for you to grace me with your presence and attention? I'm not a doll for you to play house with when you feel like it, Weston." Tears stung at my eyes as I pushed past him and ran out the door.

I heard him yelling for me, calling my name, and my pace quickened. I jumped into Charlotte's waiting car, needing to get away as soon as possible.

"Wren?"

"Go, just . . . go."

Without another word, she pulled out and away from the house that wasn't my home. As we drove, I wondered if it would ever feel like my home. Then again, the man that resided inside didn't even feel like my husband. Nothing felt real. Everything was fake. I wished for the cool fall air, my mother's arms around me, Daniel and me hanging out; that was real. That was home, and I was delusional to have ever entertained any other.

"Do you want to talk about it?"

"I think the honeymoon period is over. I don't . . . I don't know if staying together was right anymore."

Charlotte glanced over to me with worried eyes as she drove. "Just promise me you won't do anything rash, and remember I'm only a phone call away."

"Thanks, Char. And thanks for always being there for me."

"You're my kindred spirit, Wren. So that means you're stuck with me," she said with a smile. "No matter where you live."

"And I thank my lucky stars the only open seat was next to you on my first day."

We arrived at the street the party was being held. They weren't kidding when they said it was huge. Cars lined either side and people were all over the lawn. I'd never been to that kind of party. Back in Indianapolis, I was never invited to such things. Then again, Daniel and I weren't really into that, being outsiders, but in L.A. I was part of the crew.

Upon entering, we were handed little cups of Jell-O.

"Weird."

"Alcohol filled," Charlotte said with a devilish smile.

I looked at the small plastic cup before tipping it back and letting the Jell-O slide into my mouth. It held the cherry taste, but also the strong flavor of the liquor. I cringed at the alcohol burn, but it didn't stop my hand from reaching out and snatching a few more from the tray and downing another.

Damn, those were good.

It always happened in movies—facing hard times led to drinking. For the first time, I understood. I just wanted to wash it all away. I sucked down the other shot, and we made our way to the keg. We found Logan in the kitchen having a blast handing out cups, and I took one. A little while later I went back for another. I didn't care much for the taste, but I did like the lighter feeling it gave me.

Charlotte went off to find Liam, and I found a comfortable spot on a couch. I had another drink and another, until time ceased to matter and life was good and easy again, even if just for a few minutes.

My phone went off for what felt like the hundredth time and I pulled it out, brow furrowing as I looked down at the screen and saw Weston's name flashing. Another text to ignore. I'd been ignoring them ever since I stormed out.

Not even reading what he had to say, I turned my attention back to the drink in my hand. Doubts began to spread through my mind. Why was I still in L.A.? Why hadn't I just gone home?

Anger flared inside from his behavior. I was still in shock that he would ever say I was running away. He just didn't get it. I was so lonely. He was gone so much, and it wasn't like I had a huge support system. It had been over a week since Weston and I had been together for more than half an hour. We hadn't even had sex in almost two weeks. All the changes were too much.

Never in my wildest dreams did I think I would marry a good looking former movie star turned producer, and life with one wasn't easy. His schedule was erratic and jam packed. I knew he said it was a really busy time right now, but I wasn't even a thought to him lately. I wasn't part of his life, just a fantasy he delved into when he had five minutes.

"Hey, Wren," Aaron said, plopping down next to me. He flung his arm out to rest on the back of the couch, way too close.

"Aaron." I grimaced slightly as I attempted to scoot away. The guy gave me the creeps. He didn't take the previous hints I'd given him, apparently. He was skeezy and I couldn't stand him, but he had been persistent in his pursuit of me.

"I think you and I should go out sometime," he said, giving me what I thought was supposed to be some type of charming smile. It made me want to vomit.

"Not going to happen, Aaron. I'm taken," I mumbled, my tongue feeling heavy, but I hoped that would be enough to end the conversation.

Of course I wasn't that lucky.

"I bet I can take you away from your guy," he said, slurring his words, his hand moving down across my arm.

"Yeah . . . No. Not going to happen."

My phone began ringing and I knew who it was, so I ignored it.

"Oh, come on, just one date?" His had moved to resting on my thigh. The smell of alcohol was strong on his breath. He was very drunk.

So was I.

"I'm really not interested." I tried to stress it as best as I could, hoping it came out as strong as I wanted it to.

The music stopped, and the phone was silent once more. A few seconds later it started up again, and I forced myself to focus my attention elsewhere. Unfortunately, Aaron was the only thing nearby and his presence was starting to grate on me as much the ringing phone.

Over and over he called until I couldn't take it anymore.

"What do you want?" I screamed into the receiver, making Aaron jump next to me.

"Where the fuck are you?" he screamed back.

"I'm out!" Adrenaline pumped the words forcefully out of my drunk mouth.

"Have you been drinking?" His voice was low and laced with anger.

"Yes, I am fucking drinking! So fucking what?" I looked at Aaron in disgust, slapping at his hand that was moving higher up my leg. My voice lowered so that people around wouldn't hear. Aaron was too far gone to remember in the morning. "Maybe I'm hoping if I get drunk again I will wake up *un*-married!"

I could almost feel his anger through the phone.

"Wren Lockwood, where in this motherfucking house are you?"

I shivered at his words, and not just from the tone, which for some reason excited me. He found me.

"Not telling."

"Don't have to," he said harshly, and I looked up to find him standing in front of me.

I knew I was drunk then, because he looked so incredibly sexy, even as furious as he was. He looked like the king or a tyrant, and I would happily let him ravage me.

The crowd was murmuring about him, wondering why he was here, girls fawning over him.

I just glared up at him and took a sip of the drink in my hand. Before it reached my lips, he yanked it away. His eyes were slits, jaw locked tight. I'd never seen him so angry, until he turned and looked at Aaron. If looks could kill.

Aaron's arm was still around me, his hand still on my thigh.

"Get your fucking hands off her . . . now," Weston seethed low, but loud enough Aaron removed his arm and hand. Turning back, he continued, "Get the fuck up. We're going."

"No."

"Wren, get the fuck up, right fucking now before I fucking go off."

"Fuck you, Weston. The one time I want to go out, you're against it. Well, tough shit! You're always going out, leaving me alone! I'm staying!"

Furious, he reached down and grabbed my arm, hoisting me up from the couch and thankfully away from Aaron.

"Now," he spat. His blue eyes were almost glowing with the fire inside him.

"You're hurting me," I hissed through clenched teeth.

He ignored me and began dragging me by the arm through the house. It was not a graceful exit in my inebriated state, stumbling as I went.

"Stop acting like a fucking petulant child."

"Petulant child? Disgruntled wife is a better definition of my current state," I argued under my breath.

He glared back at me, and before I realized it he was pulling me down the driveway. Somewhere behind me, Charlotte called out my name. I wrenched my arm, finally succeeding in getting free from his grip, and tried to go back inside to her but I was captured around my waist. He picked me up off the ground and headed back on his path to his car.

"Let me go! God, you are being such a fucking asshole!"

"And you're being childish."

"Childish?"

I dug my nails into his arm until he released me and I pushed away from him, stumbling back. I looked around to find we'd walked about half a block, and, thankfully, there was no one around to listen.

"Who was the one adult enough to see what we were getting into instead of the fantasy? Who wanted the annulment? My mother convinced us to try, and now look! I'm miserable! You don't want any acknowledgement of what we are. I get that you're a successful movie producer, a former movie star, it would be a scandal." My lips trembled as my jaw locked to hold myself together as he just stared at me. "So, I'm this girl you keep in the closet, and Natalie is who you're with on the front page of every fucking magazine."

Tears welled in my eyes as all the loneliness of the past months came crashing down on me. Even I didn't realize until then just how long I'd felt alone. I'd convinced myself that it was okay because of our circumstances, but that was just an excuse. A way to self-soothe.

"I told you not to believe that shit. It's all made up gossip."

I shook my head. "Doesn't matter. Do you have any idea how all that makes me feel? How contradictory that is? You said you wanted to take care of me, but that's only when it's convenient to you, and dependent on who is around!"

He stared at me, and I wondered if my words were soaking in. "The world I work in doesn't look kindly upon situations like ours," he said calmly. "The press would be all over it and all over us. It is partially because you are still in school. I'll admit that, but more so because I was trying to protect you."

"From what?"

"From the paparazzi, the press, the rumors, the lies. All the bullshit in those fucking trash mags." He ran his fingers through his hair and let out a breath. "It's a cutthroat business, Wren, and you're young and naïve to its ways. What's going on right now is *nothing* compared to how bad it really gets. I grew up in this shit. I struggle with ordinary." His brow was furrowed, shoulders slumped as he practically begged me to understand.

And I did, but I needed him to understand as well, and he wasn't.

"Huh . . . ordinary. Just an ordinary girl. That's what you wanted," I said, tears spilling down my cheek. "What about what I want?"

His jaw locked down again as he glanced up and down the street. "We'll talk more when we get home, just . . . get in the car."

I shook my head, my arms crossing my body.

"Wren, please, get in the car," he asked, clearly exasperated.

Wiping the tears from my eyes, I finally conceded and climbed in.

It was silent on the way home. I couldn't look at him—I didn't want to—so I stared out the window watching the city go by with tear-filled eyes.

I fell asleep on the ride home and didn't remember the drive, but I did remember strong arms carrying me. They put me to bed, but they didn't stay.

Chapter Twenty-Five

OUR END?

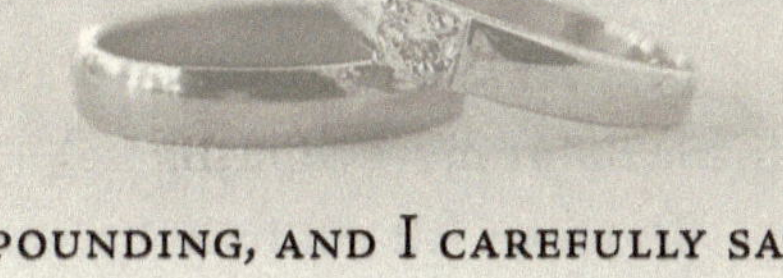

I AWOKE GROGGY, MY HEAD POUNDING, AND I CAREFULLY SAT up. It was silent, not a single sound, and when I looked to Weston's half of the bed it was still made. He never came to sleep in our bed.

With sluggish movements I made my way to the bathroom and started up the shower. The hot water felt good against my skin and helped to clear my head. Unfortunately, that brought thinking, and with it the knowledge that everything was falling apart. My life with Weston was disintegrating before my eyes.

I needed to get away, just step back for the weekend and assess what my life had become and what I wanted it to be. My backpack sat by the bed and I picked it up, throwing in a few things, including a change of clothes. I'd see if I could spend the night with Charlotte.

The house was silent as I headed down to the ground floor, but as I approached the kitchen, I could hear the murmur of voices.

"Natalie, you need to shut the fuck up about my personal life," I heard Weston say from down the hall.

He sounded exhausted, and annoyed.

"Weston, I don't see why you're so upset. She's just a little girl. You don't even love her!"

There was silence, no response from Weston, no argument.

"Let's get back to my original question," he said. "How the fuck are you getting in?"

She seemed to ignore his question, but wouldn't budge on the conversation redirection. "But, baby, how can you concentrate without getting it out?"

"Don't call me that," he argued, his form coming into view. He was sitting on the edge of the table, and he looked as tired as he sounded. "And I am not going to discuss my personal life and feelings for my wife with you!"

"Then how about we discuss us?" She smiled at him seductively, leaned forward and pressed her lips to his.

I expected him to push her away. I expected him to throw her off. He didn't move an inch.

The floor fell out from beneath my feet. She was who he was supposed to be with. She was the person who could understand his life. I really was just some stupid, little girl.

My backpack slipped from my hand, landing with a hard thud, causing both their heads to snap in my direction. Natalie smirked triumphantly at me, while Weston pushed her away from him with force.

"Wren, this isn't . . ." he trailed off, cursing under his breath. His eyes were locked on mine, pleading. "Baby, she . . ."

"Don't," I said, cutting him off. "Just . . . don't."

I reached down and picked my bag up off the floor and slung it over my shoulder. Panic filled his eyes as he stared at me. I walked past them, heading to the garage.

"Darling, she'll be fine. I'm sure there is some guy out there her age that will want her," Natalie said in her fake sweet voice.

It was all I could take.

My bag fell from my shoulder and I whipped around, punching her square in the cheekbone, sending her crashing to the ground. I stared down at her, shaking, her screams of pain echoing off the walls. Weston was looking at me and before he could say anything she was clawing at him for help.

"You disgust me," I spat down at her, picking up my bag again and walking out to the garage.

I stormed through the garage toward my car when I heard the door to the house slam and Weston's voice call out to me, "Wren, let's go back in the house."

"No!"

"Please! Let's talk about this."

"Why? Why should I? I don't even know what I am to you, Weston!" I threw my bag into the car and moved around to the driver's side. "A doll to play house with? Just some girl mooching off of you? A pussy to fuck? If any of these are the case, divorce me and we'll both be free. Because right now, every day, even with all this shit, my feelings for you are growing." I opened up the driver's side door and looked up at him. "If it's not the same for you, it's better if I go back to Indianapolis, and we'll pretend all of this never happened. You and Natalie can be together, and I'll go back to being a wallflower in a place that I'm better suited for."

Weston shook his head. "Dammit. You're not going anywhere. We're going to work this out."

I shook my head. "Weston, I'm in high school and you're a movie producer."

His voice dropped, low and quiet. "You're my wife."

My chest was tight, and I needed to get out of there. "I'm a nuisance. I'm keeping you from so many things. People . . . people don't even know we're married, and I'm tired of being your mistress."

"Natalie shouldn't have kissed me. I told her as much," he said. It made me stop, just as he probably hoped it would. "I thought we were going to give this a real try, Wren. I'm committed to us."

My anger flamed at the mention of her name, and my arms crossed my chest. "Committed to us? What interest do you have in me other than being your ordinary girl fantasy? Our worlds are so different, Weston, and there just doesn't seem to be room for me in yours. Natalie seems to fit perfectly. Get back together with her. You certainly have chemistry."

"I don't want her," he yelled, stalking toward me.

"Then find someone new," I said in defeat.

I climbed into my car and pulled out, Weston walking after me as I sped off.

Time meant nothing as I drove around aimlessly, which I realized wasn't a good idea when I ended up in a not so good area. I quickly navigated my way out of there and found myself on a stretch of road that went along the beach again. My eyes spotted a beach parking lot and I pulled in. The surf was high, the sky gray, both reflective of what was going on in my life.

With my book bag in hand and my phone silent, I kicked off my shoes, locked up the car, and headed onto the beach. I walked about fifty feet out from where I'd parked and plopped down onto the sand. Perhaps it was the relaxing sound of the waves that calmed me, but I found it very peaceful. That was why I'd stopped a week prior, and why I'd ended up there again.

An hour or two, maybe three, had passed before my eyes moved from the waves and surfers in front of me. More than once I'd almost stripped down and jumped in. I tried to think about what I was going to do, but I was facing the hard truth that Indianapolis was the best option.

I stared down at the picture of our wedding I'd grabbed and put in my backpack as I left. We looked so happy and in love then, when we didn't even know each other. The pictures might have shown love, but once reality settled over us, things weren't picture perfect. Rose colored glasses removed—reality was a bitch.

I opened one of the text books I had and slipped the photo between the pages to protect it. My eyes scanned the beach to find that even on a gloomy day, people were having fun. A father was running down the beach chasing after his little girl, a boy was flying a kite, a whole group of guys were wading out into the surf.

My life was changing, and the world still turned. I felt like a wallflower again, only this time a numb one. No one knew who I was, who I was married to, and they didn't care. Did I stay a wallflower, or step into the flashing bulbs?

A question that didn't really matter if we couldn't work things out.

"How did you find me?" I said with a deep sigh as a shadow fell over me. I knew it was him without turning around.

"Your car has a GPS locator," he said.

I snorted. "Figures." My gaze never left the crashing waves. I didn't want to look at him.

"I've been searching for you for hours." He sounded calm, with an edge of something I couldn't figure out. Fear or anger, maybe.

"You think that matters, because?"

"You're my wife."

I turned toward him, glaring. "No. I'm a drunken, fun-filled night you got stuck with."

"Wren," he began, but I cut him off.

"Why was she there?"

"She got in," he said. "Wren, she kissed me, and I swear to you I did not kiss her back."

"You didn't throw her off either," I pointed out.

"I was still as a fucking statue." He practically yelled, his anger mixed with a pleading tone. "I was waiting to tell her to fuck off when she got pissed I wasn't giving her what she wanted, but then you were there, and shit got fucked up!"

It was like he was begging me to believe him and exhausted that he was even arguing about it.

I wanted to believe him. What I saw wasn't any different than any time before—a conniving bitch and a man shooting her down. But I couldn't help but wonder, what if he didn't push her off because it reminded him of what they were together?

"So, what happens next time?" I asked.

He shook his head. "There will be no next time."

"She's always getting in."

"As soon as we get home I'm calling Joe and having him reset the whole fucking system and deactivate every single pass."

I turned back to look at the waves, wondering if I believed it or not. If it could really be done. Her actions triggered every fear I had, solidified every insecurity. She probably planned for it to happen at some point. "I don't know if I can call that place my home."

"W-what?" he stuttered behind me.

"It doesn't feel like my home." I wasn't sure anywhere did anymore. My whole center was off balance.

He crouched down, his knee touching my hip as it sank into the sand. "Baby, it is. You're my wife."

"Wife . . . right." I shook my head. "We never go out. I always see you there, never anywhere else, and especially not at your office anymore, since I'm not allowed." I wanted the words to sting him, so he'd have a little taste of how much his dismissal hurt. "I think it's not just because of the paparazzi, but because you're embarrassed by me."

"Wren, it's not that. I swear." His hand moved like he wanted to reach out, to touch me, but he held back.

"No? Are you sure?" My lip trembled. "Wouldn't your image be tarnished if people found out you were married to a high school girl?"

"I don't give a fuck about my image!" he yelled out, startling me. "It's a difficult situation."

"You say that a lot."

"Because it's true!"

I let out a sigh and watched a surfer catch a wave. "I think it's also true that I don't belong here."

"Wren . . ."

I stood and brushed the sand off my backside. "I'm going to go back and pack my stuff. I'll be on the first flight out."

His hand reached out for me as he stood, begging. "Baby, please, don't go."

"No reason for me to stay," I said softly in defeat as I looked up at him. I was tired of being alone, of trying but being made to feel like a doll and not a person.

"Do you have no feelings for me at all?"

I couldn't stop myself; my body reacted on behalf of my heart.

My hand slapped across his cheek and we both stood there, stunned, his skin pinking as our gazes locked. Tears began to slide down my cheeks.

"That's my line, Weston. And to answer . . . I'm in love with you," I admitted, then pushed past him and into my car, speeding off, leaving him there on the beach.

My eyes blurred as I raced down the Interstate. It was so stupid to think being married would work. Two different worlds and a large age gap, plus trying to avoid being in the public eye? Doomed to fail.

I wiped the tears from my eyes, clearing my vision. My heart was breaking, because I really was in love with him, just too afraid to admit it before, especially with all that'd been going on. But there was no point in staying if things were going to stay as they were. I was smart enough to know I didn't deserve to live my life unhappy and lonely.

I pulled into the garage and ran up the stairs to our room. The tears began again as I grabbed my suitcase out of the closet and pulled out my phone to search for flights. I could drive, but in my state it was not only a bad idea, but I wasn't going to take the car with me in case I didn't come back. There was a flight in about four hours. I booked it, called for a cab, and began packing as fast as I could.

My heart began to race, adrenaline pumping, when I heard footsteps on the stairs as I zipped up my full suitcase. He was breathing hard behind me, a strangled noise erupting from him.

"Please," he whispered. That one word tore at me, and I had to squeeze my eyes tight to keep from crying again. "Please, don't leave me. We can work this out, Wren. Give us . . . Give *me* a chance to prove how much I want you with me."

I turned to look at him and both of our eyes widened. His eyes were red and tear filled, panic written all over his expression and in his posture.

I shook my head. "Your actions speak louder than words, Weston."

He walked to me, his hands moving to cradle my face. "Forget about what I do, and who I am to the public. What are your feelings on me, Weston, the man?"

"He is so wonderful," I whispered, tears falling once again.

"Then please don't leave him. I need you, Wren," he begged, wiping my tears with his thumbs. "The potential of us is so beautiful. I've had a vision of the kind of woman I always wanted in my life, and you are her. That's why I asked you to marry me. I know it is. I couldn't let you go. I need you. I've waited so long . . . I live in a world full of fakeness, and you are real. I feel sane with you. You are grounding, refreshing, and real beauty."

I had to turn from him, free myself from his touch. The hardest thing I'd ever done in my life was leaning down to pick up my bags. "My plane leaves in three hours. I have to go."

"Wren, please." His panic rose.

"I just need to clear my head. I'll spend the holidays with my mom. I need a break from . . . all of this," I said, waving my hand in the air.

"A few days? And then you'll be back?" Hope laced his tone.

"I . . . I don't know," I answered honestly, because I didn't know what was going to happen.

I had to do it, leave. I needed some distance to gain real perspective on what to do. Something needed to change, so I was going to do it and see where we ended up. In my heart I hoped it would all work out for the best, that we would make it through, but I just didn't know.

Chapter Twenty-Six

HIS LONELINESS—WESTON

S ILENCE. I COULDN'T REMEMBER A TIME MY HOUSE HAD ever felt so empty. Even in all the years I lived alone. My gaze was locked on the spot she'd been standing. The sheets on the bed—our bed—were tangled on her side. I didn't even get to sleep beneath them with her the night before, to breathe in her sweetness, feel her warmth.

I hadn't slept the previous night, haunted by what she had said to me and wondering when things had become so fucked up. I crawled onto the bed, lying down on her pillow, in hopes of getting a little bit of Wren's lingering scent. It was calming and gave the illusion she was still there, that she hadn't walked out and left me. My aching heart was soothed by the falsity of it all.

How had it all gone so terribly wrong? My recent behavior had been deplorable, so I couldn't really blame her for leaving me. The realization I'd fucked up so bad that it gave her no other choice but to leave for her own peace of mind, was like poison. Acid burning me from within. Too late to take it back.

Then there was Natalie . . .

Natalie had upped her advances in recent weeks, but I knew how she operated. It pissed her off if I ignored her. If I pushed her away, she thought it was a game and came at me harder. So when she kissed me that morning I went still as stone—they weren't the lips I wanted. I was about to tell her to get the fuck out, but then

Wren was there, bag in hand with no school, and the world fell out from beneath me.

Wren couldn't see my reactions from the angle she was watching when Natalie kissed me, and she had no idea how badly I wanted to shove her away with all the strength I had. Send her flying across the room.

My heart shattered as she got into her car, saying that I should find someone new. I knew then I'd fucked up so badly it would take a miracle for her to not divorce me, let alone talk to me.

"Get out of here, Natalie. Get out of here or so help me . . ." I raged, trailing off at the end. I knew her game. She'd twist my words, tell the paps I'd beaten her, threatened her life. No, I wouldn't threaten her life, though I wished she'd leave mine, but I could end her career.

She cackled, and it grated on my last nerve. "Oh, Weston, I know you don't hit women, unless it's when you're spanking while you fuck. You always were a kinky bastard. You won't do anything to me, because I can tell the whole associated press your little secret. Married to a high school girl? They'll eat that shit up."

"Say one fucking word about my marriage, about my wife, and I will fucking end you."

Her smile faded. "You couldn't. I'm too big now."

My eyes were slits, my fists clenched in fury as I growled, "Oh, trust me, I can end your whole fucking career in minutes. You're not as good as you think you are. No one in this fucking town will hire you, except the pimps. You'd be a natural. I know how you like to spread your legs. Without me, you have nothing but that."

"Fucking asshole, always so full of yourself. I have my own name now, I don't need you," she argued, her lips pursed, chin high in the air. She was confident, full of her own ego, but I also saw fear in her features.

"Oh, really?" I asked, glaring at her. I smirked at her as my eyes narrowed. "Shall we test it out?" Her eyes widened and it made me happy, because I was finally getting to her. "Get out before I call the cops to extract you and TMZ to blast you."

She screeched in anger as she stormed out, and then everything went to shit. Wren was gone, fed up with everything, with me.

I awoke some time later, early morning light filtering in through the curtains, and laid there listening to . . . nothing. After an hour or so I moved downstairs, trying to figure out what to do. My head was spinning, my thoughts jumbled. I was at a stalemate.

My future depended on what she decided. If she thought I was worth the trouble or not.

As I walked into the kitchen, my eyes locked onto the table. Memories of us together, loving each other on the smooth wood filled my mind, my body reacting to the images of taking her. Times when I was deliriously happy. I stumbled out of the room and into the living room where I remembered her meeting Julia, and introducing her as my wife.

Pain coursed through me, my hand lashing out, smacking the vase filled with flowers on to the ground. The sound of it shattering on the hardwood floor echoed off the walls. My chest was clenched tight, and it was becoming increasingly harder to breathe.

I heard the garage door open, a small spark of hope begging for it to be Wren. My eyes were locked on the hallway, waiting for whomever it was to appear.

Julia's figure came into view and I sunk down on the couch, my head collapsed into my hands, fisting my hair.

"Weston? Are you all right?" she asked. The concern in her tone told me I looked as bad as I felt. "Weston, what's wrong? Do you want me to get Wren? Is she upstairs?"

"She's gone."

Her eyes went wide, her mouth silent, before pulling out her phone. "Is she at Charlotte's? I'll have her come home."

"No, Julia, she's gone. She left."

She stopped again and stared at me. "What do you mean she left? Weston, what happened here?"

"It's my fault . . . I've lost her, Julia." My eyes watered and I almost felt like I was choking.

She grabbed on to my shoulders. "What the hell do you mean by that? Gone? Where is she?"

"Indianapolis. She went home. She. Is. Gone."

"You Lockwood men are so damn hardheaded sometimes." She stood and pulled out her phone, walking out of the room as she dialed a number.

I sat there, unmoving, numb from everything. I didn't know for how long, but soon Miles was tripping over himself to get at me. He grabbed my shoulders and shook me. "What have you done? What the fuck have you done, Wes? "

"She's gone. She just . . . couldn't take it anymore. And I couldn't stop her." My eyes shifted down. No way could I look him in the eye after how badly I'd been treating my wife—the best person, aside from Miles, I'd ever known.

"Well, fucking get her back!" he snarled, his fingers digging in my arm. "I mean, shit, I knew things weren't good, especially that day when you and Natalie were all over the magazines. Then at school she'd been quiet and down, so much so it reflected in her music." He shook his head in disappointment.

I brushed his arms off and scowled. "How the fuck am I supposed to do that? She hates me at this point. I'm not capable of having a normal relationship!" I slammed my fists down on the couch, my jaw tight in frustration. "I thought if I could just make it through this week, if I could just get everything done without one more goddamn fucking thing going wrong or falling apart, I could take the holiday week off and make it up to her."

He glared at me. "You're so fucking stupid, you know that, Weston? A grade A moron."

"Excuse *me*?" I cocked my head and looked at him, though my head was angled down.

"You heard me." He kicked the chair nearby. "All this time, I was so happy for you to finally have something good in your life. The dream you were looking for. I couldn't even see it at first, and then you piss it all away. I mean, I guess I shouldn't be surprised. You did stay with Natalie for six years."

I snapped up to my feet, my hands pushing on his chest in anger. "What the fuck is that supposed to mean?" With Natalie it was business and pleasure, not love. I couldn't confide in Natalie on anything, because we didn't talk like that.

With Wren it was different. It nearly killed me when it came out at Thanksgiving about my parents. I was afraid how she would look at me, knowing that I'd been a drug addict, wondering if I was worth it.

It didn't deter him. He only pushed back. "It means you haven't been in a loving, committed relationship ever in your life. The closest you ever came was Steph, and she was engaged when she began working for you. That was the most you ever really cared about someone until you met Wren, and you weren't even in a relationship with her!" I stared at him in disbelief, but not at him insinuating I had feelings for my former assistant Stephanie, because I did, he was right. "Deep down you're just scared."

"Scared? Of what?" I cried, throwing my hands in the air.

"Of being happy. You don't know how to do it, do you?" His voice lowered, but he still looked ready to rip a fucker's head off. *My* head off, to be exact.

I shrugged. "I don't know . . . I try . . ." I trailed off. "What did you want me to do? I didn't have time to spend with Wren." I turned my head to stretch my neck and shoulders. Everything was stiff.

"Well, you should've fucking told her what was going on. She had no idea Julia and Amy were trying to tamp down all the lies Natalie was telling tabloids and papers, or that Paramount almost ended their contract with you over the Talia Clark shit. And you should've seen that blowout coming that happened in your office. My God, you were taking all your shit out on her. I would've left your ass too," he spat, then took a deep breath.

"When did you become her biggest fan? You hated her."

He stared at the floor and took a deep breath. "I get it now, what I didn't want to see then. I'm *your* supporter. All I want is what's good for you, and she is good for you. You think Julia wasn't telling me everything when we weren't talking?"

"Julia can be so nosey," I grumbled.

Miles's eyes narrowed on me. "She was trying to get me to see how happy you were. That's all I want for you, and Wren is the key."

"I missed her every fucking minute, but when I got home . . . fuck! She wasn't available to me, and it pissed me the hell off. I've been doing all of this for us—for her!"

"No, Weston. You did it all for you, and nobody else. She couldn't have fucking cared if you lost your company and worked retail. She wants you. I know that now. She doesn't care about how much money you make or what you do as long as you're happy and there for her." His knuckles cracked as they fisted. "You weren't there for her. You left her all alone in a strange place."

I shook my head. No. He was wrong.

"She knew I'd have to leave sometimes and be on location, but then I get back and she's off with her little friends partying. Her priorities were fucked up," I complained. "Of course I snapped. My time is valuable—and I don't have a lot of it. She needs to be there for me when I'm available." My gut tightened as the words fell from my mouth.

God, you sound like the biggest dick ever. Just shut up now.

Miles sucked in a tight breath, and I waited for the blowout. All Wren had tried to do was make me feel better, but she got sick of my shit and she was a strong enough woman, she had to respect herself and leave. She knew she didn't deserve to be treated as second best.

"Do you know how empty my hotel room felt without her? How much I wished I could've taken her along with me? I was a step away from calling her up, begging her to drop out of school so she could be with me."

"Selfish prick," he mumbled under his breath.

"I know!" I hissed, slamming my hands on my thighs. "That's what she does to me. All the damn time. I can barely breathe without her—she's become my life force."

"You're the only person I know that can leave the house on good terms with his wife, then shit all over it the moment you get home, just to make sure it gets extra fucked up." He shook his head and stared at me like I was brain-dead.

I chose to ignore that last comment. All I had wanted was to make it up her when I got home, spend as much time with her as possible, to show her how much I had wanted her while I was away. Instead, it was like I was struggling to lock down the windows for a coming hurricane, only to find out I was the hurricane.

"Everything got so out of hand." I shook my head. "I was losing control of so many things . . ." Too many things.

"That you forgot to appreciate your wife? Fuck, Weston! Let me tell you something, I know I fucked up in the beginning with her, but I'm beginning to think I know her better than you do. She's a woman. I know you didn't get a chance to date her or chase her, because you skipped all of that, but *all those things* you should have been doing over the last few months. She's a person, ripped out of her world and dropped into *yours*."

"I get that!"

"Do you? I don't think so. You don't fucking try to do anything but work yourself to death. Stop it! I'm telling you right now—that shit's killing you. And it's not worth it. *She* is worth it, though. She made you happy, even when you had no idea she did." He sighed. "I can't believe you did this."

"*I* did this?" I growled. "She fucking left me. I wasn't the one—"

"Goddammit—forget it! You don't deserve her if you can't even get it that you're the one that pushed her away." He pointed in my face. "Get a fucking clue and stop being this . . . self-centered, controlling ass. You're turning into Dad!"

I bolted up to standing. "I am not!" I yelled, leaning forward, my chest heaving. "You fucking take that back."

Miles threw his hands up in the air. "He directed your life, took every decision away from you, including what went in your body. Now you're making sure no one else can ever have that power over you again. You control *everything*, even her and what time you give to her."

"No . . . No, you're . . ." Wrong. He had to be. I couldn't be like him. I despised my father.

"You're him without a son to push into an early grave. You've taken his role, doing it to yourself and her!" His hand dropped and his eyes were wild. "If you are serious about your marriage, about Wren, you'll not do what he did! You'll back off, spend time with your wife, make a family, and be happy."

"Fuck!" I pulled at my hair and tipped my head back.

How had I let it happen?

"Get. Her. Back," was the last thing he said to me before I dropped my face into my hands and sobbed.

My body heaved as the tears streamed down my face, having faced my ugly truths. He was right, but then again, Miles was always right.

Every decision I made without her only made things worse. Every time I didn't tell her about all the shit that was going on, when I had the opportunity to just pushed her further away. I began to wonder if I was self-sabotaging.

After a while of crying, I got up and headed upstairs to take a shower. With all that was going on I hadn't even changed my clothes in almost forty-eight hours, let alone taken time to clean up. My eyes were unable to avoid looking at her side of the bed, wishing she would appear so I could apologize . . . I needed to apologize.

After turning on the shower I stared at my reflection, my fingers tracing the letters on my skin. I hadn't gotten to show her yet. I knew I'd been an ass recently. I realized it at Thanksgiving, when I was talking to John, how much she meant to me.

How much I loved her.

My actions never gave me a chance to tell her. I treated her terribly and said so many awful things to her out of stress and agitation, none of it caused by her. I used her as an outlet.

She was my light. It was because of her I was able to make it through the day without going off the deep end. Every night in bed with her I was able to reenergize just by having her in my arms.

The shower could wash away the dirt and grime on my flesh, but it couldn't rid me of the deeds I'd done and the things I'd said.

My resolve came then. I wasn't going to wait for her to come back to me; I was going to go to her. I would do whatever I had to, to get her back, to have her come home. I loved her. It was a young love, new and uncertain, but it grew stronger every day we were together. She was mine, had been ever since I saw her at the Starbucks in the lobby at the Mirage.

I booked a flight for Indianapolis. It was a long one, but it would give me time to get my head sorted out. All I knew was that I was *not* coming back home without her. I couldn't.

An hour later I was through security and on my way to one of the first commercial flights I'd been on in many years. After boarding, I stared at the clock realizing it would be a near four-hour journey to gather my thoughts.

All I could do was hope I wasn't too late. Miles was right. I needed to cut back on work. If I was going to make it work, I needed to commit myself to Wren. Work would always be there, but if I didn't slow down, I was going to lose her forever. She would divorce me.

The thought alone was heart wrenching. Her not being with me was not an option.

Thank God for first class and being in the second row. I was off the plane in no time, carry-on in my hand, and running toward the car rental area.

After renting a car, I punched in her mother's address and took off. I'd have to thank Julia for that information later.

Forty minutes later, the anxiety began to crush me as I pulled into the driveway. I headed to the front door with trepidation of what would greet me. I found I was holding my breath, hoping she'd hear me out. I needed her, and I didn't need anything.

The door opened shortly after I rang the doorbell, a very pissed off Karen staring me down.

"You have a lot of damn nerve, or a lot of guts showing up here," she said, crossing her arms and blocking the way.

"Please, Karen, I need to see her. I need to make things right."

She pursed her lips at me. "You have a lot of explaining to do, along with groveling—and I mean *a lot*! I didn't send my daughter with you so she could come back in a couple of months with a broken heart."

"I acted terribly, I admit it, but I'm here to grovel, just as you've said, until she comes home."

"She's a person in your care, and I'm not just talking physically. You have to care for her emotionally, spend time with her. She's not a pet. Do you love her, Weston? Or do you just love the dream?" She quirked her brow, clearly telling me I needed to prove myself before she let me near her daughter again.

"She is the dream, she is love, *she* is everything. I'm new at this, Karen. I admit that I don't know what I'm doing. All I know is I want and love her."

"Then prepare to get on your knees and have your balls ripped from you," she said and stepped back inside, calling for Wren.

When she came into view, my beautiful wife was filled with sadness—an emotion I'd put there. She gasped upon seeing me, her arms folding in front of her, regaining her composure.

"What are you doing here, Weston?"

I've come to take you home.

Chapter Twenty-Seven

OUR FIRST CHRISTMAS

IT WAS DURING THE FOURTH BATCH OF OUR ANNUAL Christmas Eve cookie making event when the doorbell rang, and Mom went to answer it.

"I bet it's Weston," Daniel said as he pressed the dough out on the table.

Chances were it was yet another cookie delivery from one of the neighbors. Two tins had already been delivered since we started.

"Yeah, right. It's been two days, and I haven't heard one word from him. He's probably at work right now, figuring out his schedule with Natalie," I said, my lip twitching up into a sneer.

But even my anger didn't stop the pain in my chest or stop the tears that had been falling almost non-stop since I left.

"God, I hate that bitch!" Daniel fumed.

"Makes two of us," I said with a sigh. "She might have just ended what was never meant to be in the first place, though." It hurt to say, but that didn't make it any less true.

Daniel stared at me with wide eyes. "You don't mean that, Wren."

"Don't I? Because I sure as hell think I do."

He shook his head. "No. I don't believe that. I saw you two together at dinner and when we were watching a movie that last night. Your mom's right. I mean, he hurt my BFF, which makes me want to junk punch him over and over, but at the same time, I've never seen you look at anyone the way you looked at him."

"And how did I look at him?" I asked as I picked through the cookie cutters and pulled out the snowman.

He let out a sigh. "Like he was the whole world. And he looked at you the same damn way. Made me so jealous. I hope one day some guy will look at me like that."

I thought about what Daniel said, and remembered that feeling. What if I could get it back? What if Mom was right and we were worth fighting for?

I was pulled from my thoughts by Mom coming back in the room, a cookie hanging out of her mouth and a holiday tin in her hand.

"Cookie? Marsha brought them by," she said as she offered them up.

I chuckled and looked around the room. "I think we're good."

"Says you. Hit me up, Momma!" Daniel opened his mouth wide and she popped one in. He let out a groan, his eyes closing. "So good."

The doorbell rang again and Mom let out an exasperated sigh. "You two better finish those up soon, because I've had five neighbors deliver cookies in the last two days."

We all laughed as she turned for what was probably another round of cookie delivery.

"So, remember that college guy I was telling you about?" Daniel's lips twitched up into a grin.

"Yeah?"

"We're meeting up tonight for dinner at his house," he said. "I'm going to meet his sister!"

"That is awesome!" I ran around the island to hug him as best I could with my dough covered hands.

"He is so hot, and wonderful, and hot," he said with a dreamy sigh.

"Glad to know someone's getting some." There was a sour edge to my voice.

"Wren . . ."

I closed my eyes, then opened them, my brow knitted as I looked at him. "Sorry, I didn't mean it to sound that way." I reached for his hand and gave it a squeeze. "I'm happy for you. Really. He sounds great and you deserve to be happy, especially after all that Trevor shit."

"He is," he said, beaming, "and I can't wait for you to meet him."

His statement made me wonder when I would. If I didn't go home, I'd have plenty of time. The idea of staying made my heart hurt, though. The truth was—nowhere felt like home, anymore.

Mom called me out from the other room, stirring me from my thoughts. I washed my hands before heading to the front door, wondering which neighbor had stopped by now.

But I was not prepared for what awaited me when I rounded the corner.

"What are you doing here, Weston?" I asked as I looked at my husband. Shock and confusion filled me.

Daniel was right.

Mom headed back to the kitchen, and I was stuck not knowing which reaction to go with.

Did I jump into his arms, or kick him in the nuts and send him packing? There was also the option of kicking him then jumping into his arms. Either way, the kicking part sounded like it could be fun and very liberating, but only because I was angry with him.

As I looked him over I noticed he appeared as rough as I felt. He stepped forward, and I backed up, fearful of the power his touch held over me.

"It's Christmas Eve, and I want to spend Christmas with my wife," he said low, his voice breaking. He held up his hands in surrender. "Please don't tell me to go, baby. Please . . . I . . . fuck . . . I need you to . . . Will you hear me out, please? Please, let me talk to you."

I attempted to blink back the tears that were forming, but failed. Weston reached out and brushed away a tear that fell with his thumb, and it took everything in me not to lean into his touch.

Across the street I could see the neighbor staring at Weston, and I grabbed his arm and pulled him inside, shutting the door tight behind him. I turned to look at him, shocked to see him surrounded by the house I'd lived in for six years. He looked so out of place, much like me in his L.A. mansion.

"You came," I whispered, not meaning to say it out loud, but too overwhelmed to hold it in.

"I had to. It's been so dark and lonely without you the past few days," he said. His voice was rough, scratchy. "You're my sunshine, though I've never told you. I've never told you a lot of things, Wren, about me or my life. I should have, I know that now. It wasn't to keep secrets, I promise, but more to shield you, and maybe to protect myself a bit. But that backfired on me, didn't it?"

His words crushed my heart, his voice soft and filled with longing. I had to hold strong, because his effort alone to come to me made me want to crumble. My arms crossed back over my chest, protecting me. "There is such a thing as too little too late, you know."

His eyes widened, panic rising in his features. "N-no, please God, Wren, don't say that. Please! Baby, I need you. Please . . ." A guttural sound ripped from him as he grabbed the wall for support.

It broke me to see him like that. The emotion that poured out of him was real and heart wrenching.

"Please, Wren, please. I know I fucked up," he begged as tears fell from his eyes. "I'm so sorry. I love you, so much, Wren, and I fucked it up." I gasped at his declaration, but he didn't stop. "Please don't divorce me. Give me a chance to make it right, please. I'm so sorry."

I stepped forward, unable to take it any longer, and cupped his face in my hands. The moisture seeped into my skin, my touch calming him. His head fell against my forehead.

"Shh, calm down," I whispered. His breathing regulated and a shuddered breath moved through him before evening out. "You just said you love me."

"I do," he said adamantly. "I'm not very good at it, a clumsy asshole thus far, but I promise to protect your heart and not hurt it again. If you'll give me a chance to prove it, that is?"

I looked around and found my mom and Daniel spying from the kitchen. It looked like Mom was holding Daniel back, but I could also see the tears in Daniel's eyes.

"Come on, Weston." I pulled him up. "Let's go to my room."

I took his hand in mine and led him down the short hall to my bedroom, closing the door behind us. It was sparse, just my furniture and a few decorations, my suitcase in the corner. Everything else was in L.A.

I climbed onto my bed, folding my legs as I leaned against the wall. I wanted to say something strong and forceful, but I couldn't. There was a lot at stake on this conversation, and it couldn't be rushed. Plus, he'd been honest with me so far, no need to press him.

He looked around my room for a moment before sitting as well, turning his body so he was facing me.

"You make my day brighter and full of love. And without you, I'm just wrong. My life isn't right without you in it." There was no wading into it. He jumped right in, but his fingers picked at his jacket cuff in nervous agitation. "I became engrossed with my work, as I usually do with projects of their size, and it took me away from my personal life. Normally it wouldn't be an issue for me, but that was before you came into my life."

"You told me all these things, your dreams, and I believed them. And you went against them." I had to pause, tears forming. "To go from showering me with affection, love, gifts, to almost ignoring me is too much. Tell me why I should go back to being lonely?"

He shook his head and took my hands in his. "No, I don't want you to be lonely. I want you to be able to depend on me to be there for you."

"You haven't been lately," I snapped, my hurt coming out a little more forceful than I meant.

"I know," he whispered, then huffed, looking at the ceiling then back to me. "I see now how terrible I've been as a husband. I'm the older one, with more relationship experience, but it seems I'm a novice at love. I was an ass. A big inconsiderate ass. I had thought if I could get it all done, push past it, I could make it up to you."

Looking around the room, I drew in a breath before glancing back at him. The look in his eyes nearly knocked the breath from me. "Tell me why I shouldn't turn you around and send you back to L.A.?"

"Because I love you, and I will do anything to make this work and make up for my behavior to you." He pulled my hands up to his mouth and placed light kisses on my fingers. I let him because I needed the comfort as well. "And, I'm not going back without you, Wren. No way, no how."

"And *why* was your behavior so terrible?" I needed to make sure that he knew, that he understood.

"I could list many excuses and reasons, but the bottom line is, because instead of telling you about my stresses, I took them out on you."

I pulled away from him and scooted back against the wall.

"And what were all of these stresses?" I asked. I wasn't going to allow him to hold anything back. "Besides the hell-bitch and that fucking kiss, because I will not tolerate infidelity in any form, Weston."

He let out an angry noise. "She crossed a line, and I'm done playing nice." I quirked my brow at him, and he nodded, continuing. "First of all, I did not kiss her, she kissed me. I refused to react to her, and before it all had a chance to play out, to show her that her tricks weren't going to work, you were there. Believe me, baby, I promise I have been faithful and will always be faithful." He took a deep breath, watching me for my reaction.

I sighed. "Okay, I believe you. But never again, Weston. I don't think my heart can take it."

"I know. I'm so sorry." He reached out and ran his fingers over my face. "You know those trash mags you brought to me?" I nodded. "Well, they were leaked by Natalie and an accomplice. Julia and Amy have been squashing them for weeks, but that one got through. Between her incessant attempts to get between us, and her work, I'm finished."

"What does that mean?" I asked.

"It means, Natalie is going down." There was a fire burning in his blue eyes. She'd finally pushed him too far.

"What are you going to do?"

Scooting forward, he slipped his hands into mine again. "I'm hoping it will be what are *we* going to do. I fucked up by not talking to you, not telling you things, partly because you're not used to it. To my world. I should have explained more."

"You should have explained everything," I said.

He nodded in agreement. "Yes, I should have and I will from now on. Natalie's PR stunt was a good thing for us in a small way, because it took the attention off of you. She was trying to get me back on her arm and aggravate you, which she accomplished. Your reaction was what I was trying to protect you from, protect *us* from." He sighed and tangled his fingers with mine.

"What do you have to protect us from?"

"It's not because I don't want people to know we're married, or because you're still in high school," he said, his brow scrunched up. "It's because I want time with you, to get to know you more, to fall further in love with you. Solidify us before their hateful lies try to tear us apart."

"You're an expert on it. You've experienced it before."

He nodded. "And I know from experience the harm they can cause. Fucking vultures who prey on celebrities. Spouting lies to stir up gossip. They don't care about who we are as people. They don't care who they hurt. And most of all; they will do anything to get a story, even ruining lives and destroying relationships."

"My age and status does have some to do with it, whether you want to admit it or not."

"Because it scares me, baby."

Not quite what I was thinking. "What they'll say about you?"

"No, what they'll say about *you*. I'm used to their shit, you're not. It doesn't get to me anymore, but I know how much it could hurt you. You are a sweet, gentle person. You don't have the thick skin needed to take the lies they dish out. Not yet."

I thought about what he said, and he was right about one thing—I wasn't hard-hearted like I needed to be in Hollywood. I needed to understand what awaited me when things did come out. "So, what else haven't you been telling me?"

He swallowed hard and pulled in a deep breath. "Talia's delays almost caused me to lose all future projects with Paramount Pictures."

"What?" My voice rose an octave as I leaned in.

He nodded. "It was such a clusterfuck, money flying out the window with each day of non-production, and people on the verge of losing their futures in the business. The director couldn't get through to her, I couldn't, hell, even her father couldn't. Who fucking knew it would take a stunt coordinator to get her in line." He shook his head and smirked, and I knew he was remembering Lance and Talia's first meeting.

"I knew things were bad based on your behavior, but I didn't know they were that bad. Why didn't you just fire her?" I asked. Wouldn't that have been easier?

"I should have, but I didn't think she would draw it out so long." He pulled his hands from mine and swept them through his hair. I could feel the agitation radiating off him. "I should have told you that, let you know what was going on, all of it. Everything was getting so out of control and I couldn't get it back in line. It was maddening!"

We sat there for a few minutes in silence as I processed it all. My emotions were everywhere, not knowing what to believe.

"If I come back with you, things have got to change."

"They will, I promise."

"How?" I asked. Saying things would change was just vague words. "You have to tell me how, because if you are just saying it, if you have nothing laid out, then why should I trust it?"

"I'm going to shut down Natalie's film, first thing when we get back, until we find a new lead actress. Also, I want to have a meeting with Joe, just the three of us. He thinks he finally has a lead on how she's been getting past the gates and into the house without anyone knowing. And we'll figure out how to get rid of her together."

"And work?"

"Well, with one movie off my shoulders that just leaves Talia's, and then the promotion of *Dream Machine*. Other than that, I'm going to talk to Carson and look into bumping someone up in the ranks. Lockwood Entertainment has grown into more than I ever hoped, and we're both swamped. We've worked hard for the last six years. I think some family time is needed."

"And family time would be . . ." I pressed.

"Home at a decent hour, only taking emergency calls after I've left the office. No working on weekends unless it is for filming or an emergency. And most of all; putting my wife and our family before work." He reached out and took my hands again. "I'm redirecting my priorities in life."

"It sounds perfect."

"I'll make it perfect, or as close as I can to perfect."

"What about people knowing? Being a secret really fucking sucks, especially when I walk into your office and they don't know who I am."

His thumbs made soft circles on my hands. "I want to take you out on a date, many of them, and get to know my wife outside of our home. And I want to announce us to the world, but I really want a little more time of just the two of us, and the outing to be in an avenue we both agree on."

"I like the sound of that." My lips twitched up into a smile.

There was silence as we looked at each other, and I attempted to form my thoughts into coherent sentences. I had something I needed to make Weston understand.

"I know you're busy and work a ton," I said with a deep breath.

"I understand and can deal with it, but I need you to remember that I was uprooted from my life and dropped into yours. It may seem like nothing to you, because not much changed in your life. I was turned upside down and shaken; new state, new house, new car, new name, new school, new people." I ran my hands through my hair. "Hell, the only things I had from my old life were shipped to me in a few boxes."

"I'm sorry."

"Everything is strange and so different from what I knew. I get by tripping and stumbling when I really need you to hold my hand and help me through it, because without you I'm lost and I fuck up, making you angry. I don't know what I'm doing in your world. There are all these rules and I'm stepping on eggshells hoping I don't break one." I cringed, thinking about our fight after I stormed into his office.

He sighed. "My timing was fucked up. It sounded like such a brilliant plan in Vegas. All I could think about was the feeling I had when I was with you and how I wanted to keep it. Selfish on my part, but then you said yes, and I didn't care about anything except that I was going to marry you. After that, I continued to be selfish, making decisions and not taking your opinion into account. Will you please come home and be my partner in life?"

My chest tightened. I knew what I wanted, but I was also scared. "Weston, I . . ."

Weston reached out and placed my hand over his heart. "I want to show you something, and hopefully it will help you believe how much I love and need you, and how much I want you forever." He kept my hand in place and reached back to pull his shirt up and over his head. "I got this done when I was on set last week. I needed to have a reminder of you near me, with me at all times."

He removed my hand and I gasped, my eyes locked on his chest. The area of skin above where his heart lay, in elegant blooming script, were the words *Love happened* underneath that the date 10-8-2016, and beneath that *Wren*.

"I love you."

Tears overflowed from my eyes and I lunged at him, wrapping my arms around his neck. He was shocked, but gripped me tight to him, nuzzling into my neck.

He'd made me a permanent fixture on his skin. Our wedding—a date never to be forgotten.

I needed to trust and believe that everything he said was real and things would change, and we'd find a comfortable balance between us. I needed time to see, but I also needed an out if it didn't.

"I'll give you one month," I said seriously, my voice shaking before gaining strength. "I love you, Weston, but I can't be a kept little doll wife whose sole purpose is to serve you. If things don't get better, I'm gone, and I'm not coming back. The only time you'll see me is when we're getting divorced." My voice wavered on the last word.

His arms tightened around me, his voice strong, yet so vulnerable. "You're not divorcing me. Ever. I will make this right. I promise I will work hard so you never think of leaving my side again."

"I'll hold you to that."

"You do that," he said, swiping a strand of hair from my face. "Though, you could do something to make things easier for me . . ."

"What?"

"Stop letting that fucking brat put his hands all the fuck over you," he grumbled.

I couldn't help but laugh. For some reason, at that moment, his jealousy was cute. Probably due to his expression, looking like a kid telling me some other kid stole his toy.

"It isn't funny!"

I laughed harder, and soon he joined in. "I'm sorry, really, you just looked so cute."

His brow scrunched. "Usually my jealousy upsets you."

"That's because you're usually angry and manhandling me." I played with the hair at the nape of his neck. "And I'll make sure Aaron gets the message."

"Good." He blew out a breath, his mouth so close to mine. I

fought the urge to lean forward for a kiss. "Because you are *mine.*" He growled the last part before closing the distance and crashing his lips to mine.

I moaned, peace settling over me with his touch. His hands roamed, leaving trails of tingles, lighting my body up. It'd been weeks since he'd touched me, and I'd missed it . . . a lot. The kiss deepened, my fingers gripping him anywhere I could, the need to be close to him taking over.

My back fell against the bed, his hips settled between my thighs. "Whoa, there." I pressed a hand against his chest as I detached my lips from his.

He chuckled, kissing my forehead as he reluctantly rolled next to me, pulling me close at the same time. "Sorry, got carried away."

"Yeah, my mom and best friend are down the hall. Let's wait on *that* reunion until we get home."

We sat back up and, hand in hand, headed back to the kitchen. A smile was plastered on my face and hope blossomed in my heart.

Time to celebrate our first Christmas.

Chapter Twenty-Eight

OUR NEW BEGINNING

M Y MOM WAS GRINNING LIKE THE CHESHIRE CAT WHEN we entered the kitchen, while Daniel was stuck between smiling and bitch slapping. Weston's eyes lit up like a kid at Christmas as he surveyed the bounty, and I repeatedly had to smack his hand from picking up a cookie on the cooling rack. However, Mom fed his addiction by opening up one of the multiple canisters she'd received over the last few days and hoisting it into his chest, which he began munching away at.

"Better?" Daniel asked in a whisper once Weston's attention was diverted.

"We're getting there." I gave him a smile.

His eyes lit up. "Are you going home with him?"

I nodded. "After Christmas sometime."

He smiled back and wrapped his frosting covered hands around me. "I'll miss you."

"Miss you, too. And it's only a few months till summer," I said to reassure him, but it didn't do much to lift the sadness that swallowed him.

"Yeah, but every day without you sucks monkey balls."

I laughed and nudged him with my shoulder. "Ditto."

He shook his head. "No, you're living with your gorgeous, rich, hunk of a husband. There is no ditto there, Buttercup, only envy from me."

I watched as Weston packed another cookie into his mouth, a look of pure bliss on his face as he licked his lips and devoured the sugary goodness. "I dunno, I'm kind of envious of that cookie right now."

Daniel looked toward Weston, and his jaw dropped. "Yeah, totally envious."

We finished up the cookies and boxed them up for the neighbors, separating out the ones for Daniel and ourselves, before discussing dinner. It wasn't feasible to take Weston out—Indianapolis may not be L.A., but he was too well known of a face.

"Really, we can go out," Weston said. "I want to take you all out to dinner."

"It's too risky," Mom argued. "You don't want that kind of attention here, Weston."

"We can order in," I suggested, but Daniel groaned at the idea of Chinese for the second day in a row.

After another twenty minutes we all piled into Mike's Jeep, me sandwiched between Weston and Daniel in the back, and headed out to Chili's. Not my first choice of restaurant, but when Weston said he'd never gone, Mom was determined we rectified that situation. She loved their boneless buffalo wings more than I did.

It didn't turn out to be the disaster I thought it might. Then again, introducing himself as Dorian March—his character from *Genesis*—threw people off his scent.

"You know you look like . . ."

"Weston Lockwood." He finished for the waitress when it finally clicked, halfway through our meal. "Yeah, I get that a lot."

She laughed, and then headed off to refill our drinks.

"I'm starting to get kinda jealous of the women around here," I whispered to him.

"And why is that exactly?"

"They're openly flirting with *my* husband. I want to be able to do that."

He pulled back and stared at me, making my cheeks heat before leaning back in. "Soon, baby girl."

"Soon," I said with a resigned sigh.

He leaned in closer, voice just above a whisper as he spoke into my ear. It was so low no one else could hear. "Until then you can mark me with your scent to keep them all away. I'll eat your pretty little pussy until you cream all over my face, and I won't wash it off."

My eyes were wide, hand fanning my face as my legs squeezed together.

"PG over there." I heard my mom say, and my eyes flashed to hers. They were dancing in amusement, which only made my face flame hotter.

Weston *loved* the boneless wings, devouring them like a starving man while wondering out loud if Kelly could make them. I was pretty sure she could, but it would probably be more fun if we could sneak out and get them by ourselves. My mind began to wander, trying to figure out how it would work. How could we date in L.A.? Maybe the secret was going outside of the city.

A pair of girls did come up to him on our way out to have their picture taken with the Weston Lockwood look-a-like. I couldn't help but laugh at the day they realized it really was him.

We had so much fun at dinner that it was hard to believe the reality of the past few weeks. Stress made him a different man. When he was happy about something he shined bright and was like a magnet, but when the skies grayed and took over, destruction was all that remained.

I could only hope and have faith in him that things would change like he promised. Faith that my mom was right, and the feelings I had for him were right. I didn't expect a huge shift over the next month—that was too much for him to do right away—but I wanted progress. Signs that he was taking us seriously for the first time, and adjusting me into his life.

"Here, guys." Daniel thrust a package at Weston minutes after walking in the door to my mom's house from dinner. "I was going to mail it to you two, but seeing as you're here . . ."

Weston stared from the brightly wrapped box in his hands, then up to Daniel. "Thank you, Daniel."

"You can thank me by not hurting my best friend anymore."

Weston pursed his lips and nodded in agreement. "I'll try my hardest. You have my word."

"You better, or I'll kick you in the nads."

I stared in surprise at Daniel, who gave me a small smile in return. He truly was a wonderful and loyal friend. Weston grimaced at the idea, quickly agreeing.

It was a shock that Daniel had gotten Weston anything, and I had to wonder what questionable item lay in the pretty paper. I squinted my eyes at Daniel, but he just grinned back at me.

Weston's hand tore through the wrappings, slitting the tape, and opening up the box. He moved a ton of tissue out of the way before he came upon a picture frame. I gasped when I saw what it was: the photo Daniel took at Grauman's Chinese Theatre. It came out perfectly. I was smiling up at the camera, my hands in Weston's prints, my ring sparkling in the sun.

Weston smiled, chuckling as he looked it over, his finger reaching out to touch where my ring was in the photo.

"I love it, Daniel. Thank you."

Daniel blushed a bit as Weston beamed up at him. "You're welcome, Weston. It was my pleasure."

"I know the perfect place for it."

"And where is that?" I asked as I leaned into him.

"On my desk at the office, so you'll always be with me."

I smiled, relaxing into him. "Perfect spot."

"I thought so."

An hour later, I gave Daniel a hug goodbye and sent him on his way. It was hard to have him leave, knowing I wouldn't see him again for months, and especially with the support he'd given me over the last few days, but family called.

"Wren, I think your phone's ringing," Mom said, pointing to the end table in the living room.

I jumped up from my chair and ran into the other room to get it before the call ended. We had been playing cards in the kitchen after Daniel left, Weston losing but getting an education in Euchre.

"Hello?" I answered just before it ended, but not before noticing the three missed calls.

"Wren?"

"Miles?" I asked in disbelief.

"Hi."

I blinked and glanced back to Weston. "Hi."

"Umm, I was calling to see how things were going. Did he . . . did he make it there okay?" he asked, a bit unsure.

"Yeah, everything's fine."

"Fine?" He sounded surprised.

"I mean . . . we talked."

He breathed a sigh of relief. "Talking is good. Are you coming back?"

"Yeah, we're coming home. Not sure exactly when."

"Well, we usually—and by we I mean me, Julia, and Weston— have dinner Christmas night. We'd love to see you."

I went silent for a minute, trying to work out some logistics in my mind. "If we can find a flight, I think we can make it back in time for that."

"Say hi and tell her I miss her!" I heard Julia say through the receiver, bringing a smile to my face.

Miles chuckled. "Did you hear her?"

I let out a giggle. "Yeah, loud and clear."

"Wren, I'm happy you're coming back. I don't think even he realizes how good you are for him. Thank you."

My brow scrunched as I jumped up and sat on the counter. "When did this change in your attitude happen?"

He snickered. "When I pulled my head out of my ass."

"Thanks for calling, Miles, it means a lot."

"Thanks for finally answering," he said. "I was beginning to think either you didn't want to talk to me, or you'd beaten my little brother with your phone."

I laughed out loud. "And hurt my phone?"

He laughed on the other end of the line. "We'll see you soon."

"Bye." I hung up the phone and looked up to find Weston standing in front of me.

"Everything okay?" he asked as he stepped forward to stand between my legs.

I leaned forward and planted a kiss on his lips. "Everything is great. Miles was just checking in. Apparently neither of us noticed our phones ringing. He also mentioned a Christmas dinner with them."

Weston nodded. "That's been our tradition since we stopped going to my parents."

"Well, here we do presents in the morning. With a three hour time difference . . ." I trailed off.

His eyes perked up. "Really? But, you just got here."

I grabbed onto his shirt and pulled him closer. "But this way, we can spend the day with both our families."

He pursed his lips. "That makes for a long day for us."

I shrugged. "Oh, well."

"Are you really okay with that?"

I nodded. "This is all contingent on finding a flight on Christmas day that would allow us time here and get us back there."

"Oh, don't worry about that," he chuckled.

"This is Indianapolis, not L.A.," I reminded him. "And it's *Christmas*."

He just smiled at me. "Leave it to me, baby girl." He pressed his lips to mine, stopping me from protesting the high probability of failure.

An hour later, we had an early afternoon flight booked, giving us all morning in Indiana and all evening in California.

Mom helped me make up the couch for Weston to sleep on because there was no way the two of us were going to fit all night on my single bed. All protests of "we can fit" were shot down.

Mom giggled from the doorway as he tried to explain the logistics of how we could fit, while I rolled my eyes. After a few minutes and some sighs of defeat, he let me push him out into the living room with a pillow and extra blanket.

It didn't take. I woke up as the sun peeked through the curtains caged between a wall and a strong chest. Sometime in the night he'd crawled in bed with me. Seeing as my arm was wrapped around him, I figured my body needed the closeness as much as his.

Christmas morning was spent with my mom. I caught her in the kitchen trying to make breakfast, just managing to pull the frying pan from her before the eggs became a solid mass. Mike was still asleep, unable to stop her path of food destruction.

I took over, whipping out some French toast and bacon to go with the slightly overdone eggs. We all ate at the kitchen table, talking like any other normal family. Mike had been a little starstruck when he got to meet Weston, but soon they were carrying on like old friends.

After breakfast, we headed to the living room and the tree. Weston was especially needy, his hands always on me, touching, caressing. I had shipped out my presents for Mom and Mike, so they were wrapped under the tree, waiting for us. We watched from our curled together position on the couch as they unwrapped their gifts.

I was surprised when a stack of packages formed around us.

Mom quirked her brow at me. "What? I never got to mailing them out. I was going to do it a few days ago, but you showed up instead."

I leaned forward and wrapped my arms around her, hugging

my mom tight. I'd missed her, and I would miss her when we left in a few hours.

Weston usually spent part of the day with the gang, and dinner with Miles and Julia. I didn't want to take that from him. It was a tradition he needed, and I'd gotten to spend Christmas Eve and morning with my family.

Everything was now about compromise and communication. A hard way to learn those lessons, but what mattered was that we did learn.

I was bustling around packing up, making sure I'd gotten everything, when I heard Mike talking to Weston in the kitchen.

"Marriage isn't easy, Weston," Mike said.

Weston let out a little laugh. "Everyone likes to tell me that lately."

"It's true," Mike said with a nod. "Things haven't always been perfect between me and Karen. I'm sure you've noticed she's got her quirks."

Weston snorted. "That's a good description for her."

"It's one of the things I love most about her, but it also drives me bat shit crazy sometimes. She'd probably say the same thing about me with racing." Mike chuckled and shook his head. "But I have to agree with her after seeing you with Wren. There's something special between you two, but the situation was all messed up to begin with, causing a lot of pain on both sides."

Weston rubbed his face with both hands and let out a heavy sigh. "It's been an adjustment."

"Well, here's my 'I'm Wren's father' talk. I've been in her life for eight years, so I'm more than qualified. Your adjustment has been nothing compared to hers. She gave up *everything*. Let me stress that again—*everything*—to go with you. If you can't care for her, we will." His voice was hard, but only to make a point, to stress how serious he was about what he was expressing to Weston.

Tears stung at my eyes. I'd forgotten how great Mike was when it came to my well-being.

"I love her, Mike, and I'm going to make this work. The only reason she's going to come back here is to visit."

Mike held out his hand and Weston took it. "I'll hold you to that."

After packing up our presents and my suitcase into Weston's rental car, I hugged my mom and stepdad goodbye and promised to call when we got in. A tear slipped from my eye as I once again left my mom. She promised they'd make a trip out soon to see our house and visit L.A., and then we were off, speeding toward the airport.

"Okay, so let's go through the changes again, to make sure we're on the same page." I held up a finger and began ticking off items. The list was going smoothly, but I realized with his busy schedule, it wasn't going to be an easy switch. "I want to amend the no more work at home. In home office is fine, but not all night or all weekend, and the attitude has to be checked at the door. No infecting the rest of the house. I understand being in a bad mood, but no taking that out on me anymore."

He shook his head. "Nope. But I will also have to amend that by saying, if I come home and I'm in a bad mood, don't approach me unless it's to point toward the gym to get my frustrations out that way, and then you can bake me some cookies."

"Wait, cookies?" I asked, chuckling. "When did they come in to the conversation?"

"Just now. If I'm going to be working out a lot more, I need more calories."

I turned to stare at him with my mouth open. "And you jumped to cookies?"

"Yes." He nodded, very serious.

"I'm going to send you to COA if you don't watch it."

"COA?"

"Cookie Obsessed Anonymous."

He chuckled, turning to me and giving me that beautiful boyish smile that I loved. "Then you'll also have to send me to WOA."

"WOA?"

"Wren Obsessed Anonymous."

I rolled my eyes and smiled. My chest light and bright—a feeling I'd been missing. The car had the atmosphere I loved, one that often happened at home. Lighthearted playfulness, soft caresses, and peace.

However, the peace part was short lived when he brought up the bane of our lives. "I've talked to Joe. He's investigating how Natalie's been getting in. No one has been letting her in through the gate, which means she's been getting in through one of the access cards. I don't get it. It doesn't make sense."

"Hers was deactivated, right?"

"Right, so there should only be eleven active, and he only sees eleven being used."

"Did you talk to him about deactivating them all and starting over?"

He nodded. "Joe wants to wait."

"Wait?"

"Sometimes, he has hunches and he asked for a few more days. Plus, we were gone, leaving a period of time where nobody was going to have access. We're going to get to the bottom of this. We'll meet up with Joe in the next few days to get a game plan together."

"Sounds good. I want her gone. I . . . *hate* her." Hate wasn't a strong enough word for how I felt.

He smirked. "Yeah, I could tell by the way you laid her ass out on the floor. If I hadn't been freaking out that you were leaving, I would have been laughing my ass off."

"Really?" I was confused that he would have that reaction.

"You didn't see the way she was frantically trying to climb up my leg as if I would protect her and give her sanctuary while blood dripped down her face. It was pathetic, and prophetic."

I hated the subject, but his use of one word caught my attention. "Prophetic?"

"Because we're going to leave her broken and bleeding in the dredges of Hollywood society while she begs anyone passing to give her a job." His voice was cold, sending shivers through me. The way he talked was almost frightening, if it didn't excite me to envision it so much.

"I'd like to say I'm the bigger person and we shouldn't go that far, but I really want to see it. I want to see her expression as the tabloid covers have a picture of us together, showing us happy and in love, while her life turns to misery and the only acting job she'll be able to get is in porn." I was panting when my rant ended, my fists balled up tight, but loosened when Weston's thumb stroked over them.

My whole body began to unwind at the gesture. "Oh, I like that idea. I'm sensing the next Hollywood meltdown."

I grinned. "Me too."

Weston returned the car and we made our way through security with only a small bit of recognition from the agent who checked our IDs. The flight was full and we were booked in first class—a first for me.

I watched the scenery fade away as we flew up into the clouds. Weston's fingers drifted around my skin in soothing motions, almost lulling me to sleep when he leaned down.

"I want you to go to the Oscars with me."

I turned and blinked at him, wondering if I'd heard him correctly. "What?" My heart slammed in my chest. The thought of coming out gave me butterflies, but the worldwide coming out he was suggesting? I was already beginning to shake with a full-on panic attack.

"I've been thinking about it . . . We're not going to make it to the end of your school year, and I mean both as a couple and from the public, if we stay hidden. I've realized we need to go out, we need to have dates. Because I didn't think things through, and we need all this for a healthy relationship."

I nodded and squeezed his hand. At least dates were an easier transition, and I desperately wanted to go out with him. "We do need dates, but I want to go on them now."

He slipped his hand into mine. "We will, baby girl, I promise. Starting with this weekend."

I took a deep breath. "So, the Oscars? That's in February, right?"

"Right."

I let out a giggle. "Guess I'm going to need to call Sophie about a dress."

"Ha!" Weston laughed.

"What?"

"Do you really think Sophie hasn't already picked out dresses for you?"

I pursed my lips. "She was planning on me going with you, wasn't she?"

"I'm sure she was thinking ahead like that. Do you remember she already had my tux two months ago? I bet you a hundred bucks as soon as you left that day she started looking."

I smirked at him. "That weekend."

He quirked his brow, a grin spreading. "Are we betting here?"

"Maybe," I said, drawing the word about flirtatiously.

"Hmm." He rubbed his fingers against his lips, a thinking trait of his. "Okay, if I win . . ."

My eyes narrowed at him. "You're thinking naughty thoughts, aren't you?"

He grinned sheepishly. "You caught me."

He shifted in his seat, and cleared his throat. After looking around to make sure it was clear, I reached over to pat his crotch. A moan slipped from his lips and he began to grow beneath my hand.

"We're almost home, big boy."

"Tease."

I turned the conversation away from thoughts we couldn't do anything about while flying as I was not about to join the mile high club. "Okay, if I win, we go on vacation during my spring break."

He thought about it, a sly smile growing. "And if I win I'll pick where we go, and the only thing you can wear are those little swimsuits Sophie gave you."

I didn't like the idea of being so restricted, but little pieces of fabric meant a place with heat and water. "That's not really fair, is it? Either way I win by getting a vacation with you all to myself."

"But I get you by myself, free to stare at your scantily clad ass all day long." He licked his lips as his eyes zeroed in on my breasts. "Plus, it's been a long time since I had a spring break. This could be fun."

He was exuding excitement, and it made me realize just how long ago he'd had a school vacation.

"When was the last time?" I asked. There was still so much to learn.

He made a hmm'ing sound. "I was only eleven. We went to the Grand Canyon. After that . . . Well, it just wasn't feasible. Either work or my own fame got in the way."

I slipped my hand in his. "Time for another, I think."

"I'm sensing the beginning of you trying to help me live moments I've missed the past nineteen years. At this rate, you may be asking me to prom."

"Are you saying you aren't taking me to my senior prom?" I asked in mock defense.

He drew my hand up to his lips and kissed my fingers. "Do you really think I would let my wife go to her senior prom without a date?"

"Who says I'm even going?" Sure, Daniel and I had gone to our junior prom, and my sophomore year I went to homecoming with Reece Adams. I'd had a crush on Reece, but he was more interested in what was under my dress than in me.

Weston tipped my chin toward him. "I'm saying I want to take you. It'd be fun."

"Well, I'd like that very much."

"I'm sensing a but. Isn't it a high school moment girls love to have?"

"It would be nice, show off my husband to the school, but there's an even bigger event that day we need to attend."

His brow scrunched. "What's that?"

I rolled my eyes. "Your brother's wedding."

He pursed his lips. "Hmm, I suppose it would be bad if we missed that."

"Yeah, I think Julia would make you pay for years to come, and I just got on Miles's good side. I'd hate to lose that for a prom."

He nodded. "That's a good idea. I like my family being peaceful."

The rest of the trip went by fast, and before I knew it we were back in L.A., on our street and pulling up in the driveway. For the first time since I arrived in California, I finally felt like I was coming home.

Chapter Twenty-Nine

OUR BETRAYER

I T DIDN'T FEEL LIKE I WAS COMING BACK FROM RUNNING AWAY, but home from vacation. Perhaps it was due to the Christmas spirit that was still evident in the air. I was buzzing as I climbed the stairs with Weston trailing behind me, suitcases in hand.

We were closing in on our bedroom, and the air around us was changing. It was only supposed to be a quick stop to change, but between rekindling our relationship and the proximity to our bedroom, a match had been lit. I was itching to have his hands all over my body.

I got my wish as we crossed the threshold, bed in sight, and he was on me. I turned toward him and bit my lower lip from the lust that filled his eyes. The bags dropped from our hands, arms encircling as lips devoured.

With his hands on my hips, he walked me backward until I hit the bed and fell down onto it. He gripped under my arms and tossed me farther up onto the bed. A moan ripped out of me as he crawled on the bed and settled between my legs.

"Oh, baby girl, I need you so badly."

"What about Miles and Julia?" I asked, panting against his lips.

"It's called fashionably late."

His lips crashed to mine again, our hands working in tandem to strip each other bare. Shirts were lost to the floor, followed by my bra.

With each pass of his skin on mine, the feeling of serenity filled me. We still had a lot to work through, but I was gaining confidence that we could persevere, as long as we were together.

I had his belt undone and open, while his fingers grabbed my jeans and yanked them down my legs, along with my panties. He kicked off his own jeans, then kissed his way back up my body.

"God, Wren," Weston moaned when I took hold of his cock and began to stroke. "That feels so good, baby, but I need to fuck you. Right now."

"Yes," I whispered against his lips as I released him. "Just like our first night in this bed . . . make me yours."

It wasn't a time for sweet loving; it was a time for reconnecting in the most primal of ways. He hovered over me, and I shuddered and smiled when he slipped inside me. The connection that had been frayed was solid again the second he was inside of me.

I groaned, shuddering at the perfection of him filling me. "Now it feels perfect to be home with you again."

I wrapped my arms around his shoulders, bringing him down to me as he rocked inside me. It wasn't sweet, his hips slamming into me, fingers tangling into my hair.

It was hard, needy, and precisely what we needed. All the pent-up emotions came spilling out.

He was thrusting into me like a madman, sliding in and out. Every time he entered me, the fire within grew. I was about to be consumed, my muscles tightening, coiling.

Incoherent sounds ripped out of my lungs as I shattered beneath him, clenching around him.

"Yes, fucking perfect," he hissed, his hips picking up the pace for a brief moment before slamming into me. His body jerked, overrun with force as he spilled inside me.

My pussy was still twitching as he collapsed down on me, head in the crook of my neck as he regained an even heart rate. After a moment he let out a shuddered breath, and his arms wrapped around my back, pulling me flush to him.

My fingers threaded through his hair, trying to calm him. Something about being together, back home, was almost too much for him. His lips trailed kisses up and down my neck, nuzzling as he went.

"Oh, baby, how I missed you," I whispered into his ear.

He pulled back, then leaned down and kissed me, hard, with an almost possessive edge. "You don't know how good it feels to hear you say that, baby girl."

"Did you miss me?"

He pressed his forehead against mine. "So unbelievably much. I missed you so much it tore me apart."

I smiled up at him. "Now, I know."

We stayed together like that for a bit longer, loving our little bubble, but it couldn't last. Weston was running his fingers through my hair when his watch caught his eye. "Shit! We're supposed to be arriving at Miles's right now. Julia's going to kill me."

I giggled and pushed him off me, then ran toward the bathroom. He chased after me, grabbing me around the waist and hoisting me in the air.

"Where do you think you're going?"

"If you think I'm going to walk into their house smelling like sex, you've got another thing coming. Shower time!"

I pushed him into the huge shower stall and turned the water on. Cold water splashed onto him, causing him to yell and dance around. I stood at the door laughing, but he reached out and pulled me in with him.

We spun around, but the water shot out from almost all around. It didn't take long for it to warm up, and we got back to the task at hand.

We walked up the drive, hand-in-hand, both of us grinning like the cat that ate the canary. We were over an hour late, and I blamed it all on Weston. He was quite irresistible, after all. Our shower took a bit longer than I'd expected.

The door swung open, and a relieved Julia greeted us. "There you are! You're late. I was starting to get worried."

"Well, Merry Christmas to you too, Julia," Weston said with a chuckle.

Heat spread throughout my face, while Weston unabashedly pulled me through the doorway. "Sorry, Julia. It, umm, took a little longer to get dressed than we'd thought."

Her gaze snapped to Weston, and she rolled her eyes. "Well, it's better than you two fighting, I guess, so I suppose I can forgive you for letting my hard work get cold."

Weston let out a barking laugh when I nudged him with my elbow. His arm wrapped around my waist as he kissed my temple.

Julia smiled, her body relaxing as she looked at us. "Come on, dinner's waiting." She grabbed my hand and led us in.

We walked down the hall into the kitchen, and as we went I looked around. I'd never been in their home before. It was very warm and inviting, Julia's vibrant personality coming out in the décor and furniture. The house was large, not as big as ours, but also not what I was expecting for some reason. Given Miles's own success, though, it didn't surprise me. I often forgot he was a movie score composer and not only a high school teacher. The teaching was just a way for him to give back to his Alma Mater and help blossoming composers.

Also, I was pretty sure Weston paid Julia very well.

Miles was sitting at the counter when we entered, a smile lighting up his face as we walked in.

"About time! She was so close to going over there and collecting the two of you." He rose from the stool and walked over to us, throwing his arms around Weston before turning and doing the same to me.

It was a little awkward between us, but I knew it would get better in time. I didn't miss the smiles that lit up both Weston and Julia's faces.

With Julia's urging, we all headed to the dining room where we were greeted by a huge, holiday spread; Julia had gone all out.

"Wow, Julia, there's so much. I'm sorry I wasn't here to help."

She waved me off. "Wren, you had more important things to worry about than food. Besides, I make this much every year. These Lockwood men are quite demanding and ravenous."

They, of course, protested her statement, and I couldn't help but giggle as Miles tried to blame it on Weston. Weston retaliated that Miles was starting to get chubby. It was fun watching them interact as brothers. I finally got to see how much they loved each other.

After dinner we headed to the living room and to the Christmas tree that awaited us. I recognized many of the packages; they were under our tree at home when I'd left for Indiana.

Julia stepped up beside me and handed me a cup of hot chocolate. "I hope you don't mind, I went ahead and brought them over."

I smiled at her as I took the cup from her. "Thank you, Julia. Honestly, in all that's gone on, I kind of forgot about them."

She walked over to Weston and handed him a cup as well, and my chest clenched, loving the brilliant smile that spread on his face. It reminded me that even though he was thirteen years older than me, and a successful actor and businessman, inside he was still very much a kid. He was forced to grow up in a short time, losing many family traditions in the process.

Julia didn't have to tell me the hot chocolate was especially for Weston. It was just one of the many things that showed she loved Weston as more than her boss. Even if she wasn't marrying his brother, Julia was his big sister and possible surrogate mother. Though Weston was the older one, she protected him and loved him like he was her own blood. It was a heartwarming thing to see.

I sat down on the couch, Weston taking the spot next to me, his arm draped over my shoulder as he pulled me close. Julia and Miles mirrored us on the other couch, and I smiled at the two of them together. It wasn't a scene I'd been around very much; they were usually on their own when I saw them. Miles was adorable with how he doted on Julia. The love he had for her projected from his whole body, but also very much from his eyes as he looked at her with reverence.

"Would you believe that guy pined for her for two years before asking her out?" Weston whispered in my ear.

Miles rolled his eyes. "Hey, little sister, don't listen to him. It was all part of my master plan."

I smiled when Miles called me his little sister. The last bit of distance was closed, and I felt completely accepted in their family.

Weston quirked his brow. "Master plan? Man, you were salivating over her, watching her. It was kind of stalker-ish if you ask me."

"Did I ask you? I think not. And it wasn't stalker-ish," Miles said in protest.

Julia patted Miles's leg. "Wren, he was very sweet. I was so happy the day he got up the courage to ask me out. I'd been crushing on him from the moment I laid eyes on him. Now, shall we get back to the task at hand?"

Weston grinned. "Presents!" He sat up, placed his cup on the table, and walked over to the tree. He rifled through the presents, then he handed one to each of us before taking his seat next to me.

Without further ado, Weston began ripping into his package, along with Miles and Julia, making me relax a bit. Unlike the formality of the meal and our clothes, it was all gone when presents were involved, just like at my mom's house.

My fingers found an edge of the beautiful Christmas paper and tore into the glossy rectangular package from Miles. I hadn't expected anything from him and was floored by the gift in front of me: personalized music sheets. My fingers ran over the pristine paper, my name written in elegant, cursive script at the top.

"You are a very talented musician, Wren. It's time you wrote some of it down and shared it with the rest of the world."

I looked up to him, tears welling in my eyes. "Thank you, Miles, so much. This is so beautiful and perfect."

Weston beamed down at me, then placed a kiss on my forehead before placing a small box in my hand.

"What's this?" I asked.

"Something to out-do my brother's beautiful gift."

"Hey," Miles cried out. "I was basking here. You're ruining it, you little twerp."

Weston stuck his tongue out and turned his attention back to me and the little perfectly wrapped package sitting in my hand. Julia smiled and shook her head. It was obvious that was their normal behavior.

I unwrapped it as fast I could, seeing the excitement etched in my husband's face. My fingers opened the small, pale blue box with "Tiffany's" written on the top. The lid flipped up, and nestled inside was a perfect, pear-shaped diamond pendant, just like the one on my finger. My jaw went slack as I looked down.

"I thought this might work better as a substitute for your ring to wear around your neck. I know how bulky it is. It's not for much longer, but this will always be a beautiful addition around your neck."

"Weston, I love it, it's beautiful, but I love *why* you chose it." Even though it was extravagant, it had a meaningful and practical purpose. A way to show our love, our marriage, without being obvious to the world. I leaned over and pressed my lips to his, smiling at him. It was another sign that even through all the crap of the prior weeks, he had been thinking about me.

He helped me put it on, his fingers lightly passing over my skin, sending warmth and shivers through me.

"I can't wait to wear my ring on my hand every day. I can't wait until everyone knows I'm yours." I leaned forward and placed my lips on his.

"Not much longer, baby girl. I plan to show you off to the world." He took my left hand and kissed just above my ring. It was one of the few times I'd been able to wear it.

My right hand settled into his left, my fingers caressing his ring. One day, we wouldn't need to take them off, and I couldn't wait for that day.

Weston assured me there would be no interruptions and we could enjoy the holiday. Julia rerouted the few meetings that were scheduled, which gave us a few days of just the two of us. It was exactly what we needed to jump start our commitment. Weston did something when we got home that I was not expecting and made me very happy: he turned off his cell phone and forwarded the house phone to voicemail.

The first day was spent mostly in bed, but we did crawl out for dinner. We swam, played games, made love, and relaxed in a way we hadn't been able to since the beginning of our whirlwind romance.

We were enjoying another nice, relaxing day, snuggled on my favorite giant chaise lounge watching movies. With only one day left before work claimed him again, each minute was precious. He assured me he would keep his promises, though, and I was surprised at the faith I had that he would.

We were discussing what to do about lunch when we heard a door close followed by footsteps clapping down the hall as Joe's voice rang out for Weston.

"In here!" Weston called back.

When Joe appeared in the doorway, he was very much a man on a mission; a very disheveled man on a mission. The poor guy looked like he hadn't slept in days.

"Joe?" Weston's posture straightened as he took in the head of his security.

It wasn't the first time I'd seen him, but it was the first time I got to take a good look at him. His brown eyes were almost bloodshot, the huge muscles in his arms bulged, and his brown hair was a sticking in every direction like he'd been pulling on it repeatedly.

"I've figured it out!" Joe rushed forward, thrusting a stack of papers at Weston.

I scooted closer to Weston and stared down at the high-lighted lines, trying to make sense of it all, but it was just gibberish.

"This shows Wren at home, and Wren coming in. I cross referenced it to the security in her car as well. She was almost always home when the card was used," Joe explained, pointing to the yellow lines.

"That's not possible, then," Weston said, shaking his head.

"Shouldn't be, but take a look at this." Joe grabbed hold of the papers and pulled out a spreadsheet. "After hours of looking at everything, we noticed a high usage of Wren's card. Here, we created a graph." He pointed to the document.

I narrowed my eyes and looked closer, my hand grabbing for the papers. Then I saw it. The graph represented times when my card had been used, then below were lines for everyone else. It was as high as Julia's, and I didn't need mine once I pulled into the garage. Weston noticed it as well.

"How is this possible?" Weston's head snapped to Joe's.

Joe's gaze flickered to me. "One theory is Wren gave her card to Natalie to get in."

Weston was stunned, and I was speechless.

"What?" My voice came out in a stunned shrill.

Weston shook his head. "Impossible. She hates Natalie."

Joe nodded in agreement. "I don't believe that is what happened, but I still had to suspect you, Wren. The evidence does point to you," Joe said.

"I . . . I . . . Weston, you know . . ." Tears burned my eyes as Weston and Joe regarded me like I was some kind of hardened criminal.

Weston took my hand and looked at Joe. "There has to be some kind of logical explanation. It wasn't Wren." He squeezed my hand, then pulled out his phone and called Julia.

While Weston was talking to Julia, Joe spoke to me quietly. "For what it's worth, Wren, I'm trying to exonerate any suspicion of you . . . I know it wasn't you and that there's more to this than what it appears to be."

I sighed. "Thank you, Joe, but I didn't do a damn thing to help that slut get into my home."

"Where is your card right now?" Joe asked.

"In my purse." My hand shook as I pointed across the room.

"Did you take it with you to Indianapolis?"

I scrunched my brow. Of course I did, it was in my purse. And while I didn't know if I was coming back, it was something I always kept on me. "Yes. Why?"

He let out a hard breath. "Your card was used while you were gone."

"W-what?" I jumped up and ran across the room, picking my purse up from the floor and rifling through it. "How's that even possible? I was two thousand miles away!"

I pulled the card out and handed it to Joe. He looked it over, flipping it back and forth, looking closely at it.

"It doesn't make sense. None of it does," Joe said with a sigh. "I'm sorry, Wren, but you do understand, right?"

I nodded. "With all you've shown us, I get it."

"Weston is my priority. I have to protect him, even if it's from his wife."

There was a knot in my chest, fear of being a suspect and that someone would actually believe it. After everything, I was still the outsider. While my status was high, I was the newest person in Weston's life, and the least was known about me.

Weston explained to Julia what was going on, but at the end, before he hung up, he began shouting, "No, no way!" He rubbed his face, and for the first time I noticed just how hard all of it was on him. "Julia said she'll look into it and get back to me. She's heading to the office now. She doesn't believe it either, sweetheart."

Joe left after that, heading to the office to meet Julia, giving Weston and me a little time. I knew Joe still had his doubts, but Weston was his boss, and I was the boss's wife. Joe knew his position.

"You know, I had a stalker or two back in the day, but they were nothing compared to Natalie. That's what she has become. Maybe that's all she ever was: the ultimate obsessed fan." He shook his head and pulled me closer, seating me in under his arm. My head fell to rest on his shoulder as he nuzzled my hair and took a deep breath.

I reached up and cupped his face, smoothing out the worry lines. "We'll get rid of her soon."

He heaved a sigh and rubbed his free hand over his face. "Not soon enough. I never thought it would come to all of this, that she wouldn't be able to accept I found someone else and leave me be. That she would conspire to break into my house . . . I don't think she's dangerous, but I'm not going to take any chances that she might try to hurt you, especially when she finds out her plan didn't work."

I snuggled deeper into his shoulder, my hand gripping his shirt over his heart. "What did you ever see in her to begin with?"

"She came into my life at a turbulent time and helped give me some sense of normalcy. I'd just started up Lockwood Entertainment, she was a new actress, and we kind of bonded with our shared interests." He chuckled. "It was before she turned into a vapid Hollywood slut. She was actually supportive, and caring. Over time, the more popular she became, the less she exuded any of those characteristics. I'd never really had a long term relationship prior to her, as I was always too busy, so a part of me wanted it to work. Maybe so I wouldn't have to put myself out there to find someone really worth it."

I swallowed hard, and asked him something that had been nagging at me for quite some time now, even with all that he'd said to reassure me. "Am I really worth it?"

He turned to me, taking my head in his hands, staring into my eyes. "Baby girl, you were a blessing that was unexpectedly dropped into my life. I almost fucked it up, but know this: no one is worth it as much as you are. I am thankful every day for you."

Tears of relief and happiness spilled from my eyes as I smiled up at him. "Sounds like we have a bitch to bring down."

He leaned into me and pressed his lips to mine. "And whoever her accomplice is. I have my suspicions, so let's see what Joe and Julia can find."

A few hours later, Weston and I were still snuggled together watching movies when Julia came running in the house and threw a file on the table, Joe in tow.

"I found this in Mallory's desk, Weston. We had to break open the fucking drawer! Look!"

It was an access form for my security card, but it was a photocopy, not the original. Among the papers were the specifications of the card's security details, and an envelope from Safe Form Security.

"Who sent in the original request after you both signed it?" Weston snapped his head up to Joe.

"Mallory."

"Son of a fucking bitch!" Weston cursed, tossing the file back onto the table. "I knew Mallory was helping her, but *this?*"

"I don't understand," I said looking up at them. "Why would Mallory help?"

Nobody talked about Mallory much, only that she was close to being fired and they didn't trust her.

"When Mallory was hired everything seemed kosher: her background check, references, personality. We did it all," Joe said. "Things were fine for the first year, but then things started to change right around the time Amy was hired on."

"She was your second assistant?" I asked, looking to Weston.

Weston nodded. "I don't know if it was a rivalry thing, or an ego thing, but a few months after Amy started, leaks to the tabloids appeared."

My brow scrunched as I shook my head. "I don't understand. She's jealous? Is that it?"

Julia shrugged. "Who knows. It's something we've been trying to figure out for a year. We don't know why she's done any of it."

"My guess is money," Joe said. "Some magazines are willing to pay big bucks to sources who can give them good info. Add that in to maybe being a bit scorned when Amy started gaining tasks that were hers, and add in a conniving Natalie, and you've got the perfect storm to wreak havoc."

"Did she like Natalie?" I asked.

Julia's lips formed a thin line. "She was the only one who did."

"And that's the only way you can tie her in." I mulled it all over in my brain, trying to piece it all together. "And you haven't fired her because?"

Joe cleared his throat. "Both me and Weston's lawyer agreed that keeping her on while we attempted to figure out the leaks was the best course of action. However, that may have backfired on us since you came in, though at the same time, it's provided proof of breaching company policy and aiding in breaking and entering." He pointed down to the envelope the papers were in. "Mallory's boyfriend works for that security company."

"Shit," Weston cursed. "And they were able to duplicate the keys?"

Joe's jaw twitched. "Not proud to admit it, but yes. They use the same technology. I'm looking into a few other options, new technology, to see if there's something better."

"The sooner, the better," Weston said as he mashed his teeth together.

"The first course of action is to deactivate all the access cards, and *tell no one*." Joe began going into detail for our plan of action. "I'll get all new ones set up tomorrow and give them to you, Weston, to hand out yourself. I personally will change all remotes in the cars, and change all punch codes. I trust my team, but I don't want any mouths running about the change to get back to Mallory, so I will be doing it all. Every entry to the house will go directly through me for the time being."

Weston nodded. "You want to set her up."

Joe sighed. "What we have isn't enough to do much damage, so it's best if we have more evidence, especially against Natalie."

"You think Natalie will contact her?" Julia asked.

"Yes. And since even her cell phone is company property . . ." Joe trailed off.

Weston smiled. "Any conversations can be used against her."

"But, so what?" I asked. "Even if Natalie does call, she could just say she can't get in. And, if she does say 'the card you gave me isn't working,' is that anything criminal?"

"We don't need criminal, baby girl," Weston said, smiling at me, joy circling in his eyes. "I'm going to sue her ass. Ruin her reputation so she'll never get another job in Hollywood. No one will trust her, and trust is a big part of working in this business."

"That will hurt Natalie as well . . ." I trailed off, my mind whirling.

"Exactly," Weston said.

"We just need some proof on our side, dig up some more evidence of what Mallory has been doing with company property," Joe said, plotting out details. "I'll go through her phone's records: calls, texts, internet, everything. I don't think she's smart enough to really get rid of it properly."

"I was with Natalie for a long time. She spends every Christmas with her family, then comes home a few days after. There is a very good chance she will try to get in when she gets back, thinking I'm alone." Weston looked over at me, then back at Joe, slipping into delegating mode. "Let's get on this as soon as possible. I want Mallory gone by the end of the week. Julia, I want you to call my lawyer and go through the contracts for Natalie's newest movie. Lockwood Entertainment is pulling out our support and funding."

Julia had her tablet out and was making notes. "Will do. What should we have Mallory do for the time being?"

"If they're working together, let her continue to think Natalie's plan, whatever it was, worked, and that I'm still upset about losing Wren."

Julia tapped her finger on the side of the tablet. "It's Monday. You have meetings set up on Wednesday. Are you still taking tomorrow off?"

"Yes." He smiled and looked to me. "Make an appointment with Natalie on Wednesday, sometime around lunch."

I quirked my brow at him. "What are you scheming, Mr. Lockwood?"

"Just a little acting venture for my beautiful bride." He turned back toward Joe and Julia. "This is ending on Wednesday. Joe, find what you can in that time, and make sure you and a few members of your team are in the office then. I'll fill you in more once Wren and I talk it out."

With assignments in hand and a promise to call if they found anything out, Joe and Julia left.

I sat up and turned to Weston. "So, what's your grand plan?"

He gave me a wicked sly smirk. "You, coming to the office, all decked out à la Sophie. Mallory will be caught off guard, and it'll be right when Natalie comes in for a meeting."

"You want to piss Natalie off and see what she does?" I asked, excited about the plan. He really could be scary when he was pissed off.

He grinned, big and wide. "That, and show off just how hot my wife is."

I shook my head. "You know, this could out us before we planned."

"I'm willing to take that chance in order for them to be out of our lives. How about you?"

I leaned forward and pressed my lips to his. "I'd call the press myself if it meant they were gone, but I like your devious plan better."

"Me too."

We snuggled back down and resumed our movie, returning to our cocoon. Weston's grand plan continued to run through my mind. I was happy he included and informed me of the plan, something I wasn't sure he would have done a week earlier. It was finally sinking in that we were a unit now, a partnership, and we did things together. Like take down annoying ex-girlfriends.

Chapter Thirty

OUR VINDICATION

I HATED THAT OUR LAST FREE DAY TRAPPED IN OUR LITTLE bubble was marred by getting the details of our plan laid out. It also required me taking a trip to Sophie's store and being away from Weston.

"I'm so excited!" Sophie was buzzing as she put the key in the lock. "I wish I could be there to see the look on that bitch's face! If something goes down, you *have* to take pictures."

To avoid me being seen, in case Natalie showed up, Sophie picked me up from the house and drove me to her shop. As we entered, the lights were off and it was silent.

"Where is everyone?" I asked, looking around.

"Oh, we take a little over a week off for the holidays. So, it's just me and you. Come!" She waved me her way, a conniving smirk on her lips. "I picked up a bunch of enticing dresses for some of my other clients recently, and I think there are a few that will work perfectly for your little play."

"Then what else am I going to need? Because I see that look on your face. I've been warned about it from Weston."

Her head tilted back, and she laughed as she placed her purse down on a desk. "To pull this off, you're going to have to go Hollywood. I called in a few favors from some friends. So, tomorrow, hair and makeup will arrive at your house early to get you painted up. Today, I thought we could have some fun girl time, especially since we missed seeing you at Christmas. I figured a manicure and pedicure would be enough time to catch up on what the hell has been going on the last month."

"This is sounding like an all-day event." I sighed, sad that I wasn't with Weston.

"Don't worry." She waved her hand, reading my body language. "I'll get you back with plenty of time to fuck your husband's brains out for hours before you have to go to bed."

I was stunned and felt heat rising in my cheeks. "Why do you think that?"

She quirked her brow at me. "I've been with Carson over half my life. Believe me, I know how good and how long make-up sex can go on."

"What about Ari?"

"She has Weston and her father, though poor Carson will be ignored." She disappeared behind a large rack of clothing, flipping through each article.

"I meant, can we really leave her with them that long?"

"Carson is a great dad, and he raises, not babysits. And Weston would keep her for days if I needed it." She laughed. "He'll be the best father to your kids."

I sighed and sat down on a stool. "We've got a long way to go before that happens."

"One day at a time. It's going to be an intense few months, especially when you meet Richard and Joanna."

My brow scrunched in confusion. "Weston's parents? Why would I meet them?"

Sophie pushed the clothes aside and stared at me with wide eyes. "Miles hasn't told him yet?"

"Told who what?"

She walked forward, wide-eyed. "What big event is happening in April?"

"Miles and Julia's wed . . ." I trailed off, my eyes and mouth popping open as it hit me.

"Exactly. Miles invited them to his wedding."

"Weston would have to assume . . . I mean, wouldn't he?" I asked. He had to know—he was the best man, after all.

She pursed her lips and resumed her search. "I'm not sure if he would. He's written them off. Hell, Miles barely speaks to them, and when he does, it's only to his mom. I'm pretty sure Miles didn't want to invite them, and I bet it was Julia who made the final decision. Probably as a courtesy invite. Anyway, they RSVP'd."

"I hadn't even thought about it," I said, still in shock at the possibility of meeting my in-laws.

She came out, her arms full of garments. One of the hangers was caught up in one of her long teal curls, and I helped to untangle it. "Normally, we don't. I'll tell you, your dad at Thanksgiving . . . he about gave us all heart attacks."

Thanks, Dad.

"He knows how to push buttons to get the answers he wants, and he wasn't going to be satisfied until he knew what Weston was hiding."

"It was good, though," Sophie said with a sigh. "Otherwise, I don't know if you ever would have found out. He's gotten so much better, but this way you understand why the rift."

I nodded. "I wouldn't want someone in my life who did such a horrible thing. It's unbelievable his dad drugged him."

Sophie hitched her head to the side, indicating for me to follow, and started walking. "It was hard on all of us to watch him crumble. Weston is strong, and he fought past it, but it scarred him."

I shook my head, still confused on why his parents were invited. "I just don't get why Miles would allow them to come."

Sophie let out a sigh. "That's the danger with courtesy invites—the invitees actually coming. Though, there's no way Joanna would miss it. If she brings him or not, who knows."

We stopped at the back, away from the windows, at a dressing room and mirrored area. It was halfway through the stack of revealing, short dresses when we found the perfect one.

The perfect, symbolic color for the occasion: an all-white dress. It had a very short, tight skirt with a sleeveless, looser top that had a little metal V, creating a perfect view of my cleavage. It was sexy, fun, flirty, and it was guaranteed to get Weston going.

We spent the afternoon in the salon, and I filled Sophie in on all that had gone down before and during Christmas. Every emotion crossed her face, and in the end she wrapped her arms around me in a tight hug.

"Thank you for giving him a chance and for loving him." Tears fell from her eyes, and she brushed them away. "I've been hoping he'd find someone like you for a long time. Someone genuine who could love him just for him."

I ducked down as the car pulled into the driveway and into the garage. Inside, we found Carson in the kitchen working on his computer.

"Where's Weston and Ari?" Sophie asked.

Carson lifted his head, giving us a sour expression. "My baby doesn't love me anymore."

Sophie tried not to giggle, but she did "aww" as she walked over to comfort her husband.

I walked into the living room and found Weston asleep on the couch, Ari on his chest. Her little fist was balled up in his shirt, blonde curls everywhere. I couldn't help but smile at the adorable sight of her splayed out and think about the day when I would come home to find him like that with *our* child on his chest.

Sophie walked up beside me. "How the hell am I going to get them apart without waking her?"

"No clue. Good luck with that." I patted her shoulder and stepped to Weston.

Reaching out, I ran my fingers through his hair. He drew in a sharp breath, his eyes popping open. A lazy smile formed on his peaceful face as he focused on me. His arms spread wide, mouth as well, as a yawn moved through him. When he settled back down, he placed his hand back on Ari as she stirred against him.

"Help me get her into the car?" Sophie asked in a whisper.

Weston nodded and wrapped his arms around her as he stood. When we returned to the kitchen, Carson was all packed up and ready to go.

"Knock 'em dead tomorrow, and don't forget pics or video. I expect a full report," Sophie said with a smile and a hug.

"Will do."

They all walked into the garage, and a few minutes later Weston returned.

"Have fun, baby girl?"

I smiled up at him as I wrapped my arms around his waist. "Tomorrow is going to be epic."

Weston grinned at me with a devilish look in his eyes. "Can't wait."

He leaned down, lips pressing against mine, and I melted into his chest.

"You shouldn't be allowed around kids," I said when we parted.

"Why?" His lip twitched up in an amused smirk.

"It's too damn sexy! It makes my ovaries scream out for you to fill me with one."

He took in a deep breath, his eyes darkening while his tongue swept across his lips. "Baby, you shouldn't say things like that, because you have no idea how much I want to put a baby inside you." Heat flooded my cheeks, and my hands fisted in his shirt. "For now, why don't you and I go work on our baby making skills? That way, when we're ready, we'll know exactly what to do."

I fisted his shirt and began walking backward, pulling him with me. "I like your practice-makes-perfect line of thinking."

Mallory fell into the trap Joe set, and with greater ease than we all expected. The moment Natalie arrived home from her holiday vacation, when I was out with Sophie, she tried to get in. When her access failed, she called Mallory.

The next step was the plan Weston and I devised, and it involved fucking with Mallory first, knowing she'd tell Natalie.

I smiled and winked at Julia as I got off the elevator on Weston's office floor. School was still out of session, but Weston was to the point he couldn't put off work any longer. We'd have New Year's Day together, which was only two days away. Joe was allowing us this moment, knowing it would get more concrete information, which we needed.

My wedding ring sat on my finger in full display, matching necklace around my neck. Hair and make-up professionally done. My usual wavy hair was styled into beautiful curls, and my black hair was in perfect contrast with the white of the dress. I looked very much the twenty-something Hollywood actress, and not very much the eighteen-year-old me. It was hard to admit, but I kind of liked it. I felt confident and sexy, and I couldn't wait for Weston to see.

I was in Oz, and off to face the Wicked Witch. *Watch out, bitch, Dorothy's in town.*

Inside I was giddy, vibrating with excited energy for our plan as I strutted down the hall in the fuck-me pumps Sophie found to round out the impressive outfit. They were hot and difficult to walk in at first—I'd never worn heels so high, but she showed me how to work them.

"Excuse me. You can't go in there," Mallory called, jumping from her chair as I reached out to grab the door handle to Weston's office.

Her eyes were wide—part horror, part surprise.

"Oh! Hi, Mallory. I didn't see you there." I smiled at her. It took all my inner strength to keep up the charade, when all I wanted was to slap the shit out of her. "I'm just here to see Weston."

"Mr. Lockwood doesn't want to see you." Her lie tumbled out with a little too much protest.

I quirked my brow at her. "And why not?"

She was trying hard to keep the sneer off her lips. "He's busy. You can't go in."

I decided to throw a diva-esque hissy fit, inspiration courtesy of Talia Clark. "Do you know who I am?"

Her jaw flexed, and her words were strained. "Of course I know who you are . . . *Wren*."

I cocked an eyebrow. "Then what's the problem? Who are *you* to tell *me* what my husband does and does not want? Especially where I'm concerned."

She stood straighter and sneered at me. "Mr. Lockwood does not want to be disturbed. By anyone. He's in an important phone meeting."

I knew she was going to be a tough nut to crack, so I changed my tactics back to sickly sweet. I pulled out my phone, and the last text he'd sent me minutes before. "But he sent me this, so I'm pretty sure he's waiting for me."

I flashed the screen in front of her. He'd worded it perfectly: *What are you doing downstairs? Get your sexy ass up here, baby.*

"I was going to surprise him, but he caught me." I giggled and threw the phone back into the Louis Vuitton purse Sophie loaned me.

"Yes, well, like I said, he's in a meeting. His schedule is packed because he took the last few days off."

I bit my bottom lip and smiled brightly at her. "Yeah, he's been . . . busy at home."

Her face paled, hands clenching at her sides.

"So, you two have made up, then?"

I looked at her and quirked my brow. "Made up? You heard about that?" I waved my hand as to dismiss it. "I mean, sure we had a little tiff, but we made up . . . for six days straight." I embellished a bit, but it was all working. She was growing more and more agitated by the second. I decided to drive it home. "Oh, do you think you could be a doll and get me a soda? I'm parched. Thanks!"

I put my hand on the door again, and she grabbed my wrist.

"I told you, he's in a meeting!" she snapped.

Turning toward her, I dropped my bubbly persona. I narrowed my gaze, recalled all of my hatred, and directed it at her. "Take your hand off me before you lose it." She released me, and I flipped my hair again, smiling at her. "I'd like a Sprite."

Just then, the door swung open and Weston stood before us. "Well, hello there, pretty lady." Weston smirked at me, his eyes growing heavy as he looked me over, tongue peeking out to wet his lips.

I beamed back at him. "Hi."

His suit jacket was gone, the sleeves of his white dress shirt folded up his arms. The look was too sexy.

"What brings you here, baby girl?"

I stepped up to him, placing my hand on his chest and looking up at him from under my lashes. "I missed you, baby. We've spent the last few days, just you and I." My hand moved down to his belt and I tugged on it, bringing him closer. "I was lonely and thought we could have lunch."

"Mr. Lockwood has work to do," Mallory said with a sneer, interrupting us. It was obvious she was not happy with the sudden turn of events we were shoving in her face.

I flashed my ring at her in a less than subtle gesture and turned to glare at her. "Oh, I'm sure he can spare a few minutes for his *wife*. Don't you think, Mallory?"

Weston's hands reached around and grabbed hold of my ass. "Baby, in that dress I can spare more than a few."

I giggled, playing the part but getting turned on as well, and swatted flirtatiously at him. "Sounds like a good time."

Mallory stepped closer to Weston's office door. "Mr. Lockwood has a meeting with Miss Larson in half an hour."

I gave her a fake surprised look, and Weston had trouble containing his laughter as he took in my reaction. "Oh, I'll make sure to have him finished off . . . I mean, finished with lunch by then. I don't want to interrupt his work."

"Mallory, can you make sure I don't have any calls or interruptions for a while? I plan to be busy. Thanks." Without letting her respond, he took my hand and pulled me through the door.

"Oh, and don't forget that Sprite. I'll need it . . . after." I smiled and waved at Mallory, laughing inside at the look of disbelief that covered her face.

Weston's arms wrapped around my body, lips crashing to mine. His touches held a desperate edge to them. My getup had quite the effect on him.

"Wren, while I fucking love how you look in this little scrap of clothing you call a dress, I have to wonder what the meaning is of you prancing around baring your breasts for every horny fucker to see?" His hand moved down my hip until he met skin, his jealousy flowing through them. My thighs trembled under his touch. "Those are *mine!*" He indicated that by grabbing my partially exposed tits. "I think you need to be reminded of that." He stepped away from me and over to his desk, sitting in his chair. "Come over here, right . . . now."

I licked my lips as I sauntered over to him, enticing him more. When he palmed his cock through his tented pants, I knew the outfit worked, and very well. I had a little surprise for him and I was already wet in anticipation of him finding it.

I stepped in front of Weston and he leaned forward, hands reaching out to my legs. They trailed up, and heat flooded my cheeks as they slipped under the white fabric. He groaned as he palmed my ass, grabbing it and working up higher, toward my waist.

When his hands stopped, I looked down at him. The expression he wore was confused for a short second before his eyes closed and he took in a shaky breath, fingers digging into my hips.

"Baby girl, where are your panties?"

I was so worked up that my voice came out just above a whisper. "You can't wear them with a dress like this. The lines will show."

"But it's so short, if you bend over . . . oh, fuck . . . your little pussy would be on display." He clicked his tongue, hands working around and down. He stopped again, but this time he pushed the skirt up to expose me, his eyes wide. "Damn, baby girl, you . . . Fuck, you want me to spank you, don't you? Fucking naughty. A bare pussy? So, nothing at all to shield your clit from prying eyes? And you're fucking dripping down your thighs . . ."

I bit my lip. While I always kept it manicured and styled, I'd never gone totally bare, but Sophie said it was essential to pull the dress off. So, I did it.

Pushing my thighs apart, I opened them until his head dove down between them. He licked up my slit, taking my clit into his mouth and sucking. I knew then, it was worth it.

A growl ripped out of his chest and he stood, his hands gripping me and spinning me toward the desk. He pushed on my back until my chest was pressed against the top. His fingers pulled my dress the rest of the way up to my waist.

There was no warning, just a sharp sting against my backside that caused me to scream out. Another landed on my pussy that had my eyes rolling back in my head as the tip of his finger hit my clit. A guttural moan escaped, followed by another yelp as he smacked in the middle again. His hands soothed the skin, and I could hear his breath coming out hard and heavy behind me.

"Bad girl." He smacked my pussy again, but this time he slipped two fingers inside.

I tightened around them as he pulled them out, then pushed them back in. The edge of his desk dug into my hands from my steely grip.

He leaned over me, his chest pressed against my back. "If we were at home, baby girl, I would tie your hands and feet to the bed and strap a vibrator to you as punishment for teasing me and all other men in this dress. I wouldn't let you up for hours, until your pussy couldn't come anymore."

The image he painted had me pushing back against his hand. "Fuck, I love it when you get kinky!"

He sat down in his chair, hands pulling my cheeks apart as he dove in. My eyes rolled back into my head as he devoured my pussy. A possessed man, growling against my skin as he licked and sucked up my juices. His teeth nipped my clit more than once, as well as my ass, hand smacking against my cheeks again, then gripping them tight.

"I need to be inside you. My cock is begging to be buried in your hot little pussy."

The sound of a zipper was barely heard before I felt the head of his cock nudging against me. He pushed forward, seating himself to the hilt. I choked on a scream, tensing around him, vibrating energy flying through my veins.

His fingers tightened on my hips as he drew in a ragged breath. "Fuck, baby girl, you've got me so worked up."

He pulled out and thrust back in, setting up a steady pace, slamming his hips against me, the pleasure made my eyes rolls back.

A steady in and out, a low groan coming from the beautiful man behind me. I couldn't speak as he filled me, only high pitched whines that tried to break free.

"So good, you feel so good. Not going to last."

The desk shook so hard beneath me, in time with his hard thrusts, that things fell and tipped over onto the floor below.

Everything was mute. All except his cock inside me. Driving in, driving me higher, closer to the edge.

My back arched as he hit the most wonderful spots.

"Yes," he hissed. "Come on my cock."

His hips sped up, forcing me to shatter. Clenching around him as a shuddering mewl escaped.

Weston cursed behind me, his hips jerking as he pressed me painfully into the edge. But I didn't care about any of it as I felt him twitch within me.

A few last pumps and he collapsed against me, groaning.

My hands were lax. My whole body was as we lay there over his desk, trying to calm down.

"I don't think I can handle you wearing something like this again."

I let out a giggle. "Dress slutty more often. Check."

His chest rumbled against my back. "You're a naughty little minx."

There was yelling coming from the other side of the door, and before we could move, it swung open. Natalie stormed in, but she stopped after a few feet, Mallory and Julia behind her.

"Oh, my God. I can't believe you are fucking that little bitch in your office!"

I knew from the angle she couldn't see anything, our clothes were still on, but the pose was obvious. Despite my efforts, I felt my face flame in embarrassment. I was pretty sure it was already red due to our activities anyway. I just hoped she left so we could straighten out our clothing.

Weston blew out a harsh breath, his grip tightening at her words before he regained his composure and went right into his role.

"Ah, Natalie, you're here," Weston said, and I heard the smile in his voice. She moved to speak, but then shut her mouth in confusion. "I wanted to discuss something with you. Could you give us a moment, and I'll be right with you."

"No." She gave me her diva bitch-brow, and I couldn't stop from smiling back at her.

"No?" Weston asked, rising up off me.

"What is she doing here, Weston?" She pointed to me with a look of disgust. "Don't tell me she seduced you again?"

If it hadn't been for the enraged look on Natalie's face, I'd have been so embarrassed and tempted to crawl into a hole, but instead, it made me feel strangely empowered.

Weston's hand squeezed my hip. "My *wife* can seduce me anytime she wants. Now get the fuck out, and give us a minute."

"Fuck that. Just pull out of the little bitch."

"Excuse me?" Julia's voice came out from behind Natalie. "Don't you talk about my sister-in-law that way."

Natalie turned around, and Weston took the opportunity to pull out and hastily clean up as much of the mess as he could, so it hopefully wouldn't be sliding down my leg later. I pushed my skirt back down as he shoved his cock back in his pants and zipped up.

We moved to stand in front of his desk once we were put back together.

"Natalie, I called you here today for a reason," Weston said. Natalie's attention snapped away from the argument she was having with Julia. "First off, I am hereby pulling out funding for your current project. Lockwood Entertainment will never back a film with you in it again."

Natalie's mouth fell open. "Weston, what are you talking about? We've been planning this movie for over a year."

"Yes, but at that time you hadn't been lying to the press, trying to sabotage my marriage, and *breaking into my house*," he said, his teeth clenching at the end.

She quirked her brow. "Breaking into your house? I did no such thing. I was using my card key."

"No, you were using a card key you had Mallory, my once trusted assistant, get for you. Yours was deactivated well over a month ago."

All eyes turned to Mallory, including Graham and Amy, who'd just arrived and were blocking the door.

Mallory began stuttering. "I-I don't know what y-you're talking about."

Weston cleared his throat, his brow hitching. "So the envelope with your boyfriend's security company letterhead that we found locked in your desk drawer, containing a letter from him and the access card information, doesn't sound familiar?" he asked. "The one addressed to you? It had your fingerprints on it. Joe pulled them."

Even Natalie seemed surprised at that bit of information and turned on Mallory easier than I anticipated.

"You little bitch!" Natalie screeched. "You told me you got rid of all that. Are you really that stupid?"

Mallory gasped. "Me? You're the one who couldn't break them up. I did *everything* you asked, and then some."

"Which brings me to number two," Weston said, interrupting their incriminating conversation. "Natalie, you will never enter my house again." He turned to Mallory. "And you're fired."

There weren't words to express how good it felt to hear him say those things, especially with the force and finality in his tone.

Mallory's head shook back and forth. "You can't do that. My contract states—"

"It doesn't matter what it says, you violated the contract in more ways than one. I'm not only pressing criminal charges, but I will be suing you as well . . . both of you."

Mallory's mouth popped open and she stared out, frozen.

Natalie's lips were pressed tight together in a frown, jaw locked, a murderous gleam in her eye, as she looked between us. "Weston, I'm pregnant."

"Congratulations," he said without missing a beat or being the least bit surprised.

Did she think he was stupid enough to fall for that?

Her lips twitched. "It's yours."

Weston laughed, but it was in humor, vicious humor, which surprised me. "It's been over seven months. It's not mine, you psycho, and you fucking know it. Are you that desperate now?"

She was vibrating with anger, her mind working double time to keep up. "I told the press."

I chuckled. "I doubt you did, but if you did, then you can tell them you lied," I said, then thought about it some more. "Actually, I think that's something we can handle. I don't think they've heard from the Lockwood camp for a while. What do you think, baby?" I turned to look at Weston, who'd wrapped his arm around my waist as I spoke.

Weston smiled down at me. "I think that's a great idea. They'd love to hear the truth."

Natalie screeched, her fists clenched as her whole body shook.

"Something wrong?" I asked, smiling at her.

She was to the point of baring her teeth at me as she leered menacingly.

Weston released me, turning to grab something off his desk. I watched in anticipation as he picked up the file that contained all the cancelled contracts.

It was in that moment she lost it.

I didn't even see her move before she tackled me to the ground. My hands moved to my face to block her attack as she punched and scratched at me, her weight on top of me keeping me pinned to the ground.

"Get the fuck off her!" Weston yelled at her, trying to grab hold of her when she turned and raked her nails across his neck, scratching deep.

I saw red, my hand snapping around her neck in the split second opening. Her eyes widened and she looked back at me, her claws coming back down on my arm, trying to get me to release her.

"Don't you fucking touch my husband!" I flipped us so that she was below me and flashed my ring, shoving it in her face as my fingers held tight around her neck. Not enough to choke her out, but it was enough to hold her in place. "See this?" I screamed at her. "Do you see it? *I* am married to him, *not you.*"

I continued cursing at her as hands wrapped around me. I was hauled off her by Weston and one of Joe's guys. It was Weston stepping in front of me that calmed me enough to see and hear my surroundings again.

Joe was pinning Natalie to the ground and handcuffing her. I hadn't even seen him come in. The guy let go of me and went to relieve Joe.

Joe then walked toward Mallory, holding up her cell phone. Her eyes widened, her skin paling before turning beet red.

"I was going to be her PA! As soon as you were out of his life," Mallory screeched.

There was a fire in her eyes before she spun with something

in her hand. A hard jolt, and I found myself back down on the ground.

My vision was blurry, ears ringing, as pain lanced through me.

I heard a few gasps followed by, "You goddamn fucking bitch!"

My unfocused gaze moved to her. Weston was yelling and angry as he ran over to her. Julia got to her first and punched Mallory before she pushed her up against the wall. One of Joe's guys ran to them and pulled Weston away.

He turned back to me, while Natalie screamed and writhed a few feet away, cuffed on her stomach.

It was pandemonium.

Something warm trickled down the side of my face, and I shut my eyes, holding them tight to find some clarity in the chaos, fighting against the intense agony.

"Wren!" Weston cried, trying to get my attention.

I opened my eyes, and I tried to focus on him. His face held a terrified expression as he sat next to me.

"Can you hear me?" he asked, cupping my face.

"My head hurts," I said.

He nodded. "Julia's calling an ambulance."

"Ambulance?" I winced as I reflexively scrunched my eyebrows. "Why?"

Tears welled in his pained eyes. "Baby, she hit you in the head. You're bleeding, and we need to make sure you're okay."

"Oh." I looked around the room, taking in the blurry scene before me. Mallory and Natalie were both cuffed, guarded by Joe's men. Joe was on the phone, and Julia was in one of the chairs on her phone as well, with Amy holding an ice pack on her hand.

"Not quite how I pictured it going." My voice was weak and sounded kind of far away. "The magazines are going to love this, and the trash mags will be gobbling it up and exaggerating it."

Weston chuckled as he took a cloth from Graham and wiped away some of the warm liquid on my face. "I'm a bit more concerned with you than with what we're going to tell the press."

A little while later, the paramedics were rolling me out on a gurney through a back entrance. I opened my heavy eyes and smiled in glee, watching as Mallory and Natalie were loaded into the back of a police cruiser.

Assault was being added to the many charges we were already filing against them.

And with that, I closed my eyes. *God, my head hurts.*

Chapter Thirty-One

HIS PARENTS

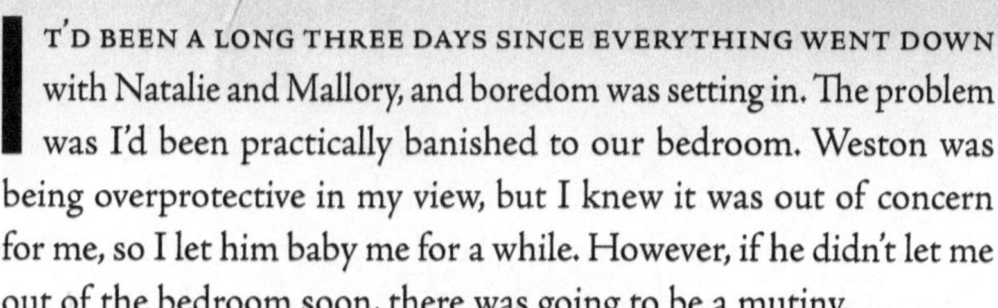

IT'D BEEN A LONG THREE DAYS SINCE EVERYTHING WENT DOWN with Natalie and Mallory, and boredom was setting in. The problem was I'd been practically banished to our bedroom. Weston was being overprotective in my view, but I knew it was out of concern for me, so I let him baby me for a while. However, if he didn't let me out of the bedroom soon, there was going to be a mutiny.

"How are you feeling?" Weston asked as he sat down on the bed beside me.

"Tired of sitting in this bed. How much longer do I have to stay here?"

Besides a nice, nasty cut to my scalp right near my hairline that bled profusely, I was left with a concussion and some bruising, along with a few stitches. The docs all said I was lucky she didn't crack my skull or worse, so it was the best outcome. They made me stay overnight for observation, and we escaped the next morning with the help of Lance.

Thank God for HIPAA privacy rules that kept them from disclosing to anyone my health information, because we didn't expect my trip to the hospital. Though, Julia did make sure they knew they'd be sued if news leaked out of my true identity as Weston's wife and not sister.

Weston snuck out the back and into Sophie's car, while Lance came through the front and picked up his "baby sister."

Needless to say, the lies were making my life more and more complicated. Especially, since almost the entire hospital heard his act. He was really hamming it up.

"It's only been two days, baby girl."

"But it's New Year's Eve." The cabin fever was strong, especially since I hadn't left the bedroom. "And besides, I don't feel that bad. We're at home. At least let me walk around the house."

"The doctor said you need rest."

"Yes, *rest*. Not bed rest!" I was getting whiny, but I didn't care.

Weston pulled me into his arms, my head resting on his chest as he stroked my hair. "There are stairs, and the last thing I want to have happen is for you to fall."

"Damn you," I said, pouting.

He chuckled. "What? I'm just making sure you're okay. It's my fault this happened."

"Is not. We didn't know they'd both flip out, even with as much as we taunted them. How's Joe doing?"

I'd been worried about him, knowing how seriously he took his job.

"He's still beating himself up."

I pursed my lips. *Great, just what I was afraid of.* "It wasn't his fault either."

"No, but he feels responsible as head of security, as he should. He is supposed to protect us, and he didn't do that properly."

His tone caught my attention. It held an edge of anger. "The way you said that . . . do you blame him?"

Weston heaved a sigh. "Like I said . . . It's his job to protect us, but it was utter chaos. It was a split second between when she grabbed the marble award and then hit you with it. Joe tried to get to her, but by the time he reached her, Julia had already pulled her back and was turning her around to punch her."

"I saw that. It was awesome!" The memory made me smile, seeing someone stand up for me.

He let out a chuckle. "It was, and Julia deserved the chance to hit her."

Julia was my new idol. The woman exuded calm, even when I watched her deck Mallory. What made her so excellent, though, was the photos she took on her cell phone of Natalie and Mallory being put into the back of a police cruiser.

She then sent them to every local news source with Weston's press release and pictures of the injuries sustained by both of us. They'd made sure not to mention my identity, and my face wasn't in view. Weston still wanted to wait for the right time, but he did say they'd attacked a woman visiting his office.

It was in the papers and on magazine covers the next day while the two of them sat in jail, unable to do anything about it.

I hoped they stayed there for good, rotting away. The sooner they were permanently out of our lives, the better. Sad thing was, trials go on for so long it could be months of rehashing that day.

From what was gathered, Natalie promised Mallory a hefty pay increase for the position of her head assistant if she helped her get back with Weston. After our fight, Mallory was ready to hand in her resignation and begin working for Natalie, but she wasn't expecting us to work things out and come out stronger. Which explains why she lashed out at me, because, to her, I was the reason her life was going into the gutter.

"How's your neck doing?" I looked up, my fingers ghosting over the white bandage that covered up the deep scratches from Natalie's nails. Another reason I wanted that bitch to rot in jail. Marring my husband's perfection was *not* okay.

"It'll be fine. I'm just keeping the bandage on so it doesn't dry out. That will help keep the scarring down."

I shook my head. "The whole thing is still surreal. I've never been in a fight before. It was kinda scary."

He blew out a breath and pulled me closer. "She was moving so fast I couldn't get a grip on her, and when I did, man, she struck hard. Graham ran to get Joe, while Julia grabbed onto Mallory to keep her in place."

"Was Mallory trying to escape?" I asked. The information was new to me.

"I think her flight response was strong. She was caught, and the person she did everything for was ruining it all. With Graham gone from the door, she tried to bolt."

"Fucking bitch. I hope they lock her up for a long time."

"Don't worry, baby, I'm going to make sure she gets the maximum sentence possible."

Maximum sentence wasn't even good enough for all they'd done, in my opinion. The wedge they'd tried to carve between us, the breaking in, was all an attempt to manipulate and it failed. In the end, we won.

But that didn't mean everything was suddenly rainbows and sunshine.

"How are we going to keep our marriage from the press?" I asked.

"It's going to be tough, but I think as long as we keep feeding them information, they won't dig too deep. It's only for seven more weeks. I think we can do it. Though, I don't doubt the paparazzi will be camped out on the lawn and will photograph you."

"I'm excited." I beamed up at him.

He looked at me like I was crazy. "Excited about being hounded by the press?"

I rolled my eyes. "No, I'm sure that part will suck. I'm excited about being able to go out with you, have dates with my husband. To really give this the fair shot we haven't gotten so far." I giggled. "I'm most excited about not being your sister anymore."

Weston's head fell back, and he broke out into laughter. "Yeah, let's not have that rumor going around, as well."

"How about we watch some TV? Maybe some *TMZ*?" I said with a devilish smile.

He looked down at me and shook his head, then placed a kiss to my forehead. "You just want to see the mug shots, don't you?"

He was right. There was a satisfaction I got seeing them

holding those incriminating numbers up under their faces. "That, yes, and you haven't told me what today's news is all about."

He grimaced at me. "*You* are today's news. Well, the fact that I have a girlfriend. We were being hounded about who the mysterious woman was. Julia told them Natalie flew into a jealous rage when she found out she'd been replaced."

"They're going to find out. Especially if they see me."

"Another reason I've been keeping you in here," he said, and pointed to the closed drapes.

Realization dawned on me. "They're already here, aren't they?"

He nodded, his expression solemn. "As soon as the news broke about Natalie's arrest. I had to call the cops once already for trespassing."

Lockdown in our own home. My favorite places now off limits.

"How am I going to get to school on Monday with them like that?" I asked.

"Joe's going to drive you for the next few weeks until this blows over."

I sighed and snuggled deeper into his chest. I could live there. "You're all mine until Monday?"

He kissed the top of my head. "All yours, baby girl."

He flipped on the TV, and Mallory's face greeted us. My head throbbed just looking at her pathetic mug.

News of Mallory's betrayal was already swirling through Hollywood. Weston had been fielding calls for days from friends offering their condolences. It seemed the worst thing you could do in Hollywood was betray a star's secrets . . . and try to kill his wife, but very few knew that part. Mallory would never get another job as an assistant when she got out of jail.

Natalie's face was next as the announcer explained all the alleged legal trouble she was in: conspiracy to commit a crime, breaking and entering, and battery—similar charges to Mallory. Although, Mallory added aggravated assault into her mix when she clocked me in the head. Both the item and where she struck took it from assault to the more serious version of the same charge: aggravated assault. It was a felony, but in California the maximum sentence was only four years. Not enough time in my eyes, so I hoped the rest would increase it.

Added to that were the civil suits Weston and I had filed against the two of them.

Two days after it hit the news, Weston received a surprising call from Natalie's father. He was appalled at what his daughter had done, and apologized. A nice gesture, and from Weston's tone, he liked and respected the man.

Speaking of fathers . . . I'd been skirting around a subject for days, ever since Sophie told me, but I was recovering well and there seemed no better time like the present.

"So, you know about your parents coming to the wedding?" I asked, my eyes still trained on the TV.

He heaved a sigh and paused for so long I wasn't sure he would answer. "Honestly, I've been trying not to think about it."

I moved my head up to his shoulder so I could see his face. "You did know."

His lips formed a thin line and he nodded. "Miles always does everything he can to protect me. He called me the day he wrote out the invitation, to prepare me. It was all for Mom, but he knew there was no way she wouldn't bring *him*."

"What are you going to do?"

He pulled me closer, his lips against my forehead. "I'm going to be my brother's best man, and avoid the people who gave birth to me as much as possible."

I didn't want him to see his father, but it was going to happen.

"You won't talk to them? Even after all these years."

"No. I've said my peace. The ball's in their court—in *his* court."

I stared at Weston for a moment, the pain and anger radiating off him. I snuggled back down and wrapped my arms around him, surrounding my husband in as much love as I could.

Later that night, Weston helped me downstairs and to my favorite room, the one with the chaise lounge couches.

He surprised me with an array of appetizers waiting for us and a few not-yet-released movies, along with a bottle of champagne for later.

"You're kinda sneaky, you know?" I stood up on my toes and wrapped my arms around his shoulders.

"Just a guy being romantic and spoiling his beautiful wife any way he can," he said and leaned down, pressing his lips to mine.

We snuggled in, gorging ourselves on food as we watched a movie. Then another movie, until time closed in. As the clock drew closer and closer to midnight, we switched over to watch the ball drop.

"Ten, nine, eight," we counted together, "seven, six, five, four, three, two, one! Happy New Year!"

His lips crashed to mine for a searing kiss. "I love you, Wren."

I smiled against his lips, my eyes closed as I breathed him in. "I love you, too."

His fingers caressed my cheeks as our eyes met. "I have a feeling it's going to be a fantastic year."

Boy, did I hope so. With the rollercoaster we'd just been on the past month, all I could do was hold on for the ride, because it was just beginning.

"Me too. Lots of obstacles, but with you by my side I know we can get through them."

"I will never leave your side again," he said.

I believed him. I finally felt more like we were on an even footing and that everything would work out. Our future looked beautiful, I could see it.

"Always stay," I whispered against the palm of his hand.

He swallowed hard. "I didn't do things the right way before, and I'm not making that mistake again."

I leaned into his hand. "I like that."

He pressed his lips against mine, soft and full of the emotions that were swirling around us. Our desire quickly grew, and he moved to lie above me. His hands moved around my body as his kisses became harder, full of the need he'd been suppressing for days. Our moans echoed off the wall as my hands pulled him closer.

His lips moved down my neck, kissing and licking as they went. His hips ground his hard cock against my clit while one of his hands pinched my nipple.

My heart began to pound in my chest, blood pumping through my veins . . . and into my healing brain.

I let out a whimper from the pain, and Weston's movements stopped.

"Baby girl, what's wrong?"

"I have a headache," I moaned, my brow scrunched.

His lips twitched before he broke out into laughter.

"Why is that funny?" I asked as I rubbed my forehead.

His gaze met mine, and he started laughing again. "Should I be worried you're coming up with that excuse not to have sex with me so early in our marriage?"

I chuckled, finally getting it, and rolled my eyes. "Trust me, baby, if it wasn't for my hurt brain, we'd be going at it all night long. And, as soon as I'm better, I will pounce on this"—I placed my hand over his erection—"the very first opportunity, no matter where we are or what we're doing."

"What if we're in public?" he asked, then groaned when I rubbed him a little.

I bit down on my lip, feeling daring. "Then people are going to get quite a show."

He smiled and shook his head. "When did you become an exhibitionist?"

I shrugged my shoulders. "Probably after our two really hot fucking sessions on your desk."

He placed a light kiss on my lips. "They were hot, weren't they?"

Yes, they were. Extremely. When he was done with that desk, I planned to bring it home.

"I'm going to hold you to all of that. Until then, I think we should head to bed."

"Probably a good idea," I said with a yawn.

He helped me up, and we walked upstairs, hand in hand.

"Oh my God, it *was* you," Charlotte said, the second I got out of Joe's SUV right next to her car. Her family had been out of the country just after Christmas past the new year, and I wasn't able to talk to her.

I grimaced, my hand drifting over the bandage. "Is it that obvious? Do you think everyone will think that, as well? God, I'm so glad you're back." I pulled her into a hug.

She gave me a sympathetic smile as she wrapped her arm around mine. "A lot of people are going to put it together, especially with that nastiness on your face. What's your cover story? Why didn't they just say it was Weston's sister?"

My feet stopped and my eyes widened, chest tightening. What was I going to say? "I can't go in there."

"Yes, you can. I'm right here. We'll get you through this together. But before we get in there, we need a plan."

"Hey, Wren, Char!" Aaron called out, walking up to us. His eyes widened when he saw me. "Damn, are you okay?"

I froze, staring at him. "Fine," I said, just above a whisper before I dragged Charlotte away, despite Aaron's calls.

I led her around the side of the building and leaned against the brick. I needed a moment to collect myself, and closed my eyes.

"Oh, shit," Charlotte said.

I looked at her as she stared back out at the parking lot. Miles was getting out of his car, and the paparazzi were yelling across to him from the other side of the fence.

Charlotte stepped in front of me and began playing with my hair. She swept it across my forehead and pulled a bobby pin out from her own hair to secure the strand by my ear. She took out another one and did some fluffing before she was done.

"There. That covers all but a little bit of bruising."

The bell rang out, warning us there was only five minutes to get to class. "What if people ask about what happened?"

She grabbed on to my arm again, and we headed inside. I caught Miles's eye, but neither of us acknowledged the other so we didn't tip them off.

"Just tell them you don't know."

"Will that work?"

Charlotte pursed her lips. "Probably not."

"Fantastic."

The new semester was in session, and Miles's class was first up. He only taught two days a week, and told the school over Christmas break he wasn't going to be able to return the next year. It had become too much for him. He'd only taught this year as a favor. I also suspected it was to keep from having to be too involved in the wedding preparations.

My grip tightened on Charlotte's arm as we walked into the class, right behind Miles. Everyone went silent as all eyes fell on us.

I tried my best to look normal, unfazed, but their gazes bore into me, trying to expose the secrets they figured lay beneath. Whispers began to spread as we took our seats.

"Everyone settle down," Miles said, right after the final bell rang. "It's the beginning of the new semester, and I have some announcements to make."

"Mr. Lockwood! Oh, Mr. Lockwood!" A girl I knew as Maya raised her hand, bouncing in her seat, trying to gain his attention.

"Yes, Maya?"

"Is Weston okay?" Maya asked.

Miles remained unfazed by the question. He, unlike me, was prepared for the interrogation.

"Yeah, and who was that girl at his office? Is he dating someone else?"

"Is that why Natalie went off?"

"Did his assistant really help her break into his house?"

"I heard she's pregnant and he refuses to accept that he's the father."

The questions were unrelenting and flying out of every student in class. My eyes were locked on Miles, who didn't flinch throughout it all.

One day, I hoped I'd be acclimated to the life and be able to react like him. He'd had years of a very famous younger brother to get used to it—I'd only had a few short months.

"I want to go over the syllabus for this semester. I'm going to challenge you to submit a piece for—"

He was cut off by another question.

"Please, just tell us, sir. Wren?"

"Did Natalie really attack Weston?"

"Could have been the pregnancy hormones."

"They were so cute together."

"Who knew she'd go psycho when she caught him with someone else."

"Cheaters are bastards."

"Who said he was cheating? If he loved Natalie, would he have her arrested and press all sorts of charges?"

"Like assault. Someone ended up in the ER after being attacked. That's brutal."

"All right, let's focus back on the class." Miles tried again, but they kept going.

"Just answer one question. Please!"

"Yeah, like who was the chick? Is it Michelle Abraham?"

"He was a producer on her last movie!"

"Poor Natalie."

I snapped at that last one, jumping up from my seat and turning to look at the class for the first time since I took my seat. "Enough! Can't you just leave it alone? Natalie is a vile, insipid bitch and I'm glad she's out of his life! Just leave us alone. We won't answer your questions because he's our family. Many of you come from famous families. Do you spill all their secrets to everyone in school? Didn't think so. Shut the hell up, and let's get back to class."

I plopped back down in my chair and folded my arms across my chest.

Miles smirked at me. "Well said, sis."

A smile broke out on my face, and I beamed up at him.

"As I was saying before you all rudely interrupted me, there is a competition for film scores, and I want all of you to submit a piece," Miles said, earning a groan from almost everyone. "The piece must be ten minutes long, and you can choose whatever you want to accompany it as your inspiration. Be it a home movie, something you found on *YouTube*, or a new score for an existing movie. It will count as fifty percent of your grade and is pass or fail only. So, either you get an A+ or an F."

Miles had piqued my interest, and my mind was already thinking about what to do. I'd played so much over the last few months, and created more music than ever before. Maybe I could take that and mold it into something . . .

"How long do we have?" another student asked.

"You have until mid-April, when I take leave for my wedding," Miles said. "I will send them all in then. Those who do not have it to me by then will automatically fail."

"What will the other half of the grade be?"

"Progress playing. Each week I want to hear how you're doing."

"Sounds hard," someone groaned.

"Sounds exciting!" I smiled, already in love with the project.

"Easy for you to say," a guy behind me grumbled.

"What's that mean?" I asked.

Maya sighed and rolled her eyes. "It means you're a Lockwood. Born with not only good looks but talent most people would kill for. I mean, look at Miles and Weston."

"We all know you're going to be something big, we just haven't figured out what it is."

My eyes widened and my face flamed. "Didn't think people thought about me period, let alone enough to talk about."

"You're a Lockwood and have blown us all out of the water in the few months you've been here. *Everyone* talks about you."

I blinked back at them, completely stunned.

Miles called the class back to attention and gave out more details. I was speechless, lost in thoughts about what my classmates had said.

I still didn't know what I wanted to major in at college, but I hoped to live up to and maybe surpass their expectations.

As the weeks passed the paps calmed down, and one by one they stopped camping out in front of our house. Weston's face was all over the place, but even that was fading. Natalie and Mallory were both released on bail, and Joe had increased the security around us. We had restraining orders against them, but, after how they reacted before, we weren't sure they wouldn't try to harm us to get revenge. Even my classmates stopped asking questions. My outburst helped, but for the first week I was accosted by people in the hall looking for answers.

Weston was doing well keeping his promises, though a few times I did have to point to the gym when he was being a workaholic asshole from the stress of everything. We'd also been practicing and honing our baby making skills, so they were ready when we were. Not that we were in a hurry on that front.

By the end of January I was able to drive to school again, which was good because I often stayed after school to work on my submission. Miles's assignment had lit something within me, and I was determined to prove to them all that *I* was talented. Not because I was born a Lockwood, as they all believed. Me—Wren Bradford. Me, before I gained a famous last name.

The music sheet stared back at me. Sitting at the piano, I was stuck. I would put notes down and erase them. Over and over. Something was off, but I couldn't place it. I'd been writing down my composition after I recorded it, tweaking it as I went. Was there a missing sharp? Did I have it in the right key? Should that be staccato? All questions that were rolling around as I focused so hard on the notes.

I rubbed my eyes and looked up at the clock, jumping when I saw what time it was. It had gotten away from me, over an hour later than when I was supposed to leave.

Weston wasn't going to be happy. He'd kept to his word and was home every night for dinner, spending quality time with me, and I was the late one.

I grabbed my bag and headed down the hall to the entrance. The school was empty, silent, nobody around the halls. In fact, many of the lights had been turned off. At the rate I was going, Weston was probably already sitting at the dining room table waiting for me.

I picked up my pace to a run toward the parking lot. Racing down the hall, I began to turn and skidded to a halt, nearly crashing into a couple walking in the dim hallway.

"Oh, I'm sorry!" I apologized, my hand grabbing at my chest as the adrenaline rushed through my body.

"Quite all right, dear," the graying brunette woman said, smiling sweetly up at me. She didn't have the fake smile many of the socialites seemed to be born with around Hollywood. The man beside her, however, seemed to be born with a nasty scowl, looking down at me disapprovingly.

The look was somewhat familiar, but with my scattered brain I didn't have time to think about it.

"Can I help you find someone?" I asked, getting sidetracked once again.

The woman nodded. "Yes, we're looking for our son."

It seemed strange for a couple of their age, but I didn't think much on it.

"Wren." I heard my name being called. "Wren!"

"What's his name?" I asked them, trying to help them before responding to whomever was calling me.

"Wren Lockwood!"

Annoyed, I stepped back to look down the hall I'd just come from, my brow scrunching. "What?"

"Weston's looking for you. He just called my phone. You better get home. You know how jealous he gets," Miles said jokingly.

There was a gasp, and I looked back to the couple, both of their faces were wide in surprise. I grabbed my bag and pulled out my phone. Sure enough, I had four missed calls and six text messages.

"Shit, I forgot to turn it off vibrate!" I cursed under my breath and looked back down the hall to where Miles was advancing. "I'm heading out now. Can you help this couple? They're looking for their son."

Miles's brow shot up, seemingly surprised there was someone in the school. "Sure."

"I'm sorry, I have to go," I apologized and moved to leave, but the woman's hand shot out, grabbing my wrist in a tight grip.

"Lockwood? Is that right? Are you married to Weston?"

"Wren?" Miles asked in growing concern as he watched the action, his pace increasing.

"I-I . . ."

"Wren, what's going on?" Miles drew in a sharp breath when he reached us and took in the couple standing beside me. "Mom? Dad? What are you doing here?"

"Is it true, Miles?" Tears formed in the woman's eyes. "Is Weston married?"

Miles's eyes widened. "Yes."

"To a high schooler?" the man I now knew to be my father-in-law boomed. "What was he *thinking* getting involved with a child?"

"Oooh!" my mother-in-law wailed, turning on her husband and hitting him repeatedly with her purse. "This is all your fault! My baby boy is married, and I didn't even know! You pushed him away, and I don't even know my new daughter!"

It was odd watching the tiny brunette woman beating up on a rather large blond-turning-gray haired man.

"Wren, you better get home. Weston is waiting for you," Miles said, and from his tone he wanted me to leave straightaway.

"Yes, I'm certain it's past your bedtime," my father-in-law sneered.

Miles's lip drew up in a snarl. "Dad, that's enough!"

I knew I'd meet them in a few months, but the sudden run-in threw me off and it took a moment for my brain to catch up.

"How so? You've just told me my youngest son married a child. How could you let him do that?"

Miles's jaw twitched in anger, and my fist clenched at my side.

"Wren is a wonderful *woman* and wife. They're happy together. For the first time in years, Weston is *happy*, and I won't stand for you tearing her down. You don't know her or what she's done for him."

My heart swelled at Miles's defense of me, and at the same time I wanted to punch my father-in-law I was so angry. "Wow, you're not out to win any father-of-the-year awards, are you?"

"Please, head home," Miles said, staring at me, beseeching me with his eyes to do what he asked.

But, I couldn't get my feet to comply with his request.

"Oh, please! Please take me with you! I want to see him, please let me see him," my mother-in-law begged, her eyes pleading with me.

Miles's voice rang out, hushing her. "Mom, you have no right to ask that of her!" he chastised, and she shrunk back, retreating. "If you want to know her, you have to patch things up with Weston."

"But he won't return any of my calls," she sobbed, her eyes trained on me, trying to break me down.

"Then write him a letter, or leave a voicemail. Hell, just go and see him! You know where his office is, and you know he's just as stubborn as Dad and will not come to you. Not after all that happened." Miles's chest was heaving as he stared daggers at his father.

"Hasn't he gotten over it yet?" my father-in-law grunted and looked away. It was clear he didn't really want to be there and had no interest in me or seeing Weston.

I stared at them in disbelief.

Miles tried again. "Wren, please go home."

"No, Miles. Is that him? Is that the man who shoved drugs down his own son's throat?" My hands shook in anger.

"Wren . . . can I call you Wren?" his mother asked.

I shook my head. "No. I don't know you, and what I know of you is nothing good."

"Wren, will you help me?" she begged again.

I took a moment to gather my thoughts and looked between all three of them. "No. Because I love my husband and don't want to see him in pain. You've hurt him, and I can't stand that. We will support and love our children, not abuse them like him." I pointed to my father-in-law, my hand shaking.

Miles gave me a sad smile and nodded, letting me know I'd done good.

"See you in a few months," I added before turning and walking off. My mother-in-law's sobs rang out through the halls as I stormed away. They swayed me, but only a little.

During the drive home I was left with nothing but my thoughts, and I became more irate at Weston's father. When I pulled into the garage, I had to take a moment to calm myself before going in.

When I entered, Kelly was in the kitchen washing dishes, and Weston was standing at the counter.

"You're late," Weston said, glaring at me as I entered.

"Sorry, baby, I lost track of time working on my composition."

"Was it worth it?" he asked, an edge to his tone.

I sighed. "No, because I'm stuck and you're mad at me." I stepped in front of him and wrapped my arms around his waist.

"I'm not mad." He let out a hard sigh. "Okay, I am mad—furious—but most of all I was worried, especially with all this Natalie and Mallory crap. You weren't answering your phone."

"I can't have it on during school, and I forgot to turn the sound back on. I'm sorry."

His fingers grabbed my chin so I would look up at him, his gaze hard. "Don't scare me like that again."

"I won't. Promise." I stood up on my toes and pressed my lips to his. That seemed to calm him, his body relaxing. "But I do have something to tell you."

"What's that?" he asked as he took my hand and led me toward the table.

"I ran into some people today on my way out."

He held out a chair for me. "Yeah? Who?"

I regarded him carefully. "Your parents."

Weston stopped all movement, his expression falling. "How?"

"They were at the school looking for Miles."

He let out a hard breath. "What happened?"

My jaw twitched. "I became very angry looking at your father."

He paused before asking, "Was he everything you'd built up in your mind?"

"Yes," I spat between clenched teeth. "He was an ass."

"To you?" he asked, his tone lowering.

"To me, to you, about me, even to Miles." I blew out a hard breath and let my head fall against his chest.

"I'm so sorry, baby girl." He wrapped his arms around me and kissed the top of my head. "I'd hoped to never expose you to him, but I knew it would happen one day. I thought I'd be at your side when it did, though."

I snuggled against his chest. "All thoughts and hopes I'd had of you reconciling with your father were blown away in less than two minutes tonight."

Weston sat down and pulled me onto his lap. "I never knew you felt that way."

I shrugged my shoulders. "Guess I just wanted you to have your parents in your life. Family is important, but after meeting them . . . I feel for your mom, really, I do. But your dad . . ." I shook my head. "If I thought Miles was bad when we met, your father was the same and probably thinking much worse. Miles's attitude was out of concern, but your father almost sounded disappointed, which made me feel like shit."

He leaned forward, resting his forehead on mine. "He has a way about him and I'm so sorry he directed it at you."

"Well, unlike your mom, I didn't cower to him." I played with the hair at the base of his scalp.

"Cower?"

I nodded. "It was like she had no strength to stand on her own, like everything she did was dictated by him. It was hard not to give in to her."

"Why did you feel for my mom?"

Why? Because I could see her love for him.

"She was very upset with your dad, yelling and hitting him with her purse before she began crying. She was begging me to help her see you."

His face scrunched up in pain and his grip tightened on me. I smoothed away the lines with my fingers and placed light kisses all over his face.

"I miss her, but she never stood up for me against him. She even defended him."

"Maybe she just wasn't strong enough."

"Maybe," he said with a sigh, his gaze off in the distance.

I stood from his lap and sat down on the chair next to him. "Come on, baby. Let's eat and then we'll go upstairs and take a bath together. How's that sound?"

He smiled at me and kissed my lips. "That sounds fantastic."

One day soon, he'd see them again. The last time was so long ago. Maybe something good would come of it, but maybe not.

I wasn't sure if time could heal that wound.

Chapter Thirty-Two

OUR COUNTDOWN

"**O**PEN WIDE," WESTON SAID, WAVING A FORK IN front of me. The tines were topped with the most delicious cobbler ever.

I opened wide and let in the heavenly dessert, moaning as the peach flavor burst against my taste buds.

"I'm going to miss this," I said, my eyes scanning the diner. There were only a few people occupying the booths, and none of them even noticed Weston.

He sighed. "Me too, but it will calm down after a few weeks."

I nodded. It was our fourth official date. We'd managed to find some pretty good places to go about an hour outside the city. A long drive, but a fair price to pay.

The Oscar buzz was out of control. Seeing it on TV and seeing it unfolding in L.A. weren't even in the same spectrum.

Weston's free hand took hold of mine, linking our fingers. "I'm nervous and anxious about it coming out, but I'm also ecstatic. I'm so tired of having this hanging over us, hindering us."

Butterflies invaded my stomach every time I thought about the Oscars. Excitement combined with fear and anxiety. My anxiety meter was at one hundred fifty percent.

"Yeah, I know what you mean. I have the same feelings you do, but once it dies down we can finally get on with our life together."

He smiled at me and brought my hand to his lips. "I can't wait, baby girl. You and me against the world."

I grinned and got up from my side of the booth. I sat down next to him and pressed my lips to his. "A most unstoppable force."

His arm moved up and around my shoulder, pulling me close into his side. He placed a kiss to the top of my head before relaxing back into the cushion.

We sat like that for about an hour, watching the cars go by on the little two-lane country road. People came and went, but nobody bothered us. We were just an average everyday couple, enjoying some country cooking.

The Natalie incident finally calmed down, and even people at school had stopped talking about it. Some other star's arrest after a hard night of partying was top of the talk.

Added to that was the fact the Oscars were just a few short days away.

"So, my stylist picked out this beautiful purple chiffon ball gown by Vera Wang. It's so beautiful and I can't wait to wear it!" Cloe said with a squeal of excitement.

Logan stuck his chest out and smiled. "Yeah, well, mine found this stylish tux by Calvin Klein."

Cloe sighed and rolled her eyes. "Guys are easy. It's a tux. How difficult is that?"

Logan stuck his tongue out, and everyone laughed. We were enjoying a lunch outside on the lawn, everyone together for the first time in weeks. The schedules were so hectic for some that days went by without seeing them.

I stared down at my plate, my stomach churning. The anxiety that had been building for weeks was at an all-time high. While excited and happy for the truth to come out, Weston made me even more anxious with his talk about the changes to come.

I let out a sigh as I fiddled with the food before me.

"Are you okay, Wren?" Bianca asked with a gentle touch to my shoulder.

"Yeah. I think it's just all these Oscars jitters floating around starting to affect me," I replied, forcing a smile.

"I'm not nervous," Cloe said.

Charlotte snorted. "I don't think you've ever been nervous."

Cloe rolled her eyes at her sister. "I just don't see the point of getting all worked up. It's part of the life, like it or not. Get over it."

"Not everyone is as cool and calm as you," Liam piped in.

Cloe stuck her tongue out at him, and Charlotte placed a kiss to his lips before reminding her sister how she felt. "Not everyone wants the life."

Liam smiled down at her. I was almost jealous of them at times. Both born to Hollywood, but down to earth. They didn't want the fame. They just wanted to be normal teenagers.

The bell rang, and we all groaned. Charlotte kissed Liam goodbye before grabbing on to my arm with a sigh. We waved to everyone as we broke off, heading in different directions.

"Are you working on your composition after school?" Charlotte asked as we walked to class arm in arm.

I shook my head. "Going over to Sophie's to try on more dresses. Want to come?"

Charlotte's eyes widened. "Really?"

"Why not?"

She giggled. "No, I was thinking about the fact that Sophie has *more* dresses. I thought she'd have *the* one already."

"She's still peeved about having had only four months to find the perfect one. Going on about how it's the Oscars and how elegant and formal an occasion it is. How the best ones are already spoken for."

We walked into the class and found our seats.

"I'd love to come. Since I'm only going to be able to see you in the dress on television, after all."

The teacher entered and brought the class to order, ending our conversation. I was happy she was coming with me, and even happier two hours later when the final bell rang.

I ran out to the parking lot to meet Charlotte after my last class. She was leaning on the passenger side door when I walked up.

"God, I love this car!" Charlotte said as she slid into the seat next to me.

"You say that every time."

"Doesn't make it any less true. Weston spoiled you with this baby!"

I laughed and rolled my eyes. "Yeah, I admit it. I fell in love at first sight."

"With Weston or the car?" She winked at me.

"I'd have to say both."

"I'm so excited you two are coming out. I mean, hell, it's a real shock it hasn't come out after all the Natalie crap."

"Julia is *very* good at her job. She, Amy, and Graham have been working their asses off to keep it quiet."

"And you're becoming quite the actress. I think Hollywood is rubbing off on you."

I couldn't help but laugh at her statement. "You could be right. This was never how I saw my life going six months ago."

Twenty minutes later, we arrived at Sophie's boutique. No sooner had we entered than I heard the familiar ring of a delighted two-year-old.

"Wehn!" Ari squealed, her little face scrunching up, smiling while her body vibrated with excitement. Then she was off, running toward me as fast as her little legs could propel her.

"Arianna, be careful!" Sophie's voice rang out from behind some rack.

I leaned down and scooped her up into my arms. "How's the princess today?"

"Goo. Where Wehtun?" Her wide eyes searched mine, then she looked behind me.

Charlotte let out an "aww" next to me. I knew then that she had succumbed to the cuteness that was our Princess Ari.

"He's at work."

Her cute little face turned into a pout and she sniffed, tears filling her eyes.

"Don't cry, sweetie. You'll see him soon," I said, trying to soothe her. Her bottom lip jutted out, but she nodded in understanding. "Until then, do you think you can help me show my friend Charlotte around?"

Ari's eyes lit up, and she looked over to Charlotte before nodding furiously and squirming to be let down.

"Come awn, Chowet." She reached her tiny hand up and grabbed onto Charlotte's before leading her around the store.

I followed behind, listening to her point out all the "pwetty" things.

A few minutes later Sophie was beside me, out of breath and looking frazzled. "Sorry about that. We got in a whole shipment for one of my clients today, and I had to check them in."

"That's okay. We were being entertained."

Sophie smiled at the sight of Charlotte and Arianna. "Her sitter was sick today so she's been here all day, getting into trouble. Carson was supposed to be here an hour ago to get her, but as you well know, things don't always go according to plan. He and Weston are stuck in some negotiations."

"And that's different from any other day?"

Sophie let out a laugh. "Nope." She sighed before grabbing my hand. "Come on, let me show you what came in. It's going to be a tough decision. You have to stand out, be elegant and fashion forward. It has to be different and make people take notice, so I made sure to get in a Versace. I contemplated a white dress for symbolic reasons, but I wanted options, so there's one."

The current front-runner of her dress debate was a multi-orange toned, frilly skirted dress with a tight bodice. However, that could be blown away based on how her newest arrivals would go.

We moved over to the dressing rooms and mirrors, Ari taking a seat on Charlotte's lap while Sophie and I went behind one of the curtains. After stripping out of my uniform, Sophie slipped the dress over my head. It was weird for me the first time she helped me into one of the dresses, being only in my panties. Sophie had just rolled her eyes, cracked a joke about "once you've seen one, you've seen them all," and the weirdness melted away.

As soon as I stepped out from behind the curtain and saw Charlotte's face, I knew the blue gown she'd put me in was a no-go.

She shook her head. "Maybe if you were Weston's age."

"Hey!" Sophie shouted in protest before laughing.

"Sorry, Sophie," Charlotte said with a laugh. "I only meant that, well, she's eighteen."

Sophie nodded. "No, I get it. It is too mature. Now that I see it on her, it's obvious."

We headed back in and grabbed another. She had five in all, and all were very different.

Sophie smiled at me. "Just think, we'll have a dress for you to wear for the wedding from one of these."

One of these? They were Cinderella-like gowns. "I didn't think it was that formal."

"Not really, but I think that blue *Elie Saab* from last week would be perfect."

"I loved that dress," Charlotte said.

"You've seen it?"

Charlotte nodded. "I've seen all the pictures, but I will say, live is so much better."

Sophie smiled. "That dress isn't as formal and the blue will complement her colors. Make her eyes pop." Sophie helped me out again, this time earning a drop-jawed expression from Charlotte. "Have his parents tried to contact you? I heard about you running into them."

I shook my head. "No. I thought there was a chance his mom would call, based on her reaction. Then again, his father may have kiboshed any idea of hers that led to communication."

Charlotte shook her head. "Based on what you've told me, sounds like a different generation issue. One where women were expected to obey their husbands. Archaic."

"Yeah, I thought about that, as well," I said. Charlotte picked the perfect word. Maybe it was the way I grew up, but the thought of anyone telling me what to do all the time made me ragey. "He seemed like a very controlling man, one that would bend her to his will. I don't think she wanted to side with him. I think she's just weak. She was afraid to defend Weston against him."

"Wow, that's a pretty big insight for meeting them once," Sophie said, staring at us.

I shrugged my shoulders. "It's just the impression I got. She was so distraught, begging me to take her to Weston. Richard looked like he couldn't care less."

Sophie sighed. "I think you're both right. Richard wasn't the warmest to begin with, but Joanna . . . she loves her boys, and having a child of my own, I know she misses Weston."

I sighed. "I can't help but wonder what's going to happen at the wedding."

"You have more important things to worry about than your in-laws. You and Weston are announcing your marriage to the world in three short days." Sophie fluffed up the back and was beaming as we looked at my reflection. "And I think we just found the perfect dress!"

I stared back at the reflection of a woman who was not me. She was older, sophisticated, and more beautiful than I was. I didn't recognize her, but I couldn't deny she was beautiful.

The mermaid style hugged and accentuated my curves. The plum color was lovely against my sun-kissed skin. It had intricate jeweled and beaded details all over, making it sparkle. The sleeveless top was straight across, both hiding and accentuating my breasts at the same time.

"I've always loved the mermaid style. Such a sexy yet classy look with the way it hugs the body," Sophie said as she adjusted something in the back. "Weston is going to go crazy when he sees you."

It was fashion forward and showed off the aesthetic the designer was known for, or so Sophie told me. Definitely Hollywood.

Charlotte agreed, and we all squealed in excitement. It even got Ari's stamp of approval. She called me a princess.

We said goodbye a little while later, then headed out to dinner. It was one of my last nights of anonymity, and I wanted to share it with the person who had become my closest friend since I'd arrived. I didn't know how I would have ever coped at school if it hadn't been for Charlotte's unwavering support and friendship.

Two hours later, I was pulling into our garage. I let out a sigh, happy to be done trying on dresses. Sophie's stress was driving me crazy. Thank God we finally found one we both agreed on.

"Weston?" I called out as I entered through the kitchen, tossing my bag down on the table.

No response.

Evidence of Kelly making dinner was gone, except the note on the counter that explained the reheating instructions.

I still didn't hear Weston, but I knew he was there somewhere, because all the cars were in the garage.

His office door was open, and I stuck my head in. "Baby?"

Empty.

I turned around and headed back down the hall toward the home gym, only to find it vacant as well. Where could he be?

I made my way up to our bedroom, an eerie feeling coming over me. It wasn't like him to not respond. Granted, if he was in our bedroom, there was no way he could've heard me from downstairs, but it was almost eight. Why would he be up there?

"Weston?" I called out again, waiting for a response.

"In here," Weston's voice called out.

The door was open and the light on as I walked in. I scanned around the room, expecting him to be within sight, but he wasn't.

The hairs on the back of my neck stood up as I felt eyes on me. "Weston?" Where was he hiding?

The bedroom door slammed behind me and I jumped, turning to find Weston running toward me. I let out a scream, but was silenced by his hand covering my mouth.

Panic filled me and I fought against him, thrashing in his arms as he pulled me across the room. We fell onto the bed, and his body fell on top of me, pinning me beneath him.

He smiled down at me, a wicked gleam in his heavy lidded eyes.

"You scared the ever loving shit out of me!" I yelled as I hit his bare chest with my hand. "Bastard!"

Tears stung in my eyes as my panic subsided, and I willed my body to calm down, but it shuddered instead.

His expression morphed, and his fingers brushed against my cheek. "Shh. It's okay, it's me."

"I know that, but it still freaked me out."

He kissed my lips and rested his forehead against mine. "I'm sorry, baby, I just wanted to surprise you."

"Surprise me?"

He chuckled and rotated his hips, grinding his erection against me. "Welcome home, baby girl."

I couldn't help the moan that slipped out. That was when I noticed he was naked and hard. He'd been a wicked sex god for the past few weeks.

"Planning on tying me to the bed and playing a game?" I asked as I smiled at him to show him I was okay. "Have your wicked way with me while I'm helpless to stop you from ravaging my body?"

He groaned and flexed his hips again. His breath came out in pants, then his lips crashed to mine.

All I felt from him was a thirst to consume. His desire for me wasn't a want, but a need. A primal need. A parched man who'd found his oasis.

His grip on me was intoxicating, so much so that I didn't even notice he'd moved my arms until a familiar "click" sounded in my ears.

I released his lips and tilted my head back. Sure enough, he'd handcuffed me to the bed. There was a pulling at my waist as he tore off my panties. He was acting like a man possessed.

The head of his cock was burning hot as it grazed against my wet entrance before he pushed against me, forcing it inside.

I shuddered as he worked his way in. It was so intense, a tearless sob erupted from me. His mouth latched onto my neck, nipping and sucking. Once he was all the way in, he pulled his whole body back and slammed into me.

A half scream, half moan tore from my chest, and my eyes rolled back as heat flooded my body. He stayed still for a moment, flexing his hips to push himself deeper.

A matching growl erupted from him as hands took hold of my shirt and ripped it open. His fingers pulled down the cups of my bra, exposing my nipples. Leaning down, he took one into his mouth while his fingers pinched and pulled at the other.

"Oh, fuck!" I cried out. His hips remained seated against mine as he played with my breasts. My hips tried to move, needing to feel him sliding in and out, but he just pushed me farther into the bed.

When I reached the point where I thought I was going mad, he slowly slipped out, only to slam back in. He repeated that rhythm over and over.

"I like you like this, baby girl. You're clenching my cock so good. Your pussy is begging for me to pound it, but you're at my mercy."

I needed more. He was driving me insane. "Please, baby. Please fuck me."

An evil grin formed on his lips. He pulled back and slammed in. "Not"—he pulled out and thrust again—"yet."

I let out a whimper, my wrists pulling at their binding. His mouth moved around my chest and neck, marking me, but I could feel his need to drive into me rising. His hips made short thrusts, giving us both a little bit of friction, but not enough.

"Weston, please! Baby, I need you to move."

"I am moving. Be more specific, baby girl," he rasped into my ear. "What do you want me to do?"

"Pound my fucking pussy!"

He grinned and nipped at my lower lip. "As you desire."

His fingers gripped hard on my hips, pulling me close to him, stretching my arms out. His hands moved around my thighs before pushing them down to the mattress.

Then he let go, moving at a fast and furious pace. I cried out as he did exactly what I asked him to, sending a fire ripping through me. He took me with relentless thrusts—it was pleasure and pain all rolled into one. I knew he wasn't hurting me, that he loved me, cherished me even, but for some reason our connection, while intensely physical, didn't feel like it was the emotional bond we usually shared.

It didn't take long with him taking my body that I came undone, back arching and screaming. He followed with a roar soon after, pressing his hips against me, pushing his cock deeper.

His body jerked with aftershocks as his muscles relaxed and his eyes slowly opened. Turmoil brewed in his eyes, despite the euphoria he was experiencing.

He released my hands from the cuffs, placing a kiss on each wrist before collapsing onto my chest, harsh breaths and sweat against my skin. My near jelly-like fingers brushed against his back. "You're not usually like this. What's going on?"

His arms wrapped tighter around me. "Only a few days left until I have to share you with the world." He sighed. "I'm anxious. I can't shield you as well then. I can't protect you."

"So you've gone feral caveman on me?"

He chuckled and kissed my neck. "I guess so."

"We'll be okay. As long as we're together."

He looked deep into my eyes, like he was studying me. "Together. Me and you as a team."

I linked my fingers with his. "Always."

Chapter Thirty-Three

OUR D-DAY

WE ONLY HAD A LITTLE TIME TOGETHER ON SUNDAY before the whirlwind began. Sophie arrived first with our clothes. The makeup artist and hairstylist showed up shortly after and began to work on getting me camera ready for Hollywood.

"Do I need to get you a sedative?" Sophie asked. She was scowling down at me with her arms folded across her chest.

I looked down at my lap to find I'd destroyed a napkin, shredding it into hundreds of pieces. Drawing in a deep breath, I tried to center myself, but it wasn't helping.

"Maybe?"

She sighed and uncrossed her arms. "Cissy, can you give us a few minutes?"

I caught her smile in the mirror as she set down the brush. "Sure. I need to get something from my car anyway."

Sophie stepped forward and took my hand in hers. "I know it's scary."

"I wasn't expecting this to happen." I held my hands out and watched them shake.

She gave me a small smile and wrapped her hands around mine. "It was bound to happen. Tonight is a lot to take in. You're announcing to the world you're married to a guy who was one of the most eligible bachelors in the world!"

Whatever blood was left fell from my face. "That's not helping."

"After tonight, the world will know about you. Yes, the unknown is scary, but think about all that this opens instead. You'll be able to go out together, hand in hand. You can wear your wedding ring and not worry about tucking it away." She leaned in and locked eyes with me. "And best of all, no one will think you're his sister."

She got a smile out of me with that one.

"Now, calm down, because if you do to the dress what you did to that napkin, I'll kill you." She smiled at me, and I couldn't help but smile back. "I'm serious here. Clothes are my life."

I let out a laugh, feeling much calmer than I had moments before. "Thanks, Sophie, that helped. And I promise I will do my best to make sure nothing happens to the dress."

A tug at my head brought my attention back up to the mirror and Cissy, and the loose up-do she was creating.

My makeup was complete, and once again I stared back at a woman I couldn't comprehend was really me. She didn't look eighteen. She did, however, look like she belonged on the arm of Weston Lockwood.

"Am I going to be able to sit in this thing?" I asked Sophie as she zipped me up and fastened all the buttons.

"Carefully. Just do it slowly and you should be fine. Your hips are a little wider—"

"Which is something her husband likes very much," Weston said, cutting Sophie off.

"Turd," Sophie said as she hit Weston in the stomach. "As I was saying, your hips are wider than the designer's base size, so just be careful when you sit."

I nodded and drew in a breath, then looked at Weston's reflection in the mirror.

My gaze moved up and down with his. "Wow. Wren, you look . . . I don't think gorgeous is a good enough word."

I smiled back at him and blew him a kiss. "Back at you,

handsome." James Bond had nothing on Weston in the three-piece tux Sophie had acquired. I had to admit, she was right—not all tuxedos were the same. It was a perfect fit on him. The pin-striped vest hugged his slim waist, giving it another dimension.

He stepped toward me, but Sophie halted him. "Back off, bucko. I just got her into this dress. You are not taking her out of it."

He scowled down at her. "Listen here, munchkin, I just want to kiss her."

"No." She held her hand up.

"No?" Weston asked.

"You'll smear her lipstick."

No matter how intense he glared down at her, she wouldn't budge. "I think I liked it better when you weren't dressing my date."

"Yes, but look how much more beautiful your date is with my expertise," Sophie said with a smile.

"How much time do we have?" I asked.

"Fifteen minutes until you have to be in the limo," Julia said as she entered the room. She let out a gasp when she saw me. "Oh, Wren, you look so beautiful. It's perfect."

"Thanks, Julia. You look beautiful, as well."

Julia was wearing a stunning navy blue empire waist dress. She was Miles's date, of course. Weston gave her the night off from standing behind him. She wouldn't be far, though, and was basically on call for any emergencies. Amy would be our shadow for the night.

"Are we ready to head . . . wow." Miles walked in and stopped in his tracks.

"I'm getting a lot of that tonight."

Miles blew out a breath. "I don't think the tabloids are going to be able to talk about anything other than your beautiful bride, Weston."

Weston was beaming. "I am quite lucky, aren't I?"

"There, all done!" Sophie said, clapping her hands together.

I broke out in a smile, which quickly morphed into hyperventilating. Weston ran to my side as I leaned over, trying to take a deep breath.

"I knew I should have gotten her a sedative," Sophie grumbled under her breath.

"It's okay, I just need a second," I said, gripping his jacket. I took a few deep breaths to steady my nerves. It took a moment, but I was able to stand straight, giving them a nervous smile. "I'm good. Promise."

"Are you sure?" Weston asked, cupping my cheek.

My lips moved into a real smile, and I leaned forward to place a light kiss on his lips. "Just the jitters."

With that, I took his arm and we headed out to the limo. There were two sitting in the driveway, Miles and Julia climbing into the first one as I very carefully slid into the second one with Weston, Amy taking the front seat to give us some privacy.

Sophie gave me a hug and wished us luck before shutting the door. Silence prevailed over us, Weston's hand gripping mine tight as we headed out.

We didn't speak, just touched, but it conveyed everything words simply couldn't at that time: *I love you, I'm here, we'll get through this together—you are mine.*

A little while later, I knew we'd arrived when the car stopped and Weston's grip became crushing. We were in the drop-off line, some unknown amount of cars back.

Weston's lips crashed into mine, kissing me hard as if it was our last. He pulled back, his eyes boring into mine, speaking volumes.

"Everything is about to change. Your life—our life—is going to be all over tabloid covers across the country. The world, for that matter. Don't read their lies this time. Don't even glance at them. People you don't even know will come up to you, calling your name, wanting your autograph or photo. Don't lose your cool, be as distant as you can. As soon as you step out, your privacy is forfeit. All you need to know is that I love you, and I'm right beside you."

His fingers stroked my cheek, sadness etched in his features.

"Weston?" I asked, my voice filled with a little more worry than I meant to let out.

"I just want to keep you locked up, hide you away from any pain to come." His voice was just above a whisper.

"Pain?" It was a word I wasn't expecting and didn't understand.

"People are going to say many things about you, about me, and about us that are complete lies. Just like the ones you read months ago. They will try to pry you apart to see how you tick, they will scrutinize every detail about you and our life. Don't listen, don't watch, don't read. And most importantly, don't believe."

I nodded, my hands shaking in his. I blew out a breath and met his gaze, centering myself on him.

I let out a little giggle when I noticed he was wearing my shade of lipstick, which helped to relax us both a bit. I ran my fingers across his lips, wiping away the dark pink shade.

"If you messed up my lipstick, Sophie will kill you."

He pressed his lips to mine again. "You look flawless."

I quirked a brow at him. "Says you, but our stylist may have her own ideas."

He pulled something out of his pocket. "Perhaps that's why she slipped this to me on our way out."

I took the tube of gloss from him and pulled down the vanity mirror. After a quick touch-up, the driver gave us the signal that we were up.

"Time to introduce my wife to the world," Weston said as he wrapped his arms around me for a hug, kissing my hair.

He stepped out of the car and I scooted closer as I grasped for his outstretched hand. Fans were calling his name, cameras were flashing. With one last breath, I pulled myself together and became what I needed to be: movie star Weston Lockwood's wife.

I climbed out, trying to hide my absolute awe of the scene before me. Fenced-off fans, tons of media, and more stars gathered together than I'd ever seen on TV. There was a long red carpet that

Weston began leading me down after tucking my right hand into the crook of his arm.

I straightened my spine and placed one foot in front of the other, smiling at Weston before turning toward the crowds of people.

We made it down the line, past some reporters who didn't have much interest in us, but still asked who made my gown and took photos. About one-third of the way down, one of them finally spoke up.

"Weston, who is the lovely woman you have with you tonight?" the reporter asked.

Weston beamed down at me. "This beautiful being is my beloved wife, Wren."

The hand that held my ring rested on his chest, his own on his hand, sat on my hip.

There was a sudden pause, and then all the reporters and cameras around were coming down on us, snapping pictures and asking questions.

"How long have you been married?"

"When was the wedding?"

"What's your name?"

"What about Natalie?"

Weston stayed silent, letting the mayhem die down a bit before delivering the speech he'd worked out.

"Our marriage is fairly new, and a very private matter. We ask that everyone respect that, please. The rumors regarding Natalie Larson and myself are very false and spun by Natalie herself. We have not been together in almost a year. I love my wife, and we are very happy. She is a wonderful person, and is beyond everything I ever dreamed I wanted in my life."

We looked at each other, smiling, and he leaned down, giving me an Eskimo kiss. The clicking of shutters increased, as did the questions.

My nerves calmed down a bit after the initial weight was off. Having Weston hold me close was a huge help, too.

One of the event people ushered us to move on. More questions and pictures were taken. As we were prepared but selective, only a few questions were answered, and only one by me.

"Where did you two meet?"

I smiled at the reporter. "We met at Starbucks."

They didn't need to know when and what city, but it still riled them up.

Amy ushered us to continue down the red carpet, and after what felt like forever, we reached the end.

I let out a deep breath of relief, my body going limp against Weston whose hand tightened around my waist.

"You did great, baby girl," he whispered as he kissed the top of my head. "Are you thirsty?"

"Now that you mention it, yeah."

"Wait right here, I'll go get us something. Julia and Miles are over there." He pointed across the crowd, about twenty feet away, where they stood talking to Amy.

Apparently, there was something she needed to speak to Julia about.

I had a hard time letting go of his hand, and once I did, I felt out of place. It was very awkward. People were staring at me, whispering to each other. I felt as though I was in the center of a stage with a spotlight on me.

Stars mingled in the open space, having a drink and talking before going in to take their seats. Across the room I saw Adam Devonshire talking with Gabriella Scott. Iris Newby was snuggled up in Nicholas Day's arms. All of them huge Hollywood actors and I was standing, breathing the same air as them.

My fingers began fidgeting with my dress, but I forced myself to stop before I ripped something off. Sophie would kill me if anything happened to the dress.

Just as my breathing picked up, and I feared I'd begin hyperventilating, the familiar sight of Cloe and Damien Clark appeared before me.

"Wren!" Cloe smiled and hugged me.

"You look absolutely beautiful beyond words, Wren," Damien said, leaning down and giving a kiss to my cheek.

I tried not to fangirl that Damien Clark had just kissed my cheek, but I'd be sure to gloat about it to Daniel when I called him the next day. "Thank you."

He placed his hands on my shoulders. "Take a breath. You did great. The cat is out of the bag now, so be strong."

"Cat, what cat?" Cloe asked, her head whipping between her father and me. It was obvious she was confused.

I held up my left hand, showing off the ostentatious ring Weston bought for me months ago. "Weston is my husband, and we just announced it to the press."

Her eyes widened, jaw dropping. "What? But . . . but you said he was your brother!"

"Technically, I said that Miles was my brother and that I was related to Weston. Which wasn't a lie, just a spin of words."

I hoped that the others in our group of friends would understand. I'd been so nervous leading up to the Oscars I hadn't even thought about what I was going to tell everyone at school.

"But you never corrected anyone," she said in protest.

"Because it was a secret," I said.

"Does Char know?"

I nodded. "And I think Talia may, as well."

She pouted. "Why am I the last? I thought we were friends."

"We are friends." I took hold of Cloe's hand and squeezed it. "It's just that Talia came to the house for a meeting one night."

Cloe turned to her dad. "How did you know?"

He smiled down at his youngest. "Honey, I've worked with Weston since he was a teenager, I knew he didn't have a sister."

"Why didn't you tell me?" Cloe gave a little stomp.

"For the same reason your sister won't go by our last name. Privacy." He gave me a smile. "And considering Weston's history with his parents, it was a pretty good backstory."

A hand slid around my waist, lips kissing my temple. "It was a pretty ingenious on-the-fly move. We'd kind of forgotten about that when she headed off to school."

Weston handed me a glass, and I gulped down whatever was in it.

"Whoa! Ease up, baby, that's champagne."

I bottomed out the glass and looked up at him. "I told you I was thirsty."

He pursed his lips and took the glass from me. "I'll go get you a water."

"I can do that, sir," Amy said, startling us and taking the glass from him before walking to the bar.

"Think you might win best picture tonight, Weston?" Damien asked, engaging us in conversation.

"I hope so. Lockwood Entertainment needs it. Have to pay for my wife's car."

I scoffed and elbowed him in the ribs. Then I turned to them to explain. "I was happy with some used car, but no, he took me to a car dealership and trotted out this beauty of a car. How was I to say no to it?"

The lights dimmed, cuing us it was time to be seated, and we made our way to our designated seats.

It was so difficult not squeal when I saw some of my favorite stars walking around, and even more when I sat surrounded by them. Jennifer Beck, kick-ass actress from *Doomed*, one of my and Daniel's favorite movies, sat right in front of me!

"You're doing great," Weston whispered into my ear as he entwined our hands. PDA wasn't something you saw a lot of in Hollywood, but Weston knew I needed it. He probably needed it, as well.

I exhaled a deep breath. "Inside I'm a wreck."

"Well, outside you are simply stunning and have everyone's attention."

"So, what is my handsome husband up for? I can't believe I don't even know that."

He settled farther into his chair. "Sorry, I should have told you. Everything has just been so busy, I didn't even think about it."

"It's okay. I know all your current projects," I reassured him.

He placed a kiss to my knuckles. "Lockwood Entertainment has a few movies that are nominated for different things, the biggest being *Westwood Lane.*"

I stared at him in wide-eyed shock. "You did *Westwood Lane?*"

He chuckled. "Yeah. Adam's an old friend of mine, and I jumped at the chance to work with him again."

He said Adam like it was nothing, but inside I was screaming that my husband was good friends with Adam Devonshire!

I thought back to the list of Weston's movies and remembered at least one he did with him.

The event began, and I stared in awe at all the cameras that were flying around. It was quite an event. My eyes scanned around the room, trying to keep in my squeals. The last thing I wanted to do was embarrass Weston.

The opening began, and soon they were running down categories and announcing winners.

When one of Weston's films category came up, his hand clamped down onto mine. The best picture category had some pretty damn good competition, but even without my bias, *Westwood Lane* knocked them all out of the park.

He took a deep, steadying breath as Iris Newby made the announcement.

"And the winner for Best Picture is . . . *Westwood Lane!*"

"Yes!" I clapped my hands together.

The crowd erupted in cheers as the cast and Weston stood. He gave me a hug and a kiss before making his way to the stage.

I watched as Weston climbed the stairs and stood beside the actors and director, and Miles, as well.

The award was handed to Adam Devonshire, the lead, who then began his speech. "Well, first off, I want to say thank you to everyone who made this possible. We had a great team working on this movie, and I'm proud to accept this award on everyone's behalf!" He smiled, then turned to Weston. "And then I want to go to left field and congratulate my friend and our brilliant producer, because without him this film wouldn't have taken off, on his recent marriage. That's right ladies . . . and gentlemen. Weston Lockwood is off the market!"

My hand covered my mouth as he spoke, hiding my ear-to-ear smile. Weston was grinning like a fool, and even blushing a little while the crowd went wild.

"Where is she?" Adam turned back to Weston. "You didn't even tell me! You could have texted me or something. I found out on the red carpet from the tabloids. I mean, how often are they right?"

My smile faltered, eyes bulging. They wouldn't put me on the spot, would they? My heart began to hammer in my chest.

"What's her name? Wren? Okay, Wren Lockwood, show yourself and be introduced to the world!" I slid down farther into my seat, trying to hide.

I gawked up at the stage and my face plastered all over the big screens.

"Quit hiding your beautiful face," Weston said into the microphone. I peeked up at him through my fingers. "She's embarrassed, and a bit camera shy." He was saying it to Adam, but it got picked up by the microphone.

The spotlight shone on me and I sighed, pulling my hand away and giving them all a shy smile. I was very much out of my element.

The stage erupted into applause, and soon so did the audience. My cheeks were flaming hot as I smiled up to my husband and waved, making sure to flash my wedding ring.

All of Hollywood, and much of the world, was focused on me.

I was going to die.

Weston returned and cupped my face, kissing me deeply as he sat down. "Sorry."

I gave him a pout. "You suck."

He chuckled against my neck. "No, baby girl, that's you later."

Once all the awards were given away, we headed to the after party. I took Weston's outstretched hand, his beaming smile infectious as we walked through the maze of stars.

Weston spotted Adam, who waved us over.

"Come say hello," Adam said.

My steps were hesitant, and I caught myself staring at Adam's outstretched hand. Besides Weston and Damien, he was the biggest star I'd ever met. It left me wondering if I would ever get used to it.

Adam smiled at me. "She's a shy one."

"Anyone would be in this arena," I said, finally taking his hand. "And it's not really shyness. I'm trying my hardest not to pass out, or throw up from nerves."

The group of people, most from *Westwood Lane*, laughed.

"How's tonight going for you two?" Adam's wife, Mara, asked.

"It's been . . . something else. Very overwhelming, but also an amazing experience." I smiled and lowered my voice. "And, it's hard not to shout out 'Hello, I'm Wren Lockwood and I'm married to the sexiest, sweetest, most wonderful man ever!'"

Mara laughed, nodding. "I hear you on that one, Wren."

After a few minutes we ran into Iris Newby who threw her arms around Weston and gave him a big kiss on the cheek.

"Wes, I can't believe you got married!"

He laughed. "Well, you know, I got tired of you refusing to go out with me."

My eyes popped open as I looked at them.

Iris glanced over to me before stepping to the side and pulling me in for a hug. "Delighted to meet the woman who stole my boy's heart."

"Your boy?" I glanced at Weston and quirked my brow.

Iris laughed as she stepped back into Nicholas Day's arms. It was hard to even look at him. He'd been a model before turning to acting.

"Nothing to worry about, Wren. It's kind of an inside joke between us."

It was then I remembered she was in *Midnight Horizon* with Weston years before. They were a couple in the film and I began to wonder if at some point those feelings ever transferred over into real life.

"This the new meat?" a handsome man that I instantly recognized as James Conroy said as he walked over, a huge grin on his face. "Or newbie, I should say."

"Hey, Jimmy, how's it going?" Weston asked.

James Conroy was older than Weston and probably in his fifties, but the man was one of those that only got better looking with age.

James nodded. "Good, Wes." He shrugged. "Could be better, you know, if *Domain* had won best picture but hey, at least we were beat by you over that horrible *Life of Death*."

Iris's mouth popped open and she whacked James in the stomach. "You're awful!"

James laughed and pulled her in for a hug. "It was a great movie. You were fantastic."

Her eyes narrowed on him, but there was a glint of amusement in her eye and then she laughed, breaking it apart. "God I've missed working with you!"

"Yeah, well, come by the set sometime." James put his hand on Nicholas's shoulder. "You know me and Nic here got one going down over at Fox."

"You know who I want to work with again?" a seductive blonde asked as she slipped her arms around Weston's other arm.

Rachel Brookes.

Dr. Brighton's patient in *Thorntown*.

"Hi, Rachel."

Rachel stepped back and looked straight at me, almost like she was dissecting me, before a smile crept onto her face and her eyes softened.

"You look a bit frazzled, my dear."

I let out a nervous laugh. "Yeah, well, let's just say I never in a million years thought I would ever meet a Hollywood actor let alone be here, mingling with hundreds."

She took my hands in hers. "Welcome. I've never seen Weston smile so much, and that makes us all so happy. Now hold on tight to him, and don't ever let go."

I glanced over to Weston who was smiling down at me. Turning back to her, I couldn't help the grin that felt like my face would split in two.

"Never."

It was a whirlwind after that. I lost count of how many of Hollywood's elite I met.

By the end of the night, my feet were killing me, and I was following untold stars on *Twitter*, *Instagram*, and *Facebook*. It was a fabulous night, and all of Hollywood seemed happy for us. I just hoped the rest of the journey could be so smooth, but I knew that was a dream.

God only knew what tomorrow would bring.

Chapter Thirty-Four

OUR FALLOUT

WESTON WASN'T KIDDING WHEN HE SAID THINGS were about to change. By the time we got home, there was already a crowd of people at the gate. From experience, Weston had the foresight to bring Joe and his crew along. Flashbulbs were going off, trying to get a picture through the tinted windows. My hand unconsciously squeezed Weston's, and he gave a reassuring squeeze back.

"Don't worry, baby girl, they can't see in. And once we're past the gates, it won't matter anymore."

The first thing I did when we walked in was rid myself of the heels that were killing my feet. Weston helped me out of my dress, and I hung it back up, quickly inspecting it for any damage to avoid the wrath of Sophie.

I searched out my phone from Weston's pocket where I kept it stowed all night. Once I found it, there was a knot in my stomach as I looked down at the screen and the ton of texts waiting for me. Many of them were angry.

You're married? Why didn't you tell us? - Logan

Thought you trusted us. How could you keep it from us? – Bianca

I knew you were hiding something, but why did you have to hide it? – Aaron

There was a lone one from Charlotte that made me smile.

You looked so beautiful! Excellent job, girl! Be waiting for you on the steps in the morning. – C

I sighed and shot back a mass text to the rest of our group.

I'm so sorry I didn't tell you guys. It's not that I didn't trust you, but this was a huge secret, for my protection, and we only told a select few. I never meant to hurt any of you. We were just trying to protect ourselves for as long as possible. I promise to explain everything at lunch. Please give me that!

I moved to the bathroom to scrub off my face. My eyes were so heavy, tired from the long day.

"Everything okay?" Weston asked as he wrapped his arms around my waist, resting his head on my shoulder while I wiped my face dry. He'd removed his tux, dressed now only in his boxers.

I pursed my lips. "My friends at school saw and aren't happy I lied to them."

He sighed and kissed my neck. "Don't worry, they'll forgive you. Tell them the truth tomorrow."

"You want me to tell them about Vegas?" I asked.

He locked eyes with me in the mirror. "Do you trust them?"

I nodded. "They're all Hollywood born, working, or their parents are diplomats."

"Then go ahead. People in the life don't spill beans. Be honest with them, they're your friends, and the biggest part of the secret is out now. People are eventually going to find out what really happened. Better they know first."

"Okay." I relaxed back against his chest.

"Come on, let's go to bed."

"Yeah, I'm beat."

"Oh, I wasn't talking about sleep yet. You looked so damn good in that dress, and I just got you out of it." He grinned at me, then leaned down to nip at my neck while one of his hands slid down my stomach. My breath hitched and my pussy clenched. "I mean, here you are, all fucking naked but for these poor excuse for panties." His fingers looped around the thin strap of my thong and pushed it down. "Unless you're too tired?"

Tired? Fuck, not anymore.

I moaned when his fingers slipped between my thighs to find my clit.

I sucked in a shuddering breath, my arm looping behind me around his neck.

"How do you want it, baby girl?" he asked as two fingers sunk into me.

My body arched into his hand, rocking against him. "Hard. Demanding."

"Tell me why." He nipped at my neck and pushed his hips against my ass.

"I need to feel how much you need me."

Without removing his fingers, he wrapped his other arm around me and picked me up, carrying me to our bed. He tossed me down, and I turned to face him. His fingers were in his mouth, and he let out a moan.

"Fuck, baby, you taste good."

He pushed down his boxers, and I licked my lips at the sight of him hard and dripping. He gave his cock a few quick strokes before crawling onto the bed and looming over me, so feral and sexy.

His hands gripped my thighs and pushed them open, down to the bed, and held them there. My breath sped up, the lust in his eyes skyrocketing my own as he looked at me.

A groan vibrated in his chest as he licked his lips. "You look so good spread out for me."

One hand released me and grabbed his cock, dragging the tip between my folds before sliding in.

My back arched against the bed, my mouth fell open, and my eyes rolled back as he filled me. A rush of fire burst through me like it always did when he entered me.

"Mmm, yeah. That's the connection I needed," he said in a breathy tone, his eyes unfocused.

He leaned down to kiss me, and my hands wound around his neck. Reaching up, he grabbed my wrists and pinned them above my head.

"I believe my beautiful wife said she wanted me hard and demanding."

I licked my lips and nodded, my hips rocking.

He grinned and pulled out, then slammed back in. A spark moved through me, cleansing my mind of all thought with each thrust. The sound of our bodies coming together filled the air, our moans creating a chorus to the beat.

Every time my body tried to move, to arch against his, to pull him deeper, he pushed me further into the bed.

I was overcome with him, with feeling him inside me. Each time he slammed into me, all my worries flew away. All I needed was Weston.

My muscles coiled tight, my breath barely coming out in pants as he pushed me over the edge, screaming as I came undone.

I shuddered beneath him, my walls squeezing around him, trying to pull his come from him.

"God, baby girl, shit . . ." He came with a roar, pushing himself as far in as he could go.

He collapsed down on top of me and released my hands. It took a moment before I could move them, my hands stroking up and down his sweaty back.

Sleep claimed us after that, hard and deep, wrapped up in each other.

The next morning, I peeked out the window and groaned when I saw the amount of photographers outside had doubled overnight, leaving me to wonder if we could even get out.

Weston's arms wrapped around me and kissed my temple as he hugged me tight. "Text me throughout the day, let me know how you're doing."

I gripped his arm and leaned my head back against his shoulder. "It's going to be a rough day, isn't it?"

He nodded against my neck. "Yeah, it is. But I'll be with you, even if I'm not there physically."

We both finished getting dressed, including our wedding rings, and headed down to the kitchen.

The butterflies in my stomach kept me from eating breakfast, despite Weston's protests, but I did grab a glass of orange juice.

"Holy shit, it's a madhouse out there!" Julia said as she entered, her arms flying in the air, scowling as she set down her bags. "Those idiots wouldn't even move to let me in." She sighed, putting on a smile as she wrapped her arms around me. "Morning."

"Good morning," I said with a smile.

Weston threw his arms around us and squeezed. "Morning!"

We giggled and pulled away, but not before I gave Weston a quick kiss.

"How's the day look?" Weston asked Julia, then took a bite of his toast.

Julia's lips moved into a thin line. "Busy. Carson's meeting us at the office, and I suggest we get going ASAP in order to get through that mess out there."

Weston sighed and gave me a pout. "Remember what I said. Call me, text me, just keep in touch. If you need anything, have any problems . . ."

I nodded. "I'll contact you. Gotcha."

He cupped my face in his hands and gave me a long, hard kiss. "I hope you have a good day, baby girl."

"You, too."

With one last peck, they headed out to the garage and through the crowd waiting at the gate. I gazed up at the clock as I took a sip of juice, wondering how early I needed to leave to push my way through the mess.

"You ready?" Joe asked, walking into the kitchen with one of his guys trailing behind him. I'd seen him before, many times, but never caught his name.

I quirked my brow at him. *How long has he been here?* "Ready?"

"Oliver and I will be taking you to school for the next few weeks," he said. I glanced over to Oliver, who gave me a wave. "You're going to be accosted and followed going out by yourself. I'm trying to reduce the amount of them."

"Oh," I said, setting down my glass. I let out a sigh, my eyes down.

Joe walked forward and dipped down to meet my eyes. "It's going to be okay. I'm here to protect you."

"You really think they know I'm in high school already?" I asked, staring up at him. He nodded. "But, Weston needs you."

"Weston knows how to handle these types of situations, and I've got a guy on him. Right now, you are our top priority."

We headed out a few minutes later, me climbing into the back of a black SUV with fully tinted windows. My stomach was tied in knots as we backed out of the garage and headed toward the gate.

At least thirty paps were snapping cameras, trying to get a glimpse inside the vehicle. Joe slowly pushed through the crowd, but the moment he was free, the gas pedal was to the floor.

"What the hell was that for?" I asked a few miles down the road.

Joe's gaze flickered to the rearview mirror. "Were we followed?"

Followed?

"We've got two tailing us," Oliver said, his eyes glued to the side mirror. "Tan Toyota three back and a red Honda left and two back."

With that information, Joe took a sharp turn right, losing one of them. After many twists and turns, Oliver couldn't identify anyone behind us.

I was still astonished they would follow me when we pulled up to the school gate and onto the secure grounds.

"Thanks, Joe," I said, opening the door.

"Wren," he called, stopping my movements. I turned to look at him. "Oliver will pick you up right here after school. Do not stay late this week. If anything happens, call my cell phone, and I'll get you out of here immediately. Even if it's because you just can't take the attention from your classmates."

I smiled at him. "Aye aye, captain."

With great trepidation and a whole lot of butterflies that were threatening to burst through my stomach, I stepped out. Charlotte was waiting for me, just as she said, but before I could reach her, I was faced with some unknown person.

I'd seen her around before. Blonde hair, entitled attitude, with a posse that fawned over her. "Do you think this is some game? Coming here and lying to all of us, thinking you're better than we are because you're a Lockwood, only to find out you're not."

"I am a Lockwood," I said, my spine straightening.

"By marriage. You're an impostor and you shouldn't be here," she sneered, then walked away.

Each of her groupies gave me bitchy looks as they pushed past. One of them even whispered "whore," under her breath.

Great. Was that what I had to look forward to?

Charlotte took the final steps toward me, glaring at the girl who'd just left. "Bitch," she muttered under her breath.

I let out a small chuckle and threw my arms around her. "You are awesome."

"I know. Come on, time to face the music."

"Is that pun intended?" I asked, knowing it was Miles's class we were headed to.

She laughed out loud and rolled her eyes. "I guess it is. C'mon."

Arms linked, we walked up the steps and into the building. I stopped when we reached the door, seeing everyone inside gathered around Miles. One girl noticed me, and then the wolves descended.

Question after question was flung at me, people touching me, and I was beginning to freak out a little bit. Hands grabbed me, jostling me.

"All right, everyone settle down and take your seats," Miles said, trying to call the class to attention.

With reluctance, they dispersed and found their spots.

"Mr. Lockwood, before class, can we talk about the elephant in the room?"

Miles leaned against his desk and nodded. "Okay, let's get this out of the way and get back to class. As you should all know by now, Wren is my sister-in-law, not my sister by blood. She is married to my brother, Weston. End of story. Now, I want to talk abou—"

"But why so secret?"

Miles didn't pay any attention to the question, and his voice rose to signal that any and all discussion over the topic was over.

"We need to talk about your compositions. Some of you seem to think this is a slack assignment and you can just throw some notes together and I'll pass you, but I want to remind everyone that progress playing is graded."

There were some groans, but at least I wasn't on the spot anymore.

My first class ended up a bit better than I thought, but that was most likely because it was Miles's class. Now they knew my talent wasn't because I was born a Lockwood.

I walked into my second class and immediately caught Aaron's gaze. Out of habit, my head turned at my name being called. Some jackass made a lewd gesture at me, and I got a bitch brow from his girlfriend.

"You going to tell me what's going on?" Aaron asked as soon as I sat down. He didn't look too mad, but he also didn't look his normal friendly self.

I heaved a sigh. "I wanted to tell everyone at once. Can you wait until lunch?"

His lips moved to a thin line, and he nodded.

"Thanks, Aaron."

I thought my first week was bad, being a spectacle and all, but it was much worse now. *Everyone* stared at me everywhere I went. Whispered words, gossip spawning. A cross between jealousy and high school bitchiness hit me more than I was expecting. Apparently, it was fine if you were related to a celebrity but not so fine when you were married to one.

Thankfully, I had an established group of friends. I just hoped they would forgive me for not telling them.

With each class, I was bombarded with question after question. It was exhausting and strange, especially when some wanted to know about our sex life. What the hell was that about?

Charlotte met me at my locker just before lunch and we headed to the cafeteria, where I was accosted by yet another person.

"You married your brother? That is so sick!" a tall, lanky blonde said.

I stared at the stupidity of the girl in front of me, and Charlotte rolled her eyes.

"He's not my brother."

"You said he was," she said matter-of-factly.

I pursed my lips and took a calming breath. "No, I said Miles was my brother. Everyone assumed that meant Weston was as well."

She threw me her best bitch brow. "How can Miles be your brother and not Weston?"

Out of the corner of my eye, I caught Charlotte trying not to laugh out loud. It was quite a struggle for her. "Wow, you're at the bottom of our class, aren't you?"

"What the hell does that mean?" she snapped back, zeroing in on Charlotte.

"Miles is my *brother-in-law* because I am *married* to Weston." With that, I grabbed Charlotte and stormed out of the cafeteria.

"Oh my God!" Charlotte was bent over, laughing hysterically.

I shook my head, my eyes wide. "I thought this was a school for gifted people?"

"Oh, she's gifted all right." She straightened out, wiping a tear from her eye, and hit my arm with her elbow. "C'mon, time to face your real friends."

My heart hammered in a staccato rhythm as we walked over to our usual lunch spot, all eyes on me. I'd been in class with a few of them, but I asked that we speak at lunch so I could get it all out at one time.

"All right, we're here. Spill," Bianca spat, arms crossed over her chest. She'd been the most irate when I asked her to wait.

I took a deep breath and looked around at my friends who were all staring back. It was a strange feeling, to have so many sets of eyes hungrily trained on me. Looking at me like I was a juicy steak.

I sat down and took a deep breath before going right into it. "Six months ago, my name was Wren Bradford, and I lived outside Indianapolis with my mom and stepdad. I spent my time with my best friend, Daniel, going to the mall, watching movies, playing video games, and just hanging out, like any normal middle-class teenager. I was an ordinary girl, with an ordinary life, and a college plan."

I paused for a drink, when Logan chimed in, "That's different."

I nodded. "My mom wanted to go on vacation for my fall break to Las Vegas. While there, she got a taste for the casino, and I was left in the lobby, reading. That was when I met Weston."

A few eyes widened at that little tidbit.

"Let me guess, what happened in Vegas didn't stay in Vegas?" Aaron asked.

I blew out a breath. "Yeah. Exactly, and, to be honest, I didn't recognize him, and he just said his name was Weston. We spent a day touring the strip, then went to dinner. We drank a little bit, and ended up getting married." I flashed them my wedding ring that I was now wearing on my finger. "Ever since then, my life has been turned upside down. We contemplated an annulment, but decided to give it a try, and so, I went home with him."

"And then you started here," Liam said, stating the obvious.

"Yeah, a week after I got here. I didn't tell anyone, because I'd only known him for a few days. I mean, we're not the conventional story, especially not for Hollywood. I'm in high school, and he's making blockbuster movies. We just thought it would be best if we could get to know each other and see if it would work. If we'd fall in love, before alerting the media and people started grilling us."

"Makes total sense," Cloe said.

They all nodded like they understood. "So, am I forgiven? I've given you the whole story. I do trust you all."

Logan cleared his throat. "I get it. I mean, you've told us more than was said last night."

"What he means is, we're still hurt you didn't trust us enough to tell us before this went public, but we understand why you didn't," Bianca said, looking straight at me. "We've all kept secrets for one reason or another."

Cloe smiled at me. "What a story that is! Holy shit!"

"Hell, yeah!" Aaron beamed at me and gave me a squeeze. "We've got your back."

"I gotta ask, though," Logan began, a smirk playing on his lips. "How's your forehead?"

Emily's eyes were wide. "Oh, my God! Yes!"

"That was you, right?" Liam quirked his brow. "Man, I hope they throw the book at those bitches."

I smiled and rolled my eyes. A weight lifted from me, and lunch turned into the best part of the day. I hated to leave them all when the bell rang as we went off into different directions.

I wasn't sure how much more I could take from the other students, but I was bound and determined to stay and not let them run me out of school. It was rough, and caused me to text Weston more than once.

Can I come to your office after school? Is it safe?

It was hard to concentrate on class and not look at my phone, hoping for a sign. It was the kind of time I was happy our school allowed cell phones. I was staring at the teacher, trying to figure out what she was saying, but all I heard was "Blah, blah, blah, blah." Then my phone buzzed, and my eyes shot down to the new text message.

It's a zoo here, baby. How about I leave at the same time you do and meet you at home?

In all honesty, I didn't think I could wait that long. I needed the emotional security and haven that was Weston, especially since I only had a few classes with Charlotte. She helped some, but it wasn't the same.

Can you do that? I typed back.

Once again, I stared at the front. I was so zoned out I didn't even notice the slip of paper that plopped in front of me. My eyes stared at it, leery of what it might say. I'd been getting a lot of crap, and I had a feeling the white sheet in front of me wasn't going to be any better.

What's it like being a Hollywood whore? It read, then continued on: *You must have a fantastic mouth and be a great fuck to get Weston Lockwood to marry you. I bet you'd let all the guys here fuck you, slut.*

I bit my bottom lip, trying not to let the words affect me, to keep the tears away. It helped some, but my eyes watered regardless.

I didn't deserve any of it, but that didn't make it hurt any less.

My hand shot up in the air as I asked the teacher to use the restroom, then ran out the door before she gave the okay. I jogged down the hall, phone in hand, and rounded the corner, slamming into a solid form, sending me falling hard to the ground.

"Oh, shit, Wren!" I heard, but my head was spinning from everything.

My eyes opened, and the familiar black T-shirt with "L.E. Security" in white letters, worn by Joe and his team, greeted me. The wall had brown hair with light brown eyes and a soft, friendly face.

"Oliver?"

"Are you okay?" He held out his hand and helped me to stand.

My hand swiped over my aching ass—the floor was hard. "What are you doing here? You aren't supposed to be here for two more hours."

"Mr. Lockwood asked me to check on you. He was worried based on your text message."

My brow scrunched. "That wasn't five minutes ago."

"I've been camped out in the parking lot." He winked.

My eyes widened. "Oh."

"Is everything all right? The way you were running . . ." he trailed off, his eyes full of concern as they scanned the hall.

I opened my hand and showed him the crumpled remains of the note. He took it, scanning over it quickly, then whipped out his phone.

"I've left the nest. Chickadee's being hunted by some snakes," he said to whom I assumed was Joe. He listened for a moment before looking to me. "Do you want to leave?"

I shook my head. "I don't want them to think they got to me so much I ran away."

Oliver went back to his code talk about birds. I didn't understand the reason, but I was certain there was one.

"Staying on the ground, will meet back at Eagle's nest before the wolves come out." He ended the call and stared down at me. "Do you want me in class with you, or out in the hall?"

I took a deep breath, and relaxed a bit, knowing help was closer if I needed. "Outside in the hall. I don't want to cause too much of a distraction."

"I need to go talk to the principal. I'll walk you back to class, but will you be okay while I'm gone?"

I nodded. "There's only twenty minutes left. I should be fine."

"I'll be back by then, waiting for you."

We headed to my class, and I worked on composing myself. It helped, knowing he was so close. Why didn't they tell me he stayed?

I probably would have told them it wasn't necessary, but after all that happened, I was happy he was there when I needed him.

I walked back to my seat with my head high. There were a couple of guys grinning at me, probably the ones who wrote the note. One of them flipped my skirt as I walked by, and I slapped his hand, glaring at him.

"Bitch," he whispered.

Another made a lewd gesture at me as I took my seat. Thank God Charlotte was in my next class, along with Aaron.

I ignored the jackasses and jumped out of my seat when the bell rang, working my way to the door as fast as I could. A hand grabbed hold of my arm when I made it through the door, but it wasn't Oliver, because I caught him out of the corner of my eye a few feet from the door to the right.

"How about we go somewhere where you can put that whore mouth on my Hollywood cock," was whispered in my ear.

I didn't even get a chance to try and pull my arm from his grip because Oliver's hand was on him, squeezing his wrist and telling him to let go.

"Fucking A, man!" he yelled.

I didn't even know who the asshole was, but I was ready to get him in trouble.

"Don't touch her again."

He scowled at me. "You brought your security? What are you, five?"

Oliver's lip twitched up. "Unless you want the entire team on your ass, I suggest you refrain from even speaking to Mrs. Lockwood any further."

"Why?" the guy scoffed. "She's a nobody cunt who only got here by offering up her pussy to a celeb. Bitches like that shouldn't even be here."

"Darren Alexander Crossman, did I hear you correctly? Are you harassing another student?" an unfamiliar, but authoritative, voice said from behind Oliver.

By her stance and the chorus of "ooooh" I knew it was the principal, and she looked pissed.

"I wasn't doing anything, Mom."

Mom? *Oh, this is going to be good.*

She held up the note that I'd given to Oliver. "You think I don't know your handwriting?"

"Shit," Darren grumbled under his breath.

"My office. Now," she said in her stern mom voice. Darren trudged off with a huff, but not before giving me a cold glare. "I saw that, young man."

She walked toward us, once confident he was heading in the right direction. "I'm so sorry about this, Wren. I'll make sure this behavior is corrected. Your security team will have our full cooperation until things calm down. I'm sure this is very hard on you, being brand new to this kind of attention."

"Thank you," I said quietly as Oliver began to guide me down the hall.

I let out a breath and grabbed hold of his arm, resting my forehead on it. All too casual of a touch, but I needed something secure to calm me down.

"Are you okay?"

"Yeah, I just need a minute." I swallowed hard, took another breath, and straightened out. "Thanks, Oliver. If you hadn't been here . . ."

"You would've been fine."

I eyed him skeptically. "How do you know?"

"Would you really have let that shithead drag you off?" he asked.

My lip twitched. "No, I would've shoved my knee into his tiny dick."

He smirked at me. "All I did was keep you from getting in trouble, and put it all on him."

"All his fault, anyway," I grumbled.

"Exactly."

We continued down the hall, and the moment I saw Charlotte I threw my arms around her.

"You okay?" she asked, her eyes flickering to Oliver.

I let out a sigh of relief. "I'm so happy you're in class with me and it's the last one."

She wrapped her arm around my shoulder, and we walked into class together. We sat in the back, and Aaron was already there, glaring at some assholes and bitches muttering insults under their breath.

He gave me a hug as I sat down. "Don't worry, we've got you. They're just jealous."

I squeezed his hand. "Thanks." It was kind of amazing and interesting how Aaron had changed. Not since that party had he really flirted with me. He stopped and became a friend like the rest of the group. Maybe a raging Weston scared him off.

Class went off without incident, but five minutes before the bell rang Oliver came in and ushered me out. I waved goodbye to Charlotte and Aaron as I snuck out. Oliver guided me down the empty hall to a side entrance. Steps from the door, it sprang open and Weston walked through.

My heart jumped in my chest and tears sprung in my eyes as I took off, running to him. I jumped into his open arms and let out a huge sigh.

He pulled me tight and whispered into my neck. "Are you okay, baby girl?"

I nodded, but refused to let him go.

"We need to go," Joe said in a firm voice.

Weston dropped me back to the ground, but kept his arm around me as we walked out to the awaiting SUV just as the bell rang. Joe climbed into the driver's seat, another one of his team members in the passenger's seat. Oliver climbed in the back with Weston and me.

I couldn't help but crawl into Weston's lap. I needed the safety and security of his touch. My fingers wound around his neck and brought his lips down to mine.

"Are you sure you're okay?" he asked, brushing a lock of hair from my face.

I nodded. "It was just an exhausting day, and I missed you."

His hand brushed up and down the outside of my leg. "I missed you, too."

I quirked my brow at him. "Really?"

He nuzzled my neck. "Oh, yeah."

Home couldn't arrive soon enough. I was in dire need of the peace and security it and my husband provided.

Chapter Thirty-Five

OUR VACATION

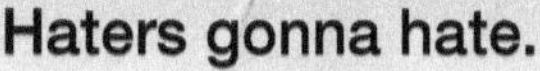

Haters gonna hate.

I smiled at my phone, a bit of calm coming over me. Somehow, Daniel always knew when I needed a lift. I typed out a quick response and threw my bag down next to the couch as I took a seat.

A week had passed since the world found out about us, and things had calmed down at school, for the most part. Oliver continued to follow me around, but he didn't have to come inside again except for after hours. However, the paps continued to stalk our every move.

"Hey, baby girl," Weston said, walking in and sitting down next to me. He let out a sigh and gave me a quick kiss.

I pulled my knees up and reached for the remote. "How was your day?"

"Good. Surprised I made it home before you."

I grimaced, nodding. "The deadline is coming up for the film score, so I needed to stay late after losing so much time."

His lips ghosted across my temple. "I know. Just make sure Oliver is always with you."

"Yes, my worrywart husband." I tilted my head up and gave him a lingering kiss.

He grinned at me as I flipped on the TV, landing on the day's gossip and my face filling the screen.

"Wren to Natalie: Stay away from my husband!" the reporter

said, then rattled on about how Natalie was trying to break us apart.

Well, they actually got something right.

However, it didn't take away from the fact that my face was all across the internet, magazines, and apparently television as well.

Weston swung his arm over my shoulders and pulled me closer. "Don't worry—Julia's making sure to give them just enough info on you to keep those leeches satisfied."

"Julia shouldn't have to worry about me so much—she's got a wedding in a few weeks!" Seriously, the woman needed to take a break. She had to be exhausted.

He tried to reassure me. "It'll blow over soon."

"I hope so. People always staring at me is getting weird. Especially some of the men."

He chuckled and kissed my neck, his hands moving down my waist and to my hips. "I'd want to kill any man for leering at you or thinking of you that way. I'm the only one who gets to fantasize about you."

"You have me, so why do you need a fantasy?"

He nipped the skin just below my ear. "Oh, I have many fantasies of different ways to take you."

I sighed, smiling as he continued down my neck. "And when were you planning on executing these fantasies?"

He gave me a sexy smile and bit his lip before wetting them. "I can go anytime."

"What do you want to do to me?" I glanced up at him through my lashes, trying to look all innocent.

"Oh, no, baby girl. It's easier to answer what I don't want to do to you than to list off what I do want to do to you."

"How about what do you want to do first?"

His hand moved under my skirt and up my thigh. "I want to kiss you." His fingers brushed against my panties. "I want to lick your pussy until you come all over me." My thighs clenched together, holding his hand in place. "I want to feel your mouth wrapped around me, wetting me before I slide into your pussy and fuck you until you're hoarse from screaming."

I climbed onto his lap, my thighs straddling his hips while my hands went to work on his belt. "I think I can handle that."

He let out a hiss as my fingers grazed his cock through his pants. His fingers worked on opening my shirt as his hips flexed up.

"We are keeping this uniform when you're done with school," he said, licking his lips. His fingers caressing the cleavage he exposed before tugging down the cups of my bra, pulling out my breasts and tweaking my nipples.

I let out a giggle. "Maybe next time we can pretend you're the headmaster and I'm the naughty student."

"Fuck, yes." He swept his tongue across my lips. "Punish my naughty girl. I haven't done that in a while."

I took him in my hand, loving the shuddering breath that left him. I leaned forward and pressed my lips to his, then whispered, "Have I been a bad girl?"

His fingers flexed and dug in to my ass. "With your hand on my cock, I'd have to go with very naughty. Trying to seduce me?"

"It's not hard."

"Oh, it's very hard. Should I demonstrate it by moving your panties to the side and slamming into you?"

My thumb brushed over the head, a bead of pre-come wetting my skin. I paused, noting the wetness seeping from me, and decided to push him more. "I'm not sure you're *up* enough to the challenge."

His lips twitched with a snarl as he jerked me closer. His hand was between us long enough to line us up before he pulled me down hard.

My eyes rolled back, and a shudder ran through me while a guttural moan escaped my parted lips. I leaned forward, my head resting on his shoulder.

"What do you think now?" He licked and nipped at my neck. "Being mouthy has consequences."

I smiled into his shoulder and continued to taunt him, excitement coursing through me. "I think you're all talk."

A low growl came from him, making me clench around him. He moved us down to the floor and pulled my knees over his shoulder.

"I'm going to punish your pussy for that."

"Yes."

He leaned forward and took my bottom lip between his teeth. "You asked for it."

His weight pushed down on me, his thrusts becoming harder and deeper. I hissed out a "fuck," whimpering as he took my body.

All thoughts left me, replaced with the overwhelming pleasure of his cock hitting deep inside. His hips slammed against me, the sounds of our skin slapping echoed off the walls. My eyes fluttered as strangled noises escaped me. Every nerve within my body was lighting off and bursting into flames.

"That's it, baby girl. Tighten that sweet pussy."

One of his hands found my breast and flicked my nipple. Not being able to move, coupled with all the other sensations, sent me toppling over the edge.

My back arched as every muscle coiled, then snapped. I let out a screaming sob as pleasure ripped through me.

Weston grunted above me, his thrusts jerking as he emptied inside me. He released my legs and collapsed down on my chest.

"I warned you," he said between breaths.

My lip quirked up. "You did, but I'm still waiting."

There was a growling at my ear. "After dinner, I'm going to tie you up and spank you before I fuck you until you can't stand."

I kissed his cheek. "We'll see."

He tilted his head and captured my lips. "Oh, yes, we will."

My fingers flicked my pen, tapping it on the desk as I stared at the clock. I had an itch to work on my composition. I was so close, which was great with three weeks left. There would be plenty of time to finish up and polish it before I needed to turn it in.

When the last bell rang, I ran out to the parking lot and the black Suburban sitting two rows down. I walked past my car and toward it.

The back door swung open and Oliver popped out. "Hey. Everything okay?"

"Yeah."

"Are you still staying after?" he asked.

I nodded. "I want to leave campus first, though. I'm dying for a snack and also need gas."

"Want me to ride with you or follow you?" he asked.

"Which do you think?"

He pursed his lips. "I'd rather stay with you, especially since you'll be out of the car."

We climbed into my car, and I took a calming breath as I drove to the gate. There were only about six or seven paps waiting, less than there had been, but still more than I'd like. They were on my car as soon as we approached, and the flashes began. I learned early on to slip on my sunglasses after I almost ran one of them over because they blinded me.

My teeth ground together.

"Keep calm, chickadee."

I blew out a breath. "I get it now and wish I didn't."

"What's that?" he asked.

"That fame is a blessing and a curse. That celebrities have no privacy and vultures are always around. I feel like I can't breathe lately, and I'm only famous because of who I married."

Really, what was so special about me?

"Yeah, I can't imagine. I've always been on this side, protecting, but I've seen the toll it takes on people. I don't blame any celeb for going off on them."

I resisted the strong urge to flip them off as we passed and turned onto the street. There was a gas station a few miles away, and I hoped to make it a quick trip back to the school so I could get home—my only sanctuary.

Or my prison.

I pulled in to the first available spot and grabbed my wallet. As I stepped out I heard the passenger door open and Oliver walk around to me.

"Why don't I pump the gas and you go grab your snack?"

I gave him a smile and slipped my card into the reader. "Thanks. I'll be right back."

I could almost feel Oliver watching me as I entered the convenience store, and that alone helped to calm me. It was amazing how I could barely function outside anymore without Weston or one of the security members with me. Everything inside me begged for it to end soon, but I knew with Weston that was never going to happen. But like with everything since our fateful meeting, it was an adjustment I'd have to make.

Walking up and down the aisles, I searched for the perfect snack and drink that spoke to my grumbling stomach. Just as I settled on a Snickers bar and a Powerade, a light flashed beside me. I blinked and looked over to find a camera not two feet from me.

"Wren, what's it like being married to one of Hollywood's elite?"

Another flash, making me blink and take a step back. When my vision cleared, I noticed a phone in front of the one asking questions, his gaze flickering between me and the screen, probably recording everything. The *click, click* of the camera had my heart hammering. They stepped forward, and I took another step until my back was flush against the glass door of the fridge section.

"We see you're here with another man. Does Weston know you're cheating on him?"

My brow scrunched. *Cheating on him? What the hell?*

I started shaking, looking for an out. I'd had about enough of them stalking me, but none had gotten so close that I felt trapped.

I closed my eyes and tried to calm myself.

"I bet since you're with this guy, Weston is being serviced by Natalie."

The shaking stopped, and my eyes opened slowly as I glared at the person. "Stop harassing me."

"We're not harassing you," the one recording said.

"You won't let me pass and have me cornered."

The guy behind the camera gave a cocky sly smirk. "You can go past us . . . if you answer one question."

I scowled and stood tall. "No." I tried to step forward, but they continued to block me.

"Yes," he said, pressing the issue and leaning in.

My jaw clenched and I moved to step forward, this time lifting my foot and slamming it down on the foot of the harassing asshole with the camera in his hand. He screamed out and I got my opening to push forward. Right when I got free, I looked up to find Oliver running toward me.

"Are you all right?" he asked, glancing between me and the guys messing with me.

"You bitch! That's assault! I'll sue you!"

I turned to him and gave him a smile. "I'm sorry, was that your foot? I was just trying to get by—I didn't mean to step on your foot. Just like you weren't trying to hold me hostage." I threw the Snickers bar at them, hitting the assmunch who was still clicking away with his camera.

Oliver grabbed my wrist and pulled me out, throwing me into the passenger's seat while he moved to the driver's side and blew out of the parking lot.

"I'm taking you home," he said as he took a hard right, not even slowing down for the turn. My car could take it.

I stared out the front window, still seething. My fingers were bunched up in my lap, and I worked at extending them. Every part of me was trembling, and I was desperate to scream. To force out some of the pent-up frustration.

Oliver was talking into his phone as we sped through the streets. I didn't care what he was saying. All I knew was that I was scared, and those fuckers had finally pushed me to my limit. I had been so close to decking that smart ass.

Tears streamed down my cheeks, and I slumped against the door. The adrenaline faded, and I was exhausted.

"Wren!" Oliver's voice broke through the fog that was taking over. "Are you okay?"

I gave him as good of a nod as I could manage. When we arrived at the house, another of Joe's guys was there, waiting to take Oliver back to his vehicle. Kelly wrapped her arm around me, and I think she asked if I needed anything. I might have answered, but was still too in shock to remember much.

With mechanical movements, I sat on the bench in front of the piano. That was what I was supposed to be doing—composing.

I sat there, staring at the blank page in front of me. After a moment, I pushed the heels of my hands into my eyes.

Why did I have to have a run-in today? I was a few short passages away from being done with my composition, but a stalking, blood-sucking vampire pap stole all my mojo with his false words as he tried to get a reaction out of me.

I didn't know how long I sat there staring at nothing, unable to do anything. So I waited, unmoving, until I heard the garage door slam.

"Wren!" Weston yelled out. I couldn't call out, just stared in to the next room. His footsteps ricocheted off the hardwood floor as he ran through the house. "Wren!"

He appeared in the doorway, his eyes wild but softening when he saw me. The muscles in his body relaxed and he closed the gap. He sat on the bench next to me and pulled me into his arms.

"Oh, my Wren."

I broke then. Tears streamed down my face and I grabbed hold of my husband, my safe place, and let it all out.

"It's okay, baby," he whispered, running his hands up and down my back in a soothing motion.

I couldn't stop the sobs. "I'm sorry. I'm so sorry."

"What?" His fingers slid under my chin and tilted it up. "Baby, you have nothing to be sorry for. I only wish I'd been there to see you go off on them." He smiled at me and kissed my forehead. "Though, I'd rather you never have had to be in such a position."

"It wasn't Oliver's fault," I said.

His voice dropped as he continued to caress my arms. "I know. He was trying to speed things up by pumping gas. He'd even made sure no one was tailing you when you left and kept an eye on you in the store."

I wiped some tears away with the palm of my hand. "I should have handled it better."

"Maybe, but I think you've been handling it pretty well so far," he said with a soft smile that turned to anger. "They were in the wrong, and trust me when I say that they aren't going to get away with it."

I relaxed at that and sunk farther into his chest. "I need a break. I just want to get away where no one knows who we are."

"Few and far between, but maybe we can get away for a while," he said against my temple.

My brow scrunched. "How?"

"Well, you've got spring break in a week. You'd mentioned visiting your mom a few weeks' back, but since then we haven't really talked about if you wanted to do anything else. We could go on a little trip."

"You have work." I eyed him. He'd already taken off a lot of time since I came into his life.

He shook his head. "Let me worry about that. You just pack a suitcase with a swimsuit and get ready for a few days in the sun."

"Going to tell me where?"

He rubbed his nose against mine. "Nope. Leave it to me."

"Have a great trip," Julia said, wrapping her arms around me.

The week had passed in a flash, and before I knew it we were packed and ready to go. All Weston would tell me was that our flight was at 7:30 pm, and he would be home early so we could head to the airport.

"Thanks. I hope you're able to relax a bit, as well."

The trip was so last minute, plus I had spent all week trying to finish up a first draft of my composition, that I almost forgot we were leaving. But I couldn't be happier that we were getting away. I needed it. Needed a break to refresh after everything.

Julia chuckled and shook her head. "My wedding is in three weeks. No way is that happening."

"At least try to have a day to yourself. Visit a spa, get a massage."

She smiled at me. "Yes, boss."

I gave her my best stern look. "Hey, someone's got to get you to slow down sometimes, and if Miles and Weston can't do it, I will."

She smiled at me. "Thanks, Wren. Can you do something for me, too?" I nodded in agreement. "Can you make sure he forgets who he is while you're gone?"

"I'll try." I gave her another quick hug goodbye and looked over to my husband, who was vibrating as he helped Joe and Oliver bring out our bags. "You're too excited about this, Weston."

He grinned at me. "First, it's been years since I've taken a vacation. A real, relax, get-away, let-real-life-fall-off-my-shoulders, vacation. Second, I've not been able to take one during spring break time since I was eleven." He gave Julia a quick hug and followed me down the steps to the awaiting car.

"Fulfilling another missed piece of normalcy," I said as his hand landed on my lower back.

"The only good thing about that is this time I have the means to do whatever I want."

I quirked my brow at him. "And what is that?"

There was a cat that ate the canary grin on his face. "You'll see when we get there."

He pushed on my butt, and I climbed into the back seat of Joe's SUV. He'd been tight-lipped about where we were going. "Why are you insisting on surprising me?"

"Because I don't get to do it often." I gave him my best pouty look. "Don't do that." I let out a little whimper. "Stop!" That seemed to affect him, so I did it again. His hand reached up and rubbed his chest. "Damn it, it makes my chest clench when you do that, baby."

He became the one pouting, and I wrapped my arms around him, giving him a kiss.

"So cute."

He sighed and pulled out his phone. After a moment, he looked at me. "I'll show you this, but I won't answer any questions about the agenda."

He flipped his phone over to show a large yacht.

"We're going on that?" My eyes went wide.

He nodded. "Going to do a little island hopping, but I won't tell you where."

"Freedom." No paparazzi hounding us down. Just us on a boat, sailing around with nobody for miles.

He nodded. "But first, a flight. You've got your passport, right?"

I smiled and planted a kiss on his neck. "Brand spanking new Wren Lockwood passport is in my purse."

The last time I'd been to the airport was to drop off my father. No one noticed me then except Cloe. Now, people were coming up to us, taking our photo without asking. More than once, a trash mag was thrust at me with a pen. I was shocked at the pandemonium. Granted, it'd only been a month since we came out. I was just going to have to get used to things being like that.

Weston kept a tight grip on my hand, moving us through the crowded arena, Joe leading the way. I suddenly remembered our bags and looked back to find two of Joe's guys walking behind us, luggage in tow.

I was expecting to have to deal with people up until we boarded while waiting for the plane, but instead of milling at a gate with a bunch of strangers, we headed out a door, down a long narrow hall, through a small security area, and popped out onto a large span of concrete. There was a small plane a few hundred feet away with a set of stairs leading up to the door that we climbed.

I gasped as we entered the lavish jet. It was small, but decked out. Weston's head just skimmed the ceiling in the very center, making him have to duck a little. We entered at a small kitchen area before passing into the seating area. Large, white leather seats sat on either side of the aisle, some facing toward the cockpit and the other half toward the rear. There was rich dark wood trim and tables, LED screens every few feet. Past the eight single seats was what looked like a couch on either side.

"Wow," I said as I looked around. It was small, but it was all ours. I'd been expecting commercial air, with special treatment in first class like when we came back from Indiana, but what we were on far exceeded any of my expectations. "What is this?"

Weston smirked. "A friend of mine loaned it to us. Nice, isn't it?"

I nodded. "Do you always travel this way?"

"Baby girl, this is the only way to travel! So get used to it, because this is the way *we* will always get around."

I sat down in one of the chairs facing the cockpit, as the thought of sitting backward for takeoff seemed weird and wrong. Weston sat in the seat next to me and took my hand, giving it a gentle squeeze.

A smile broke out on my face, unable to believe that what I was experiencing was really happening to *me*.

"Good evening," a friendly female voice said from behind us.

Weston let go of my hand so she could get by. She turned, a smile lighting up her face.

"I'm Amber and I'll be your attendant for today."

"Hello," we said in unison.

"Just a little information about our flight today. We will be flying non-stop in this beautiful Gulfstream G550 to the even more beautiful St. Thomas."

"St. Thomas?" I asked as I looked at Weston. "You couldn't have just old me that?"

"And spoil the fun?"

I shook my head and looked back to Amber who was still smiling.

"Total flight time is seven hours and twenty-eight minutes, which will put us in St. Thomas right around seven in the morning. Before we take off, would either of you be interested in a glass of champagne? Mr. Saunders arranged for one of his favorites as a celebratory gift of your recent marriage."

Mr. Saunders? Seemed Weston had friends in expensive places.

Weston nodded. "That was very kind of him. We would, thank you."

"Mr. Saunders has also arranged for a full five course menu to be served whenever you wish, and we are fully stocked on snacks and sweets."

Weston let out a chuckle. "I think Chris is trying to butter me up for something from the sound of it."

Amber giggled and shook her head. "I'm not sure about that, but he did say to take very good care of you."

With that, she left to get our drinks and I tilted my head to look at Weston.

"What?" he asked.

"Thank you."

"For?"

"All of this. To you, this is all normal, but to me, every day is an adventure."

He grabbed my hand and pulled me closer, his lips pressing against mine. "You're more than welcome. And you'll get used to it in time. After all, I do plan on spoiling you for the rest of your life."

I managed to get some sleep on the plane. The couches in the back folded down into a bed and around midnight, Weston and I curled up. It was strange sleeping on a plane, but with the week we'd both had, we fell asleep in no time.

A knock roused us and we both blinked to find Amber standing in front of us.

"Sorry for waking you. We're just over an hour out, so we will need you to return to the seats."

Weston sat up and nodded. "Thank you."

"Can I interest either of you in a cappuccino or coffee with your breakfast?"

"Mocha, if that's even possible," I said, my voice turned up into more of a question.

Amber smiled. "I'm able to do that. For you, sir?"

"Cappuccino would be fine."

She nodded and headed back toward the kitchen while I stared up at Weston. His lip twitched as he leaned down and pressed his lips against my neck, his body practically covering mine.

"And to think, we missed out on joining the mile high club."

A giggle left me as I shook my head. "Maybe on the flight home we can work something out."

We got up and returned to our seats right as Amber delivered our drinks. It was followed by an amazing breakfast.

As the plane descended ever closer to the water, my adrenaline began to spike. There was land off in the distance, but too far away to be so close. I glanced over to Weston's window and sighed in relief at the green of the island that flew by. Then suddenly the black of the runway appeared below us.

A few minutes after seven, we made our way down the steps and into the warm salty air of St. Thomas. After going through customs, a limo picked us up to take us to the docks.

I couldn't keep my eyes off the view. The blue skies and sun, ocean as far as I could see.

Excitement raced through me and I squeezed Weston's hand as the buildings opened up and the bay appeared in front of us. When we stopped at the pier, there was a huge cruise ship parked next to the docks. The driver helped unload our bags while a man in a white uniform and aviators stepped forward.

"Mr. Lockwood?" he asked.

"Hello."

"Hello, sir. I'm Alan, and I will be one of your stewards this week."

"Wonderful." Weston reached out and shook his hand. "This is my wife, Wren, and we are in your hands."

Alan took our bags from the limo driver, which was only a rolling bag for each of us, and gestured toward the dock.

We started walking and my jaw dropped at the sight of the ships in front of us. Huge catamarans, sailboats of all sizes, and a few yachts. Weston had shown me a picture of what we would be on, but it was on the small screen on his phone and I didn't get a good look, so I didn't know which one was ours.

"The Persephone is an Amels yacht," Alan said a few minutes later as he pointed to the only ship on the left side of the pier. My jaw dropped open. It was the largest besides the cruise ship and had to be at least five stories tall and as large as our house. "Amels is a Dutch shipyard, where she was built in 2011. She is fifty-two meters in length, and nine across. Currently, she houses a crew of eight at your service."

"What do you think?" Weston asked.

"I think I'm already not ready to go home and we haven't even gotten on yet."

It was exactly what we needed. Open ocean without a pap for miles. The weight seemed to lift, freeing us from the shackles of Hollywood.

Chapter Thirty-Six

MY COMPOSITION

"**B**ABY GIRL, YOU'RE GOING TO BURN," WESTON SAID, blocking my sun as I laid out on the deck of the boat. "I'm okay. It's our last day, and I want to soak up as much of the Caribbean as I can."

The week had been beyond words or expectations. Weston had gone above and beyond any fantasy vacation my mind could come up with. We'd snorkeled off the coast of St. Thomas, swam with sea turtles, spent time on the beautiful beaches in the Virgin Islands, and sailed around crystal clear turquoise waters.

Sure, we'd had our picture taken the few times we went on land, but there wasn't a pap in sight. More than once, we sat and talked with people for a while. I think it was something Weston enjoyed, meeting new people and getting to engage in conversation.

Being with Weston, we were treated differently, which was still odd for me. Having people stumbling over themselves to make me happy as going to take some getting used to.

"You should reapply."

I sighed and took the bottle from his hand and began rubbing it on my arms. I looked up and him and smiled. "Can you help me with my back?"

He grinned down at me. "I thought you'd never ask."

He sat behind me, placing a kiss on my shoulder and letting out a sigh. "I wish we could stay longer."

My vacation high was leaving me at his words. "Me too."

"We'll come back. I need to give you a proper honeymoon anyway."

"Doing this again has my vote."

"Mine too."

"But for a month."

Weston chuckled. "I don't know about a month, but maybe two weeks."

My hands continued rubbing the lotion on my stomach and legs. "I had a thought, and I wanted to run it by you."

"What's that?"

"Well, school will be out soon, and the summer is coming. I'll be getting ready for college, and Daniel will be as well."

"He's more than welcome to stay with us."

My stomach twisted, unsure of how he'd react. "Which leads me to my grand request."

"No request is too grand from you."

"Okay." I blew out a breath. "What do you think of Daniel moving in with us?"

Weston's movements stopped. "What?"

I turned to look at him. "We'll be taking a lot of the same freshman courses and can study together. The pool house is empty and would be perfect. I'd always have someone around me on campus."

"Who is male," Weston argued, his jealousy peeping through.

I rolled my eyes. "And bats for the other team."

He pursed his lips. "Just because he's around doesn't mean he can protect you."

"Daniel has a brown belt in jujitsu."

Weston opened his mouth to speak and then shut it, staying silent for a moment.

"It would help him out financially, and also emotionally."

"Emotionally?" he asked, his brow scrunched.

"It's not easy being a gay guy in a male dorm."

He heaved a sigh. "I suspect it isn't." He stared at me. "Are we talking about his whole college career?"

I shook my head. "No, just the first year or two."

"It's going to be hard to make new friends with you two joined at the hip."

I scoffed. "Baby, do you realize how hard it would be for me to make genuine friends anyway, being your wife? Same with Daniel being my best friend."

"True." He mulled over it again. "Okay, I don't have a problem with it. In fact, you're right, it would probably be a good thing to have him around."

I jumped up and wrapped my arms around him. "Thank you! Thank you!"

He kissed my cheek. "It's your house too. You get a say. And I agree that the pool house would be perfect. It has a bedroom, bathroom, and wet bar, and he'd be living with us, but not. So, we'd still have privacy."

"Exactly." I beamed at him.

He ran his hands up and down my back. "And I'd feel better with you going to school with someone, especially someone who can beat the shit out of fuckers trying to leer and touch what's mine."

I held my left hand up. "With this rock, I'm sure they'll stay away."

"Just make sure you don't forget about your lonely husband."

I gave him a reassuring kiss. "No way I could do that. No way my pussy would let me."

His hand flexed on my skin. "Say pussy one more time, and it's going to be on my dick."

I bit my lip and smiled up at him. "Pussy."

"That's it!" He hoisted me up over his shoulder and carried me down to our room.

I giggled the entire way to the huge master bedroom. When he tossed me down onto the king sized bed, I let out a shriek.

His smile was as big as mine, but his eyes were heavy, and when his tongue peeked out to wet his lips, a shiver ran through me.

"Have I ever told you how sexy I think tan lines are?" he asked as he leaned over and nipped my hip with his teeth. There was no pause for my answer before he pulled at my bikini bottom and had it on the floor.

I ran my tongue over my lips as I watched him lick and kiss his way up my body until he was fully on top of me. "No."

His hips rocked against me, almost without thought, his body's desire driving his motions. "Very fucking sexy. Nothing but pale tits and pussy. Highlighted patches of skin." His lips wrapped around my nipple.

My eyes rolled back as he slid all the way inside me.

"Yesss," he hissed before pulling out, then sliding back in.

Long, slow strokes.

It was a heady, sensual rhythm. There was no rush. Nothing that could call us away. Just the two of us absorbing every ounce of pleasure possible.

Every stroke pushed me higher and higher. My muscles tensed and my back arched as his slow torture exploded through me.

I let out a choked scream as wave after wave of intense plea-sure ripped through me.

"Fuck, baby girl. That's it."

Aftershocks continued to fire off as I came down, a lazy smile on my lips as he continued to pump into me.

My mind was clouded, lost in the euphoria of my orgasm when I felt his finger press against my tight virgin ass.

My lips twitched up into a smirk. "What are you doing?" I asked in a breathy tone as I pressed back against him.

One of his fingers pushed through and began slowly moving in and out, in time with his thrusts. "I think it's about time my dick filled you here."

I blew out a breath, keeping my spent muscles relaxed as he

worked a second one inside. "Do you?" A groan left him as I rocked my hips, drawing both his dick and fingers deeper.

"Mmm, that's it, baby. I want you to do that to my cock."

I bit my lip and looked up at him. He'd played with my ass before—multiple times with his fingers, stretching me. It'd been enough that I was more than curious, and ready for the real thing. I was still a little scared, but I was so turned on that each of his thrusts worked me toward a second orgasm.

I wanted to try it.

Raging desire rolled off him, hotter than ever, and I wanted it to consume all of me.

It ended abruptly when he pulled away from me and reached over to the nightstand, returning with a small tube of lube.

A few wet, cool drops hit my skin, and he pushed his fingers inside me again, lubing me up.

I watched as he dripped the clear liquid onto his cock, then fisted it with his free hand, working the lube around—a sight I loved to watch. He moved in time with the thrust of his fingers, opening them a little wider with each pass in and out.

With one hand on his cock, he placed the other against my abdomen in a mix of holding me down and brushing his thumb against my clit as he positioned himself.

The head of his cock pressed against me and I waited in nervous anticipation.

I drew in a sharp breath as he pushed forward, my eyes widening as I tried not to tense.

"Relax, baby girl."

It was a hard thing to do, especially with my body saying that it was wrong. I reached out, my fingertips pressing against his abs as I drew in a few deep breaths.

"Yess," he hissed as the head of his cock made its way inside.

I watched as he stared down, jaw dropped, completely enraptured as his cock slowly sank in. It didn't really hurt once I relaxed, more of a strange feeling of fullness I wasn't used to.

His thumb strummed against my clit as he began to slide in slow, full strokes. My breath picked up as he rocked against me.

I loved the way his abs tensed with each flex of his hips, and the way his chest expanded with each labored breath. Even more, I loved the way his face scrunched up and he cried out as he came.

His hips were pressed against my ass, pushing his cock as far inside as he could, twitching with each spurt. Releasing me, he fell forward, his hands on either side of me, then moved down to his elbows.

Heavy pants landed against my skin for a moment before he began peppering kisses against my skin.

"Baby girl, that has been a fantasy of mine since the first time I saw your ass."

I quirked my brow at him as I ran my fingers through his hair. "Oh, yeah? When was that?"

He let out a chuckle. "When I held the door open for you on our way to the wax museum."

I smiled at him. "Such a pervert."

"I'm all yours," he said with a yawn.

"Yes. You are."

He sat back up and moved his hips back, watching as his cock left me.

After cleaning up, we headed back out on the deck for one last snorkel adventure. I hated that it had to end, but it made coming back that much sweeter.

I hated going back to school, but the trip revived me, and I was ready to finish up my composition. Too many things kept me away, but the notes wouldn't stop running through my head. Different tones and instruments played in my mind, refusing to shut up. Demanding to come out.

"Wren!" Charlotte called out, throwing her arms around me as we met on the steps.

"Charlotte! How was your vacation?"

"Excellent! Liam and I had a great time at his dad's house in Colorado. How was your trip? Where did Weston take you?"

I smiled and wrapped my arm with hers as we headed up the steps. "We went sailing around the Caribbean, and it was fantastic!" I let out a sigh. "How'd I get so lucky?"

"You mean because of Weston?" she asked.

"Yeah."

She smiled and nudged me with her shoulder. "That's what happens when soulmates find each other."

I turned to look at her. "You think?"

She nodded. "Kinda obvious with the two of you and your situation. An attachment you were unable to understand in the beginning. The need to stay together for fear that you would fall apart without each other. Fighting for each other through everything to find ultimate love."

I stopped and stared at her, my gaze narrowed on her. "You are over-romanticizing us again. Did you watch too many romantic movies over the break?"

Her mouth popped open and she threw her hand in the air. "Oh, come on! It's true. Your story is one of the great romances of all time."

I rolled my eyes at her. "You're crazy."

She sighed and slumped into me. "True love."

I shook my head. "We're going to be late."

Grabbing her hand, we picked up the pace and walked down the hall to our first class.

I took a deep breath as I turned on the software that was connected to the keyboard. There'd been a bit of a learning curve with the composition software, but I loved watching it transfer the notes I played into notes on a page and recorded it, as well as let me edit and change things with ease.

My fingers hit the keys, crescendoing up to the melody. I thought back to our vacation, and the way I felt then. The love for him exploded from me, guiding my hands. I was lost in it. Not until the final note was played did I realize I had tears in my eyes.

I sniffed and smiled as I turned it off and moved to the computer. It was still working on converting the last few bars. The other instruments of the composition had already been implanted. I was doing my final run through of the melody.

After an hour of tweaking, I listened to the final product. Months of hard work paid off as my love and relationship with Weston came through in song. It was perfect. I couldn't stop grinning as I saved the file and burned a copy.

With a few days to spare, I dropped my envelope into Miles's school mailbox. It would be a few months until the winners were announced, and I was going to be a wreck until then.

It was just after noon when I walked into the kitchen to find Julia holding a phone up to her ear, cradling one on her shoulder, and typing away on her laptop while surfing on her tablet.

The woman never ceased to amaze me, but what she was doing was beyond one person's mental capacity. I endeavored then to find her a *Supergirl* shirt.

School was out for the afternoon for a staff day, leaving me with a free afternoon to catch up on all the homework I'd neglected while working on my composition.

"Well, that's not good enough. Weston and Carson need to have this meeting this week or they'll pull out of the project . . .

mm-hmm . . . hold on, hold on . . ." She switched to the phone on her shoulder. "Steven, I need that proposition emailed to me today by five and not a minute after. We've waited long enough. Big Bear Stunts needs access, and every day you continue to hold them up holds up production. Don't think Weston won't notice. Time is money, and the more you waste, the less you'll get in the end."

Her fingers typed furiously, emailing someone. She didn't even notice I was there, and I wondered where Graham and Amy were. Why did it seem like Julia was handling everything?

My question was answered by a door slamming behind me. Julia didn't even turn her head, but she did throw one phone down, pick up the conversation she put on hold, and then held out her hand to receive the cup of coffee Graham had in his hand.

"Hey, Wren," he said in greeting, and handed me a cup as well. I looked at it and back to him. "White mocha?"

The unsure tone in his voice made me smile. "Thank you."

It was a completely unexpected gesture, especially since I didn't tell anyone I was heading home. Then again, Oliver could be giving them a play-by-play of my movements for all I knew. My constant shadow prevailed.

Julia handed the tablet to Graham, who immediately stared at it while he pulled out his phone and began typing on it.

"What's going on?" I asked him as Julia yelled into the phone.

Graham stopped and looked at me. "Amy's down and out with a combination of bronchitis and upper respiratory infection. Julia told her to keep her contagious ass at home."

I leaned against the counter and scrunched my brow. "Amy would really have come to work?"

He nodded. "Yeah, she has a really strong work ethic, but she really needs to take the time off and get better. Add that in with Julia's wedding next weekend, being down a total of two assistants, and life is fun this week."

I cringed at the news. I'd forgotten they still hadn't replaced Mallory's position. There'd been a few candidates, but after the

Mallory debacle, none had passed an interview with each of the four of them to even get to the Joe portion. He was bound and determined to find out everything about the next assistant, in order to avoid any situation like we'd had the past few months.

"Is there anything I can do to help?"

He shook his head. "You have school and your composition to focus on. We can handle it."

I pursed my lips and looked at Julia. My normally well put together, soon-to-be sister-in-law was looking frayed at the edges. Her hair was even on the wild side, and she looked more than a few hours short of a good night's sleep.

"My composition is already submitted," I said. I looked up at him. "What can I do to help?"

Graham shook his head. "Nothing. We've got this."

"Jesus." Julia blew out a breath and dropped the phone down on the counter. Her fingers continued to fly over the keys, occasionally going down to one hand so she could grab her coffee. "Wren, did you get your appointment update for Sophie?"

I blinked at her before bringing out my phone. Sure enough, there was a calendar update for my dress fitting. "Yes."

Julia nodded before glancing my way. "Don't worry, we'll be okay, but if you can relax your husband . . ." She gave me a wink, then returned her attention to her computer.

My mouth popped open and I stared at her. "Why, Julia, are you suggesting I seduce my husband for your peaceful gain?"

"Yes."

"Well . . ." I let out a sigh and shrugged. "I suppose I could take one for the team."

With that, I took the other coffee from Graham and headed out of the kitchen and to our bedroom to change. The door to Weston's office was open, and I peeked inside to find him on the phone. He glanced up as he spoke and blew me a kiss. I walked in and set the second cup down on his desk, blew him a kiss, then continued on my path.

It was odd seeing him at home in the afternoon, but it wasn't the first time they'd worked from the house.

After changing, I headed back down to the main floor. It'd been almost a week since I'd finished my composition, leaving my afternoons open. Charlotte was still working on hers and stressing to get it done in time. Which is why instead of coming over after we went to lunch, she headed back to work, leaving me without my study partner.

Picking my bag back up from the kitchen counter, I headed out to the patio. Another beautiful day in Los Angeles made it hard to even concentrate on homework, but I wanted to get it done so I could spend the evening with Weston.

I'd been reading for about a half an hour when I heard footsteps heading my way. I glanced up expecting to see Weston, but it was Miles.

"Hey, Wren." Miles smiled at me as he walked forward.

I smiled in return. "Hey. Your soon-to-be wife is incommunicado in the kitchen."

He pursed his lips. "Yeah, I figured. She wasn't answering her cell phone."

I let out a little laugh. Between her two phones and different calls, that didn't surprise me.

"Is that why you stopped by?" I asked. "Shouldn't you be at school for the staff training?"

He rolled his eyes as he sat down in the chair across from me. "I don't have to deal with all that shit."

"Really?"

He nodded. "Part of my agreement with the school. I'm an auxiliary faculty member. I'm only there to teach the composition class."

I let out a little laugh. "Mentoring the youth, huh?"

He folded his hands behind his head. "Don't laugh, there's some serious talent this year. Present company not excluded."

I blinked at him. "You think so?"

He nodded and stared me right in the eyes. "I *know* so."

My mouth popped open, my stomach tied up in an instant knot. "You listened to it?"

He gave me a sheepish grin. "Yeah. I started verifying once about five were turned in. It was amazing to hear what was created."

"*And?*" I leaned forward, my eyes wide, waiting. I was beyond curious as to what he thought. I'd been half dreading, half crawling out of my skin for feedback from him.

He opened his mouth to speak, then closed it and shook his head. "If I was grading you would have gotten an A+. It was . . . There aren't words for the powerful emotions I felt. It was sublime and melodic. My heart twisted and my hair prickled."

I blew out a breath, then a smile grew on my face.

"You're a prodigy, Wren," he said, continuing on. "Most of the students I've taught have spent years learning music, some from the time they were only three or four. A lot of them can play beautifully, but they can't create. They're lacking the melody flowing through their veins. With you, it's obvious music is ingrained into your being. You are so much more than just talented."

I stared at him, frozen. He'd gone above and beyond the praise I'd hoped for. Prodigy? Me?

"Really?"

He ran his hand across his lips and looked around before sitting forward. "I didn't want to bring this up quite yet, but would you have any interest in a mentoring internship with my company?"

I stared at him, my mind trying to understand what he was saying. "You want me to intern for you?"

He nodded. "It's twenty hours a week. You would assist in composing scores, offering feedback, and learning hands on."

"I didn't even know you had interns." Mentoring from Miles? I'd be stupid not to jump at that chance.

"If someone really strikes me, I do. I try to get about one apprentice a year, but that doesn't always work out. This year, though, I really want it to be you."

I stared out over the view of the city, then back to Miles. There was no question I was going to do it, but I was stuck in a stunned belief of what my life had become. To have someone believe in me so much, in a passion I had, left me speechless.

"Yes. I mean . . . Yes, I would love that. You have no idea what that means to me."

A huge grin spread on his face and he blew out a breath. "Excellent. I can't tell you how excited I am to get to work with you."

I quirked a brow at him. "Seriously?"

He chuckled and nodded. "I know we got off to a rough start, but since I stopped being a close-minded asshole—Julia's words—I've been simply floored by you."

"I . . . wow." I couldn't stop staring at him in complete disbelief.

"I've never been so happy to be wrong," he said, a small waver in his voice. He'd apologized before, but what he was saying was more. Deeper. "You are exactly what Weston needed in his life, and I couldn't see that in the beginning."

"You were right to be wary."

His brow scrunched and he shook his head. "But I wasn't right to say those things to you."

I picked at the seam of the armrest. "No, but this whole conversation makes up for it."

He smiled again. "Good, because I was serious. I can't wait to work with you and see what you can do."

"Me, too."

It was the truth. What Miles was doing was giving me something I never would have imagined before we met—a direction.

I finally knew what I wanted to do with my life.

Chapter Thirty-Seven

OUR HAPPINESS

I STOOD IN THE KITCHEN WITH MY HANDS WRAPPED AROUND Julia's as she breathed hard and fast.

"Calm down. Let's pretend for this week that I'm Julia, and you're Weston."

With only days left until her wedding, Julia was going into full panic mode. In her workaholic wisdom, she decided to work until the day before the wedding, juggling her demanding job and last minute wedding details. Which left me sitting next to her on the kitchen island trying to calm her down before I needed to rush her to the hospital.

She quirked her brow at me, her chest expanding, struggling to take in a deep breath. "Wren, I can't do that."

I smirked at her. "You're a bit of a control freak, you know?"

Tears filled her eyes. "I have to be."

I nodded in agreement. "Yes, but this week it's different. Let me be your wedding assistant."

She shook her head. "It's too much." Her breaths began to slow, letting her take in a little more air with each inhale.

Gently, I pushed some loose strands from her face. "We're going to be family in a few days. It's not too much. Plus, it gets me out of the house."

"Security . . ."

"Is always with me when I leave the house, no matter what

reason," I said with an exasperated chuckle. "Hell, I caught Oliver napping at the kitchen table earlier this week." I heaved a sigh. "It'll be nice when I don't have to have a babysitter, and I'm sure he'll love to see his own house sometime."

"It's his job to protect you."

"I know, but I feel bad. He spends so much time with me. What about his girlfriend?" I asked. The poor guy. I worried that he was spending too much time away from home.

Julia smiled and sat up straighter, finally able to pull in a regular breath. "Dana understands. It was how they met, after all."

"Yeah?"

She nodded. "Dana's dad hired him to protect her as she traveled from New York to California about five years ago. She was only sixteen at the time, he was twenty-two. They ran into each other again two years ago and have been together ever since."

I couldn't help but smile at the picture her words painted, but then my gaze narrowed on her. "You were trying to deflect me."

She held her hands up. "Guilty."

I pursed my lips. "I just want to help take some of the load off you. If you keep this pace up, you'll collapse from exhaustion before you walk down the aisle. Amy is better now—she can step in as Weston's primary assistant while you take the rest of the week off."

"But . . ."

"No buts. Julia, you're getting *married*. This is a once in a lifetime event! You're marrying the man you love." I could tell by her expression that I was breaking her. "Miles won't say it, but I've seen the expression on his face when he looks at you."

"What?" she asked.

"He's worried about your health. You've been going long and hard for the past few months." If I thought Weston worked a lot, it didn't hold a candle to the hours Julia logged. "He told me that while we were gone for spring break, you were still at the office over eight hours a day every day, and then did wedding stuff until bed. You were supposed to take a break as well, and you didn't."

Her brow furrowed and she let out a hard breath. "I couldn't! There is so much backlogged work that when he was gone, I finally had time to do it."

"Isn't that what Graham is here for?" I asked. She opened her mouth to speak and then shut it. "He's *your* assistant, but you don't utilize him enough. He ends up being the errand boy. Do you think that's all he's capable of?"

She shook her head. "No."

"And Amy, she's also capable of more," I said.

Amy being sick really highlighted to everyone just how much she did, how much she helped. The first two days she was out sick, chaos had erupted. By day four, they had it back under control, but were still behind.

"I know she is."

I stared at her for a minute until I saw a flicker of confusion as she looked back.

"Control freak," I said.

Her lips twitched. "Gold digger."

I smirked at her. "Which Lockwood are you marrying? You're always with Weston."

She sat straighter and leaned forward. "The tabloids say you blackmailed Weston into marrying you."

"They also say you're cheating on Miles with Weston," I said, my lips twitching up as I saw life begin to flood back into Julia.

"Natalie's carrying Weston's child." She hit back.

"You're carrying Weston's child."

"You're pregnant."

"Pfft, Weston wishes."

Julia broke out in laughter, her head leaning back, tears forming in her eyes. "Oh, Wren." She wiped the tears away and took my hand. "Thanks, I needed that."

"Yes, you did."

A ping came from her phone and she groaned, turning her head toward it and reaching for it. I grabbed hold of her arm, stopping her.

"Why did Weston hire you?" I asked.

Her mouth popped open to say something, but then closed before starting again. "Because I said the monkeys in *The Wizard of Oz* creeped me out."

I nodded. "Weston is a monkey from *The Wizard of Oz* this week." Her eyes went wide. "Think you can step back now?"

"I-I don't know."

"Imagine him with a long tail and black fur, bouncing around while the wicked witch cackles in the background."

She shuddered. "That might do it."

"What might do what?" Weston asked as he entered the kitchen. We began laughing hysterically. He stopped in his tracks and narrowed his gaze at us. "You were talking about me."

"Yes, because I'm trying to get Julia to take a few days off and focus on her wedding this week."

Weston nodded and looked at me, then to Julia. "Sorry, Amy is my number one this week."

"But . . ."

"No buts. You're marrying my only brother, who's been gaga about you for years."

She looked between us. "You're not going to let this go, are you?"

We both shook our heads, and she sighed. "Okay, Wren. You can help me out."

I smiled at her. "See, that wasn't so bad."

"Says you."

Weston pulled Julia into a hug. "It will all be fine. Besides, you're already set for next week off. We can survive a few extra days."

Julia looked at him skeptically. "I'm not so sure about that."

"Wow. Who runs this company again?" Weston asked.

"Julia," I said without missing a beat.

Weston opened his mouth, then closed it. Julia just laughed and wrapped her arms around me.

It was the truth. Without Julia, Lockwood Entertainment would be a disaster.

For the rest of the week, I worked as Julia's assistant after school. I helped her by running errands, making phone calls, and printing off seating name tags. It was all busy work, but time consuming, freeing her up to do other stuff, including sneaking in some Lockwood Entertainment work.

"You know, one day I hope I don't have to see your face all the time," I said in a teasing tone as I looked across the table.

Oliver gave me a shocked face. "But I thought you loved seeing me every day."

I rolled my eyes. "It's the following me around all the time part."

Oliver had been on every errand, no matter how late, all week.

He shrugged his shoulders. "I don't see that changing any time soon."

"Can I ask how your girlfriend feels about all of it? I mean, before the Oscars you worked a normal day."

He let out a sigh and sat back, massaging his neck. "We miss each other, a lot. I won't lie about that. And this week's been especially hard."

"Why?" I asked.

He looked down at the tabletop. "It was our anniversary."

My eyes widened, and I slammed my hand down on the table. "Why didn't you take the night off? I'm sure someone else could've babysat me."

"We have something planned for this weekend, so it wasn't a big deal."

I pursed my lips. "To her it was."

His expression fell. "Yeah, she said she was okay, but I could tell she wasn't." He leaned forward, elbows resting on the table, and rubbed his face.

"Can't there be someone else to take the night shift? I mean, you've been with me anywhere from twelve to sixteen hours a day for the past two months."

"Yeah, I've thought about it, and we'll probably make a change after you graduate. But for now, I like the extra hours." A smile formed on his face, and he looked a bit mischievous. "It makes it easy to save up money."

I let out a gasp. "You're going to ask Dana to marry you, aren't you?"

He nodded, grinning like a fool. "Yeah."

I reached out and hugged him. "Oh, my God. That's so exciting!"

"Thanks. So, for now, get used to seeing my mug all the time."

"It's sad I see your face more than I do my husband's." I gave him a pathetic chuckle.

"I have a feeling things will calm down when the summer hits. It's already been happening. Every few days there's one or two less paps following you around."

"Natalie and Mallory's trials are coming up."

He grimaced. "Yeah, things will be very bad then. Maybe late summer, then. Hopefully you won't get any more death threats."

I stopped what I was doing and stared at him. "Any *more*? Are you saying people have threatened my life?" He cursed under his breath and nodded. "And no one decided to tell me?"

"You were dealing with enough that we didn't want to increase your stress. Besides, after investigation, they were found to be baseless."

I continued to stare at him, wide-eyed. "So, that's why the twenty-four-hour guard?"

Oliver grimaced. "I'm sorry. I wasn't supposed to tell you."

"How many?" I asked.

"Threats?"

"Yes. I think I should know how many people want me dead and why," I said. Oliver's gaze moved around, huffing and cursing some more. "Oliver."

His nostrils flared, and his gaze locked on to mine. "They're mostly from deranged Natalie fans, but a few from Weston's fan base as well."

I couldn't wrap my mind around it. *People wanted me dead?* All because I met Weston.

"You have nothing to worry about."

"Nothing? You just told me people want me dead! How do I not worry about that?" My heart began to thump forcefully in my chest.

"Because they're baseless threats," he said. "It's just them saying they hate you for no reason other than being with Weston. It's the stalker we may have to worry about."

I threw my hands up in the air, tossing the papers into the air. "Stalker? What the fuck? I have a stalker?"

"Stalker's not quite the word. Exuberant fan?" He shook his head. "Maybe I should take some time off. I'm exhausted, and apparently I don't know how to keep my mouth shut around you."

"Fuck, no. You're not taking any time off now that I know there is a stalker!" My breath sped up and a panic set in. "Does Weston know?"

Oliver nodded. "Weston is aware. He trusts Joe to do his job, and the primary responsibility is to make you two feel safe and secure."

I reached up and ran my hands over my face. "I felt safer three minutes ago."

"Please don't worry, Wren. If it gets to a point of concern, then we'll all discuss a plan of action."

I let out a groan. "Why is this happening to me?"

Oliver chuckled. "Because you had a chance meeting with one of Hollywood's most eligible bachelors and snagged him."

I pursed my lips. "I hate that word. Snagged. Like I was fishing and he took my bait, when it was nothing like that."

He leaned back in his chair. "It really isn't anything to worry about. There are a hundred other celebs in the L.A. area that have the same problem. That's why they all have guys like us—to protect them." He flexed his muscles in an effort to lighten the mood.

"All this because my mom wanted to go to Vegas over my fall break." I shook my head. "Well, I'm glad you're here with me, protecting me, and I'll try to forget everything you just told me . . . Emphasis on the word *try*."

Oliver's brow scrunched and he gave me a pleading look. "Try hard, please. I don't need Weston pissed at me, let alone Joe."

The day that Julia Moore became Julia Lockwood, and my official sister-in-law, had arrived. The event was littered with both complete happiness and stomach twisting anxiety.

"You are all set!" Sophie said. She looked so funny smiling back at me with her head covered in curlers.

Sophie had come over to help with my hair and makeup, as well as slip me into the Ellie Saab dress she'd brought with her. It was one I'd tried on for the Oscars but didn't make the cut. It was perfect for the wedding, though.

I wasn't sure I'd ever get used to people helping me get ready for an event, but I also didn't see it stopping.

"Thank you so much, Sophie. I really couldn't look halfway decent without your help."

She rolled her eyes and smiled at me. "Stop, Wren. You're gorgeous."

She began packing things up while I simply stared at my reflection. Back in Indiana, I doubted I would have looked half as good for prom.

"Can you take a picture real quick? I want to show my mom and Daniel."

"Sure." She picked up my phone and began snapping not just one photo, but a dozen.

I let out a little chuckle. "I only need one."

She rolled her eyes and smiled. "Haven't you learned yet that it takes dozens to get one good one?"

"I think they're all good," Weston said from the doorway to the bathroom. "Are you almost ready?"

I turned to look at him. "What do you think?"

He blew out a breath and stepped toward me. "I think Julia is going to have some competition in the beauty department on her day."

"Oooh, you better not say that around her," I said.

He wrapped his arms around me. "Don't worry, I'm a good actor. She'll never know."

I quirked my brow at him. "Julia can tell."

He pursed his lips, then sighed. "You're right."

"But she may forgive you, seeing as I'm your wife."

He smiled down at me and gave me a quick kiss. "I think you're right."

A sigh from beside us made us both turn to Sophie who was staring at us with dreamy eyes. She stepped forward and wrapped her arms around us.

"You two are so adorable."

Weston chuckled. "You are, too."

She stepped back and over to the counter to pick up her bags. "I better get headed out. I've still got to finish getting ready and we've got to take Arianna over to my parents."

"You're not bringing her?" Weston asked. He looked crushed by the news, but it only made Sophie roll her eyes.

"I'll see you two in a few hours." She waved as she left, her teal curls bouncing as she walked out.

At the reminder of hours, and how long I was going to be in a dress, I was suddenly very happy to have an empire waist instead of the mermaid cut from the Oscars. At least I'd be somewhat comfortable, even in the insanely priced fabric.

I'd also snuck a pair of flip flops into a bag that contained some things we were taking with us.

"The car is here," Weston said, pulling me back into the bedroom.

I handed him the bag and carefully made my way down the stairs. Weston watched each step, ready to catch me. One day I'd be able to walk around in heels with confidence. Maybe.

Weston had decided it might be a good idea if we hired a car service for the evening. However, Joe was still with us.

"How's it looking, Joe?" Weston asked after we climbed into the back of the car.

Joe turned from the front seat. "Good. I've got one of my guys following us and if all is okay, we'll head back before the wedding starts."

"I don't think there will be much of a problem," Weston said.

Joe nodded in agreement. "I don't either, but I'm also not psychic, so I'm not going to take any chances."

When we arrived at the Malibu Wines Vineyard, I was stunned. High up in the hills, the view was amazing. Vineyards filled the valleys of the rolling hills. High up in the hills, the venue sat atop a large hill, allowing for an amazing panoramic view.

"The area is small, isn't it?" I asked when we arrived. It was small enough I worried about how crowded the flat hilltop would become.

Weston nodded as we walked toward a domed building in the center. "It is, but there are only going to be about a hundred people."

"Only a hundred people?" I asked. I had helped with the name plates for the tables, but the stack seemed like a lot more than a hundred.

Weston nodded. "They wanted to keep it intimate."

We had almost made it to the small building to drop off our things when Weston stopped and tensed beside me. I followed his gaze to find out why. Walking toward us was a couple I'd seen only once before—my in-laws.

"It's okay, baby," I whispered to him. My chest tightened as I ran my hand up and down his arm in an attempt to soothe us both. It didn't help the anxiety crawling through me with each step Richard and Joanna Lockwood took to close the gap between us.

"Weston, hello," Joanna said as she stopped in front of us. "Wren, lovely to see you again." Tears filled her eyes, her bottom lip quivering, but she soon gained control over her emotions.

I gave her a small smile, then moved my gaze to Richard. He and Weston were staring at each other, neither saying anything, but the tension was thick.

"Are you going to behave and not be an ass on your son's wedding day?" Weston asked him, his jaw tight.

No "Hello" or anything. Straight to the point. Then again, with everything I'd learned, and knowing Weston, it didn't surprise me.

Richard looked to me and sneered as he let out a huff. Weston stepped forward, but before he could do anything, Joanna was between them, her hand on each man's chest.

"Your father is going to behave," she said as she looked to her husband, her hand flexed against his chest. "Isn't that right, dear?" Her death glare could be felt without being seen. "We talked about this. I'm not going to let you push them away anymore. Our sons are successful and have found love. You should be proud and happy for them."

I stared in shock, waiting on edge to see what my father-in-law would do, and I wasn't the only one. Weston was holding his breath, waiting to go off, but it didn't happen. The fire building in Richard died down and his arms relaxed.

Weston stared in shock at his mother, her hand still on his chest, right at his heart. The emotions pouring out of her were strong. Regret being the most prominent, followed by love.

She removed her hand and reached up toward his face, but stopped, her fingers clenching as she dropped it back down.

I felt her loss, her heartache.

"We'll behave or we'll leave," she said, a sad smile on her face. With that, she took hold of Richard's hand and led him away, toward a seating area.

After a minute, Weston slipped his hand in mine and we continued on. As soon as we entered the stone building, I reached up and cupped his face and brought it down to mine.

"Are you okay?" I asked in a whisper.

He let out a shaky sigh and nodded, then pressed his lips to mine. "I'll be okay, baby girl."

"Promise? You're not just saying that, are you?"

I felt his arms wrap around my waist as his lips twitched. "Promise."

Miles arrived a few minutes later, and then time flew by. Before I knew it, the hilltop was loaded with people and Julia had arrived. Everyone took their seats, and Weston went to stand next to Miles. I sat on Julia's side, next to her mother with her nephew, Deacon, in my arms. His mom, Julia's sister Rebecca, was the maid-of-honor, and I was happy to help out.

Everyone stood and turned as the music changed to look toward the end of the aisle where Julia walked slowly up the aisle with her father.

She was stunning in her gown, and absolutely glowing with happiness. I couldn't get over the absolute love that stretched between her and Miles. With every step, her smile grew, and so did Miles's.

When she reached him, Miles couldn't look away from her. I'd never seen him so happy.

I chanced a glance over to my in-laws. Joanna was crying, and Richard actually had a small smile on his face, which surprised me.

Maybe one day the Lockwoods could come together as a family again, but that all depended on Richard. It was a large gap to mend, and only time would tell if it was possible.

"I ask you now to repeat the wedding vows," the Justice of the Peace said.

I looked to Weston and he glanced my way. Our eyes locked as the justice went through the familiar words. The intensity of emotion, of love, that flowed between us with each line made my chest tighten.

Tears welled in my eyes. There was a tight hammering in my chest, and I hoped that it was the same as his own, as we silently exchanged vows.

"I love you," I mouthed at the end.

He smiled at me and mouthed as well, "I love you."

I glanced back to Miles and Julia just as the words "You may kiss the bride," were said.

There were a lot of "awws" and hollering when the kiss went past a little more than a peck.

"Ladies and gentlemen," the justice said to the crowd, "it is my privilege to introduce to you for the first time, Mr. and Mrs. Lockwood!"

The crowd erupted into cheers, and bubbles started to fly. Julia's smile was from ear to ear, her face pink. They both looked so incredibly happy, but I knew it was a long time coming.

We all headed back to the reception area, which was only a few hundred feet. I didn't get very far past the rows of chairs before Weston had his arm around my waist.

"I love you," he said as he kissed my temple.

I smiled up at him. "Hey, handsome. Better not let my husband catch you saying that to me."

He chuckled and pulled me closer. "Good thing I'm friends with him."

I rolled my eyes. "So, are we sitting with them?" I said, motioning toward my in-laws.

He shook his head. "No. Definitely not."

We found our table, which wasn't hard—Sophie and Carson were already there and waved us over. Lance and Talia were there as well at one end, along with a few other people I didn't know.

"Who knew?" I gestured over to Lance and Talia.

Weston shook his head. "I can't believe they moved in together."

I turned to him, wide-eyed. "What?"

Weston nodded with a smile on his face. "Lance told me yesterday. He asked Talia to move in with him a week ago and she had her apartment packed up and was moved in by Thursday."

Looking back over to them, they were sending off some major love vibes. "Huh. Who'd have thought it?"

"Not me," Carson said with a chuckle as he caught on to our whispered conversation.

Weston nodded in agreement. "Talia is one of the biggest divas I've worked with, but something about Lance melts her."

"Maybe it'll be a good thing for everyone, then."

When dinner was over, Miles and Julia had their first dance.

Their love was an overpowering force, and had my complete attention. The way Miles sang the words to her, their eyes locked, and the tears slipping down Julia's face.

True love. Pure.

The music changed and Julia and Miles waved people onto the dance floor.

Weston stood and held out his hand. I blinked at it, then up to him.

"Come on, let's dance."

Nodding, I slipped mine in and he pulled me out of my chair and onto the dance floor. His arm wrapped around my waist as the other took my hand and we began to rock.

"I can't say I've ever danced before," I said, right as I stepped on his foot.

Luckily his shoe was thick enough he didn't even flinch.

"It's okay," he said with a chuckle. "Just let me lead, and you'll be fine."

I let my body sway, let Weston move me around, hold me close. His blue eyes sparkled in the lights, his smile making my heart pound in my chest.

There was no way to keep the smile from my face. My happiness couldn't be denied.

The music slowed down, and I leaned my head against his shoulder.

He hummed and placed a kiss on my temple. "I want this."

I scrunched my brow at him. "Want what?"

"Memories of our wedding," he said. "I mean, I have them, but it's fuzzy. What I really want is the vision of you walking to me in a white dress as we tell the world you're mine and I'm yours."

"I'm liking this idea." A tangible memory. A fairy tale wedding with my prince.

He twirled us around in a circle, lifting me from the ground.

"I was thinking this summer, before you start college. Then we could go on a honeymoon, anywhere you want."

I pursed my lips and scrunched my brow. "That's not a lot of time to plan."

"Well, that's what wedding planners are for, right?"

One would probably be a necessity with only a few month's warning. "True."

"We have more than enough money to hire one to do it all. Plus, I'm sure Julia can give you some advice. Your mom as well, and Charlotte, and I don't know if Daniel's into this kind of thing."

I nodded. "I bet we could throw something together. I don't need something lavish, just me and you and a few close friends and family."

He leaned down and kissed my lips. "Sounds perfect to me."

My mind was already spinning, thinking about a dream wedding. Anything I ever wanted, I could have.

"Ari could be the flower girl," I said. "And I'm sure Sophie will go gaga to pick out our clothing."

He nodded. "You'll have the most beautiful dress you could ever imagine. As long as you don't involve her in wedding plans, we'll be good."

"Why is that a bad thing? Girl has mad skills."

He laughed out loud. "Yeah, you didn't see her wedding. It was over the top. It's a good thing Carson knew what he was getting into already." His laughter died down to a chuckle. "One time, I caught her playing dress-up with him. He was in this purple frilly dress with big feather boa, his hair and makeup all done. They were having tea. It was then I knew he liked her."

I glanced over to the table they were sitting at, talking to someone. The love he spoke of was there in the way Carson's arm sat across her shoulders, his fingers making circles on her skin. It was shining from his eyes as he looked at her. Amazing and beautiful.

"How old were they?" I asked.

He shook his head. "We were just kids, but even then he was smitten with her. I got an ass kicking later for laughing at him."

"Never talked about again, huh?"

"Hell, no! I was his best man. That shit was in my speech!"

I laughed and slapped his arm. "Awful! And hilarious."

We continued dancing, just soaking each other in, surrounded by friends and not having to worry about anything. Just enjoying the evening with loved ones.

"I have a good feeling everything has fallen into place now," he said against my temple.

I turned to look up at him. "Yeah?"

"Yeah," he said with a smile. "The future looks beautiful."

He pressed his lips to mine, and the world melted away. We weren't at a wedding any longer, but sealing a promise for the future.

Weston . . .

IN THE ENDING DAYS OF JULY, I STOOD OUTSIDE A HUGE estate, looking over the wedding site preparations. I scanned over the garden where the final touches for the ceremony were being put into place.

In a few short hours, I would marry Wren with all our friends and family in attendance. We would both remember it this time, and have more than just a few photos to memorialize the event.

I would have the memories of her walking down the aisle on her father's arm in a white dress. The thought made me anxious. We were doing things backwards, so I didn't think it would affect me, but it did.

Somewhere inside the large, Spanish style mansion behind me, was my wife. She was hidden away in the bridal suite with her mom, Daniel, Sophie, Julia, and Charlotte.

And I was going crazy without her. I wanted the hours to pass faster, just so I could be close to her again without some stupid barrier between us. We were already married, for fuck's sake. Normal traditions didn't apply.

While Wren was initially thinking low-key, lavish is what we ended up with. There was no culling the guest list, at least on my side, and a small wedding, like the size of Miles and Julia's, erupted into four hundred guests.

She didn't seem to mind, though, and was happy building her fairy tale wedding. We hired a coordinator, and she lucked out on getting us a venue in the small time frame we were looking at, all thanks to a cancellation.

The months passed quickly, and between her mentorship and the wedding, she was kept pretty busy. Add into all that getting the pool house ready for Daniel's arrival. He loved the pool house, and I loved seeing my wife happy to have her best friend so close.

Gifts started to pour in almost as soon as invitations went out, but the best one came in June from our lawyer.

It was the satisfaction of watching Mallory and Natalie in bright orange prison jumpsuits. They both took a plea deal, which diminished their sentences down to a few years each. Mallory's was longer, though, due to the aggravated assault charge. While Wren had fully recovered from it, a scar still remained at her hairline. It was a constant reminder of what a split second could have taken from me.

Even Natalie's fame and impressive lawyer couldn't keep her from jail after what she'd done. The two-year sentence with possible early parole was nothing, but we ruined her with our civil suit. Everyone in the industry knew what she'd done. It only took a few days for the information to fly around, and she was blacklisted in a week.

In the end, while we were happy with them in jail, it wasn't as long as I'd hoped.

"Oh, Weston, there you are," Melanie, our wedding coordinator, called out as she walked up to me with her assistant. "I wanted to discuss something with you. There was a mix-up with the centerpieces." She pointed to one of the tables and the elaborate bouquets with crystal accents. "These are more expensive than what Wren had decided on, but . . ."

I waved her off. "They're beautiful, and she'll love them."

"Are you sure?" she asked, a little hesitant.

She'd probably been around one too many bridezillas, which Wren was not.

"It's so small of a difference, she won't notice." In fact, I barely had and I'd been looking at them for twenty minutes.

She smiled at me. "You're itching to see her, aren't you?"

I nodded. "I'm used to seeing her every day. This is rough."

"Well, not long left." She glanced down at her watch. "In fact, you should start getting ready."

A hand clamped down on my shoulder. "Yes, he should."

I turned to find Miles. "Hey."

Melanie headed off and Miles stepped in front of me.

"Carson and Lance are already in the groom's room."

I nodded. "Excellent." A knot then formed in my stomach. If they were already here, then . . . "Are they here?"

His smile faltered, and he nodded. "They got here just as I did. Mom assured me he'll behave."

My stomached tightened. "He better. I won't let him ruin this in any way."

"I won't let him even attempt to ruin this day for you," he assured me as we headed back in.

"He shouldn't even have the possibility of it," I grumbled. I couldn't stand the thought of my father tainting my wedding day. It was our day—mine and Wren's.

"Wren felt for Mom at my wedding," Miles said. "She invited Mom, not Dad, just like we did. He was just her plus one."

"I know her intentions were good, but it's our wedding. I . . . If he . . ." I let out a sigh. I was a mess, worried about what my father might or might not say to Wren. At the same time, I was happy to see my mom again. When I saw her at Miles's wedding, it seemed like she'd grown a bit of a spine.

When we rounded the corner, entering the large manor, there they were, about twenty feet away. It was so abrupt, no warning, that I almost stopped in my tracks.

As we closed the distance, I straightened my spine, steeling myself.

The look on my mother's face still made my chest ache. Longing and remorse. She'd aged since I'd last seen her years ago—they both had. I noticed it at Miles's wedding, but it was more prevalent when I stopped to really look at them.

"Hello, Weston." Mom stepped forward, her arms opening, hoping and waiting.

I stared at her, frozen for a moment, before closing the space between us. I leaned down and wrapped my arms around her.

How long had it been since I'd hugged my mom? The way my arms tightened and the vice that loosened around my chest told me it'd been too long. I loved my mom, but I was so angry with her for not standing up for me, for staying with him. I'd forgotten how calming it was to be in her arms.

We parted and I looked over to my father and his bland expression. He didn't say anything, but he did look quite uncomfortable.

I stepped toward him, taking in the way he straightened, bracing himself for my attack. There was none, but I stared deep into his eyes, looking for some sense of remorse.

Wren had taught me a lot in our journey about love and forgiveness, and maybe right then was the starting point of mending our relationship.

But it all depended on my father.

"While I'll never forget what you did to me, Dad, I can forgive you," I said. There was a gasp behind me from my mom. "But that's up to you. All I've ever wanted was for you to acknowledge you did wrong."

His jaw tightened, lips pursing and relaxing as he struggled with a response. Such a stubborn mule, and sadly, a characteristic I inherited. But I wouldn't let it ruin my happiness or the happiness of those I loved. I learned that lesson the hard way.

"I did what I thought was best for your career," he said.

The blood in my veins began to boil, rising up. *My career?* I was seconds away from decking him, but when his head dropped, I stopped and waited. Miles was next to me, ready to punch him again.

When his head rose, I finally saw it, deep in his eyes—remorse. For what, though?

"It wasn't right of me," he said, then paused. "It wasn't what was best for *you.*"

"No, it wasn't. Not in the least." There was no way I was going to relent easily. I was going to hear an apology from him, or it was the last time I would ever see them.

He gave a hard nod. "Sometimes, as a parent, you make a decision for your child and it turns out to be the wrong one."

His words sounded almost rehearsed, which made me grind my teeth together. "Were you spoon fed that answer, or is that something you came up with on your own?"

His blue eyes darkened and his brow furrowed. "Damnit, Weston. I'm trying here."

He was. I could tell. It wasn't anger, but frustration at his own shortcomings that was giving him trouble.

"I didn't do it to hurt you," he said as he struggled to get words out. "I thought it would help you, and it did for a while, but then you were hooked. And that's the guilt I've had to live with."

"Hasn't seemed much like guilt to me."

His jaw clenched, and he looked toward my mother, then back to me. "I'm not an emotional man. It's not easy for me to express my feelings. I deal with things my own way, but I am sorry for what I did to you, son."

I stared at him, at the defeated face of my father. It took a lot for him to say it, but he did. And by his broken pride laid out before me, I knew he meant it. What he said wasn't to appease my mother, but the truth.

I stood there for a few minutes, just looking at him. Out of the corner of my eye, Mom was wringing her hands while Miles rubbed his hand up and down her arm.

My fingers did an involuntary twitch, waking me, and I lifted my hand up and held it out. He glanced down and gave a nod before he slipped his hand in mine.

It was the first touch we'd had since I'd pinned him against the wall, ready to punch him, years before. The last time I'd seen them before Miles's wedding.

It was the best I could manage after everything.

We each nodded, then I released him and stepped toward my mom. I leaned down and kissed her cheek. "I . . . Thank you for coming."

There were tears in her eyes when we stepped back, but there was also a small smile on her face. "We'll see you outside in a little while."

I nodded, and Miles leaned down for a hug before we continued walking.

"Wow," Miles said when we made it up the stairs and out of earshot. "I didn't expect that today."

I shook my head. "Me either. That's one hell of a wedding present." Acknowledgement. It and an apology were all I ever wanted. Some proof that he felt like he did something bad to me, his son.

"Oh, by the way, I haven't had a chance to tell Wren yet, but the results are in from the film score competition."

My ears perked up. Wren had spent so much time on her composition, and I knew how much it meant to her. Miles had even divulged how wonderful it was, and I could tell just by the look in his eyes as he spoke about it. He wasn't blowing smoke up my ass—my wife was talented.

"And?"

He grinned at me. "She won."

I stopped walking. "What?"

He nodded and kept smiling. "Over eight thousand entries, and she beat them all."

Holy fuck.

I knew Wren was gifted musically, because Miles didn't give

out glowing reviews to those who didn't earn them. But to beat out over eight thousand other people?

"She is going to go nuts when she finds out," I said, a huge grin on my face. I could just imagine her freak out, and the excited sex.

"Yes, she is. She should be getting something in the mail any day now."

I reached out and grabbed his arm, stopping him. "We're leaving on our honeymoon tomorrow. I can't go without her knowing."

A grin spread on his face. "Good thing I came prepared with a *phenomenal* wedding gift."

I shook my head. "Always trying to outdo me."

"What did you get her?" he asked, knowing I'd been having trouble.

I was a failure in the end. Besides some lingerie for our honeymoon, I'd come up with nothing. "A vacation with no phones."

He shrugged and pulled open the door to the groom's suite. "That's actually quite huge."

"What does she win?" I didn't even think Wren knew what the prize was.

"Ten thousand dollars, five thousand dollars' worth of software and equipment, and who knows what kind of offers she'll get for the song itself."

When we entered the room, Lance was out on the balcony on his phone, talking all sweet, and Carson was missing.

"Bet you're happy to have her in your pocket," I said before rolling my eyes at something Lance said.

Talia had him wrapped around her finger so badly.

"You bet your ass. As soon as I can, she's going to come work with me."

It made me happy that Miles and Wren had become not only friends, but allies. They were a lot alike, which probably added to them not getting along at first.

Their mentorship only helped them grow closer. It was interesting to watch them interact over the last month. Conversations with musical references and humming melodies—neither of which I knew much about. But Wren seemed eager to learn everything she could.

After an hour of slowly getting ready, and hunting down Carson, we made our way out to the growing crowd. The anxiety spiked then, or maybe it was just excitement. Either way, my stomach was in knots and I couldn't stop fidgeting.

Dozens of movie sets, acting like a complete idiot in front of twenty people because of a prop that wasn't visible, yet it was a wedding to my *wife* that got me.

"Are you okay?" Miles asked as we took our place at the altar.

I shook my head. "Why am I nervous?"

Miles stared at me for a moment, then let out a little chuckle. "It's a wedding, and you're the groom. Enough said."

"But I'm already married to the bride."

"Doesn't matter. Just wait. She's going to blow you away in ways you can't even imagine when you see her."

Maybe that was it. I'd seen both his and Julia's reaction at their wedding, and as corny as it sounded—my wedding day was the happiest day of my life. Because unlike our drunken night, there was a relationship. Our wedding was planned by us, and we were truly ready to start our lives together after all of our obstacles.

Karen and Mike made their way down the aisle, followed by Arianna, who was having a blast throwing petals around. The crowd laughed when she stopped and bent over to pick some of them back up, while Sophie tried to get her back on track. She eventually made it to the end and was swooped up by her mother.

Charlotte walked down the aisle next, followed by Daniel, Wren's Man of Honor.

Then, she was there. A beautiful, brilliant smile, beaming directly at me. My heart hammered against my ribs, almost fighting to get out. It was the vision I'd dreamed of—Wren walking down the aisle toward me in a white gown. Her arm was tucked into John's and I couldn't take my eyes off her.

Every word I knew for beautiful, gorgeous, or exquisite just didn't do her justice. There were no words to describe her.

It was then I understood why. Miles was right. Despite already being my wife, there was nothing to prepare me for seeing my fantasy come to life.

Everything I ever wanted was Wren.

Tears stung my eyes when I took her hand in mine. I couldn't stop staring at her. I didn't even hear the Justice of the Peace speak, but out of the corner of my eye I saw John sit down.

We were in our own little bubble. The four hundred people behind us weren't even a thought.

"Do you, Weston James Lockwood, take this woman, Wren Alexis Lockwood, to be your lawful wedded wife, to love, honor, and cherish her through sickness and in health, through times of happiness and travail, until death do you part?"

"I do."

Her bottom lip trembled, and tears filled my eyes as the words left my lips for us both to remember.

"Place this ring on her finger and repeat after me." The Justice paused before saying the words as I brought Wren's hand up and held the ring I bought her a year before at the tip of her finger.

"With this ring, I thee wed, and forever pledge my devotion," I said, my voice catching on the last word.

The Justice then turned to Wren.

"Do you, Wren Alexis Lockwood, take this man, Weston James Lockwood, to be your lawful wedded husband, to love, honor, and cherish him through sickness and in health, through times of happiness and travail, until death do you part?"

She smiled at me and as a tear rolled down her cheek.

"I do."

Two little words, and everything was perfect.

Wren

A year and a half later . . .

I stared into the mirror, bags evident under my eyes. My brain was fried after having pulled an all-nighter with Daniel. I only hoped I remembered half the stuff we were cramming into our heads.

"Morning, baby girl," Weston said, placing a kiss to my temple. I grunted back to him, and he chuckled. "What time is your test?"

"Ten thirty," I said with a yawn.

He pursed his lips as he looked at me. "You still have a few hours, you should get in a nap. Where's Daniel?"

"He's in the middle of the living room floor." I let out a small chuckle. "I think he just fell and didn't get back up."

"I think you should climb into bed for a while. One of you has to be awake to drive you two to school."

I nodded in agreement and headed back into our bedroom. "Will you set my alarm?"

I flipped the covers back and slid in, a groan escaping my lips when my head hit my pillow. My eyes were fluttering closed, but I could still see as Weston programmed my phone.

He placed a kiss on my forehead and wished me good luck before heading out to work. I was out before his footsteps hit the stairs.

I woke to my alarm going off a few hours later, though it felt like minutes. My hands rubbed my eyes, and I yawned as I turned to shut the blaring off. I stumbled to the bathroom to wash my face and brush my teeth before heading downstairs to find Daniel.

He wasn't in the same spot on the floor where I'd last seen him passed out, so I headed out to the pool house. Sure enough, splayed out in the middle of his messy bed, was Daniel.

I pulled on his leg and smacked his ass. "Wake up!"

He woke with a start and glared at me. "You were interrupting my dream."

"Yeah? Was it good?" I asked.

His lips drew up into a lazy smile. "Excellent. David Gandy had me over his lap and he was spanking me."

"Sorry, that was my hand."

His forehead crinkled. "Ew, girl cooties."

I rolled my eyes at him. "Come on, we've gotta get moving."

He groaned, but rolled out of bed while I went back into the house to grab my bag. After a double check to make sure I had my notes, I grabbed my phone to check my email. It was mostly junk, but there was an email from Miles.

Wren,

Do you have class on Friday? I'm in need of some help, and I'm hoping you're available.

Miles

I pulled up my calendar and confirmed I was open, shooting him back a quick message.

I'm free. What's up? What time and where?

"Okay, I'm ready," Daniel said, popping in.

I turned to look at him and started laughing.

"What?"

His hair was sticking up everywhere, the buttons on his shirt were off by more than one loop, and one shoe was untied.

"Two words. Hot. Mess."

He tilted his head back and groaned. "I don't fucking care anymore. Fuck finals!"

Reaching out, I grabbed his arm and pulled him toward the garage. "Come on, grumpy."

One more final and we were done for the semester. The closing of my third semester of college.

The last year and a half had been a challenge, though not as much of a social challenge as I thought it would be. While there were people that recognized me or my name, after a while, I was just another freshman.

A few hours later, I was more than happy to be home. Daniel disappeared immediately and I headed up to the bedroom. First a nap, and then when Weston got home, dinner.

Or maybe going over to the studio.

The challenging part since I started college was the mixture of my classes and working with Miles on the side, as well as being a good wife and friend. Most days I was fall down exhausted, and for the last few days, even worse.

I was halfway undressed when my stomach flipped, sending me rushing to the bathroom.

Because I really needed random vomiting added to my days.

"Baby, are you okay?" Weston asked when he entered the bedroom a few minutes later and walked swiftly to my side.

I shook my head from my spot on the floor, hovering face first over the toilet. "Think I had some bad Chinese."

He swiped the hair from my face, pinning it back with his hand. "I remember campus food being hit or miss."

My stomached heaved again, but nothing came out. "Today was a miss."

His other hand rubbed soothing circles on my back. "How did your test go? Were you able to get through it?"

I nodded. "It went pretty good, I think. Daniel was freaking out. He's convinced he failed." I sat back, my stomach seeming to have calmed down for the moment.

"Where is he, by the way?"

I let out a small chuckle. "As soon as we got home, he went to his room and crashed." I shook my head, then blew out a breath. "I'm so happy finals are over."

"You're free." He held out his hands to pull me up from the floor.

I moved to the sink, my body moving slowly, and grabbed my toothbrush. "Yes, thank God. Do we get to go on vacation?"

"As long as it doesn't interfere with your work with Miles, yes."

It took me a minute to answer, but my mouth felt infinitely better when I was done. "Miles is closing the studio down next week, giving everyone two weeks off for the holidays."

His eyebrows rose. "Really? Okay, where do you want to go?"

We walked into the bedroom, and I immediately crawled onto the bed. "Spoil me?"

He climbed in next to me, smiling as he leaned forward and kissed me. "Always."

"Actually, I've always wanted to go on a cruise."

"We cruised around the Caribbean last year."

I rolled my eyes. "I meant a cruise ship. You know, those huge boats with thousands of people crammed on them."

He grimaced at my description. "Us on a boat with thousands of people? We don't even fly commercial if we can avoid it."

I shrugged. "Would it be so bad?"

He pursed his lips. "Possibly." His forehead scrunched as he looked down at me before reaching out and placing his hand on my forehead. "How long have you not been feeling well?"

I shrugged and thought back. It'd been almost a week of feeling off, but only a day or two of vomiting.

"A few days."

"What hurts? I can go get you some medicine."

I looked up at him. "You?"

He chuckled. "Hey, I used to go shopping before you came along."

"I'm not so sure." I let out a groan as I snuggled into my pillow. "I think I just need some sleep."

He stared down at me, a disbelieving look on his face. "Tell me. Are you achy?"

I shook my head. "No, not achy. I was a little crampy a few days ago . . ." I trailed off, frozen.

Shit.

I sat straight up and grabbed my phone, a strange cross of fear and excitement buzzing through me.

When was the last time . . . ? Oh, shit. Oh, shit.

"Wren?"

I shook my head as I went through the symptoms: nausea, vomiting, fatigue. They were all things that I associated with not getting enough sleep. I was a bit crampy the other day, and my breasts were tender like they always were right before my period.

But I'd been on the Depo shot for two years and hadn't had a period since.

It stared back at me, the last time I'd gotten my shot—April 2nd.

I slowly raised my head to look back up at him. His eyes bored into mine, jaw tight.

"What is it?" he asked, clearly worried about my reaction.

"I missed my shot."

His brow scrunched. "What shot?"

"My birth control."

A noise came from him like he stopped himself from speaking as he processed my words. The concern melted from his face and was replaced with cautious joy.

"Pregnant?"

I shrugged my shoulders. "Maybe?"

He jumped up from the bed and threw a shirt on as he slipped on some shoes.

"What are you doing?" I asked.

Bright eyes turned toward me. "I'm going to go get a pregnancy test." He took my head in his hands and leaned down, pressing his lips to mine. "A baby."

I didn't even get a chance to say anything before he was out the door. Instead, I just lay back, a smile forming on my face as I placed my hand on my abdomen.

"Baby . . ."

One year later . . .

Less than one month after my twenty-first birthday, in the middle of July, Savannah Amelia Lockwood was born.

After I found out I was pregnant, I decided to take a hiatus from school. When Miles heard the news, he approached me about working with him full time. Ever since my mentorship with him, we continued to collaborate, so it was a fluid progression.

When Savannah arrived in our lives healthy and happy, I took the remainder of the year off, with the exception of one particular project that started in the fall. Weston took off the first month, then slowly eased back in. Which was all made possible thanks to the new vice president, Julia Lockwood, who was also due with another Lockwood in a few months.

Weston said it was the logical progression. He'd long ago admitted he and Carson needed another voice of authority, and Julia was the most qualified and perfect addition. Amy stepped up as head assistant and Graham continued to work under Julia, which meant that yet again, another assistant was needed.

Mallory's replacement, Audrey, was a valuable addition. It was her brother, Nick, who was hired on after Julia's promotion, which turned out to be a fantastic decision. The two of them worked very well together, despite the occasional sibling rivalry, which was entertaining to watch.

The arrival of a second child in the Brooks household, a little boy named Ander, allowed Sophie and I to get closer, swapping baby war stories.

My eyes fluttered as I strained not to fall asleep. My head nodded and my eyes snapped open before drifting closed again.

"All right, that's it. You're going to bed."

My eyes opened, and I looked up at my husband who was walking toward me, still in his suit.

"She's still eating," I said, feeling the suction of Savannah's tiny mouth and milk being released.

Weston sighed. "Baby, you haven't slept in two days between work and Savi."

"Miles and I are almost done. Just a few more days."

"You won't be standing in a few more days at this rate." He leaned down and picked her up from my tired arms, his tongue peeking out to swipe up a droplet of milk off my nipple. I shuddered at the feeling, a heat blossoming even in my tired state.

Weston picked a bottle up from the table, one that I didn't even notice him carrying, and Savannah eagerly latched on. She was so hungry lately, backed up by the rate she was growing. Six months old, and she ate like a champ.

I watched him for a moment, the sweetest vision I'd ever seen before me—my husband holding our daughter.

She was cradled in his arms. Their matching blue eyes connecting while she ate. He lightly swayed, a motion he became a pro at real quick, and smiled down at her.

"Did my precious little girl have a good day?" he asked her. "Did you miss Daddy?"

She just looked up at him with her big eyes and reached up to grab onto his finger.

Before I knew it, I was being jostled, not even realizing I'd fallen asleep. My eyes opened to the dark, the light long gone, Weston's arms beneath me, carrying me. He pressed a kiss to my forehead and laid me down in our bed, his body joining, pressing against mine.

The next time I woke, it was to the cries through the baby monitor, but the bed jostled and I went back under when the sound stopped a moment later.

Soft kisses and touches to my skin roused me next. I let out a little moan, smiling. "How long have I been asleep?"

He pulled me back, closer into his chest. "About twelve hours."

My brow scrunched. "Who fed Savi?"

"Baby, I'm perfectly capable of taking care of our little girl."

I chuckled. "Have I told you how hot that is?"

He kissed my neck. "Hey, anything that gets you hot, I'm more than happy to do over and over."

"Just keep being a great dad and husband, and I'll be hot for you all of the time."

His hips flexed, his hard length pressing against my ass. "Are you hot for me now?" His hand slid around my waist, slipping into my panties. "I've been dying to be inside you for days."

I let out a sigh as his finger moved along my slit before sliding in. My head tipped back, my hand moving to his arm, keeping him there.

"I can't wait until this weekend," he whispered into my ear as his other arm worked to pull my panties down my hips. "It's been weeks since I've been able to do all the kinky fuck-hot things I love to do to you."

The hot head of his cock touched my skin, and I let out a moan. He moved down my body, getting the angle right before his fingers left me to guide him in. My eyes rolled back as he filled me, pumping in and out.

Savannah could wake up at any moment. Time was limited, so instead of removing his hand he teased my clit, working me up more and more.

"I need you to come, baby. It's been too long."

He groaned and picked up the pace. I began panting, his fingers and cock driving me crazy. My hand reached back, gripping onto his hair.

"Fuck, yes. Squeeze me."

It was just a quickie, but he was hitting all the right places, and soon I was clenching around him, a choked scream crawling out of me. Weston tensed behind me, his mouth clamping down on my shoulder.

"I love you, Wren," he whispered against my temple as he came down.

I craned my head back and pressed my lips to his. "I love you, too."

Life was as busy and hectic as ever, but we had our balance. Family was our first priority, work second.

When I got on that plane to Las Vegas, I never imagined where it would really take me. The love I would find or the life I would lead.

I was living proof that fairy tales did exist, and that princes were real.

That love at first sight was possible.

The End

About the Author

K.I. Lynn is the *USA Today* Bestselling Author from *The Bend Anthology* and the Amazon Bestsellers, *Breach* and *Becoming Mrs Lockwood*. She spent her life in the arts, everything from music to painting and ceramics, then to writing. Characters have always run around in her head, acting out their stories, but it wasn't until later in life she would put them to pen. It would turn out to be the one thing she was really passionate about.

Since she began posting stories online, she's garnered acclaim for her diverse stories and hard hitting writing style. Two stories and characters are never the same, her brain moving through different ideas faster than she can write them down as it also plots its quest for world domination. . .or cheese. Whichever is easier to obtain. . . Usually it's cheese.

Website—www.kilynnauthor.com

Facebook—www.facebook.com/kilynn.breach

Twitter—twitter.com/KI_Lynn_

Instagram—www.instagram.com/k.i.lynn

Get my Newsletter—http://bit.ly/1U9NSoC

Abducted

The mafia never lets you go.

I thought I was safe, free, but I never expected to find myself locked in a cage.

I'm in his territory. His prison.

The beast.

A fate worse than death awaits me if I can't get away, so when the opportunity of salvation presents itself I grab it, even if I'm unsure if I can trust the hand I'm holding.

The only way out is through, exposing secrets and spilling blood.

Things aren't how they appear. Nobody is what they seem.

Not even me.

Find out more here:

books2read.com/AbductedKILynn

Forever and All The Afters

He promised me forever.

Then he boarded a plane for a college a thousand miles away and never returned. A decade later there's a ring on my finger with a new promise from a new love.

Just as my life falls into place, pretty as the pages of a magazine, my world is knocked over. The moment he touches me everything around me begins to crack, exposing all the lies I've told myself.

Every glance reminds me. Every touch ignites.

Things aren't how they used to be.

Love isn't easy.

Find out more her:

books2read.com/ForeverAndAllTheAfters

Welcome to the Cameo Hotel

I get what I want.

When I walked through the door of the Cameo Hotel I didn't expect such a beauty to be working the front desk.

The effect she has on me is intense, and I make her life a living hell because of it.

I love her spirit, her internal defiance when completing the most inane task I assign her. My two week stay has turned into unending, just to be near her.

She's under my every command if she wants to keep me happy.

There's one last thing I want.

Her.

Find out more here :

books2read.com/WelcomeToTheCameoHotel

Becoming Mrs. Lockwood

Every girl has dreams of meeting Prince Charming, or at least I know I did.

A fairy tale-like meeting of love at first site.

Real life and fairy tales are very different.

I'm just a small town Indiana girl that had a chance encounter with one of Hollywood's golden boys. You may think you know where this story goes—not even close.

Life is different. Marriage is hard. It's even worse when you're strangers.

Find out more here -

books2read.com/BecomingMrsLockwood

Six

I had a one-night stand. It wasn't my first, but it would be my last.

A gun to the head.

A trained killer.

A deadly conspiracy.

Kidnapped and on the run, my life and death is in the hands of a sadist captor who happens to be my one-night stand. Armed with countless weapons, money, and new identities, the man I call Six drags me around the world.

The manhunt is on and Six is the next target. Can we find out who is killing off the Cleaners before they find us?

Two down, seven to go.

When it's all over he'll finish the job that dropped him into my life, and end it.

Stockholm Syndrome meets bucket list, and the question of what would you do to live before you died. The questions aren't always answered in black and white. Gray becomes the norm as my morals are tested.

Death is a tragedy, and I'll do anything to stay alive.

Are you ready for the last ride of your life? Six has a gun to your head—what would you do?

This isn't a love story.

It's a death story.

Find out more here:

books2read.com/Six-KILynn

Check out the Trailer: youtu.be/fzpON3PadIA

Breach Book 1

His body was sin, his cock was sin, and I was a sinner.

To keep myself safe I hide in the world and let life move around me.

My new partner, Nathan, isn't safe. Far from it.

The darkness coils around him, hidden by a shield created by a blinding smile. But those who live in shadows see past the façade we create.

Even in darkness, there is light. A spark that ignites, then explodes.

Every filthy word from his mouth, every possessive touch—I crave them, need them. Violent and passionate and everything I need to fill the void inside me, but one thing is missing.

He can never love me.

More than my heart is on the line, and I don't know if I'll survive our breach.

Find out more here:

books2read.com/Breach

The Executive

Business is king, and I have an empire to topple.

Ivy is my new assistant and a threat to me. She's my undoing. If ever I was to believe in a cosmic connection, it was the moment I met her.

For years I've had one goal--revenge. As CEO, I have crafted a strategic plan for business, but never a life beyond.

With one touch from her, the veil is lifted. Things are different, and every moment I'm near her, my world begins to change.

A wall of propriety keeps me from her. I need her as my pawn in this war, beside me in battle. Sharing the secrets of my enemies, and her desires in my bed. Her body to claim as mine.

Getting what I want has consequences.

Collateral damage is real.

In the game of crushing kings of men, I never planned on my heart being a sacrifice.

Find out more here –

books2read.com/TheExecutive

Cocksure

Co-written with Olivia Kelley

A life altering lie, ten years, and one wild night later, the game has changed.

Niko

My life is great. I love my job, have awesome friends, and a great family.

Women love me, even if they know it's just for a night.

I always thought love at first sight was bullshit. Then she came storming into my life. She tore through my every rule, rocked my world, and knocked me on my ass.

There's only one problem. . .she lied.+

Turns out my best friend's little sister isn't so little anymore.

Everly

I stole a night with my fantasy. Lied to him.

After ten years of not seeing each other, Niko doesn't even recognize me.

So I take what I want from him, what I need from him. Without worry. Without consequence.

What I didn't count on was the lingering need for him.

Once the truth is out, the game changes. There are consequences.

I should have known nothing in my life is ever simple.

My brother is going to kill his best friend and I have nine months to figure out what I want.

Find out more here -
books2read.com/Cocksure-Lynn-Kelley

Need Book 1

Co-written with N. Isabelle Blanco

I was Kira's from the first moment I saw her. Maybe it was love at first sight, but I was only ten.

She became my best friend.

My crush.

The girl I can't live without.

But I have to.

She was almost mine, but my father took away my chance.

Now she lives across the hall from me. Instead of the title of girlfriend, she's now my stepsister.

But that doesn't stop how I feel, how I want her. Thankfully, I'm off to college two hundred miles away, but even that doesn't help.

She's under my skin, all around me, and I watch her morph from a sexy teenager to an irresistible woman.

I can't take it anymore, I need her.

Is it possible to ever be happy without the one person you *need?*

"I'm Brayden, baby. The man you've been dreaming about your whole life. And I'm about to fucking show you why."

Part 1 of a 3 part series.

Find out more here:

books2read.com/NeedSeries